welcome!
browse, sit awhile or borrow.
but, please
RETURN TO:

Also From the Author

- **A LAD FROM SARDINIA** — **The Adventures of Morgan Harmony**

   A High Seas Adventure in the Mediterranean Sea in the 1600's. Story set in prose poetry.
   ISBN #978-0-9966042-0-8

- **POETPOURRI** -- **A Labyrinth of Wandering Thought**

   A Collection of Short Stories Poetry and Prose Poetry from the Ridiculous to the Sublime.
   ISBN #978-0-9966042-1-5

- **A RANGER'S TALE** -- **Jacks' Vendetta**

   An Old West adventure revolving around the fledgling band of Texas Rangers in pursuit of the Jacks' gang.
   ISBN #978-0-9966042-3-9

Cowboy Justice series

- **COWBOY JUSTICE** -- **On The Border**

   A fictional account of an Arizona lawman who joins a vigilante group to rid the influx of illicit drugs and entry by undocumented migrants along the southern U.S. border.
   ISBN #978-0-9966042-4-6

- **A CRY FOR JUSTICE**

   Continuing the fight against corruption, trafficking, and drug-running . . . ugly, ongoing problems, not just in Arizona, but in every state . . . and now, as a couple, Frank and his bride feel a shared obligation to follow the desperate cry for help whenever and wherever it presents.
   ISBN #978-0-9966042-5-3

Gumshoe & Fox series

- **THE REUNION** -- **a Case of Revocable Trust** -- **a Gumshoe & Fox Mystery**

   A story that begins with a high school reunion . . . should be filled with fond memories, a few drinks, some dancing and some back-slapping, right? But it ends with murder . . . not one murder, but four! And that's just for starters.
   ISBN #978-0-9966042-6-0

- **THE DERELICT** -- **the Key West Caper** -- **a Gumshoe & Fox Mystery**

   When Brigadier-General Maggorie sent him $20,000.00 as a retainer to find and return his missing teen age son, Alan Garrett, a.k.a. Gumshoe, took on the assignment. The general's son was last seen on the Atlantic coast heading south. Garrett gave the assignment to his subordinate, Fox. Good plan . . . or was it?
   ISBN #978-0-9966042-7-7

THE BLACKSMITH

and the

Sheepherder's Daughter

An Old West Novel

by Myron Ferdig

This book is a work of fiction.

Names, characters, events, places or incidents are the products of the author's imagination or are used fictitiously.
Any resemblance to actual persons, living or dead -- or events or locales
is purely coincidental.

**Thank you to my friends
for the encouragement to keep
on keeping on**

Prologue

Old man Banner made his way through the swinging doors, limping at a fairly fast clip, and out of breath.

"Did anybody in here see them strange looking hombres outside the general store this morning?" he asked. "Nobody? There was at least five-six of them, Jake! Coupla scrawny kids. Didn't see but one woman amongst'em. Said they had just bought the old *Ed Dammer Homestead* up north o-here."

Owner, Jake Ruskin looked up from behind the bar and raised an eyebrow. Floyd was a regular at his establishment. The old man normally arrived sober and left half-looped, but tonight, thought Jake, he must have stopped off at one of the other watering holes in town to wet his whistle.

"Stop waving that cannon around, Floyd, before someone gets hurt! I'll buy you a drink and you can tell me what you saw."

Heads turned, ears strained to listen as small groups of clientele in Jake's Place sat and watched the old man with interest. He leaned his rifle against the edge of the bar as Jake filled a short glass with sour mash bourbon, and left the bottle on the bar. Floyd grabbed the glass, nodded toward Jake, mumbled something, and emptied the glass in one gulp. Then he cradled the bottle in the crook of his left arm, placed the glass over its neck and with his Sharps 45/70 slung over his right shoulder chose a table in the center of the lounge. He poured a second shot for himself, then lifted the glass to his lips.

"I'm good for this, Jake. You know I am."

"Oh, sure, Floyd. 'Sides, where you gonna go with that gammy leg of yours?"

The onlookers laughed as Jake wiped his hands on a bar towel, tossed it to Teresa, grabbed another shot glass and joined Floyd at the table. The old-timer filled Jake's glass and continued without missing a beat.

"Gonna run some sheep on it, they said. Dressed kinda funny. I put my scope on 'em; course I wasn't gonna shoot any of 'em, but I wanted to get a closer look.

Funny thing, Margaret seemed to know them. Gave 'em hugs and waved 'em goodbye an' all.

Yes, sir, boys, looks like we got ourselves some sheepherders in the valley. What's this country comin' to?"

One of those in the room bellowed out, "What did Margaret have to say about them, Floyd?"

Floyd craned his neck around. "Oh! Hi, Buzz. I never got that far. I was on my way to a late breakfast over at Maude's. Plumb fergot 'bout it after."

"Funny it should be such an all-fired newsworthy story tonight, ... come runnin' in out of breath and all," Buzz Calder, the town blacksmith persisted.

"Well, if you must know," Floyd scowled at Buzz, then turning back to the barman, "an' no offense to you, Jake --- I stopped by Betty's to have a snort before coming over here. She owed me," he added, looking at Jake apologetically. Jake waved him off.

Everyone over there thought the news was important,

so I figured you should know, too."

"You did good." Then turning to the others, "Buzz, you and Jefferson should go see Margaret tomorrow morning -- see what our sheepherders bought from her. Then we'll ride out to the *Dammer Spread* and have a talk with our new neighbors."

The following morning Buzz came back with a report: the family consisted of two brothers: the Brodericks, their wives, the mother of one wife, one teen brother of one wife and four small children -- ten people in all. Half had stayed at their new digs, the other half had come to town for supplies. He confirmed that they had brought five hundred sheep down from Utah that were already grazing on the *Dammer* acreage.

A few of the boys --headed by Jake Ruskin -- along with wives and children decided to pay a welcoming visit to the new owners of the *Dammer Ranch* -- in fact, three wagons-full made the twelve mile trek.

The local newspaper at the time -- The Clarion Call -- reported their findings as follows:

<u>*Clarion Call   Bi-Weekly*</u>   *June 3, 1845*

An immigrant family of ten - the Brodericks - made the wrong choice, choosing a 640 acre property known as the Ed Dammer Homestead near the Eagle Ranch to put down their roots and begin a sheep herding operation.

According to an eyewitness report yesterday, within two miles of the homestead it became evident to a visiting group that the Brodericks had suffered tragedy and loss. Dead and dying sheep bloodied the grasslands.

When the visitors reached the homestead they found the buildings still burning and in ruins. Further examination proved to be unbearable for those visiting.

Molly Broderick, age ten, was found still alive, cradled in

the arms of her dead mother --
the only survivor and witness to
the carnage.

The leader of those arriving
on scene, Mr. Jake Ruskin, called
it a most cowardly massacre of
both man and beast. Bodies of
those lost were brought back to
our community for proper
burial.

Young Molly is presently
being cared for by Dr. and
Missus Daniel Ford.

⊃ Council Grove

★ Warm Springs

THE
BLACKSMITH
and the
Sheepherder's
Daughter

Chapter 1

"Jimmy says the fish are biting real good on the *Little Black* up at the beaver dam, Uncle Buzz. We're going up there in a few minutes, soon as he digs up a mess of worms. You want to come?"

"Naw, Missy," the old blacksmith set his hammer down and smiled at the skinny teenager looking up at him. He pulled a blue-checked kerchief from his overalls and ran it across his face before continuing.

"I'm so far behind I think I can see my ass ... er, butt 'bout fifty feet up there ahead of me. But you run along; maybe I'll saddle up the mule and come check on you around noon-time."

That line about his butt was one of Calder's favorites. All the folks in town had it memorized, yet it never failed to elicit a giggle from Molly -- not once -- in the six-plus years she'd known him. No different today. Molly giggled. "Whatcha making?"

Sarge, the blacksmith's shepherd, must have heard his master speak of saddling the mule, for he stretched and came eagerly out of the shop, tail wagging.

"I'm about half-way through with branding irons for Ida Ingraham, out at the *Snake Eyes,*" he replied. She pondered his handiwork for a moment. "They look really good -- identical, Uncle Buzz. How many you making?"

"Five," the blacksmith beamed, "finished up three so far, and just started working on the other two. Don't know why she needs so many, but that's her written order. Must be expecting a good crop of calves this year. Hope to have them all done by the end of the day."

The design was unique to the *Snake Eyes* spread: two letter I's joined together by a coiled snake in the center.

Then from Buzz Calder came a reminder, "Now, you make sure your mama knows where you and Jimmy are off to."

Molly glared at him as if to say, *I'm not a child!* She turned her nose in the air with some presumption, "That's already been done!"

"Don't you smart-mouth me, young lady! Show a bit of humility, now."

Feeling her face flushing, Molly became suddenly tractable, "I'm sorry, Uncle Buzz. We did tell our mamas 'least an hour ago. I had to gather eggs and feed the chickens, Jimmy ran to the general store for his mama, so all our chores are finished up." Then she winked, "Besides, Uncle Buzz, she's not my real mama." She reached down and patted Sarge.

"'Bout as much as I'm your Uncle Buzz, right?"

"Course you're my Uncle Buzz! Everyone in town knows that," she winked again. "Anyway, if you come, bring your pole." With that, Molly galloped off to find her young fishing buddy, Jimmy Iverson.

Buzz waved a meaty hand at the young girl, shook his head, wiped his palms on his cowhide apron and resumed his current project.

"Jimmy's going to find it pretty difficult to dig up worms this early in the year," he mused aloud, "but a nice trout dinner sounds mighty fine."

Two bay horses pulling a buckboard wagon came trotting down the town's main road, sloshing through the puddles left from the recent thaw. Elmer Kaufman was at the reins. He slid down from the bench, spat at a clump of bushes, then stuck out a hand.

"Hi, Mr. Calder. Margaret says I'm to help you offload this iron and coal, and make sure I give you the bill."

"She say anything about collecting the money for the goods?" Buzz smiled. Young Elmer was about seventeen, a little slow, but a good kid. Two years before, the blacksmith had considered hiring him as a helper, but Elmer's mother had put a stop to it.

"He could get hurt around your fire and hot metals," she had declared.

Just as well, a thought flashed through Buzz's head, *I was only trying to provide a safe place for the kid. Besides, right after Margaret Chisholm had hired him on as a helper at the general store.*

"Okay, young son, hand me that paper; then drag my pushcart out to the wagon and start shoveling the coal. Make sure you use gloves. I'll be right back with her money. Then I'll join you."

Elmer handed the paper to him, and happily went to retrieve the pushcart, Sarge at his heels. He started singing an old trail song about watching over a night herd in the moonlight. Putting on a pair of gloves, the teen pushed the cart outside.

The blacksmith went through the itemized list, double-checked her line items and totals, and chuckled. As always, Margaret had added a twenty-five cent 'interest' charge to his bill.

Hell, he thought, *her business has been doing just fine for as long as he'd been here -- some fourteen years -- but to this day she wouldn't know an interest fee from a rebate. Wonder who else pays the twenty-five cents?*

Margaret worked with several tinkers -- suppliers of metal, mostly tin or iron from back east. Some they picked up in the wilderness, tossed out to lighten a wagon on an uphill climb. The tinker would bring these treasures in to her, she'd stockpile them, then send a load on to Buzz -- maybe four trips per year. The coal was locally available; if he needed it he could pick it up. But he usually waited for his regular delivery.

Buzz counted out ninety one dollars and twenty-five cents, along with a note of thanks, and stuffed the payment into a leather pouch. Then he grabbed his wheelbarrow and walked to the wagon to help Elmer empty it of the scrap metal.

"Here's the money, Elmer. I see you're almost finished with the coal. Good lad."

Within an hour the last of the supplies were stacked neatly in his crib. Buzz handed Elmer five pennies to spend at the general store, thanked him, and watched as the young man climbed back onto the wagon, spat at a large rock alongside, then whistled happily to the team of horses and drove off.

The blacksmith turned to see Mrs. Grumps standing behind the corral rails, jaws working on a mouthful of hay, tail switching at early flies. The mule reminded him of his earlier intention. He removed gloves and leather apron. A quick tug on his watch fob revealed a shiny silver pocket watch. It was an hour before noon.

"It's getting late, Old Girl," he said, rubbing behind the mule's long ears. "Shall we grab a pole and go fishing?" Then turning to his faithful dog, he added, "Yeah, pooch, if we go, you go, too." Sarge's ears received equal time.

Chapter 2

The snow melt in the New Mexico southwest had been in earnest up until about two weeks before. Flooding had receded, but even now the *Little Black Creek* levels were high -- water was flowing rapidly, with deep pools and white water eddies.

Buzz Calder let Mrs. Grumps pick and slosh her way over slippery rock, through patches of snow and thick underbrush as they trekked toward the beaver dam. They stopped a couple of times where openings allowed them to view the river.

Sarge kept busy scouting the area ahead of them, returning occasionally to prod them on ... snuffing up the air, then running off to explore some more.

The distance wasn't far -- had he walked it would have taken Calder no more than a half hour, but neither he, nor Mrs. Grumps had been out on the trail all spring. They both needed the change of pace. "Besides," Buzz vocalized to himself, "living within that corral was, no doubt, making the old gal even grumpier." She had even tried to nip his shoulder when he threw a saddle on her -- the damned old lady!

Buzz Calder loved this rugged country. It was wild and fresh, even primitive; nothing like his past life as an attorney in Kansas City, Missouri, arguing over activities of miscreants or slave ownership -- always sitting at a desk, or poring over case law. Fortunately, his dad was a local gunsmith; Buzz had spent many an afternoon or weekend working the forge, pounding, rolling metals into shape or quenching. It took four stressful years agonizing over the decision, but the day he exchanged his suit and tie for a leather apron he felt liberated.

As it happened, his dad decided the gunsmithing business would increase closer to the Santa Fe trail and the frontier. He moved to the booming town of Council Grove, Kansas, right on the trail -- and offered Buzz a partnership. The younger Calder tried it for six months, but independence and the lure of the untamed west won the argument in his head. He said adieu and joined a west-bound wagon train.

<><><>

The *Little Black* was actually a small offshoot or tributary of the *Gila River*, taking a different route through the Black Mountain Range, and then rejoining its mother river as it rushed to join the mighty *Colorado*.

The *Gila* itself was one of the longest rivers in the West, originating above 10,000 feet in the Mogollon Mountains of New Mexico, with its confluence in Arizona with the *Colorado River*, a journey of almost seven hundred miles.

In the dozen years the blacksmith had lived in Warm Springs he had never made the trek to the southern end of the *Little Black*; he had, however, seen three or four of the steaming hot springs for which the village was named. They were far downstream from today's goal.

The beaver dam lay just around the next twist of the river. It was much more than a small flotilla of logs engineered into place by an ambitious family of large, furry rodents with huge teeth. The drop from the top of the logjam to the foamy water below was a full ten feet -- maybe more. The roar of the white water below the dam was deafening, drowning out human voices completely.

Buzz simply followed the excited shepherd as he guided the mule around the bend. He expected to see the youngsters fishing in the pools above the dam.

He dismounted and dropped the mule's reins. She seemed content to forage among the new crop of shoots springing up while he scoured the ground above the dam. Fresh animal tracks of every description abounded -- both predator and game, large and small -- but no human boot prints. After five minutes of searching, Buzz straightened and pursed his lips.

"Let's look below the dam, kids," Buzz said quietly to his two companions. "Perhaps they're trying their luck down below the white water."

As the blacksmith re-mounted, he tapped his index finger on his rifle butt, hanging within reach in its scabbard next to his left knee. A modicum of anxiety crept into his mind. He tried to shake it, but as he followed the river's slight jog to the left where the fallen timbers of the dam came into full view, he grew more worried. He urged Mrs. Grumps into a trot.

There were no signs of the youngsters.

"Go find them, Sarge! Go on!" Calder almost whispered the words to the shepherd. The dog cocked his head and ran downstream a few hundred yards and barked. Then he returned a few yards and sat. Buzz had seen him do this before, but in the pursuit of a stray calf or cow, never for tracking or corralling a missing person.

Whilst easing his rifle from its scabbard, Buzz leaned forward and spoke softly, "Okay, girl, let's go see what he's talking about." He pressed the mule's flanks with his knees, urging her on.

Sarge waited for his master, then bounded down the

trail once again, stopping where he had previously stopped. Buzz saw immediately the shepherd's find: the ground had been trampled by horses' hooves -- at least two, probably more, he surmised, and all unshod.

Sarge scouted the area nearby. There was blood puddled under an aspen tree below the dam. Close by was Jimmy's brown leather duckbill hat, with a few sprinkles of blood on it, laying atop a whittled but battered wooden fishing pole. Calder found the other fishing pole further down the embankment.

Navajo? Mescalero? Chiricahua?

Calder was devastated! His young friends wounded and kidnapped! His best guess was the Mescalero, a nomadic division of the Apache Tribe, living for only a short time at any one place before moving on.

The village hadn't been troubled by Indians for five years or more. Whoever these raiders were, they probably came down to water their horses, stumbled upon the young pair; then, after a brief, bloody struggle, had overpowered them. Calder surmised that like most youngsters these two carried jack knives, but no other weapons; nothing to face an adult Apache warrior.

Calder envisioned the youngsters putting up a brave fight -- the warriors being impressed, made the snap decision to take them along.

Should he track them or head back to town for help? Sarge made the decision for him -- the dog seemed to understand that Buzz approved his first discovery, so the shepherd continued along the river, following the freshly made horse tracks, sniffing at the droplets of blood as he went. Buzz shook his head. "Damn, dog! Where are you leading me?"

As if on cue, Sarge turned to look back for a moment, then continued on at a trot. Buzz urged Mrs. Grumps to follow, keeping his rifle across the pommel. Part of his brain told him, *'Go back! Go back! Get help!'* -- but another inner voice said, *'There's no time to lose! Get those kids back, now!'*

He continued on -- determined -- following the tracks downward and eastward along the *Little Black.*

Chapter 3

They came to a point where the darkness of the forest gave way to the brightness of an open meadow. The sky was almost cloudless; after the dampness of the timber the sun felt good on Calder's arms and shoulders. Its warmth seemed to penetrate through his clothing to the very marrow of his bones -- The *Little Black* had changed as well; wider now, more shallow, with a leisurely flow. He noticed that there were areas where steam was rising, one of the many hot springs for which the river was known -- the perfect spot for a ten minute rest if he could afford the time.

He loosened the reins on Mrs. Grumps. She carried him to the stream's edge and sucked in long pulls of water. Satisfied, she turned and walked up the bank,   her head high.

Further ahead Buzz could see that the trail disappeared, replaced by rock -- an ancient bed of shale or blue-gray flagstone -- mostly flat, but with wide cracks on the surface, and the occasional, jagged spire rising as much as twenty feet vertically.

Calder wasn't a man of science, but he guessed that some part of this mountain had broken away long before the white man had ever walked here, or that for some reason two parts of the mountain collided, causing those spikes. The rock sloped off to the southwest for at least a half mile before the trees took over again.

"Damn!" Calder whispered to Mrs. Grumps, "we're right between heaven and hell!"

He checked his pocket watch; it would be dark in five hours. He couldn't afford the ten minutes.

Sarge waded into the *Little Black* to midstream, lapped at the water, and was about to resume scouting the trail ahead when Buzz stopped him with a low whistle. The dog romped back to join his master, and promptly shook himself. Water flew everywhere!

Tiny white-capped ripples changed the surface of the *Little Black* as a breeze danced across the shallow water. The breeze brought something else to both man and beast -- smoke!

Abruptly, Buzz stiffened in the saddle. He caught the definite whiff of smoke!

Surveying the edges of the meadow on both sides of the stream he looked for physical evidences of a fire. He guessed there was a campfire nearby.

While Calder was considering the source, Sarge let out a howl. The blacksmith shushed him immediately. The shepherd had smelled the smoke as well ... but had he smelled something more?

<><><>

The sure-footed mule made her way carefully over the sloping rock face, staying close to the river -- blood spatters made trailing easy.

Calder kept the dog in check, giving orders quietly. Sarge seemed to understand every word. The smell of smoke grew as they approached the treeline.

Then they saw them -- two almost identical circular mounds -- typical Mescalaro wickiups -- four feet high, six feet in diameter, with wisps of white smoke circling and dissipating above. As the blacksmith grew nearer he noted three horses tethered nearby. No one seemed to be standing guard.

Calder shook his head. "What do you make of this?" he whispered to the mule. He dismounted, rifle in hand, then reached down, grabbed a handful of the hackles behind the dog's neck and gently gave it a shake.

"You stay," he ordered the shepherd. "Keep Mrs. Grumps company. I'm just going to take a look." Then he added, "I'll have to make myself known sometime; might as well be now."

The blacksmith set off at a trot toward the two huts. When he was within twenty yards he dropped to his knees and immediately called out, "Hello, you inside! Come out! Now!"

From inside he heard, "Uncle Buzz!"

Chapter 4

"Uncle Buzz!" the excited call came again, and Molly appeared, flipping aside an animal fur that hid the entryway to one of the huts. She ran into his arms and gave him a big hug. Her long sleeve woolen shirt had been replaced by one of buckskin.

"How did you get free? Where's Jimmy? Why are you ..." Calder was completely baffled.

"It's okay, Uncle Buzz," she interrupted excitedly. "Really! We're okay. Come! You don't need your gun. Who else is here?" she asked, looking round.

"No one, just me... oh, and Sarge and Mrs. Grumps, of course."

He whistled for his animals. Sarge promptly positioned himself a bit to the rear of the mule and growled. Mrs. Grumps responded with a playful kick and trotted toward her master.

From the other hut came an old man in traditional Mescalero dress. He glanced at Calder, then watched with some interest as the dog and mule approached.

Calder guessed the man to be in his late fifties or early sixties, but he couldn't be sure. The face was lined and weathered from years of exposure to the elements, but he stood straight and tall.

Molly tugged at Calder's sleeve. She whispered, "He

speaks some English; his name is Red Hawk."

Calder looked at Molly with some disbelief, then allowed himself to relax a bit. He approached the Indian.

"I understand you are called Red Hawk," he said. "I am called Buzz Calder. I was searching for the young boy and girl. I see they are safe with you. Thank you."

The native said only, "Um."

"You're Mescalero, right? Where did you learn English?"

Red Hawk again responded with one word, "Fort."

"You were a scout for the fort out at *del Cobre*?" the blacksmith asked. He had heard there were always three or four Indian scouts helping to watch over the copper mine workers down there.

"Um," came the one word response.

"Is this your home?" Calder asked, holding out both his hands, palm up to indicate the immediate patch of land where the Indians had pitched their two wickiups.

"No," said the warrior. Then, with an outspread right arm, he indicated everything from the rising of the sun to its setting. "My home," he declared.

Sarge came close; he approached one of the wickiups. Calder ignored him, but the old Indian watched the shepherd closely.

"Him spirit dog. Good sign."

Calder frowned, then turned to Molly. "Where's Jimmy? Why are you two here? What happened back there at the dam?"

The Mescalero warrior withdrew into the same wickiup, but returned almost immediately from the entryway. Beside him an ancient woman, hunched over and barely able to walk, was trying to maintain herself. Red Hawk practically carried her into the sunshine, and steadied her for an introduction to Calder.

The blacksmith was at a loss for words. The right side

of her face was bandaged from the top of her scalp to her neck with a blood-soaked, multicolored strip of cotton. Her garb was surprising: the skirt was as he expected: leather, but the shirt was decidedly not -- it was the one Molly had worn early that morning!

Red Hawk introduced her as his mother, then he ushered her back into the hut as Calder stood with mouth gaping open. Sarge stood at the entry as if he were standing guard.

"Where's Jimmy?" Calder demanded. Molly was about to answer when Red Hawk reappeared. At his arm was a limping Jimmy Iverson. The teen's forearm was wrapped in the same patterned cloth as the warrior's mother. The boy's eyes lit up as he spotted Calder, but he kept silent.

"Now, somebody explain what went on this morning," Calder insisted, eyes darting from Red Hawk to Molly.

"It's just a sprained ankle, Uncle Buzz," Jimmy explained. "I'll be right as rain by tomorrow."

"I'm not talking about the ankle, Jimmy, I'm asking about..."

Red Hawk held up an arm. "Boy brave warrior," he said quietly. "Save mother from spirit cat."

"We was fishing in the stream, an'," ... Jimmy started.

"We were fishing, Uncle Buzz," Molly interrupted. "We didn't even see the Indians. They were relaxing and watching us from a spot in the river where warm water comes bubbling up."

"Except for the two old ladies!" Jimmy gave Molly a frown ...

Molly obviously decided she could narrate the story better than Jimmy -- after all he was only thirteen and a half -- so she continued, "Yes, two older ladies were resting against an aspen tree. We heard a horse whinny, and turned to see."

Jimmy, determined, cut in again, "We turned to see, an' that's when I saw them women and that big cat. He had his jaws around one of 'um's head. I scrambled up the bank an' ran, an' stabbed at him with my fishin' pole. He kept tryin' to drag her off an' I kept stabbin' at 'im.

He finally let go an' tried to grab me. Got my arm pretty good, but Red Hawk came runnin' an' yellin', an' he ran off. I think I poked him real good! I guess I hurt my ankle when I was a'runnin', but I didn't notice 'til after."

Red Hawk returned once more from his wickiup, this time with two other women, one as ancient as the wounded one, one much younger.

He pushed the younger one forward. Her hands were damaged, either from a fire or an illness. "My woman," he said. The other they learned, was her mother.

Calder shook his head. "Any more in there?" he asked Red Hawk.

"No," the Indian replied, "this all my family."

"But, you're all by yourselves! Why aren't you dwelling with your group or village?" Calder asked.

"Not fight white man."

"Well," said the blacksmith, "I'm taking these youngsters back with me. You're welcome to join us."

"No," the warrior stood tall, "we are Mescalero. Our home is here. We stay."

"I'm staying!" Molly was defiant! "I'm taking care of the old woman until she's healed up."

"You can't stay! Red Hawk's woman can nurse her back to health. They don't need you!"

"Look at her fingers, Uncle Buzz! The woman is crippled. She can hardly feed herself! They do need me!"

Red Hawk watched the exchange for a few minutes, then disappeared. When he reappeared he was leading a pinto pony. He handed the reins to Molly.

"Woman strong, medicine strong, but not stay. Take pony. Come back tomorrow, maybe many days until mother well."

With that, Molly relented. Buzz hoisted her onto the

pony's back, pulled Jimmy up behind him on the mule. As they headed home the girl sang out, "I'll be here tomorrow!"

Chapter 5

"You take this horse back this very morning, Buzz Calder, and tell those savages Molly will not be coming! I'll not have my daughter associate with murderers, and that's final!"

Jason and Geraldine Turnbill were sitting on the front bench of their buckboard outside the blacksmith shop. Molly sat in the back, arms folded, teeth clenched. Geraldine was doing all the talking.

Jason hopped down and busied himself loosening the Indian pony from the rig and retying the reins to the hitching post at the front. He ventured a peek at Calder but said nothing.

Calder smiled. "Come inside, please," he felt he needed to control the situation. "Molly, stay out here." The couple followed him inside. Buzz shut the door and lost no time.

"Yesterday your daughter became a woman. She's no longer the little girl you took under your wing almost five years ago. If you make demands as you just did out there you will lose her for good, perhaps marry, perhaps move away, perhaps even to the Mescalero we met. "I'm willing to take the pony back, but only on one condition -- Molly will sit that pony, both of you in the buckboard, and we will" . . .

Geraldine began to object. Buzz stopped her with a "Hush, woman!" that Molly heard outside. Geraldine sputtered to silence.

Buzz continued, "We will meet them and she will be part of any agreement as to what's best for Molly. Just remember, it's Molly Broderick, not Molly Turnbill."

"That's unfair, Buzz Calder," Geraldine moaned. She's my daughter."

"Then don't lose her," Calder returned. He looked around the shop at the two unfinished branding irons and the other projects that were stacked up.

"Damn," he said, shaking his head,"I'm so far behind I think I can see my ass up ahead about fifty feet or so."

<><><>

The sun was high in the sky; even at close to four thousand feet elevation it brought health and warmth to one's bones. Red Hawk's wife and mother were lying on a flat rock, soaking up nature's healing power.

While Red Hawk watched the newcomers closely as they inspected the exterior of a wickiup, Molly slid from the pinto, ducked down and slid beneath a buffalo hide. Once inside, she carefully removed yesterday's bandages from the warrior's ancient mother.

The wounds were cruel -- teeth from the cougar had punctured the skin covering the scalp, and claws had opened a nasty gash down her right cheek almost to the throat.

Geraldine looked around uneasily. "Where's Molly?" she asked. "Buzz, have you seen Molly?"

"Yes, Ma'am. She's inside," he said, pointing to the hut.

"Inside there? How did she get in? What's she doing in there?"

From somewhere inside came, "Red Hawk! I need your help, please."

The old man grunted, frowned at Calder, stooped under the buffalo hide. Moments later he emerged, carrying his mother outside to the open air and the sun's warmth.

"Oh! My gracious! Sakes alive!" blurted Geraldine as she and Jason viewed the old lady for the first time. "Will she survive?"

"Definitely!" Molly shot back, confidently.

Red Hawk and Molly conferred for a moment; he seemed to agree with her -- whereupon, with his mother in his arms he continued into the shallow stream and set her down in the hot springs. Molly followed suit. The two of them sat in the shallow, bubbly warmth, with the medicinal waters flowing over them. Both were smiling.

"A cougar did that to her face?" Geraldine looked directly at the Mescalero warrior for the first time.

"Um," he looked at her almost tenderly as he spoke. "Brave young warrior save mother. Strong! Red Hawk thank."

"And how would my daughter be of assistance to you if I allow her to come for a few days?"

"Daughter *strong* medicine!" He held both fists out in front of him. "See," he said, pointing at his mother laughing playfully in the water. "Good heart!" he added.

Molly gently pulled the old woman to her feet. They waded slowly toward shore. Suddenly the water became icy cold. The old woman shrieked with a mixture of pain and delight. The two giggled. Calder, watching their antics from shore, waded midstream, lifted Red Hawk's mother out of the water and carried her to sit with the other women.

The young girl then ran to the buckboard and pulled a bulging pillow case from under the back bench. She dumped the contents of the case in front of her: a roll of cotton gauze, blankets, clothing, and a few other items.

She selected a small jar of honey. Dipping into it, she

applied honey liberally to the old lady's punctured skull, across the forehead, down the right cheek and onto the neck. Then, to Geraldine's amazement, Molly wrapped the head wound deftly, using the cotton gauze cheesecloth she had purchased at the general store the afternoon before.

Turning to Red Hawk she said, "Keep her warm tonight." His simple reply was "Um."

Jason turned to his wife, "Nothing more for us to see here. Let's go home."

As they climbed into the buckboard, Geraldine called out to Molly, "We're proud of you, honey."

Molly responded, "I'll be home later, Mom."

Chapter 6

Before going home that evening, Molly went to see Doc Ford. They were just having dinner when she knocked. Missus Ford ushered her into a small add-on attached to the main house, which served as a waiting room and office. She went to fetch the doctor.

"Well, well, if it isn't my little sheepherder," he said, grinning as he walked in. "I see you around town once in a while, but we haven't talked much at all in, what's it been-- five years? How are you keeping, Molly?"

"I'm just fine, Doc. In fact, feeling great."

"So then, what can I do for you that you come in at the end of the day? It had better be important to take me away from a nice bowl of beef goulash." He raised an eyebrow and chuckled.

"Sir, I have a -- uh, a patient if you will, and I need your advice."

"A patient? You're taking my patients now?" Doc Ford leaned forward with a curious look on his face. "That doesn't set right with me, young lady. I do the doctoring in this town" ...

"Oh, no, Sir! Nothing like that! You see, I'm taking care of some Indians out along the *Little Black*, an'"...

"Oh," Doc Ford exclaimed. "I heard something about an Injun getting cat-bit, and Jimmy Iverson saving her. So it's true, eh? And you want some help taking care of her."

"No, Sir. Not that. But these folks are getting old, and they have aches and pains -- painful fingers, arms and legs, rheumatism maybe; one of them has burns up and down her arms -- an' I'd just like to know if there's something I can do for them. They're good people, Doc."

"Ah, I see." He leaned back and twiddled his thumbs for a few seconds. "Maybe I should take a ride out there with you tomorrow and meet these '*good people*' of yours."

"Not necessary, Sir, but welcome. I'll be heading out in the morning, after I finish my chores -- about eight."

"The wife and I will be ready. I'll bring a few items from my cabinet, but there's not much that can cure old age." He laughed. "Can the trail handle a gig?"

"Yes, it can." She turned to go. "Thanks."

<><><>

True to his word, the doctor was ready, along with his wife, to travel along the *Little Black* early the next morning. Molly led the way, riding the Indian pony.

After introductions, Doc Ford knelt to examine the wounds, just scabbing over on the face, skull, and neck of Red Hawk's mother. After a careful evaluation, he looked up at Red Hawk and Molly. "My goodness! You tended her?"

"Yes, Sir," Molly replied, obviously embarrassed. "I did the best I could, but I'm sure I coulda done better."

"Don't ever say that, young lady! You did an outstanding job! The use of honey was real smart!"

Molly beamed; Red Hawk added "Um," and nodded in agreement; the warrior's mother, although not understanding the language, reached out and put her hand over Molly's hand -- and smiled.

Doc Ford turned to Molly. "Is she the only one you

wanted my advice on or is there someone else?"

"Yes, there is ... sitting over there." She pointed to Red Hawk's wife. "It's her arms."

"Ah, yes," he mused -- "Old. Not much can be done at this stage; too old to bring the skin back to life I'm afraid. I do have some ointment if she's in pain."

"No pain from burn," assured Red Hawk. "Burn long time -- now, woman moan; pain at night, fingers crooked, Mescal gone."

"Ah, so the Mescal helps, eh? I brought some, but not much." Doc Ford looked up at his wife. "Mildred, bring me the jar of Agave."

He applied the lotion, looking at Molly. "It's a big desert plant with pointed leaves, been known for years as good medicine for many ailments."

"Desert?" Molly frowned. "No desert close to here. How do I get mescal?"

"Traders; just like everybody else in town gets supplies. I have more agave in my office -- enough to see you through until the next wagon pulls in."

"Thank you, Doc. I'll pay you."

"I may have a couple of ideas for you if you're interested. Come, see me in a few days."

Doc Ford helped his wife up into the gig, then turned to Red Hawk. "You know about chewing willow and birch bark, right?"

"Um," the Indian replied. "Earth Mother teach Mescalero use many trees, plants, grass, berries. Good medicine."

"What's this about chewing willow and birch bark, Doc?" Molly was intrigued. "What does that do?"

"Helps with things like sickness, headaches, fever, toothache, any number of things. Not the outer bark, mind, but there's an inner bark, and that's what you use. I'd advise you to always know where the nearest willow tree is."

"Good to know. Thanks again." Molly waved them goodbye, then invited the women to accompany her to bathe in the hot springs. They sucked in air and shrieked with laughter as they waded through the icy water toward the hot bubbles.

Chapter 7

Spring was turning to summer -- longer days, more sun -- and with summer came more activity among the villagers, and, of course, it equated to more work for the local blacksmith. Buggies and carriages needed normal repairs to things like undercarriages, springs, harness riveting and, of course, horse shoeing.

Households needed pots, pans, skillets, hinges, nails, and wash tubs. In short, Buzz Calder, like so many of his fellows in other towns and villages, became a "jack of all trades" for any household that couldn't purchase a needed item at the local general store.

Specialty jobs came around as well, like the branding irons for Ida Ingraham, various trunks and strong boxes, or a horse-drawn hay rake with a trip lever to gather hay in stacks. He had seen the rake design on display in Kansas City years before, and had put the concept on paper. This was his third such output, and with each he had made slight adjustments. The farmers were elated.

Now he was working on a job he himself had designed, a set of huge jawed tongs to hoist hay into his barn's hayloft. In theory, it should work, and he was anxious to try it. There were a few glitches to work out, such as a rolling rail to bring hay inside, and the configuration of the hoist itself. Some kind of greased wheel on an axle, or perhaps a chain with cogs -- he was still working it out. If it worked as well as he envisioned, Buzz felt it would be in demand. He was going to patent it before he made it public.

He pulled out his pocket watch; it was only three forty-five -- but it was Saturday, and he was feeling in fine form.

"I'm going to quit for the day," he announced to his shepherd. "In fact, Sarge," he said, taking the dog's face between his calloused hands and looking into its eager pale blue-green eyes, "I'm taking the rest of the week off!" He laughed. "I'm going up to the house, take a shower, then I'm going to Jake's Place for a juicy steak dinner and a couple of beers. But," he laughed again, "I'll share. Promise! I'll bring you some gristle and a bone. After all, you're my spirit dog."

Jake's Place was crowded that Saturday night, July 5th. Almost all the tables were occupied; the mood was cheerful. Calder elbowed his way to the bar, placed his order for the steak, asked Jake if Teresa could throw a couple of beef bones on the plate for Sarge, then ordered a big jug of beer to be brought to his table -- now he just needed to find a table.

A young ranch hand nodded as Buzz asked and sat down across from him.

"I have some beer coming if you're thirsty," Calder told him. "I'm Buzz Calder, blacksmith in town," he said, extending his hand.

"Yep, I know," the younger fellow said, shaking Buzz's hand with a firm grip. "Ted Willitson ... *Eagle Spread*, out 'tween the *Little Black* and *Caballo Lake*. An' sure, I'll have a beer with you. Problem with beer, it foams all over the table, then the mug drips all over your shirt, an' on a hot day it ain't all that satisfyin'. Most as tasteless as a glass'a water."

"Huh," Calder said aloud, "hadn't thought about that. I think you're right. A cold beer on a hot day sounds much better than what we have here. Cause for thought, Ted, cause for thought." Then something else twigged in Calder's mind.

"The *Eagle Spread*. That's close to that old ranch that burned to the ground a few years ago, isn't it?"

"*Ed Dammer's Spread* you mean?" Ted acknowledged. "Tis for a fact. We run cows on 'er two-three times a year. Damn shame. They's 'most nothin' there 'cept 'bout half the barn. When the boys are out that way an' it's snowin' or rainin', we head there fer cover."

"Huh," Calder said again, nodding his head. He saw Teresa coming through the crowd holding a large serving tray. He moved his elbows off the table as the waitress set the tray down; "Be right back with the beer." She looked at Ted. "And two mugs," she smiled.

"I'll take one of those steaks if you got another'n," Ted called after her. She raised her arm to acknowledge the request and disappeared through the smokey din. She reappeared a moment later with the beer.

"Your steak will be a few minutes, drover," she smiled.

"Just Ted, Ma'am," he smiled back.

"You can pick up your bones on the way out, Buzz. I'll have a few by then, and I'll wrap them up for your pup."

"Much appreciated, Teresa," Calder saluted her with a raised steak knife.

Ted's steak followed within minutes. Wearing a goofy smile, the young cowhand said, "Much appreciated, Teresa," and saluted her with a raised steak knife.

"My, you're a quick learner, aren't you?" she laughed.

"Put his steak on my bill," Calder told her.

Ted started to argue, but Teresa cut him off. "I've already written it down."

Steaks and potatoes disappeared from the plates, the second jug of beer, even though warm, was almost gone.

Calder pushed his chair back. "How long in town, Ted?"

"Paid fer tonight an' tomorrow night at the hotel.

Headin' out just after midnight, or, if I get lucky," Ted winked at Calder, "early Monday mornin' -- prob'ly four or five. Why?"

"I'm thinking on it," Calder replied. "Have an idea or two, but not sure if I have all the pieces yet. If you're sober tomorrow afternoon around four o'clock, swing by my place. You know where it is. We'll talk."

The two men stood, shook hands, Ted thanked him for the dinner and walked away. Calder watched him go, then seeing Teresa, he sat back down and ordered one last warm beer. He needed to think.

It was a shock just moments later to see a new waitress approach with a third jug and two mugs: Margaret, owner of the general store. He stood, and bowed.

"Don't worry, Buzz, my store isn't in financial trouble. I asked Jake if you were here, and Teresa was just walking up. She pointed over here, gave me the jug and two mugs. Ha!" she continued, "told me you were lonely! You lonely, Buzz?" she laughed.

He invited her to sit. "What will Rian say, Margaret?" he asked pulling a chair out for her. Rian had been dead for more than six years, but Calder played along.

"Rian won't even know," she assured Calder, "and nobody in this place recognizes me."

He poured her a beer. "So, tell me why you're really here, Margaret."

After a swig, Margaret grimaced, then grew serious.

"Buzz, mail wagon pulled in from Albuquerque late yesterday. There's a letter from your mom. I should have had it to you this morning early, but I plumb forgot until this afternoon. I had Elmer run it over to your place, but you were closed."

She reached into a sweater pocket and retrieved a

bedraggled envelope. He ripped it open and scanned the short message. Margaret watched closely.

"Damn it!" Calder looked at his friend glumly.

"Today's July 5th isn't it? My dad died, Margaret. Back on April 5th, exactly three months ago."

He downed his full mug of stout, and stood. "I need to go home."

Margaret took his arm to console him, but the blacksmith only patted her hand and smiled down at her.

"Just as well the news waited until now. I had a good day. Now, when does that wagon come back through?"

"Not for more than a week, but there's a small company of soldiers heading for the fort at *del Cobre*. Supposed to be coming through here early tomorrow morning, picking up a few here and there. You should be safe if you join up with them."

"*del Cobre!* That's a fair bit south, Margaret"...

"Yes," she cut him off, "but I hear there are loaded copper wagons going to Albuquerque every couple of days from there. Probably your best bet."

"And you're probably right."

"Anything I can do for you, while you're gone, Buzz?"

"Uh, well, yes, now I think of it. I had an appointment tomorrow afternoon at four. I'd appreciate it if you have Elmer swing by my place to feed my animals and cancel that meeting."

Chapter 8

Early morning that same Saturday, Molly Broderick and Jimmy Iverson headed for the Indian encampment, riding double on the pony.

Red Hawk, on Molly's last trip there, had specifically asked that Jimmy come with her in four days. That was Tuesday. Today was four days.

They took their fishing gear with them, figuring to share a trout with the old warrior and his cadre of female companions.

Within an hour they had four fat trout, three cutthroat, one brown. They journeyed on. The expansive flat rock finally came into view -- the wickiups lay just beyond, in the first line of white birch -- except, there were no wickiups! Molly urged the pony on.

They were met by Red Hawk, his mother and wife. The three were dressed shabbily, the two women wailing.

"What happened?" Jimmy whispered to Molly.

"I think White Otter, Red Hawk's mother-in-law, must have died," she answered softly. "They look so sad."

"She die. Two day." Red Hawk walked toward them, holding two fingers in the air. "In morning."

"When are you going to bury her?" Jimmy blurted out, then he remembered his manners. "Sorry, Sir. I mean, how are you going to handle the ceremony, and when?"

"Same day, in afternoon," came the reply.

Molly pulled Jimmy aside. "Just show respect, don't ask questions. Let them cry. Red Hawk wanted you here today, he has something to say. Be patient. White Otter's death was definitely unexpected."

"Okay, okay! I guess I, uh . . ." Jimmy looked down at the stringer of trout. "Hey, what should we do with the fish?"

Red Hawk overheard, "How many?"

"Four," Jimmy responded. "One real big one."

"Cook over fire," the old man pointed to glowing red coals where the wickiups had been. Then he asked, "You want share big one with White Otter?"

"Uh, well, sure! But how?" the lad asked.

"She there," he said, pointing to a mound under a birch tree. "We fry, put on flat rock on grave. I watch all night, keep wolf, bear away."

He pointed to willow trees along the *Little Black*. "Cut branch," he held his arms about three feet apart. "This many," he said, holding out both hands, fingers up.

"You're leaving us, aren't you, Red Hawk?" an easy venture on Molly's part. Wickiups were broken down, one of the ponies was outfitted with leather straps, a travois lay beside it -- already loaded with hides, and waiting for whatever else the Indian had in mind; just a matter of strapping the pony to the sleigh.

"Um," Red Hawk answered. He turned his attention back to Jimmy. "Bring fish. Cook now."

The man showed the boy how to split the fish down the middle, then lace a willow branch through each half until all four were as butterflies, frying over the embers.

"I found a flat rock when I was down at the river, Mr. Red Hawk, Sir. Shall we take her breakfast over there now?"

"Um," Red Hawk agreed. "Half big one." He stripped the fish from the branch and set it on top of the rock. The two of them walked to the mound; Jimmy set the fish atop the freshly-dug earth mound. "Do we say anything special, Sir?"

"Already say. You say what in your heart."

Jimmy thought for a moment. Then he brightened. "Hope you like trout, Ma'am."

Red Hawk studied Jimmy for a moment, frowning -- then he nodded. "Um." He put his arm around the lad's shoulders as they returned to the fire where they all gathered to feast on trout.

After the meal the two native women walked a few feet into the trees and unabashedly began stripping. They returned, donning fresh clothing which they had obviously stored on birch limbs. Red Hawk followed suit.

<> <> <>

"Say goodbye now," Red Hawk said, soberly. "Have something for brave. Call him Spirit-Cat Warrior." He walked into the *Little Black*'s shallow, steamy water, reached down and pulled something out from an underwater boulder and handed it to Jimmy. It was a vest made from a mountain lion pelt, fringed at the bottom, and hemmed with fresh water pearls. The women must have worked on it for hours, scraping and softening.

"Cat come back, try kill pony. Red Hawk kill. Mother say make for brave, young hunter," the old man informed them. "It big now, but you grow!" he added.

"Thank you all!" Jimmy beamed at the three natives. "This is my cougar, Molly, the one I stabbed with my fishing pole! Thank you, thank you! I promise I'll take real good care of it!"

Next, the old man turned to Molly. "Medicine woman." He held his hands out, "Much strong healing in hands. You like daughter to Red Hawk. Keep pony."

"Oh! Thank you, Red Hawk! I shall call him Spirit! *He that runs with the winds!* Thank you!"

Red Hawk's mother stepped forward. She handed Molly her favorite buckskin shirt, washed and neatly folded. Molly reached out and hugged her, a very uncommon custom for the old lady. She shrank back at first, then returned the gesture. The old lady stepped back and said, "Good." They all laughed.

"Are you leaving today?" Molly asked Red Hawk.

"No. Next day. Keep grave safe tonight."

"I hate to say goodbye, but I guess we'll be off," Molly said. "Maybe we'll see each other again." She reached for Spirit's mane and pulled herself up, then reached around and pulled Jimmy up behind her. They journeyed home; Jimmy exuberant, Molly with tears in her eyes.

Chapter 9

While the Iverson and Turnbill families were singing hymns in church the following morning, Buzz Calder, satchel in hand, was almost eight miles southeast, traveling toward the old Mexican fort at *del Cobre*. He was granted a "ride-along" spot with a U.S. Army detachment of twenty-eight recruits, given a rifle and a seat in the third of four wagons.

Of course, he had the option of pulling out at any point along the trail, to strike out north on his own, but for now he was content; he was basically going the right direction: east.

Two days later three others joined their little group -- two brothers and a friend. The commander frowned, but gave them permission to tie their horses behind a wagon and climb aboard. They were scruffy-looking characters, but they were three extra rifles in the event of a skirmish with Apaches; all three were equipped with bed rolls and their own weapons.

In Calder's mind, they had clearly washed neither clothes nor bodies for months; the stench was almost unbearable. Fortunately, they were assigned a different wagon; Buzz could only imagine the revulsion of their fellows.

Evening came. The little caravan stopped along a

small alpine lake -- actually more a pond than lake. At it's deepest it was no more than four feet.

As the men began to gather for an evening meal, consisting of pemmican and coffee, the commander suddenly declared, "Someone here stinks! Step forward!"

Everyone, including the commander, knew who the culprits were, but no one volunteered.

"Wagon one! LaRue! Does your wagon stink?"

"No, Sir!" came the answer.

"Wagon two! Wheeler! How about your wagon?"

"No, Sir!" came the answer.

"Calder! I Assigned you to wagon three. Does it stink?"

"Not bad at all," Buzz replied.

"That leaves wagon four. Osborne! Does your wagon stink?"

"Sumpin awful, Sir. Didn't before them three come aboard," he continued, pointing at the three scruffy ones.

"You three!" the commander bawled. "Step forward!"

The three men looked at each other, but didn't move.

"Boys," he continued, allowing their ignoring his order, "you ride with us, you stay clean. That means clean clothes, clean bodies, clean hair. You three smell like the rear-end of a skunk that's been dead two days."

Some of the soldiers guffawed, others nodded their heads in agreement. The three men stared at the commander -- angry and embarrassed.

"Here's your choice, gentlemen. Strip down, clean yourselves up in this little pond we have here," he said, pointing with a thumb. "I have some lye soap for you. When you come out put on some clean duds; I'm sure you have a change in your saddlebags. If not we can probably scare up some for you. Your other choice is to ride out of here now. It's up to you. What's it gonna be?"

The three men considered his ultimatum. One fellow immediately threw a leg over his horse's back and started down the trail. He looked over his shoulder for his companions. When the brothers didn't follow he reluctantly turned his horse around, dismounted and began to undress with his buddies. The commander tossed them each a chunk of lye soap as they stepped into the shallow pond.

<><><>

Calder woke to a whinny, followed by a strange noise he couldn't identify. His heart began pumping faster. It was at least an hour before first light. He raised up on one elbow, straining to listen for any other peculiar sounds. Nothing.

Slipping out of his bedroll, Calder gripped the army rifle he had been issued, and on hands and knees headed for the sentry's station, the hair on his neck standing.

The sentry was dead; throat had been slit. Calder raised the rifle and fired into the air. The camp came alive. First search revealed more sorrow: the commander and his aide had also fallen victim to a knife to the throat. Chunks of lye soap had been stuffed in their mouths to express contempt. Missing, too, was the commander's money pouch.

Panic and confusion followed. The young soldiers were without direction. Calder gave a loud whistle. Heads turned.

"Anyone here with army time under your belts? You all new recruits? Okay. Here's what we do. Take five minutes. Choose one among you as your leader until you reach *del Cobre*. Now where are the three who just joined us?"

One of the three newcomers came forward. "Those two brothers who were with me are gone, Sir. I suspect they are the murderers."

"So do I," Calder agreed. Then, turning to the nearest fellow standing by he said, "Soldier, bind this man in chains until we determine his guilt or innocence."

The soldier looked around unsure of the order, but proceeded to do as asked. In the meantime, a vote took place, and a captain chosen. Calder asked and received permission from the newly appointed leader, Henry Ware, to go after the two brothers. After some discussion, Calder chose a Benjamin Draper to ride with him in pursuit of the murderers.

They left immediately. The sun was just creeping over the eastern mountains, just enough light to make tracking easy. From his reckoning, Buzz thought the two were less than an hour ahead, and riding hard to the north. Tracks were deep, throwing dirt and grass behind the horses.

Calder chose an easier pace. There was only wilderness for at least fifty miles in any direction; he felt sure he would catch up with them within two days; sooner if they continued to push their horses as they were.

In the meantime the soldiers, under Henry Ware, were heading now almost straight east toward the old fort near *del Cobre*. From there they would join up with a larger contingent heading for Albuquerque. Calder hoped to meet up with the troupe near the old copper mine.

Mid-morning came. A small stream was trickling beside the trail. Draper suggested they stop for a few minutes to give the horses a breather and a drink.

"Good idea, Ben," Calder agreed. "We'll have a chance to let some water as well," he laughed.

Draper took the reins of both ponies and led them down to the stream; Calder had other business to attend. After a few minutes they returned to their saddles and continued on, but for only a few minutes.

"I noticed some pinkish water in little pools along the edge of the stream when I was watering the horses, Mr. Calder. Where do you suppose that came from?" Ben asked. Then he looked at Buzz with a look of panic. "It's blood isn't, Mr. Calder?"

"Sounds like blood, Son. Let's take another look." They dismounted once again.

"Stay here with the horses, Ben. I'll be right back. Keep your eyes peeled and your rifle handy."

Once at the water's edge, Buzz could easily see the snakelike wisps of blood, still bright red, on the surface, some gathering at the water's edge in small pools, some continuing downstream. He quickly climbed the bank.

"Whatever happened, Mister Draper," he whispered, "it happened close by and recently. Could be a predator just doing what it does naturally, could be something more. Don't panic, but keep a sharp eye."

The young recruit only nodded. They retrieved rifles from scabbards and kept their horses at a walk. Calder was sure that whoever was letting blood flow into the stream was within a hundred yards of them.

They found the source -- a spot where the trail crossed the stream in a shallow gully and proceeded up the other side. In the stream-bed a big bay, still with saddle intact, lay dead. Its rider, also dead, had apparently tried to scramble up the bank, but been unsuccessful. Further up the trail the dirt was plowed, evidencing several horse hooves. From the look of it, Calder concluded five or six had given chase to the other brother. He turned back.

Draper stared from the two bodies in the stream to Calder. "What should we do, Sir?"

"I'm satisfied the other one met up with the same fate. Let's pull this fellow out of the water, strap him to a horse and get the hell outta here. Take the saddlebags. May find the army money."

Chapter 10

After church Molly and Jimmy ran to visit the blacksmith, to give him the news about Red Hawk's family -- the death, the moving on, and the parting gifts to each of them. Mule and dog were there, barnyard animals had been fed, but Calder wasn't to be found.

"Wonder where he went off to," Molly said.

"He wasn't at church, neither," Jimmy added.

"He wasn't at church, *either*," Molly corrected.

"That's what I" ...

"It's *either*, not *neither*," Molly scolded her young friend. "Don't you learn anything from Old Missus Brighton?"

"I just wonder where he is," Jimmy continued. "It ain't like Mr. Calder to just leave town, especially on a Sunday when he's expected to be in church. You spoze he's sleepin' off a drunk?"

"I don't think so. He never misses church."

"I'm gonna check," Jimmy decided. Before Molly could protest, he threw a rock at the wall of Calder's house. It made a dull thud, but otherwise no damage.

Old Floyd Banner came shuffling down the road on his way home from church, saw the throw and yelled, "Hey, you kids! Git away from there! Go on now! Git! 'Fore I tell Buzz when he gits back!"

"Mr. Calder's gone?" Molly asked.

"Yeah," Jimmy echoed, "where is he?"

"Why, he's in Council Grove, Kansas. Leastwise," the old man continued, "he's on his way there. If you'd went to church this mornin' you'd a knowed that!"

"We *did* go to church, Mr. Banner," Molly said matter-of-factly, "but we left right after, so I suppose we missed the announcement."

"Weren't no 'nouncement," Floyd Banner informed them, "jus' everbody talked 'bout it. His daddy died. He's goin' back to see his momma."

"How long will it take to get there, Mr. Banner?" Molly asked.

"Well, young lady, prob'ly a week or more to reach Albuquerque, then another week to get to Kansas, mebbe more. But don't worry about his place. Margaret told us Elmer Kaufman is hired to take care of his animals while he's gone."

"Is he gonna stay there, Mr. Banner?" Jimmy asked, looking very concerned. "I was hopin' to work for him when I get bigger. I hope he comes back."

"He'll come back, Jimmy," Molly assured her friend. "He likes it here -- that's why he left Kansas City in the first place. Right, Mr. Banner?" she asked looking for support.

"Why, of course! Don't you worry 'bout that! He made his home here in the Valley, an' made lots o' friends, too." With that, Banner continued down the road, hobbling in an up and down motion, swinging his shorter wooden leg out in front of him.

"I should have gone with him," Molly said after Floyd was out of earshot.

"Who? Mr. Banner?" Jimmy shrieked. "Why on earth would you go with him?"

"No, Silly! Uncle Buzz! He's going to be gone for a long time. He'll be all alone; I could have kept him company; I could have cooked for him; I speak Apache in case he meets up with Indians; and like Red Hawk said, I have the gift of strong medicine; he should have asked me to go with him, Jimmy."

"You in love with him, Molly?" Jimmy giggled. "You are, ain'tcha?"

"No, Jimmy Iverson! I am *not* in love with Buzz Calder! Stop being so childish! I simply think he should have talked to me before he left."

Chapter 11

Calder led the way northeast, following a well-used, and in his view, dominant animal trail; his young companion was impressed with the tracking skills of the older man. Most impressive to both was that no Indian ponies had used the trail.

"What tracks do you see?" Buzz asked young Draper.

"I know those are deer," Draper answered, pointing, "but I have no idea about the others."

"It's not just the prints," Buzz smiled. "Scat tells you things as well. At this very moment I see evidence of four different critters." He pointed to paw prints of a wolf and mountain goat, and without moving forward, he identified the scat of a big horn sheep and a rabbit.

Further up the trail Draper pointed to the ground. "Mr. Calder, look! Does that black pile belong to a bear? I've never seen anything quite like it. Looks like it could be really big!"

"Son," Calder agreed, looking at the steaming black mound, "it surely does; and he is big, and he is close by! If you know any songs, now's the time to start singing. Hopefully, you'll scare him away."

"That ain't even funny, Sir."

"Wasn't meant to be. Get your rifle ready just in case," he added. "Grizzlies are mean sons-a-bitches.

Loud noises usually scare them in another direction, but if this one's a new mama with cubs she'll be fiercely protective of her kids. Could also be a grand-daddy that just may want to sharpen his skills.

Just remember this, Son, a horse can't save your ass trying to outrun a grizzly in a chase for even as much as a quarter mile. I've seen it with my own eyes, else I wouldn't have believed it myself."

"What happened?"

"A group of us was rounding up some stray cows -- five of us as I recall. Came up a rise and stumbled upon two mean old boars fighting. It was rutting time for them, and one was having the worst of the fight. When he crawled off to lick his wounds the winner spotted us watching. Didn't even stop, just came roaring. We, of course, all scattered. That old bear picked out Farley Pickens; chased him and his roan down that hill and through a meadow before he finally figured Farley was not worth the effort and gave up the chase.

When we regrouped, Farley was white as a sheet; said that bear's breath was less than ten feet from his roan's rear end. You'da thought the old boy would have been all tuckered out after his fight, but he wasn't quite ready to settle down."

Draper held his rifle tighter and started singing an old-time folk tune his parents had brought from the old country. It was about a fellow who mistook his lady friend for a swan and shot her. Calder remembered the tune and joined in. The volume increased as they rode on through Scrub Oak, Mountain Mahogany, and the various shrubs and grasses.

Even being so close to potential danger both sang as they trotted through the bush. Singing made the two feel more comfortable -- almost cheery.

The major trail they had been following opened up

to an area of high plains -- grasslands as far as they could see. Calder's watch told him it was just after noon. The trail continued northeast through the high grass, so they followed along. Other trails criss-crossed. The two men agreed to follow a smaller one which seemed to head in a more easterly direction, hoping to meet up with the north-south trail between *del Cobre* and Albuquerque.

The long day ended without finding the wagon ruts they were looking for. They camped beside a small mountain lake and feasted on two ruffed grouse over a small campfire.

Before settling in for the night they found out a bit more about each other: Buzz told of his past life in Kansas City, Ben told of stealing the horse he was riding and running away from an orphanage in Phoenix, then simply working at odd jobs as a drifter for almost a year.

"I was just like those three that came into camp the other day -- just like that one," he said, pointing at the dead fellow they had leaning against a tree for the night. "Except," he said with a wide grin, "I didn't never smell as bad as they did. When I heard the army was recruiting, I found where they was, washed up in a river, combed my hair and joined up."

"How long did you sign on for?" Buzz asked.

"Two years. I got two uniforms, a rifle and all the truck in my backpack. Oh, and two dollars a month plus rations."

"How old are you, Ben?"

"Seventeen and a half, I think."

"You know you could be hanged for stealing that horse, don't you?"

Draper stared into the fire but said nothing.

"Son, never tell that story again!" Buzz warned.

Mid-morning the following day, their trail joined up with the wagon road they were searching for. It was time for a powwow.

Calder had already decided to head north on his own, but the more he kept thinking about the young rider with him the more he wondered if it was a good decision. Hell, the kid was barely seventeen if that, and signed on for two bucks a month? He could do better as a drover.

Calder decided to pursue this new strain of thought.

"Mr. Draper. This is where we part company. I'm off to Albuquerque, then continue along the Santa Fe Trail east northeast to Council Grove, Kansas to visit my mom. You are to head south to rejoin your contingent, turn in the dead murderer and tell your story. Now," Calder scratched his head, "how many of those soldiers know you?"

"None, Sir. I joined up just 'fore you came on."

"Have a suggestion. Drop this piece of scum right here on the road, and ride to Albuquerque with me. I think we can find you a job paying as much or more than the army pays. But more than that, I think a good education would serve you even better. It's up to you: north or south."

Draper took no time in deciding; without ceremony, he untied the dead man and dropped him at the horse's feet. Calder wrote a note and pinned it to the killer's shirt:

> *One of the two that killed the army commander and others from the contingent heading for del Cobre. He died at the hands of the Apache, as did his brother.*
> *Yours,*
> *Buzz Calder, Blacksmith - Warm Springs*

"We'll need to get you some new duds," Calder smiled as he put his foot in a stirrup, "otherwise, you'll be hanged as a deserter as well as a horse thief."

Chapter 12

Elmer Kaufman sat in the rocker on Buzz Calder's front stoop, chewing on a long stem of straw. It was after three p.m. on Sunday.

Margaret said to meet somebody there around four p.m. just to tell him Mr. Calder wasn't coming. Sounded awful silly, but he'd do it for Margaret.

He was supposed to feed all the animals afterwards as well, and *that* he was happy to do. He loved animals. Plus, he was getting five pennies every day for feeding them morning and evening.

On top of that, Margaret promised a hard boiled egg each day he brought her the eggs from Mr. Calder's hen house. She gave him a collection basket; he would gather the eggs just before leaving.

Five pennies a day! Margaret had told him the blacksmith could be gone for as long as a month!

He stopped rocking. A sudden realization came over him: he would be earning more than a dollar by the time Mr. Calder returned. Another thought came right behind -- a glimmer of sentience Elmer had never before experienced. More than simply doing odd jobs for Margaret and occasionally others, he was almost a man, making real money at a real job.

He was still daydreaming when Ted Willitson rode

into the yard.

"Afternoon, young man; looking for the blacksmith. He around?"

"You the fella he was fixin' to meet here at four o'clock?"

"Yes, I believe I am, " Ted said. "Leastwise, I'm one of them." He shrugged his shoulders, smiling.

"Well, he ain't here," Elmer said with emphasis, "won't be here for maybe a month."

"Oh, what happened?"

"He's gone someplace for maybe a month or more, left me in charge of feeding his animals."

"A month, huh? Okay, young man, looks like he chose the right man to take care of his property. Do him proud. I'll be back in a month or so. Hope to see you again." Ted tipped his hat and nudged his pony in the flanks...

Elmer watched him go, satisfied with the approval of the cattleman -- especially by calling him a young man. He stood, picked up Margaret's basket and went to gather eggs, still basking in his earlier daydream.

Chapter 13

Calder and Draper reached Albuquerque at seven p.m. two days before the next wagon left *del Cobre*. The two men stopped for the night at a hotel on the edge of town -- more of a boarding house, owned by the widow Marcussen.

They noted a stable, an outhouse and a corral with two mares -- a black and a big-boned roan -- gawking at them from one end. The two men dismounted, walked their steeds into the stable, threw saddles over a rail.

Calder found a barrel of oats and a stack of oat-bags; he filled a bag from the barrel, tossed another to the lad, then fed his horse. Ben was quick to follow every move the blacksmith made.

The old two story was solidly built but in need of several repairs, and Calder noted, could use a new coat of paint. As they headed for the front door, the widow watched from the kitchen screen door.

"You may as well come in this side door boys; act like you own the place anyway," she gestured, smiling.

She guided them into the parlor, watching their every move.

"Deserters?"

Ben started to say something, but Buzz cut him off.

"No, Ma'am. I'm Buzz Calder, blacksmith from

southwest of here. The boy is an orphan. Army gave him duds, thought they were going to" ... She stopped him abruptly.

"Explain later. Right now you'd better get up to the attic and sort through some clothes." She pointed. "You'll find something for the lad. He's a bit conspicuous in those army duds. Bring your old clothes down. I'll burn them in my trash barrel."

The blacksmith tried again to explain.

"Explain over supper. Right now, do as you're told."

Calder cocked his head as he looked at the widow. "You've done this before, Ma'am." They headed for the stairs.

The attic was filled with merchandise left by tenants; some had left without settling their accounts, taking advantage of her good nature. Some had simply forgotten their goods. There were guns, boots, rain slickers, pocket watches and miscellaneous items -- even two boxes of books -- in addition to rack after rack of attire for all ages. Draper chose a couple of shirts and a pair of pants. He changed, folded his uniform and descended the stairs. Calder followed with three pocket watches, two books and the biggest bore handgun he'd ever seen, complete with holster, belt and ammunition. He brought it down to examine it a bit closer.

Mrs. Marcussen treated them to a delicious supper after which Draper washed up the dishes. Their host smiled and shrugged as she opened the back screen door, walked out to the burn barrel with the uniform. Then she joined them in her parlor with a bottle of whiskey.

She had no other boarders. She did, however, have a good supply of whiskey.

She allowed Calder to explain why he and the lad were on their way to Council Grove, Kansas.

Ben listened for only a few minutes then he yawned, "I'm plumb tuckered out. I think I'll head on up to bed.

Thanks for the nice dinner, Ma'am." Buzz and the widow watched as he headed up the stairs.

"You have that roan mare out in the corral. Interested in selling her? You see I need to return the army nag to the barracks here in town -- I borrowed it to track the killers I told you about."

The widow nodded her head. "One hundred for the mare and saddle."

"Total it up, then, Ma'am How much we owe you? We'll be leaving in the morning. There's the kid's duds, the books, three watches, and the pistol, plus a couple of rooms, of course."

"How about ten more for night's lodging for you and the kid?"

"More than fair, Ma'am. We haven't added in the meals and the whiskey -- which, by the way, we haven't finished yet."

"Ha!" the lady answered. "Your young friend cleaned up after supper. He does that after breakfast, we're square. My name is Lily, by the way."

"Your breakfast is as good as your dinner, we'll pay you double, Lily," the blacksmith smiled back.

Calder explained his journey's mission, their adventures so far, young Draper's under-age signing just one day before Calder came along.

"He's a good kid, Mrs. Marcussen -- uh, Lily. Been shoved around from place to place, never knew his folks, on his own for over a year . . ."

The widow interrupted, "Do you have a question in all this, Mr. Blacksmith?"

"I'm determined the best thing for him would be schooling, but I'll listen to alternative suggestions. Any ideas?"

"Well, Mr. Blacksmith," she said, laughing, "I had some ideas earlier, but nothing to do with the teenager. No ideas. Just an old woman with idle thoughts. You're welcome to sit in here, drink all my booze; I'm heading off to bed. My room is down the hall and to the left if you need anything before morning."

"Night, Lily. I'm sure I won't be needing anything."

He sat alone for a few more minutes in the darkness, sipping on one last whiskey, thanking the Good Lord for guiding him and the boy to the widow's establishment, and asking that the final leg of their journey would be without incident. He finally climbed the stairs.

<><><>

Morning rituals over, Buzz Calder came in through the kitchen screen door and greeted the host with a wide grin. "Had a great night sleep, Ma'am . . . I mean, Lily. Bed's real comfortable."

"I aim to please, Mr. Blacksmith. Where's your young man?"

"Still asleep, I reckon."

"Nope! I'm up!" Draper sang out as he descended the stairs. "I didn't want to, though. I've never slept in a real bed before, Ma'am. Even at orphanages we only had a gunny sack filled with straw. I'll be back in a minute." With that, he raced out the door for the outhouse.

Buzz Calder and Lily Marcussen sat drinking a final mug of coffee watching young Ben Draper happily scrub the iron skillet and police the entire kitchen.

"Now I see that lad working so hard, makes me realize I could use a handyman around here, Mr. Blacksmith. Lord knows I'd keep him busy with all the mending needs doing around here."

"The only way I could allow that, Lily, is that I'd pick him up on my way back through." He took a sip of hot coffee. "At only seventeen he's my ward -- got a good head on his shoulders -- I want to see he gets schooling."

"I understand. How about this: I have several books here in the house, including a primer; there are more in the attic. Traveling that trail is a good month and a half;

you'll be gone all summer, Buzz. Now, I'm not a school teacher, but I know I can teach him his letters. I'd have him reading a fair bit by the time you get back."

"Lily, I just bet you could. You could probably teach him his numbers as well. Let me ask him what he thinks."

"Okay, but let's both ask him. I want him to know he won't have an easy time of it here. I've just thought of two or three more jobs need doing."

<><><>

Buzz reached down with a money bag. "This should cover the bill, Lily."

They shook hands, but Lily wasn't satisfied.

"Don't I get a kiss, Mr. Blacksmith?"

He laughed, "You're making it difficult to leave, Lily. Step up in my stirrup and get up here." He wrapped his arm around her waist and kissed her. "I guess I should have come down the hall last night," he whispered, nuzzling her hair.

"I did invite," she murmured, "well -- sorta." They both laughed. She gave him another peck on the cheek and hopped down.

After giving Ben some final fatherly words of advice he poked the roan in the flanks and lead the army horse toward the Albuquerque barracks.

Chapter 14

Remains of wagons and animals were scattered along the trail -- skeleton after skeleton of failed wagons. After ten days, Calder came across two caravans of as many as eighty wagons crowded in two long lines and a hubbub of travelers in what could be considered a commercial area. He recognized the spot, even though it had been years. There were now four log buildings and a stockade at the site -- the north bank of the *Arkansas River*. Progress, Calder thought. He wondered how long it would take for it to grow into perhaps a real settlement.

He filled his canteen, listened to any news from further east, shared a few stories about frontier life and continued on. He looked back to see a crude sign: *Wheelwright, Smith & Store*. He wouldn't learn until later that this was the beginnings of Fort Mann, and later Dodge City. *Wheelwright, Smith & Store* being the army corps of engineers team to make things happen under the orders of Captain William M.D. McKissack, and directed by Daniel P. Mann, a master teamster employed by the army to protect these pioneers.

Calder pulled out his watch, looking at the lowering skies. It would normally take just three more days of hard riding to reach Council Grove, but if a downpour came, well . . . things could get a little dicey.

He pulled a slicker from his saddlebag, and stopped just long enough to pull it on, then spurred his horse on, anxious now to take his mother in his arms and console her.

The rain came in a torrent. Wagon ruts became rivers, small rivulets grew from higher elevations and poured down gullies, uprooting bushes and small trees, filling the trail with mud and debris. Calder guided his horse under a large Soapberry tree, slid off and toweled down the horse's head and ears with a blanket from his bedroll.

Within twenty minutes the sun came out. *Typical cloudburst and flash flood* he thought to himself as he shook water from his slicker. He gave his roan one more rub on the ears with the blanket, then remounted and continued east.

Ten minutes later the trail led Calder to the top of a hill. Down the other side, flash flooding had decimated both hill and trail, creating a giant lake of mud. Within that mud Calder was met with a tragedy: two Conestogas caught and almost buried by the mud-flow. One was still on the trail, its wheels were covered with mud above the axles. It couldn't move, even the horses were struggling to maintain themselves in the almost belly-high mud. The young fellow driving just sat, bewildered, on the bench; sitting beside him, crying, sat his wife. Buzz saw at least one small head poke out the front of the canvas covering.

The other prairie schooner had been pushed off the trail and down a gully by the mud-flow. It's team of four horses was still thrashing, fifteen feet down a steep ravine. The ravine itself was filling with a thick stream of rushing, black sludge from the hill. Time was critical.

Calder guided his roan to the edge of the trail and yelled down to the woman he could see.

"Everybody okay down there?"

"No! I think my husband's dead," she cried. "I haven't found him, and there's so much mud! We rolled down the hill, an' . . ."

"You just hold on, Ma'am!" Buzz yelled back, "I'll get you out of there. Any kids?"

"Three! They're banged up some, like me, but they'll be alright. Please hurry!"

He quickly assessed the situation. The wagon below was in much worse shape, but less accessible. He decided first things first.

"Both wagons! Cut the traces to your horses! Do it now!"

Willy, the young driver of the stalled wagon was quick to comply. Calder next instructed him to cut each horse free from the others, but not to cut the halters.

"What about my wife and kids?" The youngster was exasperated.

"They're safe for right now, Willy. Just do as I say! I'll need help with the other wagon as well!"

Almost begrudgingly, Willy complied.

"Now," Calder yelled, "get some long rope, and tie an end securely around one of your kids under the armpits, then toss the rope to me. Make damn sure that rope won't come untied, and make sure it isn't a slip knot; otherwise we could break a rib or do some other serious damage."

Willy was beginning to understand the objectives of the older man and agreed with optimism. A minute later he tossed the rope. It reached Buzz with plenty to spare.

The blacksmith tossed the rope over a strong tree branch some twenty feet above him. The branch would serve as a fulcrum. Then -- hand over hand he pulled his first rescue, a six year old boy through the air until the lad was swinging just below the tree branch, then into his arms.

As Calder set him gently down into the ankle-deep mud he noted Willy's horses were slowly inching their way to freedom from the muck. He smiled. Willy's ten year old girl was next on the rope swing, and then his wife, Ruby.

"Make it fast, Willy! The other wagon is getting desperate!"

"I'll just hang on! Pull me up," came the reply.

Over the branch went the rope, but this time Calder tied the rope to his pommel and pulled back on the reins. The roan backed up, pulling Willy up swiftly. The young man let go the rope to avoid crashing into the branch. He landed on his rear in two inches of mud.

Wiping himself off, he asked, "Same plan with the Cooper family down below?"

"Absolutely! Same way. Horses first! Then the kids and mom. Keep a keen eye for the dad. The missus thinks he's under the mud, but we can hope. This won't be easy. We need to drag them up, but we can save them. Tell them to take a deep breath, hold their noses and keep their eyes closed."

"I got a better idea, I think, Cap'n," Willy claimed. "See that ledge 'bout halfway down? Let Ruby use your horse. I'll lift'em as high as I can; you stand on that ledge an' catch'em an' push'em on up. My rope's long enough."

"Okay, Willy. On your way down stand on that ledge for a minute. Make sure it can hold you."

Willy rappelled down the slope carrying a second rope. Stopping at the ledge he smiled up at Ruby but before he could say anything, the ledge gave way, dropping him the last six feet and up to his crotch in slop. Ruby screamed in fear.

Calder, busy throwing shorter ropes through the halters of the four, now free, large, beautiful Ardennais draft horses, turned at the scream.

"I'm okay, I'm okay," Willy assured them. "Pull me up a bit. That's fine. Now, Mrs. Cooper, I'm going to throw this rope to you. Wrap it around a wagon wheel and toss it back to me."

He threw her one end of the rope, tied the other end around his waist while Mrs. Cooper wrapped her end around a wagon wheel and tossed it back. He tied that rope high above his head on the fulcrum rope the roan would pull on.

Willy ended up dragging only slightly through the mud as he reached the wagon wheel. From Calder came a "Well done, Willy!"

Edith Cooper grabbed Willy's hand, sobbing. "I couldn't cut the harnesses, Willy. I was too scared."

"Hand me the knife, Ma'am. I'll get it done and get you and the kids out of here."

Willy took one look at the situation. Horses were in bad shape. He made a choice.

"Calder, get over here, quick! I ain't got time to save the team, Sir. They's three kids. Wagon's gonna be full to overflowing in a minute. I'm savin' the kids first. I'll need your help to get'em up the bank quick."

"Whatever you need, Son. Let's move!"

Willy tied a boy of about four to the fulcrum attachment while he kept hold of the original rope. Calder caught him in mid-air; the lad barely brushed the mud as he rose. Then in quick succession came eight year old twin girls, and then Edith Cooper.

"I'm gonna try for the horses. Lift me a bit, an' I'm gonna swing over on one of them an' cut'em free."

He used the knife given him by Edith to cut the harnesses, but he could see that at least one had stopped struggling. Once they were out of their traces, Willy attached the others, one at a time, to Calder's big roan and one of Willy's own horses. They pulled and dragged the three big steeds to safety. The tree branch held just fine. Unfortunately, one of the team didn't survive.

Ruby had been watching, fascinated and proud of her husband's skills and strength. While watching, she noticed movement some twenty feet or more ahead of the wagon at the edge of the raging mud.

She screamed, "Edith! I think I see Gregory! Willy! Mr. Calder! Oh, please, God! I think I see Gregory!"

Everyone followed her pointed finger. They all agreed it did look like some dismal creature draped over and clinging to a tenacious shrub. Whatever it was, water and mud were flowing over it.

"Gimme some slack, Mr. Calder! I'm goin' after him."

"No! You can't risk it from there, Willy! We can't drag that man thirty feet through such a mud-flow. I'm pulling you up! We'll go up the trail so we're directly across from him!"

Willy looked wistfully to the dismal creature, then yelled, "Pull me up!"

Calder and Ruby helped Willy to safety; ropes quickly came down and separated.

Meanwhile, Mrs. Cooper had run to a place opposite that small shrub. She turned and cried, "Hurry!"

Buzz saw that there were no overhanging trees to assist in a rescue attempt. It would have to be done by walking down a muddy, eight foot bank, and then through the ten to twelve feet of deep, mud-filled gully --each way -- pulling Gregory, if indeed it actually was he, back to safety. But, Calder reasoned, it had to be done. It had to be either one of Willy's strong Ardennais or his own spirited Roan.

"I'd like to use my draft horse," Willy declared. She's rideable, sure-footed and strong. I can ride across and get him back here again!"

"Alright, young fellow. Throw my saddle on one of them. I'm going to attach a rope to your mount and two of the strong ones on this side, just in case you get stuck."

Preparations made, Willy mounted and started down the bank. The big mare slid halfway down the slope before catching her footing, but then slowly proceeded until she reached a spot level with the surface of the slime.

There, Willy held her back and looked across at his objective.

The flow of mud was now snail-like -- all but stopped, leaving a miry lake of sludge. From the bank the others watched, breathless.

"It's him, everybody! It's him! Here I go!"

The Ardennais' first step took her past her fetlocks.

She tried to back up, but Willy gently coaxed her on. Rocks and debris caused the mare to stumble and change course, but she pushed on.

They were beside the bushy outgrowth within moments. The bank on that side was easily climbable. The body hanging on the bush was limp, seemingly lifeless. Willy dismounted. He removed his own slicker and woolen shirt. With the shirt he wiped Gregory's swollen, bloody face, and with his finger he dug mud from the man's mouth as well as he could. Then he carefully hoisted the body over the back of the mare and tied him, belly down, to the saddle.

"Okay, Calder, pull him back!" Willy shouted. "Maybe I can walk this side until the trail opens up!"

"No! Hang onto her tail, Boy. We'll bring you both back!"

Minutes later Willy and Buzz pulled Gregory Cooper from the big mare's back and dragged him up the banks. Mrs. Cooper yelled, "Hallelujah!" and jumped into the muddy water to hug the big mare. The two struggled to safety from the the mud.

Gregory Cooper was a miracle -- they laid him on his side on a flat rock in the sun with his legs slightly elevated, head down. It was Calder's idea. Just using the logic of a simple blacksmith -- if water runs downhill, so too, must mud.

As the sun dried the mud on the man's head and clothing, Edith wiped his nostrils and mouth, combed his hair, and from time to time cleaned his face and eyes.

As he began to recover, Edith cautioned him repeatedly to blow his nose, one nostril at time, before taking a breath except by mouth. This he did two or three times; the amount of mud that was eliminated was astounding.

Calder was studying the wagons. "You have digging tools -- shovels, adze, mattock, things like that?" Calder asked.

"Got a plow, too. Why?" Willy asked.

"Let's get rid of that lake. It'll take a while, but we might be able to save one or both wagons. Lose some things for sure, some already lost, but some might be salvageable. If we can knock that bank down, we should be able to rock your wagon free, and then with the horses, right the Cooper wagon."

"Good plan," Willy nodded, "wagon's full of stuff. I'll send the horse back over for you while I start digging."

Once again the big mare was responsive to Willy's coaxing. The young pioneer jumped into the wagon, pulled out assorted tools, tossing them on the opposite bank. Lastly, he pulled out a plow and harness. Holding on to it, he crossed to the other bank and slipped off the horse. Buzz Calder pulled her back using a rope. Then he rode across through the mud. The digging began beside the overturned Cooper wagon.

They started with shovels, but progress was almost insignificant; Buzz switched to the plow. He strapped on the harness and put reins on the Ardennais. He then, with Willy keeping the mare calm, removed layer after layer of muddy embankment. Each layer saw a bigger, wider flow of mud stream down the hillside.

Within an hour the lake of mud had been reduced to no more than a puddle. Miry, black sludge oozed from the wagon as it lay on it's side. Minutes later it was still spilling out, snail-like, joining the slow-moving stream of mud over the bank. The two men thought the wagon could soon be carefully pulled upright.

They turned their attention to the other wagon. Most of the liquid silt from the trail had continued downward, leaving rock, sand and mostly rich, black loam in the ruts. Calder immediately saw a new problem.

"Willy, we need to back your wagon up now! If we don't, we'll be here two days digging it out!"

The hardening muck was so high the axles were barely exposed. Now, with the sun beating down, it wasn't going to be easy to free those big wheels.

The younger man tied a rope around the rear axle, the other rope end to the reins of his big mare. Calder did the same in front with his big roan.

"I'll go first, Willy! Fore and back until she's freed; then we'll back her up that little hill until the sun dries out the trail! Whatever you do," Calder cautioned, "don't pull too hard on that axle! We'll have two wheels sitting in your lap!"

Slow and easy they rocked the wheels until they felt satisfying movement. Thereupon, Willy eased the Ardennais backward as Buzz matched with forward movement. They backed the wagon up the little rise. Once the wheels were almost entirely exposed, they stopped.

Willy called out, "We got company!"

Calder was just pulling the rope away from the front

"Soldiers, Sir!"

A detachment of six army regulars and nine teamsters headed for Fort Mann came upon them at that moment. The young lieutenant in charge dismounted to assess the situation. He called a teamster to join him. They listened with interest to all that had happened -- at times, shaking their heads, at times nodding their approval.

"What's your next objective, Sir?" the teamster asked Calder as they walked, observing and nodding to the families further ahead.

"Raise the wagon in the gorge, and get it up here on

the trail above the soft ground," Buzz replied, wiping mud off his trousers as well as he could. "It's in quite a fix. Damn cruel situation for these folks."

The lieutenant looked down at the overturned Conestoga. Turning to his associate he asked, "What's your opinion, Rogers?"

"They've done the hard work. We can bring'er up in a coupla hours at most, Sir," the teamster replied.

"Just treat it carefully," Calder cautioned. "Take extra time to make sure it comes up in one piece. Sitting on its side like that, the mud could suck the side right off that wagon."

The teamster nodded, "Understood, and I agree."

"You say you're on your way to see your mom in Council Grove, right?" the lieutenant turned and asked Calder. Without waiting for an answer, he shook Calder's hand. "We'll take it from here."

Calder retrieved his saddle, spent a moment with Gregory Cooper who was sitting but still unable to keep his eyes open for any length of time.

Calder gathered the families in a circle. They offered prayers of thanks to the Almighty for their safety in this terrifying experience. They then hugged and said their goodbyes, after which Calder cinched down his saddle on his big roan, climbed aboard and headed eastward toward Council Grove.

Chapter 15

After the first week of Calder's absence, Molly rode to his residence less and less often. He, indeed was gone -- in fact, he would be gone for possibly as much as two months according to Elmer Kaufman. Plus, Elmer was being paid to care for Calder's animals.

He should have asked me! she had thought at first. Then she realized that was a begrudging attitude. She turned her pony around and congratulated Elmer. His job at the blacksmith's place did, however, spur her to seek employment of her own. *After all, it's July 24, 1851. I'm a lady of sixteen!* she thought.

Her first thought was as a waitress over at Maude's, the busy restaurant in the center of town. The girls that worked there were three or four years older than she -- and at the end of the day, they looked beat. Two were friends. They both told her she'd be a welcome addition, but to lie about her age. She couldn't do that.

Then there was Betty's, a bar next door to Maude's. She considered it, but she'd heard stories about Betty's, and decided not to try.

She had yet to try Margaret's General Store -- she felt it would somehow be disloyal to Elmer. Then she smiled. Margaret knew and understood Elmer's limitations as well as she; Margaret was a caring, gentle woman.

Now, Margaret's wasn't just a general store. She made that clear when Molly applied.

"There is no other store like this for sixty -- seventy miles. I have a little of everything. I told Rian, God rest his soul, this is not a general store; it's a mercantile. *If Margaret doesn't have it, she'll get it!* That's what we used to say, Rian and me."

Margaret locked the doors early that afternoon and walked Molly the full length and width of both floors, pointing out the different types of merchandise. To Molly's surprise the inventory was impressive -- wagons, plows, furniture, foodstuffs like potatoes and rice, even a piano.

The building was a large and rectangular warehouse -- two stories above ground with a large cellar filled with coal. Most of the commercial activity was conducted on the ground floor. Storage was on the second -- housing such things as bolts of cloth, chain, bags of salt, salt blocks, rope, and such.

To reach the second floor, Buzz Calder had fashioned a "rope-pulley lift" for Margaret some years before, fastening a block and tackle to an overhead rafter. Using it, she could easily raise or lower two hundred fifty pounds of dry goods on a 4' x 8' platform.

"I've been working this business by myself since I lost Rian, but I'm getting tired, Molly. I could use some help. Even keeping the floors swept up good and the shelves tidy. Pay won't be much but as you get more involved, I'll give you more to do and it'll increase. Start you off at a dollar and a quarter a week."

"Sounds real good, Mrs. uh". . .

"Chisholm," Margaret told her. "Don't tell Elmer what I'm payin' you. He figures he's got a real job. He'll be upset if he finds out. Doors open at seven."

"I understand, Mrs. Chisholm. Thank you for the job. I'll work hard. See you tomorrow."

Molly excitedly told her adoptive parents about her new job. She shocked them when she told them she had considered *Betty's* and *Maude's* before choosing the general store. Still, the following morning it was with trepidation that they watched her ride off to work.

Mrs. Turnbill closed the screen door, walked into the kitchen and circled the date on the large calendar with a note. *Molly's first day of work.* It was the 25th of July.

Chapter 16

Margaret met Molly with a short list of chores. She pointed out the location of the storage closet -- housing mops, brooms, scrub brushes, aprons, pails, and such.

"Today is Friday. Let's make the last Friday of the month a cleaning day. I'd like you to start at the counter and then this main room," she motioned with her arms, "then my office. I'm ashamed to say I don't think I've put a broom or mop to my office floor since Rian passed. Too many interruptions, I suppose."

"Well, Mrs. Chisholm, I'll take care of all that so you can concentrate on your customers," Molly smiled. "When I'm done, it will be spotless!"

"Oh my goodness, child!" Margaret laughed, "it needn't be spotless. Just tidy. And, by the way, call me Margaret. Everyone else does."

Molly already knew where the closet was; she walked in, grabbed an almost new bib apron. As she put it on she noted with satisfaction that she'd seen Uncle Buzz wear one just like it in his shop. Well made, heavy duty canvas, string ties going through grommets, deep pockets as well as a bib pocket -- Molly was thrilled. She felt like a real working lady. She wrapped the ties around to the front, tied it off and grabbed a big broom.

She put down a pail of sudsy water, only because

Margaret demanded she stop for lunch. "I'm just about finished with the walls in your office," Molly sang out. "Give me a minute."

"Now!" Margaret returned. "Up to the mezzanine!"

"Yes, Ma'am." Dutifully, she climbed the ten steps to a 20' long by 8' wide space overlooking the entire first floor, and with a good view of the second.

"What do you see, Molly?" Margaret asked.

"Uh," Molly replied, a bit confused, "I see the inside of your warehouse; pretty much all the stuff on the whole floor, Ma'am. I guess I can see most of your second floor, too."

"Right. You see lots of stuff. Now, what do you hear?"

"Nothing, Ma'am."

"You sure? Close your eyes and try again. Big things, little things, things close by or far away."

Molly closed her eyes. Moments later, she cried out, "I heard a dog bark; oh, and I hear pigeons up in the rafters -- noisy critters; I heard a woman yelling at a kid -- I think it was Mrs. Waller, probably yelling at Trent; I heard horses go by and . . ."

"That's fine, Molly. The point of all this is that sometimes we see or hear things and want to tell somebody else. Now, Rian and I started this business close to twenty years ago, and I've owned it without him since. Almost every day I hear all kinds of stuff and see all kinds of stuff, and I don't repeat any of it unless it's really important, and then only to someone who should know; otherwise, it's nobody's business!

Now, so far as you're concerned around here, I'm the one you report any important stuff to. You don't talk to your friend, Jimmy, or even your folks, and especially not to Ol' Floyd Banner. One drink in him and he repeats everything he knows. Do you understand all this?"

"Oh, yes'm."

"You're doing a fine job, by the way. Now, enjoy your

lunch."

"I didn't bring a lunch. Didn't know I'd have any time off to eat one."

"You can't work on an empty stomach, girl. Remember the passage from the Good Book, *don't muzzle an ox while he's treading out the corn*. Now, take that apron off and hang it up. Here's some money. Go over to Maude's and get yourself some lunch."

With or without her apron, as soon as Molly entered Maude's she was recognized as a new employee at Margaret's -- in fact, the first employee Margaret had ever had. . .outside of Elmer, of course.

"You working for Margaret?" one of Maude's waitresses asked as she walked by. Then the young lady turned around. "I tried last year; she told me she handled everything herself. How did you manage it?"

"I guess it was time," Molly responded. "I just happened to walk in at the right time."

"Lucky!" the girl said.

Jake Ruskin was sitting by himself, having a coffee. "Well, well, Miss Molly. Come, join me."

"I can't sit and visit, Mr. Ruskin. I started a new job today, and I need to get right back."

"Yes, I heard. Margaret's place. Good for you. I won't keep you, Molly. I'm in a hurry, too. But stop lookin' around for a spot to park your butt, come and join me. I recommend a bowl of Maude's beef stew. Best in town," he laughed.

"I've never eaten in a cafe before," she joined him in the laughter, "so this will definitely be the best in town as far as I'm concerned." She ordered the stew. It was ladled immediately and brought to their table.

"Well, there is the hotel across the street and the rooming house at the edge of town; they serve folks sometimes," Jake told her.

"How long do you think Uncle Buzz will be gone, Jake? Can I call you Jake?"

"You may, young lady, now that you're out working; how old are you, by the way?"

"I was sixteen two weeks ago -- on the 10th of July," she said, between sips. "Good stew," she agreed, "but hot!"

"Sixteen! My! Doesn't seem that long ago that we . . . sorry! Just an old man with memories. Happy birthday, girl! Keep your money in your pocket. I told you the stew is good! And it's on me!

Now to answer your question, Calder will probably be gone until at least the first part of September," Jake said soberly. "And for his sake, hopefully, before the snow flies." He watched as she tipped her bowl to spoon out the last of her stew and put a napkin to her mouth.

She stood. "Thank you, Mr. Ruskin. I gotta run."

<><><>

Pulling her apron from the closet, Molly's memories of more than five years ago flashed through her mind. Jake Ruskin didn't know half of what her family had endured. She kept it all inside her. Like Margaret, Molly was expert at keeping her thoughts private. Something else Jake had said: Uncle Buzz wouldn't be back until at least September.

September! That's too long! Molly pulled the apron strings tight and tied a bow. *I should have gone with him*, she thought, shaking her head.

Margaret was in the yard, talking to a jobber with a wagon full of goods to trade; Molly finished the job she had started before lunch. She poured fresh sudsy water into a pail, picked up the long-handled scrub brush and tackled Margaret's last, grungy, cobwebbed office wall.

Chapter 17

The Louisiana Purchase opened the west to wagon after wagon of settlers, many along the Santa Fe Trail. At the time -- decades before statehood, the land was commonly known as Indian Territory -- home to the Cheyenne, Osage, Pawnee, and other Plains Indians.

In the autumn of 1825, U.S. Commissioners met with Chiefs of the Great and Little Osage Indian tribes beneath a tree they called the Council Oak. They signed a treaty establishing right-of-way for pioneers along this famed trail. In the years following, Council Oak became Council Grove, the pre-eminent rendezvous point for wagon trains heading west.

When he returned there in the summer of 1851, Buzz Calder found it bustling with enterprise. His father had evidently chosen wisely in making the move from Kansas City.

Buzz urged the roan to the eastern end of town. His father's gunsmith shop was next to the livery stables and one of two blacksmiths in town. The red brick home, with its small white carriage house and barn sat at the rear of a long, winding road, all but hidden by the large square, brick shop in front.

It was almost as Buzz remembered. The shadow of a

frown traced across his face as he looked up at the large wooden sign that had identified Cliff Calder's business from his beginning days in Kansas City. It now looked faded and worn -- not how he wanted his father remembered. He vowed to rip it down and take it with him when he left.

An older couple rode by in a buckboard pulled by two smart-looking buckskins. The woman smiled and waved. Calder waved back. He pulled out his watch before continuing down the road toward the house. 10:41 a.m.

His mother kept looking at the rider on the big roan as she sat rocking on the front veranda. She stood, eyes widened, her mouth flung open in recognition . . . then tears came to her eyes.

Buzz put his arms around her. "I'm sorry I wasn't here sooner, Ma," he said, hugging her and smoothing a lock of hair from her eyes. "I'm so sorry about Pop, and leaving you all by yourself to . . ."

"Shush, now. Buzz Calder! Your father and I have built a good life here. When he got sick the whole town came by to offer whatever help they could, and when he passed they wouldn't let me lift a finger, from preacher to funeral director." She stopped weeping and continued, "Shops in town closed their doors and came to his wake. Your father was loved, Buzz."

"I came as soon as I heard, Ma. Took me twenty-nine days, but I'm here now."

"I know, Boy, I know." She put an arm around his waist. "Come on in. I'll put the coffee on. Have you had dinner?"

By mid-afternoon, news spread that Cliff Calder's son was in town. At 3 p.m. Council Grove townfolk began showing up to visit; soon potluck dishes were flooding into the home. People dropped by until after dark for a visit. A string of horses and a few carriages seemed

The BLACKSMITH and *The Sheepherder's Daughter*
perpetually tied at the hitching post in front of the Calder veranda -- only the color of the horse changed.

Everyone welcomed him home, several asked how long he would be staying in Council Grove, and a few asked if he could make some time for them the following day.

Of special interest was Homer Brookings, the young family attorney -- couldn't have been more than thirty. Buzz agreed to a meeting at 11:30 a.m. Mr. Brookings asked for an earlier time, but Buzz was adamant, "No! Mom and I are going to Pop's gravesite to pay our respects. I'm sure you understand."

Lying in bed late that night before his evening prayer, Buzz mulled over the events of the day: the genuine love and appreciation shown for his folks by the residents, the frailty of his mother, the several people requesting an audience with him tomorrow -- especially that lawyer. *Wonder what he wants*, Buzz thought. *Guess we'll find out tomorrow.*

Chapter 18

Tuesday, August 5th. Buzz took care of the morning chores, then breakfast. They were off to the Council Grove cemetery. Nearly sixty headstones graced the site. There was no particular order or dimension; Cliff Calder was resting upon a knoll under a Weeping Willow tree in the southeast corner. A modest chunk of upright granite marked the location.

Someone, perhaps Cliff himself, had placed a bench under the willow -- a resting place for the living.

As Buzz helped his mother down from the buggy and walked her to the site, he smiled at the bench. *A refreshing bit of Pop's satire*, he thought as he read:

We all need a rest at times -- some for a longer period than others.

Only twenty steps up the slight grade from the buggy to her husband's resting place -- but that short walk proved too much for his mom. Buzz wrapped her in his arms and carried her the last ten. He set her on the bench and studied the inscription on the headstone.

Here, Under the Willow
Lie The Calders
Gunsmith and Schoolmarm
Clifford James   November 16, 1772 - April 5, 1851
Louisa Grace (Logan)   May 11, 1775 -

"Your name is on here, too, Ma. You're planning on staying in Council Grove, huh?"

"Yes. It's my home, Buzz. Your father and I purchased this beautiful knoll for our burial site three years ago. We chose the stone, had the engraver do all the preliminary work and set it in place way back then. Just a matter of the end dates. He did a good job, don't you think?"

"I do, Mom, I do."

Buzz sat, holding his mother's hand, smiling down at her. His foreboding anxiety melted away as their eyes met. Hers were misty, but warm and content. His, he realized, had been severe, looking for doubt -- he found none.

She leaned her head on his shoulder.

"I'm tired, Son," she almost whispered to him.

He let go her hand, wrapped his arm around her and drew her closer. "You and Pop made a good choice, Mom."

"Thank you, Buzz," she sighed in agreement. "The tired I mean is not lack of sleep. I'm getting ready to join your father."

Minutes went by. They sat without exchanging a word. Finally she raised her head, "We should be going. We have a meeting with our attorney this morning."

Buzz smiled. "Correction. *I* have a meeting with Mr. Brookings. I'll drop you off at home before I see him."

"I'm going with you. Now, help me down this hill."

<><><>

Homer Brookings' office was in the center of town -- a small, single story clapboard, nicely whitewashed, with a circular gold sign on the front lawn: *Homer Brookings, Esq.* Buzz smiled as he remembered the day he first signed his name with *Esq.* behind it. Today he understood that all lawyers, just as all blacksmiths, put their pants on one leg at a time.

Buzz had a good idea as to the purpose of their visit, but as he walked around to assist his mother down from her bench seat, he quipped, "Well, we're here, Ma. Let's go listen to some lawyer-talk."

"This meeting is important, Son. I was afraid I'd have to make certain decisions by myself. I'm so glad you're here. Do be serious, please!"

"Of course, Ma. I was only kidding."

"Just like your father."

The attorney saw them from his window. "Come in, come in," he greeted them, arm outstretched for a handshake. He ushered them into his sitting room where they sat across from his desk in beautiful cushioned, wing-back chairs of European design. Buzz noted the other furnishing in the room were of top calibre as well. *Money*, he thought.

Homer's wife brought in a tray with coffee and tea biscuits, then disappeared into the kitchen.

"How long have you been in practice, Homer?" Calder asked.

If the young attorney was offended by the familiarity he didn't show it. "Three years, almost four, Buzz," he replied. "My father is in practice in Helena, Arkansas.

Mighty big issues in the states right now: banking, cotton farmers, slavery. Looks like they're flowing into Kansas as well. You in favor of slavery, Buzz?"

"Not at all, and I hope it never comes to New Mexico," Buzz said. "I'd hate to earn my living driving an awl through someone's ear lobe."

"Wha? . . .oh, I get it!" Brookings laughed. "From scripture, right?"

"Sure. Voluntary indenture is fine, but not abject slavery. So, you figure the territories are on their way to statehood?"

"I'm sure of it," the attorney nodded, "but arguments over free or slave is a big issue for the folks in Congress."

"Let's get to the reason we're here, Mr. Brookings," Calder's mom interrupted, not a little annoyed, "I'll need to use a facility before too much longer."

"Oh, certainly, Mrs. Calder. Sorry for gabbing so long. So, Buzz, you were at your father's gravesite this morning, right?" He continued without an answer. "You see that your mother will be living out the rest of her life here in Council Grove. She asked me to do several things for her in the event you weren't able to join us, but obviously, you're now included in decision making.

Number one," Brookings picked up a large green binder and flipped it open a few pages, "there is the homestead: the buildings and real property of six acres." He turned a page, "Number two -- all the furnishings from the home."

Calder watched his mother's face as the lawyer itemized the furnishings, mostly heirlooms his folks had brought with them from Virginia to Kansas. She seemed dispassionate, almost serene.

"Number three," Brookings continued, "the animals and furnishings from the barn. Animals: nine horses, three cows and . . ."

Calder cut him off. "Let me just take your book home for a day or so. Mom and I will go through it and talk. This is Tuesday. I'll have it back by Thursday. Is that okay, Homer?"

"Oh sure. Read through it, Buzz. You'll find it complete. There is a number four -- the gunsmith shop."

"Yeah, Homer, I know about it. Haven't been inside for fourteen years. You need any money today for services rendered thus far?"

"Of course not," Brookings smiled. "I understand you have others interested in talking with you today."

"I do, but don't let that bother you, Homer. I know the difference between lamb and mutton."

Chapter 19

"Mom, I'm assuming you've gone through this ledger with Brookings," Buzz looked up from the green ledger he had borrowed from the attorney, "so I just have a few questions about his appraisals and values."

Mrs. Calder brought two mugs of coffee and freshly baked cookies to the kitchen table. "Okay, I'm ready to listen," she sighed as she pulled a chair beside him.

"To answer, yes and no. He never showed me the pages. He always read it to me as he started to do today. And listen, Buzz, Cliff and I registered a release warrant in Topeka last year. Everything we owned was put in your name. Everything. I have a certified copy in the parlor."

Buzz sat bolt upright in his chair. "Son of a bitch!" he whispered under his breath.

"What?" his mother asked. "I'm not interested in the property or the money, Buzz. You must know that."

"No, Ma. Sorry. Something you said rang a bell; nothing to do with our property -- has to do with some property in New Mexico."

He took a bite of cookie, followed it with a sip from his mug. "Let's continue," he said. "Homer puts a dollar value of all the furniture in this house at $350.00; all of our livestock, the tack equipment in the barn and gun shop at $675.00. Personally, I think that's a little light, what do you think?"

"Buzz, if that's what he says that's what it is. This isn't Hampton. It sounds fine to me. That's $1,000.00."

Buzz continued, ignoring her Virginia comparison. "He lists the six acres at $30.00 per acre. So that's $180.00. Then he lumps all the buildings together: the main house, the carriage house, the barn, chicken coop, grain and corn cribs, and the gun-shop out in front . . . all at just $1,500. I'd say the house alone cost you and Pop more than $2,000 to build! Ma! Do you think Brookings is interested in buying this property?"

"Ask him, Son. It's your property now."

"I think I will. Do you have the keys to the shop? I think I'll walk around the property for a while, and have a look at the shop. Do you mind?"

"You run along. I'm taking a nap."

<><><>

Buzz meandered through the grounds, taking in the smaller buildings first, then the carriage house. The walls were covered with wagon wheels, axles, and a surplus of tack: harnesses, bridles, halters, reins, bits, saddles, stirrups, even martingales and breastplates.

On the floor stood the buggy he and his mom had used all morning. Behind it was a hay wagon, and beside the buggy stood a Conestoga, the one he had moved with the family to Council Grove from Kansas City, Missouri. All three were in 'as new' condition. Buzz itemized everything on blank pages of the attorney's ledger, then moved on to the barn.

Buzz counted a dozen horse stalls along one side of the barn. Nine of them were occupied. On the other side was a feeder trough with six stanchions for cattle. Cliff had no milk cows, only three head of Herefords that wintered inside the barn -- of course, they were grazing in the pasture at present.

Behind the barn was a typical pigpen -- all that remained was one sow, being fattened up for an October butchering. *She weighs probably 400 pounds already*, Buzz thought to himself.

He shook his head. "Didn't Ma know at least the approximate values of their property?" he asked himself aloud. "They were rich!" he almost shouted to the sow. She looked up at him and ran to her feed trough, expecting another pail of slop.

Again, he jotted down the inventory of plows, sickles, scythe, two horse-drawn rakes, the sow, and a huge dray on skids to pull logs or bulky materials through snow. *Quite an inventory*, he thought as he exited the barn and walked down the drive toward the gun shop.

"Mr. Calder!"

The shout came from behind him. He turned to see a horseman coming down the drive. "Mr. Calder!" the man called out again. Buzz continued walking. The rider followed, and tied his horse to the hitching post as Buzz unlocked the shop door.

"Come in and sit. It's been over fourteen years since I've been inside, so excuse me if I cut your visit short. What can I do for you, Sir? Rawlinson, isn't it? We spoke yesterday."

"Yes, Sir. I'll just come right out and tell you. I'd like to buy your home -- lock, stock and barrel."

"What do you intend to do with it?" Buzz asked. Evidently the question took the man by surprise.

"Uh, live here, Sir."

"What's your business, Rawlinson? What'll you do with this building?"

"Oh, I'm going to start a Feed and Grain Store. It's a good location, right at the edge of town with the livery and blacksmith close by."

"How old are you, Rawlinson?"

"Thirty-three."

"Family?"

"Yes. I have a wife and three kids, Sir."

"What's your trade, Son?"

"Huh? Oh, my work, you mean?"

Buzz just looked at him. The younger man continued, "I work as bartender and waiter at the hotel."

"That's across the street from the attorney's place isn't it? We were there earlier today. I remember seeing the hotel. Strange name, *Mile 120*. What does that stand for?"

"A hundred and twenty miles from Kansas City, Sir."

"Good job?"

"Hotel's always busy."

"What's your best cash offer, Rawlinson?"

"$1,700. I can pay $500 now and the balance in a year."

"Tell you what, Rawlinson. Keep working, taking care of your wife and kids. Thanks for your offer, but it's far too low. You probably knew that already. House alone is worth more than twice that; hell, Son, the livestock's worth that!" Buzz held out his hand. "Thanks for dropping by, but no sale."

Buzz shook his head and watched Rawlinson mount up and ride off. *Wonder who's next?* he thought.

<>< ><>

Buzz was again counting the inventory and the tooling equipment of his gunsmith father when the door opened. He turned to see a middle-aged couple standing in the doorway.

"Understand you're Cliff's son. What's your name?"

"Buzz Calder. And you?"

"Sam and Ellie Hendricks. Understand you live in New Mexico. That's a thousand miles west o'here, i'nit?"

"Yes, it surely is. Rugged country, mountains two miles high, deer, bear, cougars, elk; hot in summer, cold in winter. Pretty as hell. I love it. So what brings you by?"

"Just a friendly visit. Is the widow Calder in?"

"She is. She was taking a nap, probably up by now,

though. You're welcome to go on up," Buzz said. "Tell her I'll be up shortly. I'm taking an inventory of tools and such in here."

"You go on, Honey," Sam told his wife. "I want to discuss some business with Mr. Calder's son, Buzz, for a minute."

Buzz cocked his head and stared at Sam quizzically. "How's that?" he asked, as Ellie disappeared.

"I'm hopin' it'll be possible to work out some kind of a deal to buy your place?"

"Anything's possible, friend, but tell me how you have it figured."

"I worked for your Dad for five years, right up to the time he got real sick, back -- first part of November -- I actually finished up the work he had 'in the hopper' as he called it. He stopped taking on new orders -- I ended up without a job. Been out of work since, 'cept for a few odd jobs."

"I didn't know he had anyone working for him," Buzz frowned. "So, are you familiar with all his tools and equipment? Would you call yourself a gunsmith?"

"A damn good one. Ask the widow, she'll tell ya."

"Let's go up to the house and have a cup of coffee. We'll talk. If you worked for my dad for five years you can probably give me a list of the current inventory before I can walk around and write it down."

Walking up the road to the house, Buzz asked, "How well do you know my mom?"

"When your dad got sick, Ellie was at the house every day helping Mrs. Calder with the chores. Then about Christmas time Louisa hired a young kid to tramp through the snow to get all the chores done, so Ellie stopped coming 'round. Widow Calder sure looked frail yesterday, though."

"I agree, Sam. I'm a bit worried about leaving her. So, you were there yesterday? I was approached by three different people regarding this place. You weren't one of them."

"No, it was the wrong time to talk business," Sam said as Buzz opened the front door. The mixed odors of fresh bread and robust coffee met them as Buzz waved Sam inside and followed.

Mugs of steaming coffee were waiting for them, along with a plate of buttered bread and a bowl of hard boiled eggs. Buzz cracked an egg on the edge of the bowl just as a rider came into sight close to the house. It was the attorney.

"Busy place," Buzz smiled. "Ma, bring another coffee, and would you bring that green binder, please?" He looked at Hendricks, "Just stay seated. You're fine where you are."

Chapter 20

Buzz opened the door to allow Homer Brookings' entrance. "Umm, smells good in here. This coffee for me?"

"Absolutely, Homer," Buzz waved the attorney to the empty chair. "Fresh baked bread, and hard-boiled eggs, too. Help yourself."

"I won't stay long. I see you're busy," he said, cracking an egg on the bowl and peeling it. "Just want to tell you I found a buyer with a great offer for your place. Much more than my original assessment. Come by my office tomorrow; we can discuss it."

"I have a few appointments tomorrow, but I'd certainly like to hear that figure! Oh! Before I forget, here's your workbook back. I've gone through it, and I saw your original values." Buzz handed the attorney the green binder, smiling warmly at him as he did.

"In fact, as you're here now, let's hear the offer. You know Sam and Ellie Hendricks, of course. Sam, here, has shown some interest as well. He's already given me his figure, I have one from Rawlinson, and I expect one or two more tomorrow. Who made the offer, and how much, Homer."

"I can't give you the name, but it's a good offer from an out of town gunsmith."

"That's fine. I don't need a name. What's the price? If

it's the best offer, I'll swing by, sign papers and pick up my cash."

Sam was squirming in his chair over the conversation, turning the brim of his hat round and round to the point of being annoying. "We should be going, Mr. Calder. We've taken too much of your time."

"Nonsense! Have an egg, chunk of bread. We're just negotiating here. I might get more than I ever thought possible for the homestead. Your offer sure beat out Rawlinson by a mile; mayb" . . .

"But I hav" . . .

"Your livestock can wait, Sam," Buzz interrupted. "Let's hear the man out. Not like you have kids at home."

Brookings frowned as he studied, first Sam's bewildered face, then Calder's serious one.

"I think I'm looking at a poker player, Buzz," he concluded, chewing the inside of his cheek.

"Okay, then," Buzz said soberly, "let's stop with the buffalo chips. Rawlinson came in here not knowing what he was talking about, you gave me an assessed value lower than the value of my chicken coop, and I'm betting there is no 'out-of-town' gunsmith. So, one lawyer to another, what's your play?"

"You're right, Calder. I was a bit unethical. I wa . . ."

"No, Brookings! Unethical doesn't cover what you did. Men are shot for what you did. It was contemptible; pure corruption! If I were still practicing here in Kansas I'd have you disbarred!"

Louisa Calder and the others in the room stared at the verbal exchange in disbelief. The young attorney was caught in a blatant indiscretion and was being shamed for it. He tried to exit before it escalated, but Buzz wasn't finished.

"Not so fast, Homer. What was your offer?"

"I have no offer worth knowing," Homer said, sheepishly, "and I'm truly sorry."

"I'm not sure, but I think you do," Buzz replied.

"$7,250.00 cash," the man answered, softly.

"Now, that's a fair price, Homer. I'm taking a few of the house furnishings -- Mom and I will go through and choose a few heirlooms she's willing to let go. I'm taking most everything from the carriage house; I'll hire a drover to help with the trip.

I'm leaving Mom's buggy, her Palomino mare and harness. I was going to take the machinery from the gun shop, but it's too heavy, so it stays, along with everything else: cows, pig, and chickens.

All the buildings are solid, Artesian well has great flow, and there's plenty of trees for wood. At $7,250.00 that's a fair price for both sides. I had $11,000.00 in my head, but that would have included everything."

Buzz turned to Sam Hendricks. "Sam, what's your offer?"

"Nothing like his, Mr. Calder. I don't have nearly that kind of money. I suppose you should sell the property to the lawyer."

Buzz turned back to Homer. "What were you planning to do with this six acres, friend?"

"Hold onto it for a few years and resell it when Council Grove becomes a city, which it's sure to become. It's right on the thoroughfare between the east and the western wilderness."

"So it is," Buzz agreed. Once again he turned to Sam.

"Sam, where do you live?"

"First wagon road to the north after the Farmer's Feed and Grain. Got us 160 acres along the *Kaw River*. Road runs right along the property."

"So it's riverfront?"

"Oh, yeah! Right on the river."

"You got the papers?"

"Don't owe a dime to nobody, Mr. Calder."

"And, you want to buy my place? Why?"

"Oh! No, Mr. Calder. I was hopin' to go to the bank and get a loan to make some kind of deal with you, maybe rent the shop."

"Ah, Sam, my mistake!" Buzz pulled at his beard, "that pokes a log through a wagon wheel. Let me think! Ma! Can you bring more coffee, please?"

Mrs. Calder came to the table with a fresh jug of coffee. "You all look like you're going to be here all night; might as well stay for supper. Get into the parlor with your coffee! Ellie and I are going to make something out of all the pot luck vittles everyone brought yesterday. Now shoo! You're giving us a headache!"

The three retired to the comfort of the parlor. No one said a word, waiting for Buzz to speak. Finally, "Okay," he said, "here's how I see it; Sam, you want the gun shop, Homer, you want the whole shebang.

Now, here's what I want: I want my mom taken care of to her last day, I want Sam to have his gun shop, and I want you, Homer, to have the whole shebang, but to pay for your deceit. And," Buzz said with finality, "I want none of our conversation to leave this house. We all make mistakes. Hopefully, we all learn lessons." He looked at the attorney, "Especially lawyers; especially honesty. Remember the good book says: *'I didn't come to save the perfect, only sinners'*; and it also says, *'Go and sin no more'*."

Sam piped up first, "Ellie can take care of your mom if I'm down in the gun shop, and I can take care of the livestock, too."

"If I buy it, I'll give Sam a low rate on the shop," Homer offered.

Buzz scowled. "If you buy it, you'll give Sam free rent for at least a year, maybe two until he gets on his feet. Rent should be in the form of a firm lease, even if you sell, say 6-7 years."

"Done," Homer said, "but if he moves out before the

lease expires, he can't sublease."

"Done! Get your green notebook out, Homer, we'll write it up right now."

"What's the price, then? You're taking quite a bit away when you go," Homer raised an eyebrow.

"True enough. Flip over to the page in your ledger with the main house, barn, carriage house, all the out buildings, tack and all. That was, what, $675.00? I'm taking, let's say $40.00 worth. The furnishings in the house you have at $350.00. I'd bet I'm not taking more than $10.00 worth, using your assessment. So, let's take that $7,250.00 and subtract $50.00. You owe me $7,200.00, right?"

"Supper!" Ellie yelled from the kitchen.

Sitting at the table, Homer laughed heartily. "I agree. I agree to the price and terms, Buzz Calder. You are one shrewd son of a bee, but I like you." He pointed a fork at the blacksmith. "Thanks for the lesson in honesty.

Swing by tomorrow. Bring your deed and Sam, here; we'll draw up the papers for the sale and the lease, and you can pick up your cash. Then we'll go see Judge Newman and record a new deed. Is that satisfactory?"

"Perfectly," Calder said.

"Don't seem fair somehow," Sam Hendricks blurted. "I'm getting it all for nothing."

"Not at all, Hendricks," Buzz corrected. "You and Ellie are keeping watch over the property, you're feeding and caring for the livestock for Mr. Brookings. That sow, the white-faced cows, chickens, horse and such belong to him. You have the responsibility of maintaining them and any more that he brings on the property.

And most important to me, of course, is caring for Ma." Buzz took his mom's hand and gave her a warm smile as they all sat around the table.

"I won't be here. We'll be relying on the two of you as

she gets older or in the event something happens, God forbid. Could be one year or ten; doesn't matter. That's what you're signing on for, how you're paying your due."

Louisa Calder tittered and shook her head. "Won't be a year, I'll be gone. Don't worry about that, Ellie, I can hardly get around now. And I already told you, Son, I'm ready to be with your father."

Chapter 21

"You working for Margaret?" Jimmy was ecstatic. "Ma jus' told me she saw you there sweepin' the floor. How much you makin'?"

They were sitting on Molly's porch at the end of her second day on the job.

"I just started, Jimmy. Margaret told me if you or anyone else asks me that question to just say, 'it isn't any of your business'. So, Jimmy, it isn't any of your business!"

"Aw, c'mon, Molly. 'Fraid I'm gonna blab all over town? Elmer told me he's makin' five cents a day. You makin' more'n Elmer? I don't think so. He's a lot older than you."

"Wow! Elmer's making five cents a day?" Molly sounded shocked and dismayed. "But after all," she agreed, "he is a lot older. I'm still not telling you, Jimmy Iverson! You know why? Because it's none of your business! Now, what did you do today while I was working?"

"I did all my chores, then I helped Dad fix a broken fence and then practiced my sling shot. Hey! you wanna go . . . oh never mind, you gotta work."

"Do I want to *what*, Jimmy?"

"Oh, I was going to ask if you want to go fishing tomorrow, but you're working. Will you ever have a day to go fishing with me again, Molly?"

"I guess I'm getting to be an adult, Jimmy. When you're an adult you're expected to work, otherwise, nothing would ever get done. Can you imagine Uncle Buzz or Margaret practicing with a slingshot all day? Wagons would never have wheels, horses would never get shod, farmers would never get feed for their chickens, women would never get flour to bake cookies or bread" . . .

"Why?" Jimmy cut her off.

"Because Margaret and Uncle Buzz are practicing their slingshots; they don't have time to work."

"I'm not that dumb, Molly. I just wish you'd have time to go fishing, that's all."

"Molly!" Molly's mother called. "Time to wash up for supper!"

"It's suppertime, Jimmy. Maybe after church Sunday."

<><><>

For the first three weeks on the job, Molly performed mostly hard, physical labor: loading and unloading wagons; running up to the second floor for sacks of flour, wheat or whatever; down to the basement for a wheelbarrow of coal; whatever Margaret needed to fill orders -- in short, she was a lumper.

She wondered how Margaret had managed without her. The work was grueling. Every day she went home needing a bath, but at the end of every day she went home excited and thrilled.

Margaret was pleased as well, so on Wednesday of Molly's fourth week, Mrs. Chisholm decided that with some oversight, her new employee could handle certain orders.

The parson, George Marshall, approached in a wagon for his usual order: two fifty pound bags of #3 chicken feed. Margaret handed Molly the order pad. "Take care of the preacher, Molly." Molly froze.

"Nothing to be afraid of, Molly. Just follow these

three steps: 1. Take the customer to the counter and write the order. Make two copies. Include the price and delivery instructions if there are any. Lots of times the customer orders and picks up, as you know. 2. Bring the order to the counter or load it in his wagon. Make sure he sees it, so he can't deny he got it. 3. Collect his money, give him a receipt and have him sign the second copy for us. Keeps everybody honest. My cash drawer should match our receipts for the day. You've seen me do this dozens of times, Molly. It's easy! Now, go!" Margaret retreated to her sparkling clean office and shut the door while Molly walked out to greet the pastor.

"Parson! How can I help you today?"

"Good morning, young lady. You're the Turnbill girl, aren't you? I'm looking for Margaret. Is she available?"

"Yes, I'm Molly, and I'll be happy to help you today."

"Margaret always takes care of me," the preacher said with a frown, "Are you working here now?"

"A month, Sir!" Molly answered enthusiastically.

"Well," Marshall said, cautiously, "I hope the price hasn't increased, now she has hired help."

"Prices haven't gone up, Sir. What can I get for you?"

"Where's Margaret? She knows what I buy. I always get the same thing."

"Okay, let's go inside to the front counter and I'll write it up and bring it down for you. That's two bags of #3 chicken feed, right?"

Marshall wheeled and looked at Molly with new acceptance. "How did you know that, young lady?"

"I told you, I've been here a month already." She winked at him and laughed. The pastor followed, not all that amused.

But in the end his wagon was loaded, the cash drawer was given it's due, and the preacher actually waved as he urged his horse homeward.

Molly exhaled a sigh of relief as she added the receipt to the others on the spiked board under the counter. She smiled and thought to herself, *I can do this!*

Margaret came out of her office and put her arm around Molly. "Good job," she said.

The Turnbills were struck by the excitement as Molly raced through the door.

"Mom! Dad! I was promoted today! Margaret put me behind the counter for the first time! I sold chicken feed to the preacher, Mr. Marshall! He didn't want to talk to me at first, but in the end he was happy, and Margaret said I did a good job!

I was scared when she gave me the order pad and told me I could do it. She really encouraged me and that helped."

The Turnbills exchanged amused glances as Molly carried on.

"Oh, Dad, I really, really liked it. You should have seen the preacher's face when I told him what he wanted even before he told me! Margaret saw him coming and said, 'he always orders two bags of #3 chicken feed', and then she disappeared into her office and shut the door. It was scary! But it was fun! I can't wait to tell Uncle Buzz."

Again, Mrs. Turnbill circled the date -- Wednesday, August 20th -- on her kitchen calendar and noted: *Molly's first day behind the counter.*

Training continued for the next few days. Margaret had most of the store's pricing memorized, but sharing the load with Molly freed her time to create a price sheet for her new clerk.

Molly, for her part, was a quick learner. Customers became accustomed to her friendly face behind the counter, almost never questioning Margaret's absence.

Chapter 22

It was Wednesday, August 6th. Buzz had $7,200.00 in his saddlebag, but he wasn't yet ready to head west. He had a few more things to do.

A wagon train was being assembled along the *Kaw River*. So far there were four wagons; the wagon master, Monte Coulter, was hoping for at least eight. Buzz agreed to join them, so long as they moved at a decent rate. Monte assured him they would.

"I'll be bringing two wagons. I need a drover to run one of them. Anyone in your train you recommend?"

"You might try the Potts wagon. Got a son, Johnny. Just a kid, but looks big and strong."

Calder discussed his needs with the Potts. Both were pleased that he had asked them, and agreed with his terms of service at fifty cents per day for the trip to Santa Fe. As they walked, Calder noticed the three younger faces peering at him from behind the canvas flaps. He smiled and waved at them -- probably twelve down to eight he surmised.

The youngster, Johnny, accompanied Buzz to the homestead forthwith. Buzz put him to work loading the contents of the carriage house into the hay wagon.

"Load just about everything, Johnny; leave out the riggings for the two horse teams and the buggy."

They worked together for a few minutes, then Buzz left Johnny to continue on his own, satisfied the lad would follow through with zeal and maturity.

Next was a quick trip to the new gunsmith. Sam was already at work checking the inventory, cleaning the shop, and oiling the machinery which had lain dormant and untended for months.

"Looks like you're hard at it, Sam," Calder smiled. "Pop would be pleased to see his shop look as good as he kept it. I have something to show you." He unwrapped the big handgun he had taken from the rooming house in Albuquerque.

Sam saw it and immediately whooped, "Where'd you get that gun, Mr. Calder? That's my gun!"

"Hell it is, Boy! I found this gun in an attic. Bought it."

"No, I mean that's my design. I created that gun. I'll show you." Sam went behind a counter, grabbed a stack of diagrams, thumbed through it until he found what he was looking for.

"See here?" He flattened the paper on the counter, showing the gun in detail: the barrel length, grip size, the bore, the trigger, and ejection mechanism. "I have the mold for casting the shells. Got twenty-thirty casings in a drawer over there in the corner cabinet. I can buy all I need outta Independence, Missouri. It's a new type; center fire cartridge they call it."

Buzz opened the drawer, pulled out a hollow casing with the little button on the end of it. "That gun uses these cartridges? They must be 50 calibre!"

"Yes. The cartridge is packed with gunpowder, then a piece of lead is squeezed on the open end. That little button on the other end explodes when the trigger hits it, causing the gunpowder to explode inside the cartridge; and the pressure and force of the gunpowder shoots the bullet through the barrel. That gun is mighty powerful; you shoot it, be prepared for a strong kick -- like a mule."

"Well, I'll be," Buzz said.

"That ain't nothin', Mr. Calder. There's a fella, Colt, in Connecticut who has made some improvements on it. Shoots five bullets before you need to reload it. They spin on a cylinder. In fact if you have two cylinders and lots of bullets you can hold off twenty or more by shooting one and reloading the other."

"Damndest thing I ever heard of," Buzz said, shaking his head.

"I'm going to send off to Mr. Colt for one. Maybe he'll send me a couple. If so, I'll send one to you. If he won't, I'll figure it out for myself."

Sam reached into the drawer again and pulled out a cylindrical paper tube, about 4" long. "Your dad developed a smooth bore scattergun. It works real good. He made three or four of them before he . . . well, before he got sick."

He went to a gun cabinet, pulled a shotgun out and handed it to Buzz. "Take it. I'll make up a box of shells and a box of bullets for that big handgun for you to take along with you. Pick'em up tomorrow morning."

Buzz walked out into the sunlight, grinning from ear to ear. Sam was going to be just fine. He mounted the big roan and urged her up to the carriage house.

Johnny Potts was sitting on a rail, drinking a ladle-full of water. He was sweating profusely.

"Hi, Mr. Calder, I'm about done loading up the wagon. I pulled the tools out of the barn just like you asked: the pitchforks, shovels, a scythe, the plow, a few odds and ends I thought might come in handy, and most of the ropes. Take a look; it's all on top. If I overstepped and you want some returned, just let me know, I'll put it back."

Buzz was impressed. The lad had pulled everything from the walls, stacking the merchandise neatly in the large hay wagon and tying it down. Saddles, bridles and other tack was added on top. The tools from the barn went on last. He looked the load over. It was eighteen inches above the wagon rails.

"It looks fine, Johnny. Be here at eight tomorrow morning; we'll tackle the schooner. Mostly household furniture, so it won't be a full day. We agreed on fifty cents a day. Would you like half a dollar now, or a buck tomorrow?"

"A buck tomorrow, Sir. I'll be here."

<><><>

Ellie was just walking out the door to join her husband when Buzz approached the house.

"Good evening, Mrs. Hendricks. How was your day?"

"Oh! Mr. Calder!" she laughed nervously. "You took me by surprise! I was deep in thought," she continued.

"Oh? About what?" he encouraged.

"Your mom. She seemed so bright when we were here yesterday; today she's been very fragile -- hasn't livened up at all."

"Humph. Maybe yesterday wore her out. She is over 75, you know. I'll be around most of the day tomorrow; let's see if she'll perk up. Appreciate your being with her."

Calder thought for a moment then continued, "Glad I caught you privately, Ellie. Did I load this job on you against your will? Tell me the truth, now."

"Oh, Mr. Calder, don't you worry none about that! I'd'a been here for your mom no matter what. I think the whole town showed you the other day what we think of Cliff and Louisa."

"Thanks," Buzz tipped his hat and stepped inside.

"Your supper is on the table, Buzz. I'm going to bed," Buzz' mother called from the hallway. He didn't even have the chance to see her or say hello to her. He simply answered with, "Okay, Ma. G'nite."

Buzz took his mug of coffee and full plate out on the front porch, sat in the well-worn rocker and enjoyed the stillness of the late autumn afternoon. Thoughts rocketed through his mind: how long would his mom remain alive, wonder what happened to Willy and the other travelers he was helping on the trail, how the widow and young Ben Draper are doing in Albuquerque, wonder how folks back home are doing without a blacksmith.

He took a bite of smoked bass. "This is really good," he commented to a fox squirrel who was foraging in the lawn in front of him. Looking down at his plate he continued, "Quite a smorgasbord, Mr. Squirrel. Nice to have friends, huh?"

He broke off a bit of bread, rolled it into a ball and tossed it toward the small, red creature, but it rushed off as the projectile approached. *So much for friendship*, he thought.

Faces flashed before his brain: Margaret, Jake, Molly, Jimmy, Elmer, that young drover, Ted Willitson . . .

Back to Molly! What was it that Willitson had said? *We run cows on 'er two-three times a year.* Buzz shook his head. *That's not free range, mister! I know the owner!*

He swallowed the last of the grapes that remained on his plate, sat and watched the cautious squirrel scoop up the ball of bread to give it a taste. Then he stood, swirled his mug and tossed the last of his coffee out on the grass. *I may have to head north to Santa Fe on my way home.*

Chapter 23

Twelve hours later Buzz was sitting in the same rocking chair, mug of coffee in his hand. It was just after six a.m. Light was beginning to creep up from its hiding place, overflowing the flat, eastern landscape. *Mornings are the same, don't care what part of the earth you're sitting on,* thought Buzz. Everything on the slate from yesterday is wiped clean; today is fresh, new.

He heard the clang of a dish or dishes from inside. He stepped in.

"The aroma of coffee woke me up, Son. Here's my cup. Pour me a coffee," she said, practically dancing. "I suddenly have this urge to visit the outhouse. I'm afraid if I pour it, I'll pee myself. I'll join you when I get back."

"Sure, Ma," Buzz laughed as he walked her outside, then watched her almost trot, hobbling to the end of the veranda. She negotiated the slight ramp to the ground, then disappeared around the side of the house. Calder walked back inside, poured two more coffees and took them outside, still chuckling.

He finished his coffee and contemplated a third but decided against it. While sitting there waiting, some special mother-son childhood memories knocked at the door: especially the time he climbed forty feet up in a tree, waved to his mom and yelled, "Hi, Mom! Look at me!" . . .

and then was too afraid to come down. His mother climbed all the way up to him and guided him, one foot, one branch at a time, back to earth.

He looked up to see his mother struggling up the ramp to the veranda. He ran to assist her.

"Don't you have a walking stick of some kind, Ma? I'm going to take a measurement and have Sam make you a stick to lean on. Just sit. I'm taking your coffee back and getting you a fresh one."

They sat rocking in silence for a few minutes, drinking coffee, then Buzz recounted the tree climbing episode. She laughed, "I surely do remember! Pretty bold child at 8 years old, until it was time to come down."

Then she countered with a story of her own: "Do you remember when your father gave you your first rifle and told you never to use it except on wild predators or for food? You promptly went out and shot our prize rooster. You said we now had Sunday dinner." They were still laughing when Ellie walked up from the gun shop, carrying a package.

"What's so funny?" she asked, grinning.

"Buzz and I were just reminiscing, silly stuff from years ago."

"Carry on. I'll get breakfast started. Package is from Sam for you, Mr. Calder. It's quite heavy. Bullets, I think."

She disappeared inside. Twenty minutes and three more amusing stories later, Louisa and Buzz were invited to breakfast.

Seated, Louisa asked Buzz to offer a prayer of thanks. As he did, Johnny Potts rode up to start his day. Buzz said, "Amen," set his napkin aside and excused himself.

"I know I'm early, Mr. Calder, but the wagon master, Monte Coulter, asked me to fetch you for a time schedule. We had five wagons join up yesterday. He's ready to go."

"You had breakfast?" Calder asked him.

"Oh, yessir. Hour ago."

"Okay. There's canvas to cover the wagon you loaded yesterday. Go cover it. Tie it down really well. When you finish, ride back and tell Monte we'll have our two wagons in line by nightfall. By the time you get back here I'll have the schooner sitting right here at the house. We'll get her loaded in no time. Thanks, Johnny."

Buzz watched the lad head toward the carriage house, turned and sat back at the table. He looked at his mother. "We leave tomorrow, Ma. First light."

"I understand, Son. I made up a list already -- Ellie and I did. I think you can get it all in the Conestoga."

<><><>

Calder brought the eight draft horses from the barn to the carriage house and tied them to the hitching post just outside -- four buckskins, four dapple grays. He harnessed and hitched the four matching dapple gray steeds to the big Conestoga tongue, tossed a pitch fork in the bed, then drove it to the barn.

His dad's big, covered wagon was different from most. It was twenty inches longer, six inches wider -- making the wagon 118" long by 53" wide, and the bed 40" high.

Each wagon had a grease bucket hanging under the rear axle full of lard, and each had weather-proofed tool cribs on the outside, housing such things as hammers, chisels, axes, knives, chains, jack, extra wheel spokes, and chocks. Smaller five gallon kegs hung from the outer walls on either side, the front one held water, with a tin cup chained to it. The rear one -- with a big red X painted on it held linseed oil for more wheel lubrication. Buzz checked that one. It was full. *Dad thought of everything,* he smiled.

Once at the barn, he rolled two large, empty barrels and his dad's large funnel to the opening and set them inside. Next into the wagon went four gunny sacks of oats for the horses. He grabbed some feed bags as well.

Satisfied, he closed up the barn, headed the big wagon

the three hundred yards to the house and parked it beside the ramp. Then, pitchfork in hand, he walked into the house.

"Ma, come here a minute, please." She obliged. "Now, hold onto this pitchfork like it's a walking stick. Where's it most comfortable?" She looked at him with a frown, but again obliged. With his knife he notched the place on the handle where it seemed to him most natural and comfortable for her to grip.

"Thought for sure you were going to attend my funeral before you go," she smiled.

"Not even funny, Ma!" he yelled as he took the steps two at a time. "Going to see Sam. I'll be right back!"

<><><>

"I'll make two or three," Sam declared, when Calder asked for a cane for Louisa. "That way she can keep one in the kitchen and one on the front porch." He measured the length from notch to end of handle.

"That's fine, Sam, maybe a cane and a staff. Make them of ash. Ash is good and strong.

Another thing I want you to do for me. My mom needs a railing along the ramp she uses to get down off the porch. Would you take care of that for me?"

"This afternoon, Mr. Calder."

"No. I'm using the ramp today. Loading some of Ma's stuff. Wagons are heading out at daybreak. We need to be queued up tonight."

"Tomorrow then," Hendricks agreed.

"There's one last thing, Sam. Might not seem much, but my dad's sign out front needs to come down. I was going to freshen it up a bit, but as you're here and a legitimate gunsmith, you need your own sign. Take my dad's down and hold it for me. Always saw it hanging, shiny bright on a post. Looks beat and haggard. Like to keep it as a memento."

"I've been thinking on that sign as well, Mr. Calder,

and I have a better idea, with your permission. Ellie is a sign painter. I'll pull the sign down and send it to you, and in its place she'll make a copy in the same style. We'd like it to say *Calder and Hendricks, Gunsmiths.*"

"Oh, no! You don't have" . . .

"We already talked it over, Mr. Calder. We want to."

Buzz shrugged his shoulders. "I won't argue, Sam." The men shook hands. "I might not see you again, Sam. The best to you and Ellie. I'm happy to have played a part."

"You never played a part, Mr. Calder. You made it happen."

<><><>

Buzz was walking out of the carriage house when Ellie walked out on the veranda with the list in her hand.

"Looks like you're ready, Sir," she said, looking at the big covered wagon sitting beside the house.

"Yes. As I told my mother, we need to put our wagons in line by sundown. Hand me that list. I want the bigger items in and tied down before we proceed with the smaller."

"I can help you with that," she volunteered.

"No, but you can get a bucket and fill the two barrels with water. I'm leaving the lids on, but the funnel's in the back of the wagon."

Ellie ran inside, returned and proceeded to the artesian well, filled the eight gallon bucket and ran back to begin the fill. That's when Johnny rode into the yard.

"Only a couple of trunks need two of us for the lift up, Johnny. If I know Ma, one's filled with foodstuffs, and the other with skillet, pots, and utensils. She doesn't know how I travel. Give me a hand, we'll get them loaded."

They brought the trunks out, lifted them inside, and Johnny pushed them all the way to sit on the front axle, one on either side of the opening for easy access. He tied them securely in place.

"Take over for Mrs. Hendricks filling those drums with water, Johnny! Make sure you roll that second drum to the other side. The well is almost beside the wagon. Don't even need to pump. Make sure the lid is sealed tight and the bung valve is visible. More stuff will be coming out in a few minutes."

<><><>

The schooner was loaded. Buzz peered into the wagon. Two 30-gallon drums of water, four 50-pound sacks of oats for the horses, two trunks, two wooden crates filled with inherited treasures -- heirlooms such as sterling silver, a mantle clock, a few pieces of crystal, a few of jewelry, and daguerreotype pictures of his parents, all carefully wrapped in burlap or cotton. The entire wagon load couldn't have weighed more than eight-nine hundred pounds. Calder was pleased.

"Still plenty of room inside," Ellie announced. "What else should we load?"

"Nothing, Ma'am. I'll stop at the mercantile in town for some hardtack and a few things to eat."

"Speaking of that," Ellie said brightly, "we put together a basket of food for the first couple of days on the trail."

"Thanks, Ellie." He dropped five double eagles into her hand. "For you and Sam. I appreciate your kindness." He turned sharply on his heels, ignoring her protest. "Johnny! Ready?"

"Yes, I am ready, Sir!"

"Okay, Son. Go harness the horses to our hay wagon. I'm going in to say goodbye to my mother." He placed a silver dollar and a silver half dollar in the lad's hand. He winked at Johnny, "Buck and a half. I appreciate your hard work. I'll be stopping at a general store to pick up a few more things. You go on ahead. I'm going to say goodbye to Dad as well, but I'll catch up. Oh! Tie my roan on the back of your wagon as well," Calder said handing

Johnny the reins to his big riding horse.

Chapter 24

Molly was busy off-loading three wagons from Santa Fe. It was Thursday, August 28th. The teamsters tended their mules, greased their wagon wheels, then leaned against the front columns smoking their pipes, laughing and watching the young girl hard at work. She had one pallet of paint almost loaded on the lift to go to the second floor when Margaret returned from lunch.

"Shame on you men! Get your asses moving and help off-load your wagons. Then two of you load that elevator, and the other one get up top! My girl will help you and show you where it goes!" Margaret handed Molly a copy of the requisition sheets she had mailed to the supply house weeks before.

"Make sure everything tallies, Molly."

"Oh, Missus. We was jus' havin' some fun," said the one called Warren.

"Yeah! 'Sides we just got here. Long trip! It's the girl's fault for starting out by herself!"

"It's true, Margaret. I picked up a pail of paint and put it on the lift. I guess I just expected them to step down and work alongside me."

"But they should have!" Margaret turned and glared at the three men. "Isn't that what you get paid for?" she asked. "I thought you fellas work when there's work to be done, and relax after."

"Absolutely right, Ma'am. Move aside, Missy. We have wagons to unload. C'mon, Marv. Trace, you git upstairs with the girl."

"Stop calling me a girl! I'm not a girl!" Molly lashed out to everyone in the room. "Call me Molly or Miss, but not *girl*!" She stomped up the stairs, Trace on her heels.

"Time you git up there this first load'll be waitin' for you," Marv called out.

Molly was thrilled Margaret had entrusted her with the reconciliation list. That had always been Margaret's domain. The youngster showed Trace how the ratcheted crank worked, to bring the lift to the top floor. Once there the products were quickly offloaded and the apparatus lowered for another fill.

Just minutes later one of the two on the ground yelled up, "Hey! haul that thingamajig up there again! We're tryin' to git on the trail."

And so it went, up and down to the sound of the crackling gear. Trace reversed the cranking mechanism and lowered the lift once more. Marv was waiting. He and Warren stacked the first two of twenty bags of #3 chicken feed, a large crate of sewing materials, another containing the latest gadget: sewing machines -- two of them. Margaret cautioned the men not to overload her elevator. They nodded. Up it went again.

As time went on, the loading and unloading grew more difficult as everyone tired, but an hour later the three wagons were emptied. The elevator had gone up and down nine times.

Upstairs, items from the last three loads were scattered in mounds haphazardly, but the two from the first floor walked up the stairs and under Molly's direction the three men moved things around to her satisfaction.

She checked off the new inventory as it was set in its proper place. A rush of excitement went through her as she realized she was also checking off another milestone in her own progress as Margaret's underling.

"You have a real good material lift system," Trace said, descending the stairs, soaked in sweat. "We could use a system like that."

"Thinking the same thing," Warren commented. He'd come down shirtless, dressed only in his trousers and suspenders; sweat was dripping from his head and beard and on down his chest.

Margaret frowned when she came from her office.

"Excuse my appearance, Ma'am," he apologized, "it's like an oven up there." He continued expressing his thoughts concerning the hoist. "We'd have to rework that lift some, but it does a good job. Maybe build some kinda platform contraption on rollers, pull it around with a mule to load it, then . . . uh, I gotta think on it fer a bit. I'll have it figgered out by the time I git back to Santa Fe."

Margaret, scarcely paying attention to the teamster's ramblings, reached for the itemized list in Molly's hand.

"You sure we got everything?"

"Yes, Ma'am, nothing missing, nothing added. It's all here. I checked it off just like you do."

Margaret disappeared into her office, checked the pricing against the quoted price, and satisfied, she handed Warren a piece of yellow paper with a writing on it. He looked at the paper blankly.

"What's this Ma'am? We're supposed to collect $614.37 in U.S. dollars, gold or silver. This ain't but a yeller piece of paper."

"Put some clothes on, and go down four buildings on the other side of the street. That's our bank. Royston's the manager. Just show the note. You'll get your money."

Trace grabbed the paper. "He don't read, Ma'am." He scanned the paper, nodded his head. "It's okay, Warren.

She even bought us a drink at that place we passed. *Jake's*."

"What does the note say, Trace?"

"Says *Mr. Royston, give these three teamsters $614.37, plus $1.50 for drinks for them at Jake's. Have them sign for the money. Keep the receipt for me, Abel. I'll collect it Friday.*"

Trace looked up. "That's it. Oh yeah, and it's signed Margaret. It's been a pleasure, Ma'am. Truly has. C'mon boys, let's git to the bank."

They all mumbled something similar. The three men climbed aboard their empty wagons and started down the road. Warren waved back, and shouted, "Nice meeting you, Miss," he tipped his hat to Molly. "Hope to make a delivery here again real soon. If I do, I'll show you my design on that lift thing."

Molly frowned and shouted back, "It's not your design, Mister! It's our blacksmith, Buzz Calder's design! All you're doing is working it a little."

He laughed, "Whatever you say, girl."

"Arghh!" Molly ranted. She kicked at a pebble, but only raised a cloud of dust. Margaret had been watching from the big, open wagon doors. She laughed.

"Molly, some people, mostly men, will try to get under your skin over the most trifling of things. But that only means they admire you. Take that Warren fellow. He, for sure, really admires you.

But -- a word of caution about that very thing. Now that you *are* becoming a woman, Molly, you must think, act, and speak like a young lady. Kicking dirt isn't very lady-like now, is it?"

"I guess not, Ma'am." Then she smiled, "I shoulda picked up that rock and thrown it. Bet I coulda hit him!"

They both laughed. Molly grabbed and began to roll one of the sliding wagon doors, Margaret the other. As they pulled them together and chained them, Margaret smiled.

"Last thing, Molly. Tomorrow is payday and Monday is September 1ˢᵗ. I appreciate your hard work, young lady, so starting next week I'm giving you a twenty-five cent raise to $1.50 a week."

Chapter 25

Monday, August 11th -- only the fourth day out. The wagon train of eleven wagons headed by Monte Coulter came across two wagons struggling alone along the trail -- an older couple and a younger one, the Morrison's, their son and daughter-in-law. Unprepared, these travelers had suffered injury to one of their horses.

"What's the problem, Old Timer?" Monte asked the older Morrison.

"Looks like one'a our horses got a laig broke. We're jus' sittin' here discussin' if'n we should turn back."

"Where was home? and where are you headed?"

"Left Fort Smith, Arkansas, back in April, headin' fer the gold fields in Californy. Don't look good now."

"No, it doesn't," Monte agreed. "Let's take a look at that horse. I have a blacksmith in our group, let me ask him to take a look as well."

"First of all," Buzz said when he was called upon, "let's take those traces off that horse, so we can determine the problem." The son jumped down to start the process.

In the meantime, Monte asked them what caused them to travel on their own.

They hadn't, they replied. They were initially in a train of forty wagons, but figured the train wasn't traveling fast enough, struck out on their own, got lost, crisscrossed several trails, and finally hit upon this well-traveled road, not knowing exactly what it was, just figured others would come along soon.

"We only dropped down on this road a week ago, makin' I guess, maybe five or ten miles a day."

"How long have you been running this horse with a broken leg?" Monte asked.

"Two days, I reckon," the old man said.

"Three," piped up his wife.

"Three, then," he agreed.

Monte shook his head, "Your horse is fortunate the ground around here is relatively flat."

"Good news!" Buzz shouted as he knelt down with the horse's lame foot between his knees, probing the hoof with his jackknife. "Leg's not broken; your horse has thrush. It's pretty bad, but treatable."

He went to his wagon's tool crib. Johnny joined him, and watched as he pulled a jug of horse liniment from the box, along with a large strip of cotton. He handed the items to Johnny, then reached into the box for a long handled chisel, a large rasp, and a pair of shears.

"What's thrush, Sir?" the lad asked.

"Come with me; I'll show you."

The four Morrisons, along with some others were gathered around the horse when Calder and young Johnny Potts returned. Buzz picked up the lame foot, scraped the hoof, and with the chisel, carefully probed and cleaned the "frog" -- the very center of the hoof pad -- revealing black, oozing, foul-smelling pus.

"You see this?" Buzz asked the Morrison men. "Your horse was wounded by a sharp rock or stick or perhaps a thorn, like from the honey locust or something. Now it's infected. Have any cotton padding, soft cloth, anything like that -- and some strong twine or leather lacing?"

Young Morrison went to ask his wife. While waiting, Calder used his rasp to file the hoof down a bit. Then he went back to washing out the soft inside pad of the hoof when the young man returned with some strong cording and a piece of cotton -- probably a part of their bedding.

When he was satisfied the infected, putrid flesh was cleared away, Buzz stripped some small pieces of the cotton and soaked them in the horse liniment as Johnny and the younger Morrison watched.

He dripped liniment into the horse's pad, making sure it seeped into all the cracks and folds of the "frog", then packed the saturated cotton pieces into it.

Next, Calder wrapped the entire hoof completely in the length of cloth he had brought from his wagon. He finished it off just above the fetlock and tied it off with the cording.

He turned to the Morrison family members. "You can't go on with us. There's no way. What you do is up to you. What you must do is let that horse rest -- change her dressing once every two days for a week, and as needed after. If you don't you'll have a dead horse on your hands.

Each time you change the dressing you must apply an antiseptic like the liniment I have. I recommend one of you take this road back to Council Grove, pick up bandages, antiseptic and such. Mercantile might recommend something better. I haven't shopped for the medicine in years. Now, that's what you should do. We've traveled maybe a hundred miles. You have a saddle?"

Young Morrison replied, "We got three or four of'em."

Buzz looked at the folks standing around staring. "It's important for all of us that we look to our horses' feet from time to time, maybe once a week. We depend upon them to take us two, maybe three thousand miles. They need us to be there for them while we're traveling."

He turned back to the Morrisons, "Can't help you any further, folks. Good luck."

"Johnny, please take this liniment to my tool crib."

The younger Mrs. Morrison was upset that the wagon

train would move along without them. Monte walked up to her wagon. "You're just leaving us here?" she asked.

"Yes, Ma'am, we are. Perhaps you should all consider heading back to winter in Council Grove. There's always next spring. Pick up a train. Two wagons wouldn't be safe, especially heading for California this late in the year. Think on it, Ma'am. Talk it over before you do anything foolish." He turned to the small group standing around.

"People, it's time to move out." Then to Buzz, "I think you've done all that can be done for these fine folks."

The Coulter group swerved around the two Morrison wagons and continued their journey.

Monte rode from the front of the line to the last wagon, reminding them all that should there be a problem to sing out, then he went back to chat with Buzz.

"Thanks for the lesson back there in caring for your horses. You have training in horseshoeing?"

"We blacksmiths get involved with everything, Monte. Speaking of the Morrisons, though, I didn't offer to leave any liniment for them. Damn fools would . . ."

"I know!" Monte interrupted, "damn fools would probably have applied the liniment and continued west."

"They probably still will," Buzz shook his head. "They'll probably end up killing that poor horse. Some folks see a problem head on, ignore it until it stops them in their tracks, then lay the blame on someone else."

"Sounds about right," Monte nodded. "Tonight, would you mind if I have you give a talk about horse hoof care to our whole outfit, usin' that Morrison pony and her thrush problem as an example? A few of our group saw it, but not all. Wasn't a pretty sight."

"No problem," Buzz replied. "Next mercantile we come

across will run out of liniment real quick."

"Prob'ly." Monte rode off, laughing.

Chapter 26

Finding a mercantile was a problem. The map Buzz had picked up in Council Grove showed a place called Zarah. Calder remembered some ruins on his way east; must be what was left of Zarah; now it was only a resting place with fresh water. Barring any mishaps, it was at least a six-day journey.

A day west of Zarah was what later became known as Larned. A few people had seen great potential there because of its beautiful location along the *Arkansas River*, but each attempt for development was met with crushing opposition from the indigenous peoples of the plains.

Beyond that, it would take another week to reach the fledgling Fort Mann. On his way east, Buzz had witnessed the teamsters constructing the buildings of the fort under the direction of *Wheelwright, Smith and Store*. Perhaps these pilgrims would find a mercantile there. Two hundred sixty miles, at twenty miles per day; that is, if all went smoothly.

Buzz considered all this as he urged his team up a slight grade, following Johnny in the hay wagon. *So far we're doing just fine*, he thought to himself . . . *outside of the Morrison family problem, and that wasn't even of our making. Wagons were lucky to make fifteen to twenty-five miles per day, depending upon the topography.*

Things won't be so rosy once we get to that fort. We could take the lower road at Cimarron Crossing which would cut ten days off the trip according to Monte, or we could choose the higher, mountainous road, going into the Colorado Rockies.

The higher road would lead us to Bent's Fort and civilization. We could probably spend a couple of days there, even sleep in a hotel bed, Calder mused, *before dropping down to Santa Fe. But the going would be arduous -- making perhaps as little as six to eight miles per day along the rugged mountain trail. That trail reached heights well above 8,500 foot elevation.*

Buzz took one last look at the map before folding it and returning it to his pocket. He was happy with Monte's lower road plan, especially as the weather was changing.

<><><>

The eleven teams of the little caravan were well matched. Monte did change the order of the wagons on the fifth day, putting two mule teams at the head, and one mule team, the Potts wagon, at the rear. The mules were stronger, had more stamina, and pulled the horse teams along at a slightly faster pace. Monte figured, rightly so, that they had gained as much as a mile a day by the action.

Most days Buzz joined with the Potts family for meals. It became a ritual. Except for the bags of beans, flour, and coffee, the provisions his mother had packed in one big trunk were almost gone, as had half the hard tack and the pemmican he had purchased at the Council Grove general store. But the Potts had done the same with him. They agreed, sharing a meal was better than eating alone.

Of particular interest to Buzz, Johnny's younger brother and two sisters, along with three or four of their traveling chums often sought out his wagon at the end of a long day.

He always had a yarn to spin or a quiz to exercise their minds. They especially enjoyed hearing bible stories like *Daniel in the Lion's Den*, or *David and Goliath*, but his own life experiences were also in constant demand.

He became known as Uncle Buzz. He shook his head and wondered why and how, but the name seemed to find him here in the hinterlands as well as at home in Warm Springs. *Was he everyone's uncle?*

Chapter 27

The wagon train reached Fort Mann in the late afternoon of day seventeen -- Sunday, August 24th. They had hoped to make it by Saturday, but it was not to be. Instead of walking into a church that Sunday morning, most of the emigrants sat, surrounded by creatures of the prairie, to thank their Creator for His providence and safety thus far. After a prayer and a hymn the train continued westward.

Fort Mann was bustling with activity -- filled with another caravan of forty-two wagons, a score of teamsters, a small army contingent, and a few Indian scouts. The small hotel was packed; no availability whatsoever. The teams lined up just outside a new section of the 14 foot finished wall close to the entrance gate which had a continuous series of hitching posts along the wall. The travelers climbed down, tied off and entered what was to one day become Fort Dodge, on the outskirts of the future Dodge City, Kansas.

Calder followed suit. He walked through the open gates, following the others, and smiled at the welcoming soldiers. He noticed a few of Monte's group walk directly to the mercantile only to find it closed. It was Sunday.

A soldier pointed out the regiment headquarters; he headed there, being informed that the Lieutenant may be out. The soldier was correct. He turned to leave when a man on the boardwalk to his left called out, "Hey! Aren't you that Blacksmith?"

Buzz faced the man but didn't recognize him. "I am a blacksmith. Who might you be?"

"Nick Perryman, Sir. You don't remember me, but I was one of the teamsters on the trail when those two families were caught in that flash flood. I want you to know we all thought you were a hero that day.

That fellow, Willy, said you saved them all, and your advice to the lieutenant and Boyd -- that's our foreman's name -- sure saved that wagon. The lieutenant wanted to hurry the process, but Boyd said no, he was going to do as you said . . . slow and sure. That wagon was damaged, but we were able to pound the side boards back and save it, axle, wheels and all."

"I'm glad to hear it, son. I'm no hero, Nick. You've heard that expression -- 'be careful, no need to find yourself in hot water.' Some people jump first. Those people are called fools, Nick. Stop and take the temperature first, then move quickly. I've tried to do that all my life. Works for me."

"Thank you, Sir. Good advice."

"Not really my advice, Nick. There are scriptures that give that advice much better than I. Remember Jesus told the folks to count the cost before they begin to build their houses -- same principle."

"Kinda like using your brain before you use your muscles, right?"

"Just right. You have a good day, Nick."

Buzz next visited the hotel. He was the fourth from the train to do so.

"Sorry, no room." the manager said before Buzz opened his mouth.

"I expected that before I came in here," Calder smiled. "Wondering where all or even a few from our group could get a bath."

"Not ours," the manager said firmly. "Guests only. You might try the army boys. They have their own barracks. Must have a bathhouse."

"Yes, I was looking for the lieutenant. Haven't seen him."

"Try the Cimarron. He's generally there when he's in town."

"Thanks." Buzz walked out and headed for the small saloon. Monte caught up with him and walked with him.

"Looking for a place for our folks to have baths," Buzz explained. "I'm hoping to rustle up the base commander. I was told he may be over there at the Cimarron," he pointed.

Monte only nodded. They walked on for a few moments. "I'm thinking we should stay here a couple of days. Give everyone a chance to stretch their legs, wash their clothes, relax a bit before heading out again; teams as well. Next comes Santa Fe. That's going to be a tough leg. Almost 400 miles. What do you think, Calder?"

"Well, one day won't hurt us. Santa Fe is not quite halfway for most of these folks -- they're heading for California, right, Monte?" Buzz asked.

"Yeah, taking the Old Spanish Trail, southern route, through Utah and Arizona territories. No one here has talked to me yet but I expect to pick up a few wagons right here, or maybe in Santa Fe."

"I'll be leaving you in Santa Fe as you know. I'll pick up a teamster there to drive my other wagon south to my valley."

By this time they had reached the Cimarron. A group of men was playing poker in a corner. The lieutenant recognized Buzz immediately, stood and waved. "Mr. Blacksmith!" he smiled, "pull up a chair!"

After introductions Buzz stated his purpose.

"How many in your group, Calder?" the commander

asked.

Monte spoke up, "We have a total of forty-seven, Sir. Twenty-six adults sixteen and above, and twenty-one kids."

"By all means. Tell the On-duty at the barracks that R.W. says you are to have full use of the bathhouse, stove, tubs, coal and all -- this evening. And Calder!"

"Yes, Sir?"

"This is between us. It's not a public bathhouse. Understood?"

"Yes, Sir."

"And Calder" . . .

"Yes, Sir?"

"Fine work on the trail last month."

"Thank you, Sir."

Chapter 28

Saturday, September 6th.. Margaret counted out $1.50 into Molly's hand, thanked her for her hard work and told her to enjoy her day off. Molly was ecstatic. She rushed home to tell her mom.

"I'm proud of you, Molly. What are you going to do with all that money?" Geraldine asked her daughter.

"Spend 10%, tithe 10%, and save the rest," Molly answered promptly.

"What are you saving for, Molly?"

"I'm not sure, but I think books. Uncle Buzz told me there are hundreds, even thousands of books about almost everything. He has a dictionary book on his shelf. It explains words -- most of them I've never heard of before. I've read through some of it. I'd like my own copy."

"I thought we knew most every word there is," Geraldine frowned. "What words are there that we don't know?"

"Lots! I wrote some down when I was at Uncle Buzz' house. I have the paper in my bedroom. I'll go get it."

"Not now. Get it after supper."

"Okay. Then after books maybe buy something real special for you; maybe even a piano. Margaret has one in the store, but it would take almost a year of saving up."

"You just keep working hard, Dear; save your money for yourself. Don't worry about us. Your father and I have everything we need. Besides," she laughed, giving Molly a hug, "we don't have room for a piano, anyway."

"Well, something smaller then, but nice."

"Fine, Girl. Right now, go wash up. You can roll out the crust for pies. We're going to have strawberry-rhubarb. Mrs. Kinney brought me the biggest strawberries you ever saw."

Mrs. Turnbill looked at the clock on the mantel. "Your father will be here in a half hour. I want to pull them out of our oven just before he gets here. Go on now, Honey."

Molly's mom chirped after her, "And you can tell him about your raise in pay at the supper table."

Ten minutes later Molly had rolled out all the crusts, added the strawberry-rhubarb, put slits in the top crusts and was just pinching the edges of the last pie when there was pounding at the door. The pies and supper would have to wait.

Chapter 29

"We need every able-bodied man available for a bucket brigade! If we don't hustle, she's gonna be a goner, sure as shit!"

"Jimmy Iverson! That kind of language will not be tolerated in this house!" Molly's mom scolded the out-of-breath young man standing at the door. "Now slow down! Take a breath, and tell us," she continued.

"I can't Missus. I gotta tell everyone. Mr. Jake, he told me to run! It's Margaret's place!" He was gone.

"I gotta go, Mom!"

Before her mother could say a word Molly had raced out the door. Already neighbors were running toward the general store, some with buckets; already smoke was visible above the trees. She heard herself screaming, "No! No! No!" as she ran.

She turned the last corner to see angry yellowish, red flames enveloping the mercantile, shooting high in the air above the second floor's roof and boiling out from the basement's coal chute.

Molly's lungs were bursting with pain, her mind was almost delirious with dread and dismay; she began to cry uncontrollably at the sight. Adrenalin pushed her on.

She broke into the middle, and joined a line of

residents passing buckets of water toward the flames. She could see at least two other bucket brigades stemming from other wells, all racing against time to save the venerable old structure, one of the first buildings in Warm Springs. Molly's pounding heart began to slow; she was able to breathe.

Looking at the scene, her eyes again filled with tears, this time tears of gratitude for the response the residents were showing -- even, she noticed, some of the younger children were doing their part, running empty buckets back to the wells for refilling. She saw Old Floyd Banner in a different line. Normally unsteady on his feet, Old Floyd was resolutely passing bucket after bucket along the line without stumbling. Next to him, Maude, owner of the cafe and three of her employees continued passing the buckets of the water toward the angry flames.

A horrible thought struck her! *Margaret!* She apologized to the two on either side of her, excused herself and ran toward the huge, closed wagon doors.

"Molly!" She turned to see her step father, Jason Turnbill. "Get away from there, Molly!" he yelled. "Don't even think about opening those doors!"

"But Dad! Margaret might be in there!"

"No, she's not. Elmer Kaufman found her. He went in to pick up his wages, so he says."

"That's true enough, Dad. He's taking care of Uncle Buzz's place. Margaret pays him. But where is she?"

"She's at Doc Ford's."

An explosion from inside startled them both. "There can't be much left in there, Molly. I'm sorry, Hon."

He put his arm around her; they watched from a safe distance as they heard another explosion, then another. She pictured cans of paint and turpentine exploding. Margaret had warned her to store it carefully. She was sure that she had.

A fellow named Jefferson walked up and put his hand

on her shoulder. "Sorry, Missy," he said, shaking his head. Then turning to her father, "Deliberate, Jason! Jake an' me took her to the Doc. She's bin shot. Whoever 'twas thought they'd set the fire to make shore."

A wall on the north side of the building collapsed, sending thousands of sparks flying in the direction of the adjacent building. Fortunately, a few people had prepared for such an eventuality -- no fires ignited.

Molly ran to the exposed north side. Making sure she was at a safe distance, she peered in. It was an inferno -- completely aflame. *Strange,* she thought. *It's like the bible story Uncle Buzz told her. The one about the fiery furnace and those three Hebrew friends of Daniel.*

"Who would shoot Margaret?" she asked aloud. One of the bucket brigade men came over and stood behind her. It was Jefferson again.

"We don't know yit, Missy, but we're gonna do our darndest to find out. You don't remember me, do you Missy? I was one of the fellas that found you when you was ten. You're all growed up. I was proud when I saw you was workin' fer Margaret."

The bucket brigades had given up and the crews were resigned to watch as the old building collapsed in upon itself. Again, sparks flew, this time making a spectacular display in the night sky.

Molly, face blackened with soot, clenched her fists. "We'll rebuild, Mr. Jefferson. We'll rebuild, Margaret and me. You just wait and see."

Her father came and stood with her. "Let's go home, Molly. There's enough help here to keep the fire from spreading."

"You go on, Dad. Mom has a nice dinner for you. I'm going to see Margaret at Doc Ford's."

Chapter 30

"Molly!" Mrs. Ford opened the door wide, to greet her young visitor. "The Doctor is busy as you probably already know."

"How is she, Ma'am? Is she bad? I mean, will she die? Can I see her?" The words tumbled out of Molly like water down a spillway.

"Slow down, Child! Catch a breath!" Mrs. Ford exclaimed, grabbing Molly by the shoulders and pulling her close.

"Now, I'll go in to see the doctor; you wait right here in the kitchen. I'll be right back to let you know."

Molly sat as instructed for only a few moments; then she paced the floor, confused. *Things were going so well; how could this have happened? Shot? Why would Margaret get shot? Robbery? Elmer found her. Wonder if Elmer saw anyone leaving. Maybe some. . .*

Mrs. Ford was back, a frown on her forehead.

"She's in bad shape, Molly. Doctor Ford says he'll be out here in a moment to discuss her condition with you. I'll put the kettle on for tea. Tea always calms us down."

The two women were just finishing when the doctor walked in.

"Not good, young lady. She pushed me to the top of my expertise. It's in God's hands now."

"No!" Molly blurted out. "Margaret can't die!" the young lady continued. "I'll see she gets well. I'll stay with her, take care of her." She looked up suddenly, realizing what she had just said. "Can I? I mean, may I stay and nurse her back to health? I'll treat it like a job, bring my own lunch. I won't be a bother."

"No, young lady, you may not. I need that room for other patients; but . . . you just gave me an idea," the doc said, tapping his fingers together. "I've been wondering how to handle Margaret. You just may have hit upon the only reasonable solution. Margaret's own home is a mile out of town. Would you stay with her there?"

"Oh, yes! Yes, I can!"

"Alright, then. Go find your pa and maybe Jake and another fellow. Tell them to bring a wagon with some straw in it. We'll load her up and settle you both in her place. You and I will sit and discuss her wounds and needs. Right now, suffice it to say she was shot three times -- lost a lot of blood. Now go!"

Margaret was still unconscious when she was tucked into her own bed. Mr. Turnbill told Molly he would check on her the next morning, and with that, he and Jake Ruskin said their goodbyes and left, leaving Molly alone with the doc and the patient.

"Why is she still asleep, Doc? She's breathing, I can see that, but the men carried her in like a sack of spuds."

"It's a medicine, Molly. Chloroform. Very strong. I almost never use it, but bouncing around in that wagon might have caused her too much pain. I'm not going to leave any here. I have a jar of pain medicine for you to use. It's called ether. I'll show you how to use it, but use it only when it's absolutely necessary.

Now, Molly, Margaret was badly wounded. She was shot in her belly, leg, and shoulder. I'm a good doctor, but I'm afraid of the bullet that went through her belly. It ended up against her backbone. One wrong move and she could be a cripple for the rest of her life if she survives the shooting."

"But she'll still be Margaret, right, Doc?" Molly asked anxiously.

"She'll still be Margaret, Lass. Now let me show you how to change her dressings and nurse her back to health."

The old doctor went through the steps he wanted Molly to use in caring for Margaret: how to administer the ether, and the precautions to take in moving her.

"She probably won't be able to move, Molly, at least at first. You'll be doing a fair bit of cleaning as well as nursing."

They moved into the kitchen and sat at the table. "Now," the doc continued, "I'll come by every afternoon; the Missus will prepare meals for you so you"...

"Thanks, Doc. My dad said he would come by with food, too, so Mrs. Ford shouldn't fuss over me. And Doc, don't let all that other stuff worry you none. I figure a nurse has to do what she has to do." Doc Ford only smiled.

<><><>

From the kitchen they heard Margaret begin to stir. Molly said, "do I make her breathe the ether now?"

"Let's go in and talk with her. Maybe she's not really awake yet. I'll stay with you until she's fully awake. Maybe she'll tell us how much pain she's in. Fact, I think I'll stick around for a while," he determined, nodding his head.

"Ha!" she said. "You make decisions the way I do, Doc; talk things through to yourself, then nod your head when you've decided."

Ford smiled again. "Caught me."

Margaret was groggy, but awake. Her eyes darted back and forth as realization and recognition came back little by little. She finally opened her mouth.

"I'm hurt bad, ain't I, Doc?"

"Yes, Margaret, you are. First off, I'm relieved to see you're able to talk and move your head. I'll tell it to you straight. There's a bullet still in your back, Margaret, right alongside your backbone. I couldn't get it out for fear I'd paralyze you. I'm still afraid you might be, so don't try to sit up. I'll come by every day and when the time comes, we'll decide. Also, Margaret, I brought a bell with me. I want you to use it when you need help.

I took a bullet out of your shoulder, but you may have lost the use of that arm; and the last bullet went all the way through your leg, but that one cost you a lot of blood.

Molly here, offered to be your nurse. She's here full time to take care of you. She going to feed you, change you and your bandages, and give you something for pain if it's unbearable."

"You mean like right now?" Margaret tried to smile; her face was ashen white as the effects of the chloroform were almost gone.

Doc Ford nodded to Molly. "Warm up the jar in the warm water, Molly. Not too hot, now."

Molly put the warmed ether below Margaret's nose, and encouraged her to breathe in the fumes. Within seconds the pained expression subsided. "That's enough, Molly. Not more than once every 4 hours."

"Can you eat anything, Margaret?" Molly asked.

"Oh, no, Molly. I'm a little sick to my stomach. I couldn't eat a thing."

Doc Ford broke in, "You were just belly-shot, Margaret. Anybody'd be sick after that. Now, you just rest. If you need help, use that bell."

Margaret smiled faintly and rang the bell. The gong was surprisingly loud. "Like this?"

"Exactly. I'll be leaving now. Be back tomorrow." He turned to Molly. "A few minutes in the kitchen, Molly?"

<><><>

"She won't be able to keep solids down for a couple of days. She's lost a lot of blood, so she's weak, but I'm happy she can move her head and talk.

I've asked Mrs. Ford to render down some venison and some carrots; she's already made a broth, I'm sure. I'll bring it by later tonight.

Encourage Margaret to sleep. She'll want to talk -- that's fine, but in short bits only. Keep the conversation as cheery as possible, take care of business that's needful, then leave the room."

Doc Ford walked out, stepped up into the buggy, and turned his horse homeward. Molly felt, somehow, all alone. A shiver of fright went through her at the awesome responsibility on her shoulders, but she shook it off as she walked into the bedroom. Margaret was asleep.

Molly explored the parlor; she had never visited Margaret's home before; the furnishings, but for a desk, were simple, elegant, feminine, just like the bedroom. Interesting, though, she thought, the desk, large and ornate, backed up to a large window. On either side of the window were shelves filled with books -- more books, even, than Uncle Buzz had. *I'll be spending some time in here, for sure,* she thought.

Next was the kichen. *A cup of tea sounds good,* she thought. *I'll put the kettle on, check on Margaret, then sit in the parlor with a book and a cup of tea.*

Margaret was still asleep. Molly took her tea into the parlor and began to go through the titles of Margaret's books. There were dozens, perhaps hundreds.

Among the titles:

The Federalist (1788)   by Thomas Jefferson
Meriwether Lewis, History of the Expedition Under the Command of the Captains Lewis and Clark (1814)

edited by Nicolas Biddle

A curious Hieroglyphick Bible (1788)

edited by Isaiah Thomas

New England Primer (1802)

American Cookery (1796)   by Amelia Simmons

A Grammatical Institute of the English Language (1783)
                              By Noah Webster

Experiments and Observations on Electricity (1751)
                              by Benjamin Franklin

The Legend of Sleepy Hollow (1820) by Washington Irving

Molly decided upon the electricity book by Benjamin Franklin, sat back to read when Doc Ford's buggy drove up. She looked out the window to see the doctor accompanied by Elmer Kaufman. She opened the door to receive them. The doctor held out a brown ceramic jug.

"Here's the broth. It's almost full so it's heavy," he cautioned. She took the jug by the handle. "And," he continued, "it's still hot. How is she?"

"I've checked twice. She hasn't moved; still asleep." Molly turned, "Hi, Elmer, what brings you out here?" She already knew the answer, but wanted to hear him say it.

"I came to see how Margaret is, but I won't come in," he replied.

"Oh? Why not?" Molly asked.

"I've been out here lots of times. Every time I come out she says, 'wait right here, Elmer, I'll be right back with your money'. So I don't come in."

Doc Ford watched the exchange and took over. "Today is a bit different, Elmer. I want you to see Margaret today. She's in rough shape, and may be in bed for a long time. So, wait here for a moment. I'm going in to see how she is, and I'll come and get you so you can see her.
Molly, get a pot, a cup and spoon from the kitchen,
then come with me, please." Molly, with items in hand,

followed him into the bedroom.

"Does Margaret pay Elmer for something?" he asked.

"Yes, Sir. Twenty-five cents each week to care for Buzz Calder's place, and other money for making occasional deliveries," she said. "I think he made two deliveries this week."

"I see."

Doc Ford gently woke Margaret up by squeezing her right arm. She opened her eyes, and focused them on the doctor. A wistful smile followed.

"I'm still alive, Doc, but I feel like I lost a fight with a grizzly bear; I hurt everywhere."

"I want you to eat something if you're able, Margaret. It's a venison broth. Molly will feed you. If you can keep it down it will be good. If you need to vomit, use the pot Molly brought."

Very carefully, Ford and Molly propped Margaret up against a pillow, then Molly poured a small amount of broth into the cup, and spooned it into Margaret's mouth.

"Good!" Margaret said between slurps. "I think I can drink from the cup."

"Maybe, but not too much, now, Margaret!"

She kept it all down and asked for more. The Doc relented, but only half a cup more.

"You have other company," Molly said. "Elmer came out to see you."

"Oh! Poor Elmer!" Margaret moaned. "I owe him money. You'll find coins in my top desk drawer. Give him a dollar plus another ten cents for two deliveries he made this week. The dollar will cover this week and three more. But make it all in pennies and half-dimes and count it out and explain it all so he understands. Maybe I should do it . . ."

"No, I got it, Margaret," Molly interrupted. "I know just how to let him know. He found you, you know. He thought you were dead. That's why he's here. May he come in?"

"Oh, Dear Boy! Of course!"

"Hi, Miss Margaret," Elmer blurted out, full of emotion. "I'm sure glad yore okay. I found you laying there, I thought you was dead for shore with all that blood."

"Well, Elmer, I'm not, thanks to you. But I'm not getting up anytime soon, so Molly is going to pay you for a whole month, starting with this week and then three more weeks. Just take care of Mr. Calder's place like always. Any extra deliveries you make, Molly will pay you."

"Don't look like there will be any more extra trips with the fire and all."

"Fire?" a startled look swept over her face. "What fire?"

"We can discuss everything when you're more rested, Margaret," Doc Ford took over, and tried to smooth things out.

"No! I want to know now! Oh! I'm going to puke!" Margaret leaned forward just as Molly's quick reaction brought the pot under the older woman's chin. When she was finished, Molly stood and motioned for Elmer to follow her.

She walked outside to the well, rinsed the pot, threw the liquid as far as she could, rinsed the pot twice more and walked back into the house.

"Wait here. I'll be right back with your money, Elmer."

She hadn't seen so many coins in her life. She counted it out and closed the drawer, pleased that Margaret had entrusted her with such responsibility.

Counting out the money, she gave Elmer fourteen half-dimes and forty pennies. He looked at each one before he stuck it in his cloth sack.

"A lot of money, huh, Elmer?"

"Shore is, Miss Molly. I'll be off now."
"Aren't you going to wait for a ride with Doc Ford?"
"Naw, I'm going to run home. It's only a mile. G'nite."

Chapter 31

Buzz Calder checked his pocket watch. It was a little before 5 a.m. Friday, September 12th. Monte's wagon train had increased by two wagons at Fort Mann. The addition changed the positioning of the teams as well. His wagon and Johnny's were still together, but were now numbers seven and eight in the train. Buzz grumbled a bit, because the new wagons were oxen-driven and slower. He tried to convince Monte to turn the newcomers down but to no avail. *I suppose the added hundred bucks each is good money for Monte* he thought.

They were now just days away from Santa Fe. The train had been climbing steadily since leaving the grassy plains of Kansas and the Oklahoma Territory; Buzz had looked forward to this leg of the journey -- in fact, he had packed light in preparation. He would collect discarded items, especially metals, from overloaded wagons struggling to make the uphill climb into the Rocky Mountains.

He figured he could be selective in scavenging these cast-offs; he judged he had room in his wagon for at least five hundred, perhaps as much as seven hundred pounds of extra weight.

One of his trunks was, at this point, completely empty -- poised for such things as cutlery or sterling pieces, and should Buzz become overladen himself, he could always discard some of his loot; after all, he had no attachments to the stockpiled items.

He was correct in his anticipation: the discards included pot-belly stoves, spinning wheels, lanterns, a wood-burning cook stove, coffee grinders, and one large, rectangular wooden box with galvanized interior and two insulated doors which sealed almost water-tight. He examined the bulky item carefully before he set it into the wagon, and thought about it until nightfall. He determined it was a food storage container, but a full assessment would wait until he had the luxury of his workshop in the valley. In the meantime, he used it to store small items.

The traveler in the wagon behind only laughed when Calder slowed to analyze an abandoned item, but happily assisted him loading some of the larger items.

Johnny's brother and sisters began running from one discarded item to the next, hoping to find "treasures for Uncle Buzz" along the trail. At times he rejected their discoveries, but other times he would put their finds in the back of his wagon.

Soon the whole train became aware, providing a few laughs or groans around the evening campfires. Around the Potts family campfire, however, things were slightly different . . . half-penny rewards were given by Calder to the Potts children, along with one or two young friends, for their additions to his wagon.

"How much further to Santa Fe do you suppose, Mr. Calder?" Johnny Potts asked, as they prepared the two wagons for day 37 on the trail. "We're getting low on feed for our horses as well as coffee and beans for us."

"I know," Buzz answered. "We're probably eight-ten days out. I've been scraping the bottom of my larder as well. Horses can manage just grazing for the few days without any oats, so they should be alright. Do you know which grasses they need to stay away from?"

"No, Sir. I'm pretty green when it comes to plants growing wild. Monte hasn't told us anything either. You live here. Maybe you ought to let us all know how to recognize the good plants from the bad."

"Let me think on that for a while, Johnny," Buzz answered. The more he considered the more he realized the value of such a talk. "I'll ask Monte," he shouted as Johnny climbed aboard the hay wagon.

Calder heard the Wagon Master from far ahead yelling, "Move'em out" to the lead wagon, and the train continued its journey. He smiled to himself; Monte was right -- those two ox teams weren't slowing the train down at all. If anything they were pushing the horses on.

Monte, following his daily routine, started to pass Calder's wagon on his way to the last of the travelers.

"Monte!" Buzz called out

"What's up, Calder?"

"Johnny Potts suggested someone give a quick talk on the plants our teams should and should not be allowed to forage on; it's probably a good idea. Some of us are getting low on bags of oats and such. Maybe you have ideas on it, but I'd be happy to do it if you agree."

"Damn good idea. I've been suspicious of some of these plants myself; last time out we lost a horse. Never found the cause, but the animal kept stumbling and frothing at the mouth. After a couple of hours it just keeled over dead. Tonight?"

"Tonight's fine, Monte."

All that morning Buzz enlisted his crew of youngsters to wear gloves and collect plants as he directed. He would separate them into two groups: those edible for the teams, and those poisonous.

That evening folks gathered around in a circle to hear what Monte had to say. He started with words of encouragement: "Folks, we've made good time. Weather's been favorable, and our teams have done remarkably well. Most importantly nobody's been shot, no one is ill. This little train is doing well. Keep it up!

We're getting low on supplies, I realize. Anybody in need of food or water? Anyone have plenty of either and can share? See me before you retire tonight. How about your animals -- low on oats? Hay? Same thing, see me.

Now, allowing your animals to forage on the plants for the next, maybe, two hundred miles can be hazardous to them. Buzz Calder, our blacksmith-rag-picker knows the area." Calder laughed along with the immigrants. Monte continued, "He has some tips to keep our teams healthy. Buzz?"

"Just a few things to keep in mind, folks. Your horses, mules, even oxen are smarter than you when it comes to what they're willing or unwilling to push down their throats. Remember that. But, if they're hungry, well, watch them closely."

Calder had Johnny bring out four bushes and lay them side by side in front of him.

"These are some wonderful supplements for your teams -- this is Bunch grass, most common and nutritious grass in the area; this one," he said, pointing, "is Fescue, very common. Now, here is Bluegrama, and here," he said, "is Wheat grass. There are others as well, but these are the most common.

Then, there are others which can kill your animals, so pay attention!"

Johnny brought out the next bunch. "Stay away from thistles; they look pretty, but are deadly to horses." Then displaying a plant with tiny bunches of white flowers, "Yes, this, some of you know, is Hemlock." Buzz laid them all out, identifying each one.

"Here's Johnson Grass; And these," Buzz continued, "are sprigs from Arrow grass, Sorghum and Hogweed. Don't allow your animals to forage around these plants.

We'll be in Santa Fe in a few days; you'll replenish your supplies. Don't forget your teams. If you think they can forage for themselves they might get themselves into trouble, and you'll end up with a sick or dead animal."

Each of the travelers walked up to the plant display, nodded and went to their separate wagons.

<>< ><>

Buzz walked back toward his wagon. A chill in the night breeze let him know the season was changing. He knew only too well how swiftly Old Man Winter could overpower and strangle the high country with its icy fingers. Calder felt a niggling urgency to get home. He'd been gone too long.

Chapter 32

There was already a fair amount of daylight, but it was cold -- almost down to freezing. The wagon train had scared up several mule deer the previous day, one especially large buck, probably close to 300 pounds on the hoof. Calder hoped a few of its brothers would show up today. His rifle, normally in its scabbard and strapped just inside the wagon flap, was today beside him on the bench.

Looking ahead, Calder saw the trail was about to make another sharp rise in elevation; looking behind, he caught glimpses of where they had been just three or four days before. He figured they had climbed close to a mile above the valley floor.

The wagon train stopped. Monte rode back along the trail, stopping at each wagon to caution the wagoner of the upcoming narrow stretch of trail. He came alongside Buzz.

"Treacherous mile or so comin' up, Calder. We'll be winding around this hill you see in front of you. We'll probably climb a quarter mile in this stretch, but they's a resting place half way up, sorta like a meadow. Teams can rest up before tackling the second, steeper half; gonna be a hard day. Glad we got here before the weather changes."

"Weather looks like it could be changing right now,

Monte," Calder said pointing to the whitish cast in the morning sky. Monte considered the mountain and frowned.

"Not good! Last time through we had a bracing wind comin' at us full force -- damn near threw a couple a'wagons down the cliff. Twas the wagoners' fault. They got spooked, spooked the teams.

Keep a'huggin' the mountain, you'll be alright. Keep your team right up close behind the one ahead'a ya. Just ten feet or so, an' make damn sure your brakes are workin." Calder nodded. Monte rode on to the following wagons to repeat his words of caution. It was 8:22 a.m.

Buzz stepped down from his wagon and walked up to have a quick chat with Johnny. "Feel okay about the trail ahead, Son?"

"Oh! yes, Sir. Me and my team'll be fine!"

"Good lad. You'll be okay, just follow Monte's orders. One thing about horses; they sense danger, and will stay away from the edge of a cliff. Normally, unless you have a real skittish horse, you can let her have her head."

Buzz looked ahead. The front wagons were beginning to move again.

"Slow and steady, Son." Buzz patted Johnny's arm and returned to his own team. He pulled his watch out. 8:26.

Five minutes went by before Johnny's wagon lurched ahead. Buzz coaxed his big dapple grays forward. He put his rifle back in it's scabbard. Ten minutes later, Calder watched as the wagon ahead of him begin a steep incline. It's load shifted, slamming into the boards at the rear. He half expected the boards to give way completely, wagon wheels, plows and leather harnesses crashing down in front of his team; but the boards held; the wagon continued to climb.

After an appropriate distance Calder touched his reins and yelled, "Ha!" The team responded. He waited for the trunks, the barrels, that oblong box or any of his other treasures to fly noisily around, but aside from a definite shift toward the rear, the cargo inside the wagon was secure.

Calder, at times, could see only Johnny's wagon in front. The six others up ahead were hidden from view by the rock wall they were hugging. Sometimes it seemed they haltingly covered only inches a minute, sometimes a few feet, but they were progressing up; so far so good.

He heard the wind before he rounded the next bend; then it hit him full in the face. He appreciated Monte's tale of a previous trip and the panic caused by the wind shear and nervous wagoners. It was a biting, cold wind; Buzz was thankful there was no sleet mixed with it.

Johnny's wagon stopped. After a few minutes Calder once again pulled out his watch. It was 11:08 a.m. *Curious,* thought Calder, *almost three hours of arduous travel and now stopped for over eleven or twelve minutes on the edge of a cliff in a blowing wind.*

He stepped down and walked to the rear of his wagon. The traveler behind saw him and yelled "What's going on?"

"Damned if I know!" Buzz shouted back, "but horses been working all morning. They deserve a reward!"

He grabbed some oat-bags, put one on his roan, filled four more and walked to feed his horses. As he slipped a bag over one head then the next, he rubbed each horse behind the ears and spoke encouraging words. "Best I can do, Ladies. Can't stop the wind."

He repeated the process for Johnny's team of buckskins.

"Why do you suppose we've stopped, Mr. Calder?" Johnny asked.

"No idea, Johnny, but I'm going to find out before we run into a serious problem on this mountain. I'll be right back."

Buzz walked toward the front of the line, assuring each driver he passed that he would let them know what had stopped them. Everything looked normal until he reached the third wagon. The team looked fine, wheels looked okay, but the owner was missing. Buzz called out,

"Hey, Mr. Goodwin! Hello!" He went to the rear and peeped under the canvas. "Mrs. Goodwin! Where is Darrell?"

"He's here. I think he's dead. Damn fool! I told him he's too old to pick up and move at his age!"

"We need to move this wagon, Ma'am, and right now!

She looked at Calder angrily. "How we gonna do that, Mister, if he's dead! Didn't I say he's dead?"

"Yes, Ma'am. Mind if I check him out?"

"Please yourself, but he's dead. I'm so sick of everything. I should be laying there, so he could go off gallivanting up and down mountains; and Coulter says we have two more months, crossing rivers, deserts who knows what? And when we get to where Darrell wants to go, what then? *You Happy Now, Darrell?*" she screamed, pounding his chest with clenched fists, tears flowing down her cheeks.

Calder climbed in. Ignoring the wife's hovering, he tried to listen for sounds of life. As he reached for an arm to find a pulse, he thought he saw the chest move a bit.

Buzz looked up at Mrs. Goodwin, "He's alive, Ma'am. I think he must have had a heart attack. That, with the thin air caused him to faint. You may just have saved his life by beating on his chest. At any rate, Ma'am, he's alive."

"He is?" the woman asked incredulously. "Oh, Honey, Darlin', you're alive."

Calder watched them for a few moments with his own private thoughts, then said, "We're going to need to move this wagon, Ma'am; he needs rest. Can you drive it?" Her shocked look was answer enough. "I'll find someone." He crawled out. The two lead wagons had long disappeared from view.

He ran back along the wagons. "I need a driver!" he yelled as he went. "Man up front is sick!"

Luther Hoskins, one of the ox team drovers yelled, "Polly! We need you out here!"

A girl of no more than fifteen poked her head out of the canvas covering, "Yeah, Pa?"

"Bundle yourself up and take over, here, Girl. I'm goin' up front. Just pretend you're plowin' the field back home, stay close to the wall an' don't look over the edge. You'll do fine."

Buzz and Luther raced to the needy wagon. Luther climbed aboard, tipped his hat, and without another word, he urged the team forward with a flip of the reins and a "Giddup!"

As Buzz passed the girl he thanked her. She was taller than Johnny, he thought.

"You going to be okay?" he asked.

"Oh, sure, Mister, been drivin' oxen since I was twelve."

Calder shook his head as he seated himself and picked up the reins.

<><><>

Almost two hours later, all thirteen wagons were in a circle in the meadow Monte had mentioned. There was still the second leg to this upward climb. It was 2:45 p.m. Calder tucked his watch away, and went to find the wagon master.

He found Monte surrounded by most of the other drivers. Some were for stopping for the night, some for carrying on. Mrs. Goodwin wanted to stop to care for her husband. Others to care for their wagons and teams.

Monte's advice was to press on. "Two hours, maybe three tops," he said. "Then it's green grass and level or a bit downhill the rest of the way into Santa Fe. We could wait until morning, but we've all been looking at the skies. At this altitude weather can change in fifteen minutes."

After much discussion, it was decided: they would continue in forty-five minutes. Enough time to take care of personal needs, grease wagon wheels and tend to their teams.

Calder found a lady among the group who agreed to assist Mrs. Goodwin with her husband.

"Is Darrell awake yet, Ma'am?" Buzz asked, poking his nose into the wagon.

Mrs. Goodwin answered, "Not yet, but he is breathing steady, now. I think you're right about pounding on his heart," she beamed.

"Not the recommended procedure, I suppose," he laughed. "Keep him warm, and for heaven's sake, Mrs. Goodwin, keep him calm."

"Well, of course I will!"

"Good. We'll be moving out in 15 minutes."

Monte was right. The last leg was terrifying but short. For the last half hour -- the steepest part -- the skies grew darker and spat rain mixed with sleet, the trail began to ice up, the drivers carried lanterns and walked in front of their teams, holding halters or ropes to coax their teams forward. But they reached the top before complete darkness -- 6:10 p.m. Saturday night.

Sunday morning found them on a high plains with a panoramic view of where they had been. The ground had a dusting of snow, but grasses were very visible, wherever they looked. They were delighted with their decision to proceed.

A small herd of about ten elk were grazing, not a hundred yards from their camp. Monte pointed them out to the travelers.

"They're always here, folks. They're sorta a tame herd. We wagon masters have an unwritten rule: we never shoot at them unless we're starving. Anybody starving?"

No hands went up. "Alright, then, let's enjoy this elk family. If we see an elk or muley all by itself, well, fair game, but not these."

Buzz nodded his appreciation of the wagon master even more. He made a promise to himself to follow that same practice.

<>·<>·<>

And so, on Wednesday, September 17th they came into Santa Fe, capital of New Mexico Territory, population just under 4,600 residents. Here is where Buzz Calder would say goodbye to Johnny, The Potts family, Monte and the rest of his newfound friends, and head for home.

He and Johnny pulled his wagons into a livery stable.

"How much do I owe you, Son?"Forty-one days, Sir. $41.00."

"Exactly right," Buzz placed two gold Double Eagles and a Lady Liberty silver dollar in Johnny's hand, patted him on the back and thanked him for the fine work.

Calder watched as the lad trotted toward the other teams. He then pulled his saddle and accessories from the wagon, threw them on his roan, making sure his saddle bags were secure. The stable owner watched with studied interest.

"You a horseman, Mister?"

"No, Sir. Blacksmith from Warm Springs, down below here about 150 miles." Buzz held out his hand, "Buzz Calder. Why?"

"Torres. Manuel Torres. This place is mine," the keeper smiled, taking the blacksmith's hand. "Just don't handle yourself like a green Easterner, that's all."

"I'm probably going to be in town overnight; possibly one more day. We'll see. Can you watch over my teams and goods until then?"

"Got all the room you need, for as long as you need, Buzz. Figure nine horses and two wagons -- buck-ninety a day, includes hay and water. You want oats as well for the horses figure another half dime apiece.

"So, oats and all, I'm looking at $4.70 for the two days, right?" He didn't wait for a reply. "Tell you what, Torres, take a curry comb to my draft teams. Do a good job on them, we'll make it an even $5.00. And, I'll pay you right now. He climbed into the saddle and tossed a $5.00 coin.

Torres bit down on it and smiled, "You got yourself a deal, Mister Blacksmith. I'll take good care of them."

Chapter 33

Calder had never been in Santa Fe before, but in one of his history books he thought he remembered reading that -- *in 1610 a certain Vasquez de Coronado came with troops, built a church there and a government building, called it the palace of the Villa Real de la Santa Fe de San Francisco de Asis. Something like that.*

They taught some 100,000 Pueblo Indians until, in 1680 the Indians rebelled, killed most of the Spanish, and pushed the rest into Mexico. Then the Indians burned everything but the church and the Government Building.

Fighting between the Indians and the Spanish continued for years, but the Spanish were in control even up to 1821 when Mexico gained its independence from Spain. Mexico quickly made Santa Fe a trading center in the area, and opened trade opportunities with American trappers and traders. Now it had become a U.S. Territory, and would probably one day become a state.

Calder reached down, patted his roan, "I'm sure I have a few recollections wrong," he said, "but that's what I remember. Now help me find the Government Building. Should be right in the center of town."

The tall building on the left a block ahead looked promising. "That's probably it, huh, Girl?" The roan only snorted. Turned out to be the Mission de San Miguel. He was wrong, the roan was right.

The Palace of the Governors was further down the road -- a single story building with clay roof and fronted by columns -- not palatial at all. He tied the roan to the hitching post and walked inside.

The large room was laid out in a horseshoe shape, three offices on each side and another straight ahead. A man directly ahead motioned for him to advance. His footsteps echoed throughout as he walked. He poked his head in the three offices on his left as he approached; all were unoccupied.

"What can I do for you?" the man asked. Even his voice had an echo. Buzz looked at the man; dignified, as tall as Calder, graying hair, but Buzz noted, the fellow looked tired.

"Buzz Calder from Warm Springs, about 120 miles below Albuquerque. I'm here on behalf of an orphan girl. Just want to make sure her ownership is still in good standing on a homestead her parents had when they were murdered."

"Name?"

"Broderick."

He wrote the name on a piece of paper. "Indians?"

"Never proven one way or the other."

"Bring a deed, records, bill of sale, any papers -- anything like that?"

"No, Sir. Hoping I could get something like that from you, actually."

"What's your relationship to this orphan girl?"

"Friend."

"Just a friend, huh? You rode 150 miles without any papers to find out if this orphan girl owns a piece of property."

Buzz started to explain, but the agent interrupted.

" How long ago did this girl become an orphan?"

"Almost seven years now. June of 1845."

"Do you read, Mister?"

"Ha! Yes, I read!" Calder chuckled.

"Why's that funny, Mister?"

"Sorry. It just struck me funny. I spent three years in University, spent four years as an attorney in Missouri before coming west."

"So, you're an attorney in this, uh, Warm Springs, south of here."

"No, Sir. I'm a blacksmith."

"Ha! Now, that's funny, Mr. Colter. Lost your license, huh?"

"Name's Calder. Does sound funny, I agree, but, no, I didn't lose my license. Just feel liberated. I can create or repair something and feel good about it. At day's end I walk into the house and wash good, genuine dirt off my hands."

The agent studied Calder for a moment. "Tell you what I'll do, Mr. Calder I have some ledgers," -- he disappeared for a few moments. When he returned he had two giant ledger books under his arm. "I'm not supposed to hand these out, but sit over there so I can see you, and see if you can find the young Broderick claim to the land. Take all the time you need.

By the way, my name is Calhoun. Norm Calhoun. One of three Capitol attorneys. Been one for fourteen years. Wish I was a blacksmith." They shook hands.

<><><>

Calder chose a chair facing Calhoun and began. He knew only the tragic day of the family massacre and fire: June 2nd, 1845, written up the following day in the <u>Clarion Call.</u> When did the Brodericks file the deed? He may as well start at the beginning of the year.

They came out of Utah, Mormons -- that much he knew. What else? They had sheep. That, too, was obvious. The remains of sheep that littered the landscape near or on the six hundred acres was sickening. Calder had seen with his own eyes the horrific tragic end of the Broderick family . . . not to be forgotten.

He found nothing in January, nothing in February or March. He wished he had the plot numbers, the surveyor's coordinates -- the longitudes, latitudes, but he had nothing.

Finally, he put a slip of paper in the ledger and walked to the counter.

"Norm, I'll be back," he said, handing Calhoun the ledgers. "I need to grab a hotel room, freshen up, maybe get a bite to eat. But I'll be back."

"I'll be here, Calder."

<>

Calder had three hotels to choose from. He picked one called *La Plaza de Santa Fe*, next to the old church.

Saddle, saddle bags and rifle went with him to the lobby. He secured a room and asked directions to the bathhouse. Once he dropped everything on the floor by the bed, he sorted through his saddle bags for clean clothes, then headed to the bathhouse.

After a good scrub-down he looked at the bathwater, then at the mirror on the wall. No wonder that Calhoun fellow thought him just an illiterate drover -- six days' worth of untrimmed beard and enough dirty water to challenge the muddy banks of the *Gila River*.

He laughed as he put on clean clothes and combed his hair. *Calhoun will think someone else wants to look through those big registers.*

Lobby assured him they'd have his laundry ready -- bundled, tied and at his door by early morning. That done, he walked into the patio and ordered a steak dinner and a beer. Steak was good; beer was exceptional . . . ice cold!

"How did you get the beer so cold?" he asked the waiter.

"Easy. I'll show you."

A wall separated the kitchen from a supply room. Against the wall in that room was a horse trough of ice chunks, and in that were two beer kegs on their sides -- slightly angled downward toward wooden taps on the bottom outside ends.

"Ah!" Buzz nodded his head. "So simple! Just gravity fed. Where do you get the ice way up here?"

"Make our own seven or eight months out of the year. Store it out back in a stack of straw. In summer we bring in big blocks of ice on wagons. And," he paused, "if we run out of ice, we force ourselves to drink warm beer." He winked.

<><><>

The livery was at the end of town; just a good walk, Calder thought. He needed to stretch his legs anyway. He walked out into the sunshine, loosed the roan from the hitching post and walked her to the stable. Torres took the mare off his hands.

"This one is a beautiful animal, Mister Blacksmith. I'll take special care of her."

"Thank you, Manuel. I appreciate that. Are you, perchance interested in any of my goods? Saddles, harnesses, tack of all sorts. Give you a good price."

"Ah, Señor Buzz, no. But check with the general store. They will be needing to resupply -- very soon I think. They just received a big order. General store from down south somewhere. I heard it burned to the ground. The mail wagon just pulled in with the news, not even twenty minutes ago.

I wondered why they were late. Seems they had some kind of skirmish with bandits along the way. Normally they would have been here yesterday. Anyway, I'm to have three teams ready by Friday sun-up.

Very sad. They just had their big fall order delivered three weeks ago. Now they must order a second time." Torres shook his head, "Very sad."

Buzz frowned. He mulled the information over for a few moments. "Do you know the location of that general store?"

"No, Señor Calder. Only south. Maybe Albuquerque."

"Yeah, maybe. Thanks, Torres. I'm at La Plaza de Santa Fe in case you change your mind."

A few minutes later he was walking up the steps of the Palace of the Governors. As he stepped through the doors, his new friend, Norm Calhoun called out, "Mr. Blacksmith!" The interior resounded with echoes that seemed to bounce off the walls . . . even Norm winced.

"Been waiting for you. I think I found something for you! Come, take a look!"

Norm chose a table and placed an open ledger in front of Calder.

At the top the ledger said <u>Deed of Title -- Transfer of Ownership</u> then below were columns. Calhoun pointed to line 37

DATE	PLOT#	SELLER	BUYER	WITNESS
10/12/1844	364--L51/22	E. H.Dammer	M. P. Broderick	N. R. Planter

"Now, to confirm," Calhoun continued, "we go to the land plot on page 364, and there it is L51 and L22. Shows 640 acres assigned to Edward Henry Dammer by Mexico in 1827, and later sold to Merithew Peyton Broderick in 1844, witnessed and registered by Nelson Reginald Planter on October 12, 1844."

"So, she owns the land!" Calder exclaimed.

"She has no papers to back her up, Mr. Calder; we have a problem. There have already been conflicts over the property having to do with Mr. Dammer's original claim to the property, and now the fact that the young lady has no title deed in her possession.

The latter problem can be resolved if the young lady presents herself before a magistrate and proves she is who she says she is. The other is a legal head scratcher;

may need to be resolved in court. The U.S. doesn't recognize Mexican Land Grants."

"But, New Mexico isn't a state, Norm!"

"I'm not done quite yet, Blacksmith. There's a seven year statute on filing a title claim in the Territory. This means"...

"I know what it means, Norm. Means the seven year clock is approaching midnight for Molly Broderick. We have only 28 days to act. And you say there are already two vultures circling. Who are they, Norm?"

"You know I can't say, Calder! But I will tell you this -- fees and paperwork have already been witnessed and submitted."

"I have a good idea, anyway, Norm. You have been very helpful, my friend. Let me write everything down, and I'll be on my way."

"There's a judge in Albuquerque, if that helps!" Calhoun shouted as Buzz opened the door.

"It does! Thanks!"

Chapter 34

Darkness spread over the house. Margaret was asleep. Doc Ford had been given the chore of giving her the details of the fire -- a complete loss; now he was gone.

Molly had found the candles before sunset, and had two lanterns sending forth shadows and light. It was eerie being in a strange house.

By lantern light she sat in the parlor on the overstuffed sofa she had decided to use for a bed. She tried to continue the book she had started, but couldn't concentrate. After reading the same line for the third time, she closed the book and blew out the lantern; she had left one lantern burning on the kitchen table.

She tried to empty her head of the goings on of the day, but it was so hard to do. *Margaret had been shot! Three times! Whoever it was certainly tried to kill her.* Molly finally drifted off to fitful sleep.

She was awakened by a stifled cry of pain. She grabbed the lantern from the kitchen, headed for the bedroom.

She stood over the bed and looked down at her patient. "I'm here, Margaret," Molly said reassuringly. "I have pain medicine for you."

"Okay, Molly, but stay with me awhile. Is the doctor gone?"

"Yes, he left hours ago. You've been sleeping soundly

for a long time."

"I need to go to the outhouse. You'll have to help me, Molly. I can't hold it any more."

"No, Margaret, we can't do that. You still have a bullet in your back."

"Shush! The chair in the corner is a chamber pot. Pull it close to the bed. I can manage. I know I can! Now bring it here, Molly!"

Molly dragged the chair close to the bed. "Where did you get this chamber pot, Margaret?" she asked, removing the seat.

"Not now Molly. Bring that medicine over here and give me a dose. Quick now."

Molly held the small jug of ether above the lantern for a few seconds to warm it, then held the jug under Margaret's chin. The older lady lay motionless for a moment, eyes closed, breathing in the fumes; then she whispered, "Okay, now help me get to the chair."

Molly kept saying, "Not good, Margaret, not good," but she took Margaret's offered hand and aided her to her feet.

"I have a stack of paper I normally use in the outhouse. It's in the back porch. Bring some in, then you can leave. Take the lantern; I'm fine."

Dutifully, Molly brought the sheets of plain paper to Margaret, then walked into the kitchen, still shaking her head. Everything that had just happened was against Doc Ford's instructions. How could she explain it to him? She could only hope Margaret would be okay.

A few minutes went by, then Margaret called out, "Can I get some help, Molly?"

It took Molly great effort even with Margaret's help to wrestle the woman back into her bed. Beads of sweat poured down the widow's forehead.

"Prop me up a bit, Molly. We need to talk. I don't even know what time it is. There's a clock in the parlor. Would you check?"

"I'll be right back, Ma'am." Molly removed the pot from the chair and took it to the outhouse, then rinsed it well and returned it to the bedroom chair. She pushed the chair back into its corner spot. Then she took the lantern into the parlor.

"Molly, I don't know what I'd do without you." Margaret was almost crying when Molly returned.

"Are you in pain, Ma'am?"

"Not too much. What's the time?"

"Just before" . . . the grandfather's clock in the parlor chimed out the hour. "4 a.m., Ma'am." They both laughed.

"Molly, Doc Ford told me about the building and everything in it. We need to replenish stock or this town is going to dry up, especially with winter coming on. Rian and I practically put this town on the map, and I'll be damned if we let Warm Springs become a ghost town.

It will be light in an hour. We'll put a list together for Albuquerque and one for Santa Fe. Send them off with the next express wagon which tries to make it here on the 10th and the 24th of each month, so one should be rolling in here on, I believe, Wednesday."

""Yes'm, it is."

"But Molly there's more. I didn't tell Doc Ford, but I'm telling you. They were looking for you, as well. I heard one ask, 'The girl?' and the other one say, 'No.' First one said, 'Damn!' . . . Then one came around the corner into my office and shot me.

I tried to figure that out, but I was confused, with the medication and the fire and all I just couldn't put it all together. I still haven't, but I know you were -- and probably still are a target! Those men planned to murder us, Molly. It's just the *why* I haven't put together yet."

"Did you recognize him?" Molly asked.

"No. I only saw him for a split second. Didn't recognize the voices either."

"That's scary, Margaret. Do you have a gun in the house?"

"Several. Can you shoot?"

"No, Ma'am. Uncle Buzz was supposed to show me how, but never had the chance. But I do know the difference between a rifle and a shotgun, and I know that a shotgun can break your shoulder unless you hold the gun butt tight against it."

"Right. All my guns are in the closet. I have four revolvers hanging from a peg. Bring me two of them. There's a shotgun leaning against the trunk in there. Take that out, bag of shells as well."

"What are you thinking, Margaret?" Molly asked.

"I want you to keep that shotgun in the parlor with you at night, and take the revolver with you when you leave the house. Hopefully, no one knows we're here, but you can never tell.

On my desk in the parlor is a stack of orders, the last one was the one just delivered by your three friends from Santa Fe. Bring that whole stack and the pen and writing pad beside it."

"Right now, Ma'am?" Molly was dumbfounded. The woman had just been shot, lost a lot of blood, had surgery, bullet still lodged in her back and now wants to start a work day.

"It's Sunday, Ma'am, that's all. We're both usually in church today. If I'm not there someone may get suspicious. They may even think you're dead, but I don't have an excuse."

"You're probably right, Molly, and there's still time before the mail wagon comes through. Maybe it's best you go to church.

Bring me the stack from the parlor. I'll go through it while you're gone. Pen and paper, too. Oh! Bring me the shotgun, as well."

By lantern light Molly found the stack of orders and the shotgun.

"One last thing, Molly. In the closet there's a rifle in a scabbard. Grab that for protection, and be on your way."

<><><>

It was only a mile, but the longest mile Molly had ridden in her life. She stopped at what was left of the general store -- she just had to. There was still a wisp of smoke or a smoldering glow in one or two spots. She made out the remains of the piano, now just a charred hulk on the ground. It had fallen with the rest of the merchandise when the second floor collapsed.

It was still very early; she rode home, tied Spirit to the back porch doorpost, walked in, carrying the rifle, expecting no one up; but her dad was at the stove, brewing coffee.

"Good morning, Molly, you're up early. How is Margaret this morning . . . and why do you have a rifle?"

"Hi, Dad. You won't believe this, but Margaret got up this morning. Can you imagine that? She was shot three times yesterday, and Doc Ford operated on her belly, and she got up already."

"She's a strong woman," Mr. Turnbill said, "now why do you have a rifle?"

Molly thought quickly, "Dad! I'm a woman, traveling alone in the dark. I was being cautious."

Her dad seemed satisfied with her answer. "Cup of coffee?" he offered.

"No. I think I'm going to bed. I've been up most of the night. If I'm still asleep by 8:30 would you wake me? I don't want to be late for church."

Her father didn't say a word, but he began to wonder about his daughter.

Chapter 35

Doc Ford found Molly as she was walking into church.

"Molly! What are you doing here? Shouldn't you be home with Margaret?"

Molly took him by the arm and half-dragged him inside. The doctor's wife followed meekly behind. She pulled him into a seat and sat beside him.

"I'm not sure what to do, Doc. Margaret remembered something from yesterday that is very disturbing. She was shot by two men. They weren't robbers; they went there to kill her!"

"What makes you think that, Molly?"

"Not think, Doc. We know, Margaret and me. Just before she passed out she heard one ask about me, like they were really sorry I wasn't there as well."

"Hmm, what did he say?"

"One asked about me, the other said I wasn't there, first one said too bad, or something like that. They were going to kill us both, Doc."

Ford wrenched up his face in a look of disbelief. "Molly, she was just shot; she'd lost a lot of blood; people get light-headed and don't think straight."

His wife jerked his arm. "Listen to Molly, Daniel." Then she turned to Molly. "I believe you, child. Do you think they will try again?"

"I don't know. I just don't want the word out that I'm out at Margaret's place taking care of her."

"Jake and your dad know -- and Elmer," the doctor cut in again. "What about him? He'll tell everyone he meets."

"I already told Dad. He'll explain to Jake. Elmer could be a problem," she agreed, "I'll work on him."

"Question you haven't answered -- how is Margaret?"

"She got me up this morning just after 3:oo. Toileted, back to bed, then" . . .

"She got up?"

"Yes, and she returned to bed herself, just needed help propping up. When I go back, we'll put together two orders to replace the inventory."

"Where will you put the stock."

"She thinks Uncle Buzz will allow her to use his barn while her building is being rebuilt. I'm going over there to check it out right after church, then I'm on my way back to Margaret's."

"That might be big enough. I've been in that barn," Doc Ford said. He turned to his wife, "Mildred, I need to see Margaret. She's being a damn fool. She's probably bleeding on the insides. I'll leave right after church. You want to go with me?"

"No, I'll stay. Why not go with Molly to Calder's place, then go to Margaret's together?"

"Fine with me," Molly agreed. "Right after church."

"No. I'm going to see Margaret immediately. I'm sure you will be able to get a ride home with Mrs. Brighton the school marm." The doctor kissed his wife goodbye and returned to his buggy.

Mildred and Molly sat together for services; afterwards, they hugged. Molly looked for Elmer, but couldn't find him. She left immediately for Calder's place. As she rode up she saw Elmer sitting on the front steps.

"Hi, Molly!" he called out.

"What are you doing here, Elmer?" she answered.

"Watching over Mr. Calder's place. I spend a lot of time here since the fire at Margaret's. Is that why you're here, too?"

"Kinda. I want to look at Uncle Buzz's barn, to see if it can be like Margaret's General Store for a few weeks. We're ordering some stock so the townsfolk won't be without supplies and we need someplace to keep it."

"I don't know if Mr. Calder will like that. We should ask him first."

"But he's not here, Elmer. Margaret says he'll be happy to help us."

"Margaret said that? Then I guess it's okay. Do you want to see inside the barn?"

"Yes. But one other thing, Elmer. No one is to know about where Margaret is, and no one is to know about our plan, okay?"

They walked inside. The barn doors were easily wide enough for a wagon. Inside was a wide open space. There was a loft above, filled with hay. Elmer looked at Molly, a frown on his forehead.

"Margaret's not here yet, so how could I tell anybody she's here when she ain't?"

"Here's what I meant, Elmer. If you have already told people she's home healing up, don't tell any more people. It's a secret. And, don't tell any people we're going to store stuff here in Mr. Calder's barn. When we get the stuff here, then we'll tell people. In fact, then you can tell them, but not before. Okay?"

"Shore, I can do that."

"You're doing a great job, Elmer. I'm going to see Margaret now. Remember, keep everything a secret."

"I will, Molly. When will Mr. Calder get back?"

"I hope soon, Elmer. We all miss him."

As Molly mounted her pinto. Elmer noticed the rifle in the scabbard.

"First time I ever saw you with a rifle, Molly. How come?"

"Lots of varmints and snakes out at Margaret's, Elmer."

<><><>

Doc was preparing to leave when Molly returned. "Damn fool was sitting on the bed, trying to figure how to get to the commode when I walked through the door."

"I woulda done it somehow, Daniel. I ain't helpless!" the lady bristled. Then she laughed, "Okay, so I'm helpless; I sat here for a quarter hour trying to work it out in my head. I'm sure glad you came by, Daniel."

"Just please don't try it again, Margaret. You could start bleeding on the inside and we wouldn't know for a day or so, and by the time I figured it out you could be on your deathbed. Fortunately, things look normal in your situation. No blood in your stool or urine, no bruising around your naval, no weakness, numbness, nausea or faintness. You listening, too, Molly?"

"Yes, Sir. I heard," Molly said, "I'll take the commode out; be right back."

When she returned she heard him still on a rampage with the wounded woman. He turned to his nurse.

"Keep tabs on her, Molly. If she gets frisky, tie her to the bed."

"I promise." Molly walked him to his buggy and waved as he touched the horse's rump lightly with his whip. She listened to the crunch of both horse and buggy on the gravel, then she walked back inside; Margaret was waiting.

"No faith!" Margaret said, shaking her head.

Chapter 36

The Treaty Of Guadalupe Hidalgo in 1848, ended a two-year border war between the U.S. and Mexico. The treaty ceded a part of Mexico to the U.S. for the sum of ten million dollars. This new section of land became a part of Arizona, New Mexico, even parts of what was later to become Utah, Nevada and even Colorado. The biggest prize was California.

Later (in 1853) U.S. and Mexican authorities would meet to finalize their border negotiations. Mexico would reluctantly agree the U.S. would end up with the southernmost strip of land below the *Gila River* all the way to the *Rio Grande*, and that river would become the border eastward all the way to the Gulf of Mexico. This acquisition and agreement was the final step in gaining all of the southwest, including Texas, for the U.S. The final agreed-upon price was $15,000,000.00, and would be known as the Gadsen Purchase.

Most of it was untamed wilderness. Warm Springs was in this new part of the American frontier.

Before the advent of stage coach lines such as Wells Fargo, Butterfield or Overland, and before rail -- *mail wagons*, as they were called, sprang up of necessity.

There were several mail wagons, all of which were

privately owned, and each finding a niche carrying mail, news, and the occasional passenger along various routes.

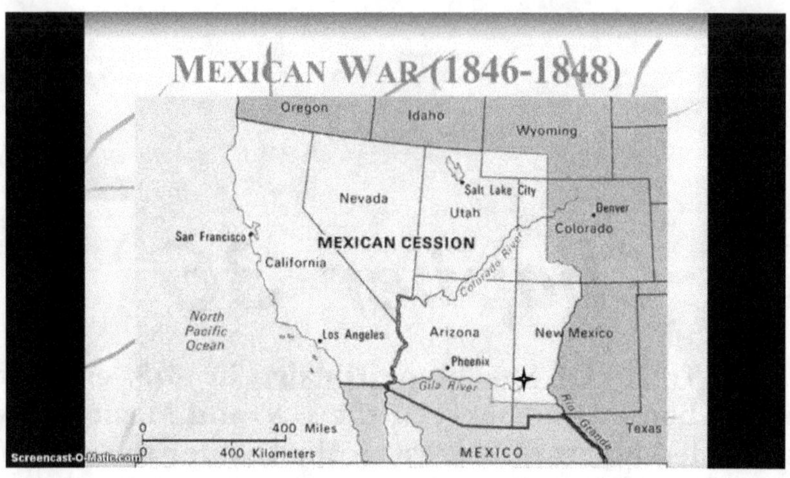

Orren Juneau was a driver of one such mail wagon, following the old Dominguez-Escalante route the Spanish had used from 1777 until they relinquished the territory to Mexico in 1821. The wagon's route led from Tucson -- the southwestern edge of the New Mexico Territory, with major stops in Warm Springs, Socorro, and Albuquerque, and a few minor stops at fledgling hamlets such as Piños Altos, and at times Mogollon before reaching Santa Fe. Then it would turn around and return to Tucson. Of course, the teamsters were masters at gossip. Visiting wagons usually brought the latest news.

Wednesday, September 10th, 1851 was no different. Molly had two letters in her hand for Orren Juneau. He pulled into town about 2:30 p.m.

"Who lit up the general store, Molly?" Orren asked.

"Not sure yet. Just make sure these are delivered, okay? We need merchandise as quickly as we can get it." She handed him the letters and twenty cents.

"Is Margaret okay?" he asked.

"Touch and go."

"Any other mail to go?" Orren stood and asked the crowd.

Someone said, "Most everything burned up, but I think the bank has a few things. I'll go check."

Orren announced, "I'm going over to Maude's for a bite. Be leaving in an hour. Anything you wanna send, remember, regular letters are five cents, packages that fit in the bag are ten cents, quarter for big packages that won't fit in the bag. Put the stuff in the bag, money and all."

The fellow who trotted to the bank came back with a handful of letters. He dropped them into the bag with some change.

Molly watched the bag for a few more minutes. Another two letters went into the bag with some change. She didn't recognize the sender. *Hmm, town's growing,* she thought. Then she walked across the street and headed toward the bank.

The manager saw her coming. "Hello, Molly, getting colder isn't it?"

"Hi, Mr. Royston. Yes, it is. I'm here for Margaret. She tells me I need to come in and be added to the check signing sheet. She may not be up and around for a few weeks."

"Oh, she did, did she?"

"Yes, Sir. She gave me this note to give to you. I think I can tell you -- she's at home. I'm taking care of her."

Mr. Royston put his glasses on to scrutinize the note and signature; then he shrugged his shoulders. "Okay," he said, "do you need money?"

"Oh, no Sir, not now. But we have some inventory coming, probably first part of next month."

"So, she's going to rebuild, huh? I'm not surprised, but I did wonder. You know, of course, that there's a consortium of some kind looking at properties to set up a large general store in the center of town. Two fellows came in here yesterday, asked the bank for our property, then they went and asked Jake Ruskin and Maude, as well. They even had the audacity to ask if Margaret would consider selling the land, now that she so unfortunately lost her business to the fire."

"Did you know these people, Sir?"

"Nope! Suited, ties, real professional gents."

"No one in town knows this, Mr. Royston, but the fire was an excuse. Margaret thinks they were trying to kill her and me. One of the guys --there were two of them -- was hoping I was there, too, so they could kill us both."

"Do you think they know you put an order in just now?"

"Yes," Molly said, simply. "I think I just saw one of them as a matter of fact, putting two letters in the wagon bag. You think they might be orders?"

"They could be, young lady. I think I need to go see Margaret. When are you heading out there?"

"I'm going to see Jake. Then I'm heading out."

"Let me know. I might join you. Bank's open only one more hour anyway."

<><><>

Jake was behind the bar, as usual "Molly! good to see you! Where have you been?" Jake knew exactly where she had been, but he wasn't about to yell, *how is Margaret.*

"I need to speak with you, Jake," she answered.

He jerked his thumb toward the back room. She headed that way. She noticed several new faces in the crowd . . . In fact, she thought she could feel eyes were on her as she made her way to the bar. A chill went up her spine.

"Is Margaret okay, Molly?" he whispered.

"Tough as nails," she smiled. "We're having new inventory coming; I sent the order off today with Orren. But I'm afraid something dreadful is brewing. You were approached by some people to sell your place weren't you?"

"Yes! How do you know that?"

"So was the bank and so was Maude's. They even asked if Margaret's place might be for sale. I think they think she's near death. But, Jake, that's not why I want to talk with you." Molly went through the words Margaret had overheard from the two would-be assassins. "They're out to kill not only Margaret, but me, too. I'm scared, Jake."

"Is Orren still here, Molly?"

"Yes, I think so, why?"

"I'm going to put a shooter on his wagon to make sure Orren gets to Santa Fe, that's why." He excused himself, asked Teresa to cover behind the bar and walked out the door. When he returned, Floyd Banner limped in with him.

"Floyd, run home, grab some clothes. You're going to Santa Fe for a few days. Bring some extra shells for your scatter gun."

"Goin' on a paid run, eh, Jake?"

"You sure are. With your pal, Orren. There's cargo that needs protecting. Don't let Orren leave without you. He's having lunch over at Maude's."

Floyd limped to the door. "Coulda picked a better day, Jake. It's gonna rain before nightfall. I'll ketch my death a cold, fer shore." He walked out.

"You hiring Floyd to protect those orders? What can he do?"

"Floyd is probably the best shot in the valley outside of one or two. Rifle or pistol, young lady.

Now what about you and Margaret? If you're right, one of our townsfolk should be there with you at all times. May I make an announcement? I'll get ten or fifteen volunteers within minutes."

"Not an announcement, Jake. Maybe in private. I saw strangers in town."

"You're right. Wait here." Jake walked out again. When he returned he had Antonio Muñez and Charlie Eversole with him.

"Muñez will ride out with you, and Charlie will spell him on Friday. One or two more before the week is done. If something is going to happen it will probably happen soon," Jake said. "Hopefully, we're being a bit panicky, but if Margaret is right" . . .

"Margaret is very savvy!" Muñez interjected. "I believe her! I'm ready to go now, Señorita."

They stopped by the bank; Mr. Royston had already told his staff he would be gone for the rest of the afternoon. His pony was already saddled. He joined them.

Chit-chat ended as they turned onto Margaret's private graveled road. A light sprinkle was beginning to fall.

Years before, after Margaret's buggy wheels kept sinking in the mire, Rian brought in a wagon load of slate. He and a few friends broke it up with sledges. They repeated the process with more loads. It made a very suitable graveled drive. Margaret had bragged about her rock drive for weeks.

Margaret was asleep. Molly ushered the two men into the kitchen.

"Señorita, I should perhaps take the horses to the barn. Señor Royston, would you prefer I leave yours just outside the door? If the rain becomes heavy" . . .

"No," Royston interrupted, "let her go with the rest of them. No sense in leaving her out in the rain. I'll get her later, Antonio."

Muñez walked the three horses through a gate to the small barn. There he found Margaret's own steed in a large inside paddock. She perked her ears up and whinnied a greeting. He tossed saddles over a rail and spent a few moments currying the horses down, then loosed them with Margaret's.

He decided to put his own bedroll in one of the stalls on a straw mattress. After trying it out, he determined it was very comfortable. Then he pulled his rifle and Molly's from their scabbards and started back to the house.

He had gone only four or five steps when he was certain he heard a crunch on gravel. He backed into the shadows. Nothing. He waited a full two minutes . . . still nothing.

Must have been a deer or some other critter, he thought to himself, *but I'll stay in the barn a few more minutes, just in case.* Then he heard it again; something or someone was definitely stepping on and crunching the gravel.

Both rifles under the crook of his arm, Antonio stayed in the shadows of the doorway and waited.

Chapter 37

Rain began falling steadily; the last rays of the sun hid themselves behind black clouds, Muñez strained his eyes to see the figures that he felt were surely making their way to the house.

Abruptly, two men leading their horses came into view, but they weren't headed for the house, they were heading directly toward the open barn doors. Muñez was shocked! They hadn't seen him . . . yet. He backed further into the barn and crouched down.

The men were engaged in a conversation, speaking in low tones that Muñez couldn't make out. They pulled off their rain slickers and shook them out, then put them back on.

"Damn rain," one said to his friend, laughing. "Remember the last time this happened?"

"Yeah, up in Utah . . . hey, Buddy! Looky here! Isn't this the pinto that gal was ridin'?"

"Sure looks to be. If she's here we can do her as well. Make sure we do it right this time. Grab our cash and skedaddle."

Antonio had heard enough. These two were hired guns to eliminate Margaret and Molly. From his crouched corner he had a clear view of the one called Buddy. He took aim, then yelled, "Hey, Buddy!"

The shot echoed throughout the barn; Buddy's horse reared with fright as it's owner fell. Buddy's partner let out a string of profanities.

"Show yourself, Señor," Antonio yelled, "and we won't shoot you! Fight and we will drag you into town behind your horse!"

"You just shot my friend, Asshole!" He fired his weapon in the direction of Antonio's voice, missing him by only inches. Antonio saw a hand reach up to grab a rifle from its scabbard. *Shit!* he said to himself. *Now we have a shoot-out for sure!*

Then a shout from the house came, "Antonio! Is everything okay? We heard shots!" The banker started out the door.

Buddy's friend, in a knee-jerk reaction, turned and fired his rifle. His shot grazed Mr. Royston's jacket, but did no damage to the banker. It did, however, give Muñez the chance he needed. The stranger was framed in the doorway. Antonio stood and fired.

"Is there a lantern in the house you can bring out here, Mr. Royston? I'll tie these two to their horses; we'll take them to town tonight. Maybe someone can identify them."

Royston returned from the house with a lantern. "I saw this one in town today," he exclaimed, peering down at the body. "Didn't see the other one, though."

"They're definitely not from town," Antonio agreed. They tied the two strangers to their horses and went back into the house.

The rain had let up; down to a light drizzle. The banker was ready to head home. "You ready, Antonio?"

Muñez nodded. "You finish your business, Señor?"

"Yes, I'm satisfied," the banker answered.

"I'd like to see the bodies before you leave!" Molly called out from the bedroom. She walked into the kitchen carrying a lantern.

Antonio accompanied her to the barn. "I'll be back later tonight. I'm going to go with Señor Royston," he held the lantern while Molly inspected the faces of the lifeless bodies, "then," Antonio continued, "I'll be back. I won't bother you in the house, I have my bed already made here in the barn. So I'll see you tomorrow morning for coffee."

Royston joined them. Antonio had just saddled their horses. "Do you recognize either of them?" Royston asked.

"This one for the first time earlier today," she pointed at Buddy. "I remember his beard and his shirt. He was with a group of about five or six rough looking out-of-towners at Jake's. The other one, I'm not sure. Probably in that same group." Molly shivered at the thought. "I'll take my rifle with me. You be careful, the both of you."

Molly walked back toward the house. Rain had completely stopped, stars were twinkling overhead.

There were at least five, maybe six in that group at Jake's, she thought. She shook her head and walked inside.

Chapter 38

General store from down south somewhere . . . Place burned to the ground . . . skirmish with bandits along the way . . . fees and paperwork have already been witnessed and submitted . . . Calder's mind was bing-banging from one thought to another as he strode down the street, trying to bring it into focus. Could it all be connected?

"Naw, couldn't be," he grumbled aloud, kicking at a pebble, "but I'm going over to the general store to talk to them anyway."

A wagon was approaching at a fairly fast pace from further up the main street. Calder moved aside to let it pass. He looked up in time to see two familiar faces.

"Floyd! Orren! Hey, stop! Whoa!" Buzz almost stepped in front of the wagon. Orren pulled the horses to the side of the road and jumped down, Floyd climbed down the other side. The three shook hands.

"Yore shore a sight fer sore eyes, Buzz!" Floyd said, slapping Buzz on the shoulder. "Are you jus' returnin' from Kansas?"

"Just got in today. Why are you riding with Orren?"

"If he hadn't," Orren chimed in, "I'd be dead, layin' in the bushes somewhere down below Socorro."

"Jake, he's a very smart man," Floyd continued, "as soon as Molly told him she saw some scary-lookin' fellas in town, he hired me to tag along with her order. Two of''em ain't so scary no more."

"Wait a minute!" Buzz protested. "Molly placed the order for Margaret. Let's go to my hotel, *La Plaza de Santa Fe*. They have an outdoor pavilion where we can have a cold beer and talk. You can explain it all to me."

<><><>

"Those sons'a bitches!" Calder exploded! "Margaret's going to be okay, right? Rotten scum! Still has a bullet in her?"

"*Touch an' go's* the way Molly described her, but she sounded like the lady was on the mend," Orren said.

"Jake called her *'tough as nails'*," Floyd added. "She's gonna be all right. I feel it in my bones."

"When did Molly go to work for her?" Buzz asked.

"Maybe July or August, can't rightly remember," Floyd said. "She shore ain't no kid anymore. People in town love her."

"I bet they do," Buzz smiled. "So, you heading out tonight, Orren?"

"No. I stay overnight here. I usually grab a room at the *Santa Fe House*. I'm off first thing tomorrow morning."

"What if I take Floyd, here, off your hands, Orren? Will you be okay?"

"Hell, take him! Been doin' this run for five years! Never had a problem I couldn't handle," Orren laughed, "but when four or five come at you at once, an extra scatter gun comes in handy. I don't think they'll try it again."

Floyd was frowning all this time. "What you got in mind, Buzz?"

"I need a driver. I was going to pick up a teamster and head out tomorrow, but I think we'll stay one more day and escort Margaret's order. I was heading over there when I met your wagon."

"C'mon, then," Orren said, we'll take you over there."

"Not Floyd," Buzz said; then turning to Floyd, "here's a buck. You can bunk with me, but you need a bath. Tell the desk you're with me; tell him we'll be here through Thursday night, and that we need another pallet.

And Floyd, I want a receipt and the change. And don't forget the bath, you hear me?" Buzz and Orren stood to go. Orren chuckled. "A little ripe, all right."

After they left, Floyd ordered another cold beer.

<><><>

"So, Hobson, you're telling me Margaret placed this order, and this similar order from someone else came in the same bag?" Buzz asked, holding up Margaret's four page order in his left hand, and a two page order in his right.

"That's correct, Mr. Calder. First one is from Margaret for sure. She signed for it. Second one is signed Alex King, never heard of him, have you?"

"No, never!"

Hobson shook his head. "Looks fishy, huh?"

"Sure does. Where is King's order to be delivered?"

"In front of Margaret's burned out place."

"Which reminds me, Hobson, where will Margaret's order be delivered?"

"Your place."

"Wha . . .well, I'll be! Good thinking, Margaret!"

He thought a moment. "Have a favor to ask, Hobson."

"Sir?"

"Put Margaret's order together and send it out first light, Friday morning as scheduled. Put Mr. King's order together and send it out the door a week from now -- say next Wednesday."

"You got it, Mr. Calder, but not even sure we can fill half of King's order. Margaret just about depleted us. I'll be ordering more goods from Leavenworth, Kansas, from Colorado Springs, Colorado, and our spring inventory order from Kansas City, Missouri. It'll be our biggest yet."

Chapter 39

Friday morning September 19th, 1851. Six wagons pulled out of Santa Fe, four teamsters with wagon-loads of goods and supplies for Margaret's "new" warehouse and Buzz Calder's two wagons. Buzz said goodbye to Torres, tied his roan to the back of his wagon and brought up the rear of the small caravan on its way to Albuquerque and beyond.

They reached Albuquerque Saturday night around 7 p.m. The teamsters always stayed in the center of town at the *La Casita del Campos*. Calder was more interested in heading for Lily Marcussen's boarding house, to visit with the widow and his young friend Ben Draper, whom he had left with her.

When Mrs. Marcussen saw the two wagons pull into her drive, she yelled at Ben to get his rifle and accompany her outside. She lifted the lantern over her head to get a better view of the man stepping down from the lead wagon.

"Oh, my lord!" she screamed. "It's Buzz Calder, Ben!" She set the lantern on a tree stump in the yard and ran to put her arms around him before he had the chance to get a breath.

"Whoa! What's all this?" Buzz laughed, embarrassed at the show of affection. "Lady, we hardly know each other!"

"Coulda fooled me," Floyd chuckled under his breath.

Lily caught herself, equally embarrassed. "Sorry," she giggled. She stood back and looked at him. "Guess I just thought we'd never see you again; got a bit carried away."

Ben Draper came out the door and rushed to shake Calder's hand. "Mr. Calder, it's so good to see you. It's been, what, almost three months?"

"I left Warm Springs on July 6th, so you're right, Ben. This is September 20th."

The widow led Buzz into the house while Floyd and Ben unhitched the teams and led them and the roan to the corral. By the time the two came into the kitchen, Ben had been informed of the fire, Floyd's repelling of the attempt on the mail wagon and now escorting the new order going to Warm Springs . . . all very intoxicating to the young man.

"Before you ask, Mr. Calder," Ben said, proudly, "I can read, I know my numbers, fractions and percentages, and I can recite the *Bill of Rights*; I know who Jefferson, Washington, Samuel Adams, and of course, John Adams were, and mostly what they did."

"All in two or three months? I must say young man, you have a good teacher!" Buzz grinned.

"Oh, wait a minute!" Lily exclaimed, "I have a good student!" Draper beamed at her words.

"While we're all sitting here," Buzz said, "I have been mulling over a thought all day -- tell me what you think. I need to find the judge here in town, I understand there is one, and here's why."

Buzz went through the property rights that would be disputed in just over twenty days.

"If it's just a matter of finding him tomorrow morning, go find him; I'll wait," Floyd blurted out.

Buzz smiled, "Not that simple, Floyd. Tomorrow's Sunday. I can't see him until Monday. Here's my thinking: Ben, if you're willing, you take one of my wagons down to

Warm Springs, along with Floyd and the four teamsters. It may take three or four days to get there. I'll be straight with you, though -- there may be trouble."

Ben looked at the widow, full of excitement. "Yes!" he answered enthusiastically. "I'm ready to go!"

"Are you coming?" Floyd frowned.

"Of course! I'll follow after," Buzz replied, "but it may take a day to obtain a hearing with the judge. Just make sure you take the *Gila Cutoff* or I'll miss you altogether."

"Maybe we should sit and wait a day or two at the *Cutoff*," Floyd drawled, winking at Mrs. Marcussen.

"Have you boys had anything to eat?" she asked, ignoring his coarse, unspoken signal. "I'll rustle up some supper. In the meantime you can wash up. You know the way."

<><><>

The following morning as the four supply wagons passed the rooming house, Floyd and Ben joined them. Buzz warned of ambush as they neared Warm Springs, but that he and his big roan should be able to catch and join them before they reached the *Gila Cutoff.* They waved their goodbyes -- the six wagons journeyed on.

Calder turned to Mrs. Marcussen. "The lad's been busy, I'll say that," he said, looking at the new veranda railing and the fresh coat of paint.

"That's just the beginning, Buzz. He's done amazingly well with chores around here, always looking for things to do. I'll miss him if he doesn't return -- Oh! and his studies continue to amaze me! He reads almost as well as you or I. He's been working on his writing; it still needs a bit of practice, but coming along. He's a bright, young lad, Buzz; I'm happy to have helped with his education."

"Mrs. Marcussen, I couldn't have left him in better hands. Glad we met up with you."

"It's Lily, Buzz, and I'm glad, too." They walked arm in arm into the house.

Lily continued, "Cedric Houghton, Joel's younger brother, is usually there by 9 a.m. He's very well respected, I doubt he'll stay in Albuquerque long. He's as ambitious as his brother, maybe more. Joel will probably be the governor soon, and bring Cedric on as head of the state court system."

"Lots of clout, these two brothers, eh?" Buzz laughed.

"I can accompany you to the courthouse tomorrow," Lily offered.

"Won't be necessary, Lily. I passed by the courthouse yesterday; I know where it is." He patted her arm.

They sat in her parlor sipping tea and chatting. Then came an awkward moment. She rose from her chair, crossed the room and sat beside him.

"Buzz, I know I'm being a bit forward, as I was when you headed east, but I've never been so smitten. I almost asked if I could accompany you to Kansas. I felt then, and still feel we could be very good for each other. I've never felt that way with any travelers who've come through here. Never!" She reached a hand out to touch his face; he pulled her to him.

The night was spent in each other's arms.

<><><>

Cedric Houghton was a young man, perhaps above forty, though Calder thought younger -- obviously ambitious and full of himself -- abrupt and in a hurry.

"So, what's so all-fired important that it can't wait, Mr. Calder?"

"Has to do with larceny, Judge."

"Sure it does. Seven cases in ten are larceny. What happened? Someone steal a bag of copper from you?"

"No, Sir. Much more than that."

He showed Houghton his research in the ledgers at the Office of Title Deed Ownership and Title Transfers in Santa Fe, explained the murder of the Broderick family, the fire destroying the title deed, Molly being the sole survivor, the time constraints due to the seven year statute of limitations, and the two unknowns who were filing in Santa Fe courts to take over the 640 acre ranch.

Houghton, now interested, took it all in without a word. His only reaction was stroking his beard and an arched eyebrow. When Calder was finished, Houghton opened his mouth for the first time.

"How soon can you have that girl in front of me, Calder?"

"We won't have time, Sir. Going to Warm Springs and back will take six days, maybe seven. Molly is taking care of Margaret Chisho". . .

"Hold it, Calder! Are you talking about the fire at Margaret's General Store?"

"You know of it?"

"Everyone in these parts has heard of it. Dammit, Calder! Why didn't you say so when you first walked in? So this young girl . . . is she the young girl they're afraid might be bushwhacked?"

"Yes, Sir, she is."

"Orren and his shotgun took care of two of them on their way here. Told the story to the town Marshal. Justifiable shootings."

Houghton reached for a pen and a piece of official stationery, and at the same time shouted, "Ferdig! Bring me a deputy marshal, pronto! Then saddle my horse!"

The judge wrote two paragraphs, tucked the note in an envelope, and while waiting for the deputy, he asked, "Why so long to begin this action? You should have started years ago, man!"

"Never dawned on me. I was in Council Grove when I wondered if all the paperwork was in order. I stopped in Santa Fe only on a hunch."

The deputy came in. "Sir?"

"I need this dispatch in the hands of Norm Calhoun, the Attorney at the Santa Fe Government House, as soon as possible, please."

"Sir!" The federal officer spun around and was gone.

"That, Calder, is a thirty day stay against any action to transfer title of your friend's parcel of land. So we have time to sort it out. Ha!" he laughed cynically, "won't that just piss off the parties fighting over it!"

"You know who, Sir?"

"I think I do, Calder. I think I do. And if I'm right there'll be hell to pay! Now I'm assuming you're ready to travel."

"I just need to pick up a change of clothing at a boarding house at the south end of town."

"Talking about Marcussen's?"

"You know it?"

"Indeed! Lily's a great hostess. For years my guests stayed there, but it began to fall into disrepair. Someone's been sprucing it up for her. Might begin to use it again."

Chapter 40

Calder and Judge Houghton caught up with the supply wagons just after 5 p.m. Tuesday evening on the *Gila Cutoff* Route, which joined the Old Spanish Trail with the Santa Fe Terminus, thus bypassing Socorro, and cutting some sixty miles and normally two full days off the wagon trip.

But the six wagoners were being extra cautious. Only Floyd and two of the teamsters had ever traveled this route, in addition to which Floyd had spent two nights around the campfire filling their heads with fears of scoundrels, be they hired assassins or Apaches.

Houghton pointed, "There's your Prairie Schooner, Calder. I must say, I'm a little surprised we came upon them so soon. Still must be three days to your town."

"Yes, at least. There's one hard, uphill pull just before we drop down into the valley. They do seem to be picking their way," Calder agreed. "Perhaps we can speed them up a bit with added security."

"You're talking to only one of seven judges in all of the New Mexico Territories as if I'm but a hired security guard. Like that -- what's the fellow's name in Chicago just started a security business? Pinkerton? Wonder how long Pinkerton'd last in New Mexico?" His laugh was satirical; nonetheless, he touched the butt of his rifle.

An hour and a half later, travel stopped; the eight men gathered around a campfire enjoying a supper of big horn sheep steaks and beans, washed down with a swallow of whiskey. The empty bottle was tossed into the fire where the last few drops flared up in the flames. One of the teamsters, Marv, brought up the general store in Warm Springs. "We were just there, weren't we, Trace?"

Trace answered, "Yes, we surely were. That young girl sure talked it up about you, Calder. Understand you're her uncle."

"Yeah," Marv added, "an' it's too bad Warren isn't on this run. He was lookin' at yore lift an' sayin' if'n it was changed a mite we could use it loadin' our wagons."

"Well, I'm gratified and impressed to think your friend thought my invention had such merit. Probably should patent it.

Regarding Molly -- she's not my niece, but since she came to Warm Springs she, like most of the kids there, started calling me Uncle Buzz. I probably should have stopped it, but I let it slide. I figure, if they need an uncle to bounce ideas off, they can come and talk. I try to be straight up with whatever advice I give them."

Houghton was intrigued. "Sounds like the country lawyer is very much alive in Warm Springs," he laughed. "How long were you an attorney in Kansas?"

"Little over four years."

"Miss it?"

"Not for a minute! Happy to be a blacksmith."

The others around the fire were awed to learn of Calder's history, especially, Floyd. He stood.

"I gotta go take a leak; then I'll take the first watch. Trace, you spell me at two in the mornin'. Judge, you an' the lawyer, here, can sleep like babies -- nuthin' to fear."

He disappeared from sight. Twenty seconds later they heard a startled shout, cursing, and finally a gunshot, followed by more cursing.

"I'm okay!" they heard Floyd call out. Then they sat waiting for Floyd to reappear from the darkness. Finally, he shuffled into the firelight, a sheepish grin on his face.

"Just got the boot on my gammy laig. Almost shot my own foot." He tossed the snake into the glowing coals-- an almost seven foot rattler -- "I lost my balance an' threw my wooden laig out to steady myself. He," Floyd said pointing at the snake "raised up out of the other side of some bushes and got me."

"Western Diamondback," Calder observed, "almost time for them to hibernate."

"I bet he wishes he'd a'ready snuck under a rock. I'da bin a mite happier, too. Took a coupla minutes to git a good stream goin' after that, lemme tell you." Floyd laughed along with the others.

<><><>

Thursday noon, September 25th. The six wagons were lined up in a row, heading toward the blacksmith's shop and barn. They passed Margaret's general store, paused, then continued up Main Street.

Residents waved and shouted greetings to their blacksmith. Some followed the train up the road.

As Buzz brought the four teamster wagons into the barn, Sarge lifted his head and began to growl. Then the big shepherd recognized his master; he ran to Buzz, put his paws on his chest and tried to lick his face. Buzz laughed; grabbed the dog's head in his hands and said, "Did you miss me , Sarge? Now, you know I don't like licks on my face, Boy! Stop it! I need to show these men where to put things."

Calder started to direct the operation; within three or four minutes Marv stopped him.

"Not how Margaret had stuff arranged," he said. "We'll arrange it. You got a big place here. Everything's gonna fit jus' fine. But somebody's got to check off our packing list against the lady's order, to make shore she only pays for the goods she gets."

"You're very right, Marv. Hey, Ben!" Calder shouted, "take the inventory, please. They'll arrange it the way it should be; just make sure to check it off as it gets unloaded. I'll be back as soon as I can." Ben nodded, and took the papers.

"I'm going to see Margaret, Judge. Do you want to come along?"

"I think I'll wait until later. I'll register at one of the hotels I saw earlier, have a bath, change of clothes, then look around your pretty little town. Nice setting; never been down this far before.

You say there was an article in your town paper years ago about the Broderick murders. I might just check to see if they keep copies going back that far."

"Alright, Sir. You're welcome to stay at my place, there's plenty of room; but I understand. I'll be back soon."

Buzz and Sarge went to the corral to visit with Mrs. Grumps for a few minutes. She came running to see him with obvious recognition. He scratched behind her ears, said goodbye, then headed for Margaret's, Sarge trotting alongside.

Calder saddled the big roan and headed out.

Chapter 41

As Calder clip-clopped down Margaret's graveled drive a familiar voice rang out, "Identify yourself! Do it now!"

"Buzz Calder! Lamar! Is that you?"

"Buzz? Get out of the shadow and into the the light so I can see you!"

Calder pushed the roan ahead. Sarge pranced along as well.

"Well, aren't you a sight for sore eyes, Buzz!" Lamar Jefferson walked out of the barn, rifle on his shoulder. Buzz stepped down from the roan and shook hands with his friend.

"How long you been in town?"

"We just now pulled in. Four wagons of merchandise for Margaret. Floyd's with me and a couple of others. Haven't done a thing yet. Wanted to see Margaret first. How is she, Lamar?"

"As well as can be expected for a woman without the use of one arm and the inability to ever walk again. Don't say that to her face, though, or the girl's either; they are determined she'll get out of that bed and walk as she did before the shooting."

"If anyone can do it" . . . Calder changed the subject. "Why the security out here, Lamar? Was there some kind of threat right here at Margaret's?

"Hell, you *did* just get here, didn't you?" Lamar recounted the shooting of the two would-be killers in Margaret's barn, including the conversation between the two assassins.

"They were hired to get rid of Margaret and the girl, collect their money and hit the road. I don't know who their boss is, Buzz, but has to be someone right here in the valley."

"Appears so. Jake sent Floyd off with the mail wagon and Orren" . . .

"Yeah, I remember," Lamar said. "What happened?"

"Wagon was attacked by three or four fellows the first day out. Floyd killed two of them with his scattergun; the others didn't wait around. Floyd didn't recognize either one. He notified the folks in Socorro, but left them where they fell."

Lamar shook his head. "What's this world coming to? I'll go up to the house with you. I could use a cup of coffee anyway."

Molly heard the door open from where she was sitting in the parlor, and called out, "Lamar, is that you?"

Calder answered, "No!"

There was a squeal, followed by footsteps as Molly came running around the corner into the kitchen.

"Uncle Buzz!" she wrapped her arms around Calder's waist and hugged him tight. Lamar grabbed a mug from the kitchen counter and helped himself to the percolator. He nodded to Molly and stepped back outside, heading for the barn.

Buzz was flabbergasted! "Molly! You've grown! Has it been that long? My goodness, Girl, you must have grown a foot taller!"

"And, I'm no longer a girl, Uncle Buzz," she laughed. "I'll have you know, I'm a lady!"

"You certainly are!"

"Buzz Calder!" came a cry from the bedroom. "Get yourself in here! Bring an extra chair so we can visit for a while!"

"I'm going to get a mug of coffee, Margaret; can I pour you one?"

Molly gently pushed him toward the bedroom, "You go on in, Uncle Buzz; I'll bring your coffee. Margaret drinks tea. I'll bring that, too."

Calder picked up a chair and entered the bedroom. He steeled himself, determined to stay positive. Margaret surprised him; she was sitting up, smiling, a plush pillow at her back.

"I am so damn mad at the two that shot me, Buzz. I've been sitting here now for two weeks -- but I am getting stronger, Buzz. Doc Ford didn't think I'd walk again, but I've been getting up every day. Molly helps me. I'm up to two steps, then I get so shaky she has to almost carry me back to bed.

But, I can move both legs. Do you know what that means, Buzz? I'm not paralyzed! Doc Ford was so doubtful, because there's a bullet still in me, close to my spine. I think if I had a permanent pole or something that couldn't move I could spend some time exercising, and get back in bed by myself."

Molly brought a tray with three mugs and some homemade bread.

"Okay, enough about me," Margaret said, taking the mug of tea and a piece of bread. "How was your trip, Buzz? How's your mother? Don't leave out any details. Did you run into any Indians?"

Buzz laughed, thanked Molly, and took a sip of coffee. "Too much to tell in one day, Margaret, but I'll start. Then if you invite me back, I'll continue my story."

"Tomorrow!" Margaret insisted.

Buzz started at the beginning, from the time he joined the army detachment that Sunday morning back on July

6th. He was just beginning to narrate the flash flood episode when he noticed Margaret's eyelids begin to droop. He stopped and announced that he must get back to town.

"Oh, by the way, Margaret, teamsters need a check. They're probably finished and waiting at Jake's."

"Molly will go with you. She'll take care of it."

"Oh! Okay, then. We'll say goodbye for now." He bent over and kissed her cheek. She reached up and touched his in return.

"Until tomorrow, then, Buzz. Welcome home!"

Chapter 42

Lamar Jefferson waved to Calder and Molly as they rode out of Margaret's drive onto the main road.

"Did I hear you right, Uncle Buzz, that you brought a judge down here from Albuquerque?"

"A judge accompanied me, yes, Molly."

"Whatever for?"

"A few things actually, but probably Margaret's attempted murder, the fire, the attempt to stop Margaret's order, and possibly other things as well. You see, Molly, we have very little established law down here, no sheriff, no marshal, just what would be called vigilante law, like Antonio shooting those two villains at Margaret's place. There's times we need a jailhouse. We rely on Jake and some of the other town leaders to"...

"Like you!" Molly interrupted, "and are you saying those two didn't need killing? Oh, I know what you're saying, but we know what's right and what's wrong, and people like you and Jake and my dad and others can make smart decisions. Do we need a judge from Albuquerque to come down here and make our decisions?"

"A little more complex than that Molly. You'll meet him today or tomorrow. Maybe you'll change your mind."

"Hah! I hate him already!"

"He's here to help; you'll see."

Floyd was the center of attraction at Jake's. He had finished his oration of his travels with Orren and was relating his rattlesnake adventure in graphic detail when Molly and Calder walked in. The place was full, and the mood was gay. Floyd was definitely feeling the liquor that was being donated by his attentive listeners, and his current story was embellished just a tad.

Calder expected to see Jake's face, but Teresa was tending bar. She smiled, waved a hello and pointed. He followed her finger and found Jake sitting with Antonio Muñez, the judge, and one other whose back was to the newcomers; the four were deep in conversation.

Jake spotted the blacksmith and stood. "Here's the Wagon-master now!" He motioned Molly and Buzz to their table. The others at the table stood as well.

Molly balked at continuing through the crowded lounge. She whispered, "Buzz, the teamsters are probably waiting for their money. I need to go see Mr. Royston at the bank."

"Hey, Miss! Remember me?" The four teamsters at a table adjacent to Jake's stood as well.

"Trace!" Molly blurted, "Of course, I remember you! and Marv! Did Warren make it?" She started for the two tables.

"Not this trip. He headed for Colorado Springs a week before we left. This here's Mo and Tito," Trace introduced the men. They nodded.

"You're waitin' to get paid, I expect. I'm heading for the bank right now. Be back soon."

"No need, Ma'am, We been paid in full," Tito said. "Even bought our table a bottle, an' a night's hotel room."

"Yup! Nice town," smiled Mo.

Marv spoke up, "We stacked the goods like you like it, Miss, and Ben checked it all off like you do, but we'll walk over with you and re-stack it if it's wrong."

"Don't bother. It'll be fine." She turned to Buzz, "Who

is Ben?"

Buzz pointed at the fourth man at Jake's table. "C'mon, I'll introduce you."

She couldn't back out now, especially since she was curious about this Ben fellow. She followed Buzz. Chairs scraped as they made room for the two. Buzz grabbed two more chairs. He placed Molly next to Judge Houghton, and took the chair next to her.

"Cedric Houghton," the judge said, holding out a hand.

"M-M-Molly Broderick," Molly stammered, then regained her composure. "Are you the judge that came down from Albuquerque?"

The others listened as the young lass bristled and continued, "Why? Don't you think we can handle our own affairs?"

Calder tried to intervene, but Houghton denied him.

"999 times out of 1000, Miss, but there comes the one time that a judge is needed to settle an argument. That judge should be unbiased; you know what that means?"

"Yes, I just read it at Margaret's place. It means without any favoritism."

"Exactly. Now I came down here to settle a couple of arguments and to take a good look at this beautiful country; and it is beautiful!"

"Don't you judges show bias in kicking the Mexicans and Indians out of New Mexico?"

"Hmmm, that's a tough one, Molly. Fact is, the U.S. paid money to Mexico and bought most of New Mexico. Paid them ten million U.S. gold dollars. Right now they are negotiating on the rest of it. Most Mexicans down here are not aware of it, but it's a fact."

Houghton stood. "How many Mexicans are in here tonight?" Eight men stood, including Tito and Antonio. "How many of you know that the United States bought New Mexico from Mexico back in 1849?"

Except for Tito, no one stood. Tito looked at the judge and shrugged, "You just told me."

Houghton sat and looked at Molly. "Do you think some Mexicans will argue?" He didn't wait for her thoughts. "Yes, they will. But a legal piece of paper, signed by both parties will settle the matter, and after years it will be settled in the minds of everyone, and any judge will rule in favor of the agreement."

"Fine!" Molly said defiantly, "but what about the Apache, the Mescalero, the Pueblo? I have a Mescalero friend, Red Hawk, who says he wanders wherever he wishes because the land isn't owned by anyone. It's owned by God and He allows us all to use it."

"I like your friend, Molly. Mescalero you say."

"Yes," she said defiantly. "I speak Mescalero. I healed Red Hawk's mother after a cougar attacked her. Jimmy Iverson's dad, sitting over there, can tell you that. Jimmy saved her, then I healed her.

You say you like my friend. If the government tries to kick them out of New Mexico, would you kick them out or would you try to help them?"

"I would try to be unbiased and make a fair judgment."

"Right! And kick them out!" she said.

Houghton smiled. "You and I have more to discuss, young lady. I'm going to meet with Margaret this evening. Perhaps we can continue our discussion there."

No answer came. Jake broke the silence, "How about another round, fellas? Molly, perhaps a ginger tea?"

"Nothing. I'm fine, but thanks, Mr. Ruskin."

Calder took the opportunity to make a complete break from territorial rights.

"So, Molly, meet Ben Draper. Ben, this is Molly Broderick; she works for Margaret."

Molly realized she had used too much of the last ten minutes in expressing her opinions. She looked up at the young man. "Hi," she said meekly.

"In fact," the blacksmith said, "let me introduce Ben Draper to all of you. Ben, here, was a drifter."

Ben looked up sheepishly, smiled at Molly with a raised eyebrow. "Yeah, that's me alright."

"Anyway," Buzz continued, "I met Ben on my way to Albuquerque. We tagged along with some army regulars just for company, it being Apache territory.

A couple of *'No-goods'* rode in and tagged along as well, but turns out, they were thieves and killers. They killed two or three soldiers including the commander, stole money and hightailed it on army nags. Ben and I chased them for a day or two, but they, as it happened, ran into some Apaches who did our job for us.

Long story short, we reached Albuquerque, dropped a note and the horses off at the army base. Ben and I stayed the night at a rooming house. Owner there offered him a job and I went on to Kansas. Needed a driver on my way back, hired Ben. Here he is."

"Well, I'll be damned!" Houghton exclaimed. "So it was you that brought those saddlebags and the horse into town and dropped them off at the fort! The whole town heard about it. Over $2,000 in those bags! I'll be damned," he breathed.

Antonio Muñez was studying Draper. "Changing the subject, are you stickin' around, Son?"

"I guess I'll look around and make a decision. I know I have a job if I go back."

"Let me know," Muñez said. "I'm putting together a crew to rebuild Margaret's general store. I could use another hand."

"You are?" Molly yelped! "Count me in! I need to help design it just the way Margaret and I want it!"

"Jake and I already figured that, so we were going to ask you to sit with us before we did anything on the property. We need you, too, Buzz, to take whatever metals you want to keep, then our crew will take the debris to the dump, and we'll get started."

"I need to go," Molly said abruptly, and stood. The Judge and Calder stood as well. "Margaret needs me. Who has my receipt and inventory sheet for the delivery, and how was it paid?"

"On your way, stop to see Royston at the bank, Molly," Jake answered. "He has the paperwork."

She started out the door, then stopped and turned back to the table.

"Are you're really coming, Judge Houghton? Because Doc Ford usually comes out in the evenings. You can probably ride out with him."

"I'll keep that in mind. Thank you," he said.

<><><>

Abel Royston was expecting Molly. "Oh, good you're here," he said, handing her two large envelopes. "I've marked them. One is for the delivery, the other is just marked 'Margaret'. Tell her everything is in order."

"I will. How was it paid?"

"It's all there, Molly. Sorry, I need to leave. I'm late for a meeting."

"Okay. Thanks."

Molly settled herself on Spirit and headed for Margaret's, puzzled at Mr. Royston's manner, a frown on her forehead.

Lamar Jefferson welcomed the occupants of the buggy -- along with the roan and its rider into Margaret's barn. Doc Ford introduced Lamar to the judge, the two visitors stretched their legs then walked to the house. Calder spent a few moments chatting with Lamar.

"So, Calder, what's a judge doing all the way down here?"

"Lamar, I'm not sure, but he has an agenda . . . one of them is to involve himself into everything that's been going on around Warm Springs."

"You mean the attempted assassinations?"

"And the fire. I'm not sure, but Houghton seems to have a suspicion as to where it's coming from, but hasn't shared it with me. We'll see, I guess."

Buzz pulled his rifle from its scabbard and followed the others into the house.

Doc Ford had gone directly into the bedroom to check on Margaret and tend to her shoulder wound. Molly showed the judge and Buzz into the parlor, then excused herself to disappear into the kitchen.

Minutes later she took a tray into the bedroom; it was a hearty chicken soup Doc Ford's wife had made . . . enough for a troop. Margaret enjoyed it, asked for more.

Ford joined the others in the parlor. "Damnest woman I've ever worked on. She should be in pain. I lift her arm up as far as I dare, she says 'push it harder, Doc, I can handle it'. If it were my shoulder, I swear it'a been pulled out of the socket."

The others laughed; Molly excused herself, took care of Margaret's personal needs, went outside, returned and re-entered the bedroom. "Busy young lady," Houghton remarked. They all nodded, impressed.

"Judge Houghton, Margaret would like all of us in the bedroom," Molly announced, popping her head into the parlor. "Bring two more chairs."

The four sat around Margaret's bed.

"I couldn't believe my good fortune in having so many witnesses; but we even have a judge. Judge Houghton, so good to meet you.

I asked Mr. Royston at the bank to draw up two papers. I have two copies, or originals of each. One copy of each will stay with me, the other will be secure in the vault at the bank.

One is my final will. The other is a directive or contract -- I've read both, and am satisfied Mr. Royston wrote exactly as I dictated to him the other evening. Both need my signature which I'm doing in a few minutes. I have no blood relatives. Whatever I do will be binding. I have the option of changing my mind, but I doubt I will.

Judge Houghton, would you read my will, please? It's short, only half a page. Then I'll sign them and you and the Doctor witness them, please.

"Certainly, Ma'am." He read the usual opening statement about being of sound mind and spirit. Then:

I leave my homestead and business holdings, both real and personal, which includes the forty acre homestead and the five acre property on which the business stands. Included are all livestock, equipment, and all inventory, and chattel, including bank accounts to Molly Broderick.

Elmer Kaufman is to receive $1,000 on May 1, 1854 -- his 21st birthday.

Dated this day _________________ 1851

Signed ___________________________ Dated __________

Witnessed __________________________ Dated __________

Witnessed __________________________ Dated __________

Molly needed a minute to register what had just happened. She stared at Buzz, then Doc Ford, then at Margaret. Then she turned to Judge Houghton with a look that said, 'surely, you read that wrong'!

"You can't mean that, Margaret!"

Judge Houghton shook his head as he passed the paper to Margaret for her signature. She signed and dated it, and passed the will to Doc Ford for his signature, then it went back to Judge Houghton for his.

"This was certainly a surprise to me," he smiled as he signed and dated it, "but it is the right of ownership to take whatever steps he or she thinks prudent. You realize, young lady, that Margaret can tear this will up and change it as many times as she wishes, the newest being the binding one."

Molly breathed out a "*phew! -- I can't believe it, Margaret!*"

"Just know that I'm not planning on leaving you all anytime soon, but if I should, well, this is my choice.

And then I have this other form the banker drew up for me." She started to pull another form out from the envelope when Judge Houghton stopped her.

"Wait a minute, Margaret. I have a form I put together earlier today; this seems the fitting time to bring it out, as it goes along with what we just witnessed."

"By all means, Sir," Margaret said.

"Molly," he began, turning to the young Broderick, "Have you ever seen this newspaper article?"

He showed her *The Clarion Call* page from June 3, 1845. She read it through then handed it back to him.

"No, Sir. Never. But it happened."

"Do you remember, was the killing done by Indians, Mexicans or white men?"

"White men. I still remember, very plainly in my mind, the face of the leader. Ugly! Scars! White hair! Oh, I'll know him if ever I see him!"

"Oh?" *This isn't the direction I had planned to pursue,* thought Houghton, *but it might prove interesting. However, first things first.*

"Your father and your uncle bought those 640 acres from Ed Dammer way back in 1844, and moved your families down here from Utah to start a new life. Then tragedy struck; the fire burned everything. You're the only survivor. Now what, Molly?"

Molly shrugged, "I suppose that's the end of, . . . wait! Are you saying no one's ever bought that place? I've never laid eyes on it since Uncle Buzz, Jake, and them brought me to Warm Springs."

"*No one's ever bought that place, you ask?* . . . Interesting statement or question. Who would they buy it from, Molly?"

Stark realization came to Molly in waves. "Do you mean I own all 640 acres out there?"

"From everything I've seen, -- from *The Clarion Call,* from Buzz, from the Fords who took you in at first, there is no doubt in my mind. As a judge, I say you still have legal claim to that land, Miss. Now we have a legal problem, but I think we can overcome it."

Judge Houghton told the story of Buzz poring over the ledgers in Santa Fe to find the date her father and uncle first filed, then coming to him to discuss the statute of limitations and the other two claims; then of his letter to put a stay on the property until he could determine legal title.

"I'm dispatching an affidavit off to Santa Fe tomorrow morning signed by you and certified by Mr. Calder and Doc Ford if". . .

"If what, Sir?" Molly asked.

"If you agree to sign it and," he winked at her.

"Yes?"

"If you agree that a duly-sworn-in, honest, federal judge has some value after all."

"Oh, I do, Sir, I do. I'm sorry I said those things and acted so childishly this morning." She reached out and hugged the judge.

Houghton laughed, "Miss Molly, you spoke from the heart. We all make decisions based on information we've received; I've seen decisions made based upon a hunch or misinformation. I vowed I would examine all the evidence I could find before doing anything rash, and there have been times I've changed my mind.

Thank your friend, Uncle Buzz Calder, here, for bringing it to the attention of New Mexico's legal authority; because of him your property is now safeguarded."

Molly signed two copies of the affidavit, Ford and Calder attested with their signatures.

"Alright, Margaret, I'm done. You had something else to discuss with us, right?" the judge laughed.

"Yes, short and sweet. Judge, you read my will so well, would you read this one as well?"

"Certainly, Margaret." He took the form and began.

I, Margaret Chisholm, being of sound mind and spirit do hereby take on Molly Broderick as a 5% partner in all my business dealings here in Warm Springs, New Mexico. Further to this, on the anniversary of her birthday each year the percentage shall increase as follows:

at 17 -- 10% partner   at 18 -- 15% partner

at 19 -- 25% partner   at 20 -- 35% partner

at 21 -- 50% partner (full partnership)

Should I be dead or incapacitated before Molly reaches her 21st birthday, and unable to carry out my functions as senior partner I appoint Jake Ruskin, Buzz Calder and Louisa Brighton to act as her advisors in making all business decisions until she reaches majority.

Dated this day _______________ 1851

Signed_______________________ Dated________

Witnessed____________________Dated________

Witnessed____________________Dated________

Margaret signed the document, Houghton and Doc Ford witnessed it.

Molly sat with her mouth wide open. "I can't believe what I've heard here this afternoon. I'm overwhelmed." She went to Margaret's bedside, held the woman's hand, and whispered, "Thank you."

"Margaret, may we chat privately for a few minutes?" Judge Houghton asked.

"It's not like I'm going anywhere soon, Judge," the widow in the bed answered. The others retired to the parlor to enjoy a cup of tea while she and the judge held a powwow. It was dark by the time the three men walked into the barn to retrieve their horses.

Chapter 43

It was early Friday morning. Buzz was just finishing a second coffee when he heard Mrs. Grumps bray. He walked outside to see Elmer Kaufman walking up to begin daily chores. The lad stopped to pat one of the four Dapple Gray draft horses on the neck, then continued.

"Hi, Mr. Calder, I knowed you was back, Jimmy told me. Then I saw all these horses, so I figured you was home for shore.

I guess you won't be needin' me no more around here. Do you think Miss Margaret will want some of her money back?"

"I'm not sure, Elmer. What money are we talking about?"

"She paid me five pennies a day to take care of your animals and gather eggs. She even said I could keep some eggs."

"No, I want you to stay on, Elmer. I'll talk to Margaret. Thanks for doing such a good job."

Elmer walked with him into the barn. The floor was piled high with merchandise. In the very far corner were his two wagons, still loaded. The horses were outside in the corral with Mrs. Grumps.

"There's sure a lot of stuff in here, Mr. Calder. How are you going to get rid of it all?" Elmer asked.

Buzz laughed. "That's going to be up to Margaret and Molly, Elmer. Hopefully soon, though," he said, looking at his barn floor, rubbing the back of his neck and whistling low. "It is a lot though, isn't it?"

"Yup. I'm gonna go do my chores now, Mr. Calder."

Looking over the new inventory, Buzz was quite impressed. The store hadn't opened officially, but was ready whenever the newest partner decided to do so. *How indeed are you going to get rid of it all, Molly?*

There was one more load coming in from Albuquerque; Margaret had asked that it be delayed a week. It was mostly gunnysacks of spring planting products -- crop seeds: barley, rye, wheat, and varieties of potatoes. It could be put in the loft with the hay.

<><><>

"You're expecting another delivery aren't you, Calder?"

Calder stepped down from his roan in front of the ruins of the general store and looked up to see the judge.

"Yes, as a matter of fact, I am . . . actually Margaret is. Should be coming in by the end of next week."

"No, no, no. The one ordered by King . . . that Alex King fellow. Didn't you say it would ship out a week following Margaret's order. I'm going to stick around your town for a few days, Calder," Houghton said, "if you don't mind that is."

Buzz laughed, "Why should I mind? But I thought you'd head back with those teamsters."

"Saw them off early this morning, Calder, with your wooden leg fellow and his shotgun, carrying my dispatch."

"Floyd's going all the way to Santa Fe?"

"I told him to turn around in Albuquerque. If there's trouble, it'll be between here and there. Besides, I haven't seen much of your town yet. What's the population here in Warm Springs?"

"Last count we took was April of this year. It was 1,322 as I recall, that includes the whole of the area of course -- probably a fifty mile radius. A new couple came in just after I left, two kids. So, as far as I know there's 1,326."

"You know, Calder, there's only but 1,850-1,900 folks in all of Albuquerque's thirty mile radius. Now there's nothing, really, between Albuquerque and here. We need this general store, Mr. Calder, for New Mexico's growth as a territory and soon, statehood.

Pretty valley," he continued, almost to himself -- then he turned abruptly. "What are your plans for today, Calder?"

"Right now I'm going to sort through the pile of metals salvaged from the fire, then I'm back home to empty my wagons. Also, need to see Royston sometime today to discuss a couple of financial matters. Why are you asking?"

"Oh, I was hoping you and I could take a ride through the surrounding areas to get a better feel for Warm Springs, but it can wait a day or two."

"Well, let's see," Calder laughed, "here to Tucson is 250 miles -- a five day ride southwest through Pueblo country, here to the copper mines at del Cobre is at least a 125 mile -- three day ride southeast through Apache country, and northwest of here is," . . .

Houghton rolled his eyes, shaking his head. He looked at Buzz, "Funny man," he smiled. "More local -- perhaps some of the ranches near the *Little Black Creek.*"

"Oh!" Buzz frowned. "There are a few fellows in town who would be happy to show you our valley."

"No, Calder, I'll wait for you. Perhaps tomorrow?"

"Perhaps tomorrow," Buzz agreed.

"Maybe I'll swing by your blacksmith shop in a bit to give you a hand with those wagons."

"Hah!" Buzz chuckled. "You'll need to change that suit for a pair of coveralls and a plaid shirt, Houghton."

"Don't you worry 'bout this ol'boy, Calder, I have no problem sweating and getting my hands dirty."

The judge left Calder there to sort through the metal.

An empty wagon pulled up in front of the general store property. Antonio Muñez climbed down.

"Glad I caught you here, Buzz. Do you see anything of value to your business in this stack of metal? Otherwise, I'm hauling it to the dump."

"A few things, Antonio. I set them over there." He pointed to a small pile of metal. "The rest can be tossed; I'll give you a hand." They piled the scrap into the wagon. Antonio looked over the ground. It had been raked clean.

"I'll be bringing in a few loads of materials Monday morning. We'll start putting this building back up pronto."

Buzz pointed to the mountains behind them. There was a dusting of new snow just a few thousand feet above them.

"Oh, I saw it," Antonio said, "weather's coming. But, I think we can get'er closed up before it sets in for the season."

"Remember, Molly and Margaret need to be involved in the design, Muñez. Otherwise, you'll have two upset ladies on your hands."

"Good point!" he yelled as he drove away.

Calder swung his leg over the roan's back and headed home; more work awaited him.

Both wagons were pulled through the rear barn doors and brought to the Blacksmith's yard. Buzz unhitched the Buckskins and led them back into the corral. Then he started unloading the hay wagon.

He was down to the yokes, harnesses, martingales and other tack; wagon wheels and parts were beneath.

"Need some help?" Before he looked, Buzz smiled, "Absolutely!" Then he turned and burst out laughing.

"Cedric Houghton! You look absolutely, uhh," . . .

"Ready to empty these wagons, Buzz!" the judge retorted.

The covered wagon was finally emptied. Houghton whistled at the treasures Calder had picked up along the trail. When the offloading was complete, Buzz pointed to the large rectangular wooden box with its two doors.

"I haven't quite figured this one out, but I think it's for food storage. Any ideas?"

"Yes, of course I do!" Houghton answered, opening one of the doors. "I have a similar one at home. It's an ice box for your kitchen. I like yours better than mine because it's walls are thicker. You put a block of ice in the top; then meat, milk, butter or veg in the bottom.

See the hole in the back corner of the shelves? The ice melts and the water runs down to this." Houghton pulled out the tray under the shelf in the bottom compartment. "The tray must be emptied every day, but your meat or milk will keep for days. Just don't open the door too often."

Buzz grinned, "Now I need to find a way to store ice -- what's funny is, I've been thinking about that for months. Beer is better cold," he winked at the judge.

"Someone said pack it in straw," Houghton suggested, "so you might try that."

They wrestled the ice box into the back stoop off the kitchen and set it in a corner.

"Thanks for your help, Judge."

"I'm wearing coveralls right now, Buzz. It's Cedric. C'mon, I'll buy you a warm beer."

As they rode toward Jake's, Buzz noted a sharp change in the weather -- a biting wind from the north started swirling up dust and blowing leaves and debris on the streets; but, Buzz acknowledged, September was quickly coming to a close. Winter was, indeed just around the corner.

Another thing Calder noticed -- several unfamiliar faces in town -- almost all scruffy-looking men. Perhaps he was wrong; perhaps the population of Warm Springs had grown even more in his time away. *Or, perhaps* . . . he tried to block out dark thoughts, but the judge was observant.

"Do you know those folks, Calder?"

"Not yet."

Chapter 44

Saturday morning began crisp, calm, and clear. Buzz sat on his veranda sipping steaming coffee, watching his corralled horses and mule blowing out the steam of condensation through flared nostrils. It was cold!

"Time to move you girls into the barn, I suppose," he told them.

There was a large common area inside the rear of the barn where the wagons had been. Buzz had designed it with long troughs or mangers lining the walls. Hay was dropped into the mangers from overhead catwalks.

Calder set his mug down to begin the move when Elmer showed up, so Buzz turned the project over to the lad and went back for another mug of coffee.

"Elmer, would you saddle my roan please, and leave her out?"

"Yes, Sir."

Today, he, the judge, and Ben Draper were supposed to ride into the valley to visit some ranches and *to get a better feel for the Warm Springs area*, as the judge had put it. But it was cold! The newfangled mercury thermometer hanging on his porch wall said it was 18° Fahrenheit. He was for calling it off, and tomorrow being church day, he was sure Monday would work fine for the others.

They met at Maude's for breakfast, agreed that it was too cold to traipse off into the wilderness. Change of plans . . . a quick check at Margaret's, and call it a day. They would meet at Maude's again on Monday for a trip into the valley.

As they stood up to leave, Antonio Muñez and two others walked in. Muñez spotted Ben.

"You ready to start work, young man? It will be a matter of laying things out Monday, marking off exterior and interior walls over at the general store."

Buzz answered, "He'll be busy Monday. Make it Tuesday, he'll be there. Have you spoken to Margaret and Molly? We're headed there now if you want to tag along."

"I do," Antonio said, "I planned on seeing them this afternoon, anyway." He turned to his companions, "I'll be back. If I don't see you here, I'll meet you at Jake's."

All was quiet at Margaret's.

"Still here I see, Lamar," Buzz called out as they rode to the house.

"Last day. Jason's supposed to be here at nightfall. Been a boring four days, Buzz."

"Better than the alternative, Lamar."

"The alternative?"

"Exciting for a few minutes, then dead."

Lamar nodded his head. "Guess you're right."

The judge raised an eyebrow and glanced at Calder with a wince.

Molly welcomed the men into the house and ushered them into the parlor.

"She's down in spirit," she told them in a hushed voice. "You'll be good for her."

"If you're not too busy, Miss," Antonio said, "we can go over the general store plans."

While Antonio and Molly discussed the building, Buzz and the others visited with Margaret. She was propped up with pillows, reading over the inventory sheets.

"Hello, Margaret. We understand you need to see some friendly faces. You already know Judge Houghton, but you haven't seen him in his working duds"...

"And probably never will again," laughed Houghton.

"And this is Ben Draper, my young friend from Albuquerque."

"Hi, Ma'am." He smiled and offered his hand. Margaret hesitated, then, with none of her usually cheery flair, she simply said, "Hi, Ben."

"Now, Margaret," Buzz continued, "you want to walk?" He turned to Ben. "Ben, she wants to walk. Take her hand, and help her walk again."

Ben took Margaret's hand. She hesitantly put her feet on the floor, but after a second step she began to shake as she had before.

"It's no use, Buzz. I'm sorry, Mr. Draper. I guess I'm not going to get out of bed again."

"Hey! Stop talking that way, Margaret! You've never given up that easily! You've always been a fighter! Remember what you said? -- *if I had a permanent pole or something that couldn't move I could spend some time exercising, and get back in bed by myself* -- remember that, Margaret?

Ben and I are going to build you a rail, like a long hitching post. I'll nail it to the floor so it won't move. When you don't need it anymore we'll pull it up."

"You mean, when I'm gone."

"Stop feeling sorry for yourself, Margaret Chisholm!" Calder bellowed. "Do you have tools in the barn or a tool shed anywhere around here?"

"Rian kept some hand tools in the barn behind a chicken wire door. I don't know what's in there."

"Fine! We'll build it this afternoon; I'll be right back. Ben and Cedric, share some trail stories with Margaret."

Calder rummaged through the tool crib and came up

with a saw, hammer, and some long square nails which he was sure he had made for Rian many years before. Inside the barn was a stack of peeled Balsam poles leaning against a wall; he grabbed a short one. Then he found some rough boards that Rian hadn't yet planed. Everything he needed except iron angle brackets to nail the rail to the floor. Damn! *He had'em. I made a dozen of them for him!* he thought to himself, *with holes bored in them just like he asked!*

Lamar walked over. "You lookin' for these, Buzz?" he asked, handing Buzz a couple of the angles.

"Where did you get these?" Buzz asked.

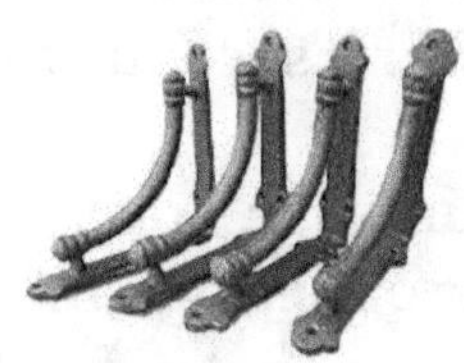

"Sorry, Sir. I didn't think she'd ever use them. I have a use for them."

Buzz shook his head. "Damn, Lamar! Give me six of those, and pay two bucks to Margaret for the rest."

"Two bucks?"

"Worth every penny."

Snow was spitting from the sky as Calder went back into the house. He stopped just long enough to stomp his boots on the front porch floorboards -- then he entered.

"Beginning to snow," he announced to Antonio and Molly, then continued into the bedroom, where he repeated the news. Houghton pulled the curtains back and peeked out the window to verify.

"Damn!" he breathed. "Do you have a good supply of wood, Miss Chisholm? Could be a long winter."

"I use coal, and yes, I have plenty."

Buzz and Ben were already making progress on the

railing, and within fifteen minutes they had it set up, using the brackets to stabilize the vertical boards to the floor, three each.

"Now, Margaret," Buzz said, "try this. Get out of bed and try the rail!" he demanded.

"It seems sturdy enough," she said meekly. "Thanks, Buzz. I promise I'll try to use it every day."
Molly and Antonio walked in to observe the rail. Both were impressed. Margeret smiled, "See what they built for me, Molly?"

<><><>

Jason Turnbill brought his buggy as he took over the security detail at Margaret's. In turn, Margaret instructed Molly to take her mother to church.

"Are you sure, Margaret?"

"Of course, I'm sure. I'm going to spend the time walking along my new rail. Your daddy brought the buggy just so you can pick up your momma. Do you realize," she gave Molly an open-mouthed look of delight, "I can now pee without your help? Run along, now."

Unfortunately, Sunday morning services were cut short; Preacher Marshall was just getting wound up when Floyd Banner burst through the rear doors and limped up the aisle, shook Jake Ruskin's shoulder, and whispered something in his ear. Jake stood, motioned to Buzz and Doc Ford to follow. They rushed out of the church to the road. Of course, that set up a hubbub of activity . . . the preacher had no choice; he could only say, "God loves you. Now please show respect for God's house as you leave." Then he ran as fast as he could to catch up with those already assembled around a wagon that was stopped across from the church.

Molly assisted her mother to the buggy; they started out of the churchyard. Then Molly looked closely at those around the wagon. In addition to those that had rushed out of the service, she recognized someone who shouldn't be there.

Chapter 45

"Marv!" Molly jumped down from the buggy and ran to the wagon, excited yet bewildered as she ran. *Wasn't he supposed to be on his way to Santa Fe?*

"We only got a day and a half out of Warm Springs when we ran across'em," Floyd was saying. "All four of 'em bushwhacked, it appears."

Molly was able to get close enough to the wagon to see the four bodies. She cringed back, stunned.

"You don't know any of them, Miss Molly," Marv said, "but they were friends of mine. Floyd and I sent my other drivers, Trace and them, on to Santa Fe, but we brought these four back."

"Me an' Marv figurred they was haulin' the order fer that other bunch," Floyd continued, "uh, the one Buzz told us about, comin' in here about a week after ours."

"Where are the wagons, Floyd?" Jake asked.

"We don't know, Jake. They just plain disappeared."

Marv looked around at the troubled faces. He directed the narrative to the judge. "Weather was dicey up there, Judge Houghton. Wind was blowin' sideways at times. We took the reg'lar trail not the *Gila Cutoff*. Tito was in the first wagon. He saw two-three big rocks in the middle o' the trail, didn't want to break an axle, jumped down to roll'em out th'way, an'" . . . Marv's voice broke, but he raised the volume and carried on, "them rocks was bodies, Judge! Snow-covered teamsters! Some of the best Muleskinners ever handled a team! God rest their souls!"

"Amen," Pastor Marshall repeated. Others removed hats, said their amens, mumbled or shook their heads.

"Injuns?" someone asked.

"No!" Floyd replied, "murderers! thieving swine!"

"And no way to track them in the snow," Buzz said. "We had new snow up there this morning; wherever they are, tracking them is out. But we do know about how far they can move the wagons in a day."

"I say, we find 'em an' string'em up!" came a voice from the crowd, which had now grown to about forty. Others echoed the sentiment. Preacher Marshall tried to quell the crowd by reminding the menfolk that they shouldn't think hateful thoughts on a Sunday, but to no avail.

Molly stood back and watched Judge Houghton. Was he about to make some kind of "judging" order? She shook her head. *Just as I thought, we can take care of our own business down here. We don't need Albuquerque or Santa Fe telling us how to deal with crime.*

But the judge fooled her. He stepped up on a wagon wheel and asked for quiet. A few knew him, others wondered who he was, but his was a voice of authority. It grew relatively quiet.

"Fellas," he began, "and Miss," he acknowledged Molly, "there are seven federal judges in all of the New Mexico territory. I'm one of them. I hold court in Albuquerque.

Now Albuquerque is better than a hundred and fifty miles from here. I came down here because of the fire at the general store and one or two other things. Let's say I have a vested interest. By the way, it's cold out here. Can we go back into the church and have a discussion?"

"If you don't mind, Sir," Marv said, "I think, out of respect, I should put my friends in the ground."

"They can stay in the wagon for another hour, Marv," Floyd said. "Ain't like they's had too much sun. Side's, it'd take you an' me a day to dig through this frozen ground, an' that's fer each one."

"Guess you're right, Floyd."

The two men followed the others into the church.

Preacher Marshall stood at the pulpit and offered up a prayer, then turned the lectern over to Houghton. The judge looked out over the fifty or so men and three women that had crammed into the little sanctuary.

He looked around and smiled, "What's the largest meeting hall you have in this town?" he asked the preacher.

"This is the only one in town, Sir," Marshall said. Square footage of Margaret's was greater but it was always full, uh, when it was there. An' then there's a couple of barns," ...

"Who owns the barns?"

"Blacksmith for one, The Wesleys for another."

Houghton turned to the crowd. "Are the Wesleys here?"

Doc Ford was close to the front. "No! Mr. Wesley's been sick for three months. Won't last much longer. Mrs. Wesley doesn't come out to the church meetings any more. They're up there in years; I think she's close to eighty-one, he's a year or two younger."

"Folks! Have everyone you know meet at 9 a.m. at the Wesley's tomorrow morning." He spotted Mr. Royston sitting in a pew. "Mr. Royston, please meet with me in my room at the hotel in fifteen minutes."

Ten men volunteered to bury the four teamsters. It took most of the afternoon. Buzz accompanied Molly to Margaret's. They were anxious to see her progress with the bar.

Houghton, Doc Ford and the banker knocked on the Wesley's door. They heard noises from inside, then a raspy female voice, "Come in."

Mrs.Wesley struggled to get up from her chair. "Let me fix you some dinner. You must have just come from church," she said starting to shuffle toward the kitchen.

"No, no, Annie," Mr. Royston said, "no fussing. We're only here for a couple of minutes to ask you and Wally if we can use your barn tomorrow morning. You'll be paid, of course."

From the bedroom they could hear continuous hacking and coughing.

"You'll need to ask him. I don't make those kinds of decisions."

"How is he, Annie?" Doc Ford asked.

"Still here."

Annie led the men into the bedroom. "These men want to use our barn, Wally. I told them they need to ask you."

"Annie, I ain't got but days or hours left. It's time you make those decisions." Wally lay coughing for a few minutes more, then coughing between almost every word he continued, "We ain't but a few chickens left anyhow. I see no problems letting them use the barn, but it's up to you."

Annie turned to the men,"It's fine, then," she said.

"How are you feeling Wally?" the doc asked.

"I feel like shit, Doc!" he continued coughing between words, "what do you think? Annie says I look like death warmed over, and I don't hear angels singing, so it worries me."

"Still have a sense of humor, Wally."

<><><>

Buzz and Molly heard the shotgun blast before they reached Margaret's private drive.

"Go back! Get some men, Molly!" Buzz instructed.

"It's too late, Uncle Buzz, let's keep going!" She pulled her rifle from its scabbard as she prodded Spirit forward. The roan passed the little pinto as they rounded the corner. Ice and snow covered the road, but they were able to negotiate the gravel without slipping.

Calder pulled his rifle and fired at the nearest of three horsemen. The man screamed, but continued to ride. A shotgun blast came from inside the barn and another of the riders fell. The horse fell also, but quickly recovered and galloped off, kicking and bucking as it went.

Molly left Buzz in the yard and raced her pinto to the house. She dismounted as she heard another blast erupt from somewhere inside the house. She started inside when Calder grabbed her.

"Rifle's too unwieldy in close quarters, Molly," he whispered. "Go tend to your dad. He's hurt."

Calder had never fired the handgun that he'd found in the widow's attic up in Albuquerque, but it was going to be tried today. He pulled the big pistol out of it's holster and crept into the kitchen.

Chapter 46

"Who's next?" Margaret shouted! "C'mon! Shotgun's ready for you. Poke your head through that door! C'mon!"

Buzz backed against the door jamb as he heard male voices in the hallway between the kitchen and bedroom. He listened.

"You told Dunkin to stay outta there, Bart. Damn fool. Now he's gone. Let's rush the old lady. She can't have loaded the gun that quick."

"She could have, Shorty, an' I ain't about to chance it. I say we torch the place. Shudda done it sooner. Let's just kick that kitchen potbelly over an' stand outside 'til we're sure the job is done an' done right this time."

They walked around the corner, so intent upon the big stove in the middle of the floor with their backs to Calder they didn't notice him standing in the open doorway. "Gents," Buzz shouted, "don't move a muscle!"

Instead, the taller one wheeled, trying to jerk his gun from its holster. Calder's pistol went off, tearing a hole in the man's chest. At the same time Buzz felt his arm fly in the air and spinning him sideways by the unexpected kick.

The second man turned enough to see Buzz recover and re-cock the pistol. Instead of drawing his weapon, the fellow sprinted back to the safety of the hallway, just before a second blast from Calder's gun splintered the hall door jamb.

Calder heard a cry of pain. He decided to pursue the man. As he rounded the corner he found the would-be assassin lying, back to the wall, holding his right arm. He'd already lost a lot of blood.

"What kinda gun is that, Mister?" the man gasped. "Damn near shot my arm off!"

"Which one are you -- Shorty or Bart? And who do you work for?"

"I hurt real bad, Mister. You're the blacksmith ain'tcha?" Buzz could see the man was fading.

"Who are you working for?" Calder repeated the question. But it was too late; the man was either dead or unconscious. Buzz took the gun just to make sure.

"Margaret!" he called out. "Are you okay?"

"Buzz! Thank God! I'm good."

Calder stepped over the one called Dunkin and entered the bedroom. "You're safe now, Margaret." He smiled as he pried the shotgun gently from her frozen grip.

"Are they gone?"

"Gone or laying around somewhere. Three inside, and at least two outside. One rode off, but he's wounded."

"Are you alone?"

"No, Molly's with her dad. He was shot, I don't know how bad. I'm going out now to find out, then I'll be back."

The gunfire outside was over. Two of the riders were down; both dead. Calder strode to the barn to find Molly sitting with her father. Jason was holding a tourniquet on his leg between his thigh and knee. She had cut his trousers off just above the bullet wound, then used his knife to dig the bullet out. Then she used his knife to cut strips off her skirt and used squares of it for bandages and some strips to tie those bandages in place.

"Help me get Pa into the house, Uncle Buzz. Need to warm him up and wash the wound out better. Margaret has some gauze and cotton batten. What happened inside, anyway?"

As they assisted Molly's dad through the snow and into the house, Buzz filled her in on the gunfight in the kitchen and bedroom, then told her of the one still alive.

"I can use your nursing skills if he's still alive, Molly. We need to learn who he works for."

Molly and Buzz guided Mr. Turnbill into the parlor, set him in an easy chair.

"Please check that guy in the hallway, Molly," Calder urged. "Keep him alive if possible. I'll keep your dad company."

"You might pull his boots off!" Molly suggested as she walked toward the hallway.

She was back five minutes later. "He didn't make it. I stopped to talk to Margaret for a minute. She showed me some cotton batting I can use for Pa's bandages. I'll take over here, Uncle Buzz."

"Good. I'll take these three outside and stack them up with the other two, then I'm going into town to get a wagon to pick them up for burial. I'll bring the doc back if I can find him."

Calder took the bodies outside, one by one. He came back inside, looked around and commented, "We might need some help cleaning up in here as well."

On Margaret's drive was a blood trail on the snow. It continued, going right on the main trail, away from town. Calder decided to change his plan. He followed the blood.

The trail followed the *Little Black Creek*, winding through a dense stand of conifers, then coming out into a clearing. There Calder spotted the riderless horse standing, reins on the ground, it's saddle and haunches soaked with blood along its left side. Buzz drew his big gun and approached the nervous pony cautiously.

"Whoa, Boy, whoa. Where's your rider?" He picked up the horse's reins and looked to ensure the horse wasn't wounded. It was not, but the snow was red all around and trampled with the horse's hooves.

Seconds later Calder found his quarry lying a few feet away in the shadow of pine trees at the edge of the clearing. The man was still breathing, but very weak. He'd been shot through the left side, just above the hip. Calder roped the fellow to his steed, and led him back the way they had come.

They reached Warm Springs within the hour and knocked on Doc Ford's door. He was home. Calder brought the scoundrel into the doc's examination room, still breathing.

"He's in tough shape, Calder. I'll do what I can do, but" . . .

"Keep him alive, Doc!" Buzz insisted. "We need some answers. I'm going to see Molly's mom and a few others, but I'll be back."

Chapter 47

Geraldine Turnbill met Calder at the front door. She sensed something was wrong.

"It's not good news, is it?" she asked.

"Afraid not, Ma'am. Your husband's been shot. Leg wound. He should recover, but he's lost a lot of blood."

"Molly never did unhitch my buggy. I'll go out there right now." She threw a woolen muffler around her neck and shoulders, followed by a warm coat and winter boots, and was out the door.

Buzz continued to the town graveyard where the four teamsters were being laid to rest.

"I need to borrow your wagon, Marv!"

"Take it, Sir. Our boys are just fine. The ground is softer than we thought."

"When are you heading home?"

"Sun-up tomorrow morning."

"I'll have the wagon back in a couple of hours, thanks."

Buzz tied the roan to the wagon and returned to Doc Ford's office.

"He's going to live, Calder," the doc advised him. "You brought him in just in time, but he's almost too weak to move his head. He'll be in bed for a week at least."

"I want to ask him a few questions. Is he up to that?"

"Not right now, I put him under. Maybe in an hour." Buzz nodded, "I'll be back." He urged the wagon team toward Margaret's.

<><><>

Without ceremony, Buzz dumped the five miscreants into the wagon, then walked to the house. As he stepped into Margaret's entry he shouted, "Hello the house!"

Mrs. Turnbill answered from the hallway, "Mr. Calder, is that you?"

"Yes. I thought I should announce myself before I walk into the house. I took the shotgun away from Margaret, but you never know."

"Took you long enough to get back. Where have you been?" Margaret shouted.

"I was just outside picking up trash in your yard, Margaret," Buzz answered. "I have a wagon-full, ready to go to the town dump. I stopped by to make sure you're all fine."

He walked into the hallway to find the floor scrubbed clean and smelling of the soda-lime mixture Margaret had in the kitchen closet. Geraldine was sitting with Margaret in the bedroom. The two women greeted Buzz as he entered.

"How's the husband, Geraldine?" Buzz asked.

"In pain, the bleeding has stopped, thanks to Molly. She cauterized the wound; says she learned it from that Mescalero friend of hers."

"Good for her! And how are you doing, Margaret?"

"Buzz, I'm a new woman. Your horse hitching post gives me new confidence! I'm going to walk again! Want to see?"

"Later. I'll be back for a visit soon, but right now I'm going to pop in to see Jason and Molly, then I'm heading back to town. Doc Ford is trying to keep one of the culprits alive. We need to know who's behind the murders and the fire."

Buzz stepped into the parlor, chatted with Molly and her dad for a minute, complimented Molly for her quick thinking in cauterizing the wound, and patted Jason on the back.

"Are you up to going home, Jason? Your buggy is here; I can help you climb aboard, take you right to Doc Ford."

"No, I'll stay here a bit longer. Molly's taking real good care of me. Maybe stay here until Doc comes out to see Margaret next trip out. Maybe go home with him."

Calder bid them goodbye and headed for town with five bodies in the back of the wagon. The temperature had dropped considerably, and by late afternoon it was near freezing. His plan was to empty the wagon, return it to Marv, then question the fellow they were able to keep alive. He pulled the wagon to a stop in front of the churchyard. Most of the men were gone -- only Floyd, Ben Draper and Marv were sitting in the foyer with Marshall, the pastor.

"Do you mind if I set these men up outside the church, leaning against the wall, Pastor?"

"That seems a little sacrilegious, Mr. Calder. Are you sure they wouldn't be more" . . .

"It's perfect where they're headed," Buzz interrupted. "*Outside the assembly* is how I remember you saying in a sermon, Sir. We're having a meeting tomorrow morning in the Wesley's barn. I'm going to ask everyone in attendance to swing by here. Perhaps someone recognizes one or more of them. We also have one still alive at Doc Ford's. I'm on my way now. Marv, thanks for the wagon. If I don't see you, have a safe trip."

"I'm goin' with'im, Calder," Floyd piped up. "Ridin' shotgun all the way to Albakerk."

"So am I," Ben said, "but I think I'll be back."

Chapter 48

Mrs. Ford greeted Calder at the door. "Jake and that judge are in with the doctor. You can go on in," she pointed. Buzz nodded to her and opened the door into the doctor's small surgery.

"Is he awake?" he asked.

"Not yet; it's been over an hour. Should be any time, now," Doc Ford replied.

"Then we wait," Judge Houghton decided. "By the way, Calder, I hear you had a commotion out at Margaret's place. Did it end well?"

"Beautifully, Judge. I rounded up the five participants, brought them into town, took them to church, told them to sit still and be quiet. I think they're still there."

"Five?" the judge asked. "And then this fellow? That's incredible!"

"That fellow, Marv, is heading back to Santa Fe tomorrow morning if you need to catch a ride," Calder continued. "Floyd and Ben are riding shotgun as far as Albuquerque, then both are returning."

"Oh, no! You don't get rid of me that easily," Houghton laughed. "I'll be sticking around for a few more days at least. Besides, we have a meeting tomorrow morning, remember?"

Doc Ford interrupted them, "He just moved; he's

coming to."

The wounded man stirred, opened his eyes and tried to raise his head; he grimaced and lay back, exhausted.

"Don't try to move!" Doc ordered. "You have a gunshot wound in a very tender spot. I've sewn it up, but it could pull out if you waggle about. You've lost a lot of blood and you're very weak. If you hope to stay alive, you can't lose any more blood, Mister."

"You're gonna hang me anyway," the man, in just barely a whisper, replied. "Why hold off?"

"Depends on your answers to our questions," Buzz said. "For starters, we need to know who hired you."

"I gotta think," the man mumbled. "Gimme some time. Mebbe I will, but mebbe it ain't no use tellin' you nothin' if'n I'm dyin'."

"Were you part of the gang that stole the wagons of goods and bushwhacked the four drivers on the trail from Albuquerque?"

Pitifully fragile, the man made a miserable appeal, "Leave me alone, let me think."

Jake grew impatient. "Mister, we'll drag you outa that bed and string you up in about five minutes if you insist on stayin' quiet!"

Buzz turned to Doc Ford, and in low tones the injured man couldn't hear, asked, "Is he a threat to you if he stays the night?"

"Naw! I'll give him a dose of chloroform and strap him to his bed. He'll still be here in the morning."

"I suggest we leave the man to clear his head and think," Buzz said to the others. "I have a feeling that when he's stronger he'll open up to us."

Houghton spoke for the first time, "Sounds like a plan. I'm not one for empty threats," he said, looking at Jake.

"That wasn't an empty threat, Houghton!" Jake snapped. "Stringin' him up is the best way to handle murdering scum like him. Eye fer an eye."

"Sometimes snap judgments are later regretted, Jake. Cool heads must prevail," the judge advised. "Remember the scripture: *'in a multitude of counsel there is wisdom'*. Maybe ten years ago, *eye for an eye* worked, Jake, but things are changing, even in the territories."

"Huh! There'll be plenty of counselors tomorrow, Judge. See you fellers in the mornin'." Jake stormed out.

"I told you," the wounded man groaned. "I'm as good as swingin'."

"You going to be at the meeting tomorrow, Doc?"

"Yessiree, see you there." Judge Houghton and Calder said their goodbyes and saw themselves out.

<><><>

Monday morning was bitterly cold but clear. Doc had the wounded fellow heavily sedated. He was no good to anyone as an informant.

Looking out over the more than 300 people in the Wesley's barn, Mr. Royston the banker asked for quiet.

"Thanks for meeting with us this morning. As most of you know, we had an awful thing happen. Four teamsters were killed on the road between Albuquerque and here four or five days ago. The wagons were filled with goods slated to be delivered here . . . not for Margaret, mind, but a competitor.

The point is, four innocent teamsters were killed; we buried them yesterday. The goods never came to town. I'm going to turn this meeting over to Judge Houghton from Albuquerque. He has more to say."

"Hi, folks. I represent law in New Mexico. I'm one of only a fewjudges. Now, we have some problems down here in southern New Mexico. It's a sign of growth -- and with growth, unfortunately, comes crime. Crime such as the men who robbed and murdered those teamsters; set fire to the general store here in Warm Springs and tried to kill Margaret; the ones who, seven years ago burned down the old *Ed Dammer Homestead* and killed the Broderick families; the ones who tried, just yesterday, to kill Margaret and Molly out at Margaret's. By the way, those that tried to harm Margaret and Molly yesterday have been eliminated -- I saw them myself over at the churchyard.

Now, here's what I'm prepared to do: I'm going to authorize federal funds to build a jail and a courthouse right here in Warm Springs. I'll get that done by the middle of next year. When the job is complete I'll either bring a federal judge down here with me or appoint one from your ranks.

Right now, I want all of you to follow me to the churchyard. We'll take a look at the five men who raided Margaret's yesterday. Anybody who saw them in town, remembers them, recognizes them from anywhere, speak up!"

Most of the residents mounted their steeds or rode buggies to the church and a procession passed by the five dead men. Several had seen two or three in town recently, but could make no other connection. Finally, one fellow said he was sure he had seen three of them in Mozura, a wide open, flash-in-the-pan, gold mining town some sixty miles almost straight west.

Mozura grew to 1,000 overnight back in the 1820's, gold-seekers, complete with the usual gamblers, whores, and other riff-raff; then when gold disappeared the town dried up, leaving only hell-raisers, robbers, and a couple of houses of ill repute behind.

The judge stood on the church steps. "I want at least four teams of five or six men to sweep through the countryside in search of the missing wagons. I'll swear all volunteers in as deputies at $3.00 a day. I'm asking Jake Ruskin to head a team going to Mozura, Buzz Calder to head a team going toward the *Eagle Ranch*, Lamar Jefferson to head a team going toward Tucson. Now, do I have a volunteer to head one more team?"

Antonio Muñez waved an arm. "Sure! I will!"

"Excellent! Take a crew toward the copper mines at *del Cobre*.

All of you: if you find the wagons, bring them back here. If you find evidence of the wagons and their direction, send a man back with your news.

Jake, I expect you'll be gone longer than the others. We'll expect you to be back here in six days at most. You others, I'd expect four at most. Choose your teams carefully -- no more than six, including yourselves."

In his final words of instructions to the team leaders, Judge Houghton asked that they use every restraint possible should they encounter the culprits. "Take them alive if you can, but use force if necessary.

I'll be riding with Calder's team. He promised me a ride along *Black Creek* toward the ranch lands of your beautiful valley . . . this will serve that purpose as well as our main objective.

Finally, put your teams together, send them home to prepare for the trip, kiss their wives, then go find these bastards. Good hunting!"

Chapter 49

Houghton and Calder turned their attention to Doc Ford. "How's the prisoner, Doc?" Calder asked.

"I tied him to his bed," Doc Ford chuckled. "I expect his head is clear enough to think and talk by now."

"Then let's go speak with him," Houghton smiled, "should be interesting. Do you need a few minutes to gather a crew, Calder?"

"No. I talked to a few fellows already. We'll pick them up at my place."

<><><>

Calder began the conversation, "You feeling more alive today?"

"A little. Hurt bad, though."

"Can you tell me your name?"

"Friends call me Buster."

"Listen, Buster, you were shot while acting like a damn fool out at Margaret's place. You had five others with you. They're all dead. We'll be burying them today or tomorrow. You're lucky you're alive."

"I guess so. They all dead?"

"All dead, Buster. Friends?

"Just one, my cousin, Roger."

"You have a family. A wife, kids, that kind of thing?"

"Just Roger. You shoot him?"

"No, but I saw him fall, and I did shoot you. Now, where did you come from, Buster? You certainly aren't from around here."

"No place. Drifters. Roger'n me was in Mozura fer a coupla weeks, up til last week. That's some town. I think it's mostly filled with drunken hooligans. Anyway, Roger'n me was fixin' to leave when some guy came into the bar we was in an' offered us a payin' job.

Said it wouldn't take but a couple three days at most, but he'd pay us $30.00 apiece. That's more'n two months worth a'ropin' steers up in Colorado. Bunch of us took him up on it. Stowed us away with a couple of his boys in a bunkhouse he was buildin'" . . .

"A new bunkhouse? Where?" Houghton was curious.

"Who knows? I ain't from around here. In the wilderness, somewhere. Bunkhouse is big enough to fit all us plus mebbe six-seven more when it's done. Building a corral next to it, too."

"Did this guy have a name?" Buzz asked.

"He said to call him Whitey. He dropped off food and whiskey and told us to stay put til he needed us. Then he pointed to half the fellows, said, 'come with me' and left the rest of us."

"Did you see those fellows again?"

"Nope. They never came back. Course, we wasn't there much longer ourselves, Mister Whitey came back fer us. Said everyone in the little town was busy, it bein' Sunday and all, and we could do a job fer him. They was only his three fellers along with Roger, me, and another feller name'a Baldy.

We was told to ride into this place, screamin', shootin' it up, trashin' it, maybe even burn it down, then ride out. We thought it would be a lark, that's all. An' $30.00 to boot! When the shootin' started it was exciting until Roger got shot, I started to go to help him; that's when you shot me, an' I ran off. That's about it."

"That's quite a story, Buster. This Whitey fellow, can you describe him?" Houghton asked.

"You have any more of that pain stuff, Doc? I hurt!"

Doc Ford applied warmed ether under Buster's nose. The young man closed his eyes and lay exhausted for a moment. He nodded his head, then continued without opening his eyes: "Real short, mean-looking, white hair, black beard, scar on his cheek. That's all I remember."

"That's a lot," Houghton said. "Get some rest. We'll be back in a day or two."

"You gonna string me up like that other fella said?"

"Haven't decided, yet. Don't think so," the judge said.

"Me'n Roger was just gonna have some fun; didn't even think nobody was there. Honest."

"I think we believe you, Son," Calder replied. "That's what happens sometimes. Bad decisions are made and people get hurt. Unfortunately, you can't undo some decisions . . . it's like trying to put a bullet back in a gun."

The two men walked out. Calder checked his watch; it was 10:41 a.m.

Three young men from Warm Springs were waiting in front of Calder's shop. He ran into his house and picked up a few clothes. "Ready," he announced.

"We'll take the *Little Black Creek* trail past the beaver dam, and from there we can take the southwestern trail toward the *Snake Eyes* spread or northwest along the *Little Black* toward the *Eagle Outfit*. Your choice, Houghton. It hasn't snowed since Saturday night so any tracks will be obvious in the snow."

"Then tracks or no," the judge said decisively, "we follow the trail toward the *Eagle*. We can check those boys out, ask a few questions, and if we're happy, we can double back and ride toward the *Snake Eyes*."

Calder nodded. "Unless, of course, there are obvious signs of riders going toward *Snake Eyes*."

"Of course," Houghton agreed. They started out.

After traveling past Margaret's drive they realized the snow had been so trampled they couldn't really distinguish how many riders had passed.

Houghton stopped and pointed up a slope. Buzz shook his head, "No, those tracks go only about thirty feet. That's where I picked Buster up. Let's just stay on the trail."

The snow from that point on seemed untouched but for a few deer tracks. They reached the fork where the trail split -- westward along the *Little Black* or southward toward the *Snake Eyes Ranch*

"How far is the *Eagle* spread?" Houghton asked.

"About eight miles from here; trail runs along the *Little Black* another three or four miles westward, then leaves the creek and goes northeast." The creek takes a turn south, cuts through a steep canyon, and meets up with the *Gila* someplace down south."

"And where is the *Ed Dammer Homestead*?"

Calder laughed, "You mean the *Molly Broderick Sheep Ranch*, Judge? Her quarter section parallels the *Little Black* just beyond the point where the creek turns south. The buildings were on a knoll in a very nice spot, overlooking the creek.

About a thirty minute ride in summer; not sure what to expect with snow on the ground. It must be seven or eight years since I've been up there, nothing left of the place but six or seven charred poles holding up half a barn roof."

"I'd like to take a ride over there before we go on to the *Eagle*."

"That's easy, we'll head in that direction."

They came to the cut-off, headed south and began to climb. The *Little Black,* once on the same plane, was suddenly ten feet below them, and a wall above them on the right side, barely enough for a wagon to move along.

Minutes later the distance to the water was thirty feet, then fifty, rushing along at the bottom of the gorge.

"How do we follow the creek, Buzz?" one of the young fellows asked, "There's almost no room to ride; no banks, only cliffs, above and below."

"It comes out in a few minutes; just wait . . . ah! There! Fifty feet ahead!" Buzz pointed. "That's what we're looking for, see the clearing up ahead?"

The moment he uttered the words, a dynamite blast sent half the cliff above out over *Little Black,* spewing rock, trees, and debris down twenty feet in front of them, effectively blocking the trail west toward the burned out homestead. The five men, after a few minutes of calming their ponies, turned around to head back. As the air cleared, rifle fire suddenly rang out from above.

"Ambush!" one of the group yelled. There was no cover. They spurred their horses back the way they had come. One of the group was wounded by a high-powered rifle. Buzz pulled his weapon, but could see no one above. They rode hard, rounded a bend and were back in the timber away from the cliff.

"Where were you hit, Chuck?" Calder asked the young man who had been shot.

"Barely nicked me; like a bee sting," Chuck replied.

"It appears we're not welcome," Calder said, frowning.

"Yes," Houghton agreed. "Someone doesn't want us to visit the homestead. Makes me think that's where we should head." He looked at the others for their opinions. They all nodded their heads in agreement.

"We could head for the Eagle Ranch," suggested Chuck, "then cut west through the hills at the base of the Black Mountains, swing south and come at the ranch from the north. Probably add about an hour to the ride, "but those sons-a-bitches sure wouldn't be expecting us."

Another of the youngsters, Petch, suggested, "Why don't we dismount, leave our horses, climb up this grade," he said, pointing to the rocky slope they had just skirted,

"I like that idea even better," Houghton said, "what do you say, fellas?"

"I like it too," Calder decided, "but we'll use the horses. They're more sure-footed than we are, and they can pull us up and over some of the steeper spots." They all nodded.

Buzz looked at his watch. It was 12:20 p.m.

"There's nothing like a noon-time hike followed by a gunfight."

Chapter 50

The climb was surprisingly easy but for one spot about halfway up. One of the younger fellows lost his footing on a shale-filled ravine and slid down, horse and all, almost to the trail below. The others waited for him to recover lost ground. Once done, they continued to the top.

Cautiously, they crept through the rocks toward the point from which the dynamite and rifle fire had come. Tracks crisscrossed the snow, both human and equine, but the bushwhackers were already gone.

They looked down at the devastation caused by the blast. It would take a crew of four or five to clear the damage done to make that section of the trail usable again.

From here they could see the trail below as it rose to a point ahead and level with their position just beyond a shale wash. They picked their way across the wash without mishap and were back on the trail.

"I'll bet we can catch them if we hustle," one of the young fellows said, "they're probably laughing, taking their time up the trail. Even if we can't catch them, we've saved a lot of time, thanks to climbing that rocky slope."

"All true," Houghton said, "let's catch them; keep them alive if possible."

Calder agreed, "They knew we were coming. They must

have been in the Wesley barn or at the churchyard. But how they knew we'd take the *Black Creek* cutoff is a mystery. For now, let's see where those tracks lead," he said, pointing.

After a few more minutes Buzz turned to his fellow riders, "You know, Molly's property is only a half mile or mile from here. These tracks can only end there, it's a helluva long way around to the *Snake Eyes*. We're headed for that old burned out homestead, I'm sure of it."

<><><>

They were close enough to hear the voices even before they saw the horsemen -- four of them, astride their mounts -- laughing and joking, just as one of Calder's fellow riders had predicted.

Calder signaled his fellows to follow him. He spurred the big roan up a bank and rode through a rocky outcropping until he came to a grassy knoll. The others followed. They were ahead of the four riders below. They dismounted and settled in. The trail was just beyond their position.

Now, in a strange twist, they became the ambushers waiting for their prey. Within minutes they saw movement in the trees. The four villains were visible, slowly walking their horses up the grade.

"On my count, we all stand and aim our weapons at them, but don't fire unless they make a run for it," Calder whispered. When the four were within 30 yards he stood, rifle aimed at the group.

"You there!" he shouted. "Raise your hands high so we can see them!"

One of them reached for his rifle. Calder shot him before he had taken it from his sheath. He fell instantly.

"Now, the rest of you, come down from your ponies and lie down on the snow. Don't try to run! My boys are crack shots!"

Calder's group approached the three still alive, noted that the fourth was beyond help, and tied the three securely, leaned them against some trees, and wrapped more ropes around them. Satisfied, Calder and company left them there and continued up the trail.

"Why are we continuing?" one of the three young men asked. "Don't we have who we were looking for?"

Houghton answered, "I want to take a look at what's left of the homestead buildings."

"Not much to see from what I remember," Calder said, "but we've come this far, and it's close, now."

They were shocked! Instead of the burned out barn with a partial roof and a wall held up by a few poles that they had expected, a new log building with a corral attached stood in its place!

"What's our play, Houghton?" Buzz asked.

"Your territory, your decision, Calder," the judge responded, staring steadily at the blacksmith.

"My whaa? . . . What did you just say, Judge?" Calder squinted his eyes and cocked his head at the judge.

"Let's go up and check it out, Mr. Calder," Chuck interrupted. The other two younger men agreed.

"We're in plain view from the trail," Buzz said, still frowning at Houghton. "We'll go up there, but we'll approach through those trees," he said, pointing at a stand of birch along the side of the corral. "We just don't know who or how many scoundrels might be up there."

"I don't think there are any, Mr. Calder. There aren't any horses in that corral."

"Let's find out," Calder said, moving toward the trees.

Chapter 51

Doc Ford was pleased with Margaret's progress. "That rail has made a real difference, Margaret. Soon you'll be up walking around in the kitchen, cooking."

"I don't know about that, Daniel," she replied, "I'm tired just thinking about getting out of bed; I don't think I'll be moving around in the kitchen very soon."

"Oh, yes you will!." A voice from the kitchen rang out. Molly walked into the bedroom, smiling. "You're just feeling sorry for yourself, Margaret.

Doc," Molly continued, "I need to talk with you. Cup of tea?" She motioned for him to join her in the kitchen.

"I think that bullet needs to come out. I was reading in one of Margaret's books about blood lead poisoning, and Margaret's showing some signs. She gets dizzy, lacks energy, forgetful, I'm worried about her."

"Let me see that book, Molly," Doc Ford said. "Is Jason still here?"

"No, Sir, he rode out this morning," she said, handing him the heavy medical-pharmaceutical reference work:

United States Dispensatory by Wood and Bache, 1845

"Okay, thanks." Ford looked inside the cover at the frontispiece. "Only a few years old, should have the most current recommendations."

He sat in the parlor with a cup of tea, thumbing through the pertinent areas of the book. After each paragraph, he took a swallow and went *Ummph*, or *um-huh*! Finally he spoke, "I'll do the operation here, tomorrow, Molly, but I'll need your help in the meantime. Give Margaret a regular supper no later than 6 p.m. tonight and only some coffee tomorrow morning. I'll be here early."

The doctor went in and discussed the operation with Margaret. When he returned, he said, "Tomorrow then," and started out the door.

"Oh! Did you know that on Sunday night Buzz caught up with one of the vermin that tried to kill your pa and Margaret? We have him at my office with a bullet hole in his side. You may have shot him."

"I didn't know that, but I'm pleased he was caught," Molly said. "Have we found those four wagons yet, Doc?"

"Not yet, but we have teams of men scouring the country in different directions. Jake has a few with him, Calder has the judge and three young fellows with him, and" . . .

"I suppose that young Ben Draper is out there looking as part of a team."

Doc Ford frowned, "No, as a matter of fact, Molly, he left for Albuquerque early this morning with Marv and Floyd."

"Albuquerque; that's where he lives, right? Is he coming back?"

"Both he and Floyd said they were coming back, but he does have a job there. Why?"

"Oh, no reason, Doc. Just thinking. Antonio is interested in hiring him to rebuild Margaret's, and I was thinking about hiring him at Margaret's after it's built."

"Ummm, right," Doc chuckled as he walked out the door.

Less than ten minutes later a knock came at Margaret's door.

"Who can that be?" Margaret frowned. Molly grabbed Margaret's shotgun and went to the door.

"Who is it?"

"It's me, Molly. I need to see Miss Margaret if I can."

"Is it about money, Elmer?" Molly asked, ushering him in, ""Cuz I can pay you whatever you think she owes you."

"Oh, no, Ma'am. I just need some help, Miss Molly. I'm seventeen, my dad's gone, my mom's not much help. I kinda always relied on Margaret for good advice."

"Elmer? Is that you?" Margaret called from the bedroom. "What do you need, Son?"

Elmer barged into the bedroom. "Hi, Miss Margaret. I've been thinking, I'm pretty much a man, and I think I should be doin' somethin' more important with my life. Mom just wants me to feed Mr. Calder's chickens and take care of her, but, well, she's always put me down, as you know, an' I can do more. I know I can."

"Okay, Elmer, make some applications. Try Roberto's carpenter shop, or Maude's. Go out to the *Eagle Ranch*, the *Snake Eyes*, try the blacksmith shop again. You have to put in some effort. You never know."

"Really? Do you think I have a chance at a real job?"

"Elmer, it was your idea," Margaret reminded him. "Are you getting cold feet?"

"I have an idea, Elmer," Molly had been listening. "Next time teamsters come to town, ask if you could ride to Santa Fe and apply to become a driver, a teamster -- now, that's a real job, Elmer, and you'd do well. They just lost some men, they might be happy to hire you."

"Those men were shot, though. My mom wouldn't let me try."

"It's up to you, Elmer. Just an idea," Molly shrugged.

"I don't know Miss Molly, I'll think about it. Would I git a rifle?"

"I'm sure you would; Indians, outlaws, food, even predators like bears and cougars make it necessary for anyone on the trail. I've seen you target shooting with Jimmy and his dad, Elmer. You shoot really well."

"Yeah, but I've never owned a gun. My mom says I shouldn't never have one."

"She's worried you're going to be like your pa, Elmer," Margaret rejoined the conversation, "seems like he was always drunk, raising hell and getting shot and all. I can understand her worry, but she can't keep you tied to her apron strings forever."

"Oh," he laughed, "she don't tie me up or nothin'."
"For goodness sake," Margaret grew annoyed, "you know that's just an expression, Elmer. Every man in this territory carries a gun to protect those he loves, so it's time you make some determinations. Are you a man yet, Elmer, or will it be sometime in the future?

Go home, think about it for a few days. Talk to a few of the men in town -- men you respect -- ask them what they think you'd be good at, or ask them for advice or even ask them for a job. Then come back to see me with your decision, Elmer."

Elmer was satisfied with Margaret's answers. "I'll do that, Ma'am. Thanks." He walked out.

"You were really hard on him," Molly said, turning to Margaret, "Is he ready for such strong talk?"

"Molly, Elmer is sitting right on the border of taking care of himself for the rest of his life, or always relying on someone else to take care of him. His mother hasn't done him any favors, that's for sure.

I've told Virginia for more than five years to give him more responsibility and freedom. We've argued many times over coffee, Molly. I just can't help him anymore. I'm so tired. You'll have to be his counselor from here on."

Chapter 52

The five men crept up through the birch trees toward the new structure. No one spoke.

At the rear corner was a wide open entry door. Just beyond were two saddled horses tied to a hitching post. As the five neared the door they could hear chairs scraping and voices inside.

"Lucky we ain't playin' fer saddles like you wanted to, Abbot. You'd be walkin' least 'til payday."

"Gotta admit, quite a stroke'a bad luck, a'right, Moe. I gotta go take a leak. Be right back -- say, Moe. Speakin'a bein' right back, wonder why it's takin' the boys so long? They shudda been here a half hour ago."

"Prob'ly blew themselves off the mountain with that dynamite," the one called Moe said, jokingly. "They must have used all six sticks. Prob'ly felt the blast all the way to that town yonder. If they ain't back in another ten minutes maybe we should take a ride down to see."

"Thinkin' the same thing. Be right back," Abbot said as he went the door to relieve himself.

Buzz motioned for the others to scurry for cover as the man walked straight toward their position in the birch grove, so intent on his objective he lost all caution or sense of vigilance.

Abbot stopped in front of the nearest tree. While he

was busy, he didn't hear the blacksmith come up behind him.

In a coarse, loud whisper, Buzz warned, "You yell, you're dead, Mister! Finish your business, then put your hands behind your back!"

Abbot tried to turn around, Buzz shoved him back to face the tree. "Hands behind your back!" he demanded. The fellow complied. Buzz tied the fellow's arms together at the wrists, wrapped the rope tightly around Abbot's neck and back to the wrists once again.

Next, he turned Abbot around. "Who else is in there besides Moe?" he asked.

"Nobody."

'Okay, here's what you're going to do," Buzz said. "you're going to yell 'hey, Moe! Come out here and look at this!'"

Abbot did as Buzz demanded. Moe came out without his weapon. "Yeah, Wha" . . . .

Immediately he was surrounded. Both men were tied to birch trees. Now came some questions. *Who are you? With whom are you affiliated? What do you know about four wagons full of goods and the dead drivers?* Neither man gave up anything.

"Go check the building," Buzz said to the three younger fellows. "Keep your weapons handy."

Minutes later they returned. "Nothing but bunks, a table and eight chairs inside, Sir," Chuck said.

"And, of course," another fellow said, "a pot-bellied stove, stack of wood, and eight bottles of whiskey."

"Each of you grab two bottles. Consider it a bonus," Calder grinned. Then he continued "Let's go down; bring those others back up here. We should get some answers before day's end."

"We'll bring them up, along with the horses," Chuck told him.

The three young men mounted and disappeared down the trail, leaving Calder and the judge with the two scoundrels.

Three shots rang out. Chuck and his companions froze momentarily. There was still more than 400 yards of twisting trail to the men they had left tied in the trees below. *Who was doing the shooting?* Chuck raised his rifle to the sky and fired an answering shot, then the three spurred their horses forward.

They rounded the last turn to see six newcomers, two of whom were questioning Calder's three prisoners.

"Hellooo!" Chuck shouted. "Coming in!"

The men looked up. "Who are you, Mister?" one of them asked.

"Name's Chuck Grossinger. This here's Brody an' Petch. Now it's my turn. Who are you, and what's your business in this part of the country?"

Petch interrupted, "Hey! I've seen you in Warm Springs a few times," he said, pointing at one of the six men. "You a local rancher?"

"Now you mention it, Petch," Chuck nodded, I've seen most of these fellows as well. *Eagle Spread*, right?"

"That's right. We're here because we heard the dynamite go off, saw that cloud of smoke and wondered who in hell is blasting this time of year. You set it off?"

"Course not," Chuck answered. "These three," he said pointing to the three still shackled to the trees. "They thought we'd be easy pickins once we were stopped by the slide, but Calder pulled us back, an' we climbed to higher ground. Ended up above them, and when the time was right we swooped down and, well, you see them as they are."

"Calder? Is Calder with you?" one of them asked.

"Yes. You know him?"

"Sure do. He had some idea he was going to share with me earlier this year, then he disappeared on me; never saw him again."

"He's up at the *Dammer Homestead* right now," Chuck said. "We came down here to take these three up to him and the judge."

The speaker stuck out his hand, "With no objection, we'll ride along. Name's Ted Willitson, by the way."

Chapter 53

Judge Houghton poked his head inside the door of the new structure. "There's quite a bunch of riders coming, Calder. We only sent down three to pick up three; must be what? Twelve? Fifteen?"

Buzz walked outside and shaded his eyes as he watched the incoming troupe. "Looks like some of the boys from the *Eagle Ranch.*"

"Must be nearby," the judge commented.

"Yeah. Starts where Molly's property ends on the north side; runs up to, and along *Caballo Lake*, about six miles east of here."

The riders stopped at the stable and dismounted. Buzz and the judge walked out to greet them.

"What the hell's goin' on here, Mr. Calder?" one of them asked.

"This isn't your work, Wilbur?"

"You kidding? The old man would never build on another's property. We've put cows on'er, ever summer since that unfortunate event several years back" . . .

"Yeah," another of the *Eagle* outfit took over, "but we wouldn't never have the gall to waltz in and take over like we owned it. No, Sir!"

"When's the last time you herded cows down here, Ted?" Calder asked.

"Actually, right after you disappeared, Sir. I drove six hundred head down here from *Caballo Lake Meadows*; as I remember, we were here for the rest of July. After that I came into town, found out why you disappeared -- sorry 'bout your dad, by the way -- then, we turned the herd to the western range along the *Little Black*."

"So you don't know what happened from August until now?"

Wilbur piped up, "We never come this way, Calder. No reason to. Only reason today was that blast."

Turning to the five men in shackles, Buzz posed the question once again to Abbot, "Who's your boss, Abbot?"

No answer.

"Okay, I'll ask all of you. Who do you work for?"

Still no answer.

"Chuck, grab a rope. Toss it over that birch branch. Petch, pick out one of the younger fellows -- any one you care to and stand him under the rope."

Petch grabbed one of the dynamiters and pushed him roughly toward the tree.

"What's his name, Petch?"

The young criminal spoke up, "My name's Reginald Montgomery. I'm from Oklahoma territory."

"I want you all to look at Reginald Montgomery, here," Buzz shouted, "because you are all going to end up swinging from this tree!"

"You c-c-can't do that, Mister!" Reginald sobbed. "You can't just hang us. It was Moe that gave us the dynamite and told us to blow the trail and then pick off any survivors. The problem was the blast went off a minute too early."

"Did you hear that admission, Petch? They planned on murdering all five of us. Penalty for that is death."

Without stopping for a breath, Buzz continued with a roar, "So, it was Moe! Then take Moe over to that tree!"

"So-o-o, you ain't going to hang me, Mister?" young Reginald asked.

"Not yet, Boy! But there's still plenty of time to watch you swing along with the others. Looks like Moe will be first." Calder turned to Petch. "Petch, throw that noose around Moe's neck!"

Petch complied. Moe stood under the tree with the noose tightly drawn under his chin, the other end of the rope tied to the pommel of one of the ponies. Buzz held the pony's reins.

Moe began to cough with the strain of the cord against his larynx. Up to this moment he had stood in almost casual disbelief that his life was about to end; now it had become starkly evident.

"Anything to say before we string you up, Moe?" Calder asked the man.

"-- Y. . *cough, cough* . . yes I d. . *cough, cough* . .*u-u-u*. . *cough, cough* .."

Chapter 54

"Got it! -- at least most of it." Doc Ford heaved a sigh, as he dropped a flattened piece of lead into a teacup, and gave Molly a look of relief and satisfaction. He wiped his brow.

"I can't risk probing any further. There are still specks and shards in there, but any more digging around may do more damage than good. Now to suture that gash in Margaret's back." The doc bent over his patient and began; a few minutes later he stood, heaved another sigh, removed his glasses and rubbed his eyes.

"We're done, Molly. I'll wait around until she wakes up. Then once she's stable, I'll turn her care over to you. For right now, let's leave her on her stomach, open to the air."

"Okay, but first I'm going to wash it with warm water and soap. Then tonight I'll wash it again, put a layer of honey on it, then cover it with gauze. If you have mescal would you bring me some tomorrow?"

"That Injun, *whatsisname*, taught you some good medicine for sure. Yes, I have a jar or two of agave. I should have some in my bag."

"Red Hawk," Molly said, as she prepared water on the kitchen coal stove, "and he's not just an 'Injun', he's a proud Mescalero." Then, thinking out loud, "I wonder where he is?"

"Beg your pardon?" Doc said.

"Nothing. Just wondering to myself where Red Hawk is right now."

A knock came at the door. "Now, who can that be?" Doc Ford said, frowning.

"Wait! Don't open that door!" Molly instructed, running to the bedroom for a weapon.

Another knock. "Molly! Margaret! Is Doc Ford in there? It's Elmer. My ma's real sick!"

Ford opened the door. "What's the problem, Lad?" Molly invited them to sit at the kitchen table. Elmer sat, took off his hat, and began --

"I don't rightly know, Sir. I told her I was thinking about becoming a teamster driver, like we talked about, you know, an' she fell down on the floor just after that. I got her up and set her in a chair. She got up an' went to bed. She won't eat nuthin. Been cryin' all day."

Doc Ford shook his head. "Just leave her be, Elmer. She's afraid that as she gets older, you won't be there to take care of her."

"Elmer," Molly added quickly, "you go tell your mother you have a job with the general store for now. Assure her you will always be there to take care of her."

"And If she still wants to stay in bed and cry," the doctor said, "there is nothing you can do. I'll swing by sometime today to look in on her. In the meantime, let her cry. You might encourage her to have a bite to eat, and a cup of tea."

That satisfied Elmer. He left in a positive mood.

Doc Ford turned to Molly, "She's got what we in the medicine business call the melancholies. I've seen it before; can get so bad the patient loses all control of the mind. Might be the reason Elmer is a bit slow in his thinking."

"I have some ideas to keep Elmer busy for a few

weeks," Molly agreed, "but you'll have to deal with his mother. Let's go look at Margaret. She should be waking up about now."

Doc Ford was surprised at the young lady's accuracy; the patient was waking from the effects of the anesthetic. He sat next to the bed; their eyes met.

"Jugit, Doc?" she asked.

"Yes," Ford said, laughing. "I got it out, Margaret," he said slowly, pronouncing each word with precision. He held her hand and continued, "I put it in a teacup for you to see."

"Goog. Is mmm'bud cover?"

"Yes, your behind has a sheet over it. Now you get some rest. Molly is staying with you. She will fuss over you, and I'll be back tomorrow morning."

Margaret faded off to sleep.

"I'll be okay, Doc," Molly assured him, "you go take care of Elmer's mom."

Doc Ford smiled as he picked up his hat and coat. "Oh, thanks."

Chapter 55

"Loosen the rope, Petch!" Buzz ordered.

"-- Uhh. . *cough, cough* . . Uhh!" Moe panted . . " *cough, cough* ..shit, man. . *cough, cough* .."

"Thanks," Moe said, finally gathering himself. "Yes, I do," he rubbed his throat, coughed a few more times and began.

"A bunch of us boys drove a herd into El Pueblo, Colorado Territory, back in the springtime. Fella walks up, says, 'where you boys off to next?' We say, 'back home to Texas.' He says, 'how 'bout comin' down New Mexico way to do a job fer me?' I says, 'herdin' cattle?' He says, 'partly'.

We stop at Santa Fe. He goes into the court house . . . we don't even stay the night; we just keep on comin' south 'til we get to some place called *Old Horse Springs*. There we pick up near 400 head of beef; says he bought them from some ol' boy name'a Tyler. Says 'anybody question my ownership, shoot'em'. A few of us got a problem with that, he reaches into a satchel and pulls out a paper showin' title to the whole damn herd, says it's why he stopped at the Santa Fe courthouse. Everything looked legit, signed and all.

Anyway, we push the cows a day south through the brush, stop by a crick an' he gives us brandin' irons, says 'start brandin' em' -- which we proceed to do."

"Where are you going with this yarn, Mister?" Calder asked, annoyed, yet intrigued.

"Tryin' to save my skin, Sir -- an' my friends."

"Fine. So how long did you stay by that 'crick' -- branding?"

"Three days."

"Anybody come after you?"

"Yessir. Ol' man Tyler hisself an' four other fellers come after us."

"What happened?"

"We shot'em."

Calder looked from the judge to Chuck and the other young men with him. He shook his head in disbelief.

"What's the fellow's name, Moe?"

"Only name he gave us was King."

"Title document from Santa Fe . . . did it say 'King'?" Houghton spoke up for the first time.

"I think so," Moe replied," but I don't read too good."

"Were there other signatures on the document, Moe?"

"Must have been four or five. Looked real official."

Calder broke in again, "Where are all those cows now, Mister?"

"We put'em in pasture other side of that stream that runs just below and west of here. You call it the *Little Black*."

"Part of that land belongs to you, doesn't it Willitson?" Buzz asked.

"Yup," Ted replied. "Runs right along the creek to *Twin Granite Spires*. Then the *Snake Eyes* spread takes over. Far as I know, been that way long as the two ranches been in existence. Ain't no other ranches down this way . . . except fer this here homestead which appears has been bought recently with this construction goin' on.

Far as us boys from *Eagle*, we thought nobody owned it. I was thinkin' on buyin' it, just didn't know how to go about it."

Calder tipped his hat back and scratched his head. "Seems this King fellow is trying to move in on the *Snake Eyes* as well as the *Dammer Ranch*.

I have a few more questions for Moe, here, but while we still have a few hours of daylight, why don't you other fellows -- Chuck, Petch, Ted -- take these bushwhackers down to the blast area and have them clear the trail so it's usable again. I don't think they'll try to run, but if they do, just shoot them."

Abbot spoke up. "Mr. Calder?"

Calder turned to him. "You have something to say?"

"Yessir. I don't think we turned them cows out on that pasture by mistake. We branded them with irons looked like two snakes, either side of a pole."

Chapter 56

"A few questions for you, Moe. Think carefully."

"Ask away, Mr. Calder. I'll give you much as I know."

"You and your boys -- was it you that built the bunkhouse and corral?"

"No. They's a sawmill along the *Little Black* 'bout two miles up-river. Mule team wagon an' crew was runnin' down here 'bout once a week, before they stopped cuz they had another job to finish up first."

"What was the other job?"

"Up at the ranch. They're building a storage lean-to fer new merchandise -- puttin' it against the barn so they only need three sides. Understand it's big, but temporary. They're hopin' to move the whole shebang by the end of the year, spring at the latest."

"You mean?" . . .

"Take'er down and put'er back up in Warm Springs soon as they git a place. Least that's what one of the fellers told me."

"How do they expect to do that?" Houghton became curious.

"Raise'er in sections, mark the sections, replace'em like they took'em down."

"So this new storage building, why do they need it?"

"All's I know, they got goods to go in'er."

"Did you kill four teamsters and take their wagons, Moe?" Calder asked.

"Hell, no! Wouldn't do that, Sir. That's murder!"

"You killed old Man Tyler and his men; you tried to kill us with those explosives, was that not murder?"

"No!" Moe said adamantly. "Tyler was tryin' to steal them cows back after King bought'em from'im fair an'square.

Far as you folks, I'm real sorry. See, last night King and that ramrod, Whitey, dropped by an' said be on the lookout for some hired killers tryin' to sneak to his ranch to kill him. Said you'd be comin' this way. We just figgered". . .

"Say no more, Moe." Calder heaved a sigh and shook his head. "I'm taking this rope off my saddle pommel, but you stay where you are," Calder warned.

He took the rope from the big roan's pommel and slapped her on the rump. She grunted, took a few steps, then pawed at the snow to find something green underneath.

Calder walked to where the judge was sitting on one of the new corral rails, watching with interest. "I think I could use a drink, Judge. Watch him while I grab that bottle of hooch in the bunk."

He returned, handed the judge a cup, poured from the bottle, first to the judge, then to himself. "Does Moe expect us to believe his yarn? Is he really that simple? How do you figure it?"

"A couple of questions you might ask him, Buzz. How much is his crew being paid, and where is the old lady, Mrs. Ingraham? Her name was still on title to the *Snake Eyes*, last I checked.

Now, I've been watching Moe. A fellow can learn a lot by simply sitting back and listening." The judge took a sip, "I think this Moe fellow," Houghton jerked a thumb toward the hoodlum, "is just trying to do a good job for

King -- following orders, counting on a fortune for his loyalty."

"You said something when we first left Albuquerque, Judge, something about thinking you knew who is behind Margaret's fire and the other destruction. Maybe it's time to let me in on it."

"Yeah, probably so. You've been in Warm Springs how long, Calder -- eighteen, nineteen years?"

"No, no, Judge. Going on fifteen is all. Margaret's the old-timer in town. She and Rian journeyed here from Utah, bought two quarter sections from Mexico over twenty years ago, started the general store on one of them and a homestead on the other one.

She says they brought in a small wagon load of merchandise for neighboring miners and homesteaders like the Wesleys and Dammers; the general store brought folks from all around, and the town of Warm Springs blossomed." Buzz drained his cup and poured a couple more ounces.

"Your story is right about everything, Calder, but do you know where they got the money to buy the land from Mexico, develop it and bring in that first wagon-load?" Houghton reached his cup out for a refill.

"No, and don't tell me they robbed a bank, Cedric," Calder laughed. "Probably just like me, I expect. Family money and hard work."

"Not quite," Houghton said wryly, "but hatred within a family ofttimes leads to retribution, and I think that's what we have here, my friend.

A few years ago up in Santa Fe there was a big Irish fellow, *Brendan something* looking for his wife. Made the rounds in all the bars -- said she had run off with his cousin from their home back in Texas in 1829, and he'd been looking ever since. Been up in Montana, Wyoming, Utah, sent folks to Nevada towns, looking."

"How do you know so much about this, Cedric?"

"Brother Joel knows everything that goes on in Santa Fe, just as I try to do in Albuquerque." The judge raised the enameled cup to his lips, brushed the corners of his moustache with his thumb and fingers, and continued, "There's more.

Rumor is, the bride was beaten almost daily by her new husband -- until the cousin, Rian Reagan, stepped in, beat Brendan almost to death, rescued her along with a wagon and all her earthly goods, including a cache of gold. The two of them disappeared."

"We're talking about Margaret and Rian aren't we, Cedric?"

"We are indeed. There's even more, but perhaps you're done for the day."

"No, Houghton," Calder squinted and looked sideways at the judge, trying to take it all in. He took a sip, "You seem to know most everything that goes on around here. I'm listening."

"Do you know Margaret's maiden name, Buzz?"

"Hah!" Calder grinned, "that's a good one, Cedric -- I don't think I do . . . as a matter of fact, I don't think anyone in town knows."

"And no one is to ever find out, Calder, not even Molly."

"But you're going to tell me, aren't you, Houghton?"

"Broderick."

"What? -- say again!" Calder couldn't believe what he was hearing.

"Broderick," Houghton repeated.

"Well, I'll be damned!" Each word came out of the blacksmith's mouth with slow realization, punctuated with disbelief! "You mean?" . . .

"Margaret's brothers. Molly is her niece."

"Shit!" Buzz frowned. "Queerest thing I've ever heard, Cedric. So, is that it? I mean, you're done with the news?"

"Not quite, Buzz. Margaret's married name is Chisholm. You knew her husband, Rian, didn't you?"

"Sure, sure. Margaret was always proud of her Irishman. Now where are you going, Judge?"

"But you didn't know her first husband did you?" His name was Reagan. Both popular Irish names, right?"

"Yeah, I guess so. Rian sure is, anyway. But Chisholm isn't. Where'd that come from?"

"Margaret told me they changed their married name from Reagan to hide from her violent husband. They chose Chisholm; figured it was a nice, safe name.

Now, both Rian and Reagan come from an old Gaelic name for King or King's son. I believe our Mr. King is actually Brendan Reagan, Margaret's bitter husband."

"Hell of a long time to carry that rage within; he must be on the fringe of insanity."

"And shrewd with it," Houghton agreed. They drained the bottle; Buzz set it atop the nearest post.

"Now I'll go ask Moe those questions you posed." Calder strode to where Moe was still leaning against a birch tree, hands tied, noose dangling above his head.

<><><>

"So, what's the play, Calder?" Houghton asked as Buzz rejoined him. He noticed the blacksmith was walking much slower, obviously deep in thought, as he returned to the corral.

"We're taking them all to Warm Springs, Cedric. Should be there before nightfall. Then tomorrow morning we'll pull about ten-twelve men together and ride out to the *Snake Eyes*.

Moe claims he spent two days up at the ranch, where he first met Whitey and a few of the regular crew. Says he watched the new warehouse being built, picked up the pay for the cattle drive, and was asked to stay on, as King said, *until the job is done*."

"Did he know what the job was or is?"

"Doesn't have a clue unless it was to get rid of us 'assassins'."

"Did he tell you what he and his boys are being paid for their work so far?"

"$35.00 a month each, and promised a huge bonus when the *job* is done."

"And Old Lady Ingraham?" Houghton asked.

"If she was there, Moe says he never saw her. Says the only women he saw was kitchen help -- two young Mexican women in the kitchen."

Chapter 57

Not surprisingly, no other teams of men were back when Calder and those with him arrived. They had decided on the Wesley's barn to house the five prisoners.

"Petch!" Buzz called out, "you and the other fellows tie these five to the posts; the judge and I will bring you back some grub."

The last of the sun had already slid over the top edge of the western slope and most of the sky's color was gone. It was bitterly cold, Calder noted. Large flakes of snow were beginning to swirl to the ground around them. Difficult to read the weather at this altitude. *Glad to be home.*

The two men walked into Maude's, stamping their boots on the mat before seating themselves. The blacksmith's watch said it was 5:40 p.m. Some of the regulars were already gone, but there were still a few waiting for their suppers.

A group of four men at a far wall caught Calder's eye. The four seemed in sober and serious discussion, not noticing the two newcomers. *Not residents,* Buzz thought. *Rough looking, all of them.*

"Any of your stew left, Billie?" Calder asked the smiling young waitress who came to their table.

"Sure is. Don't know where most of the men are tonight. Almost a full pot left."

"Ask Maude how much for the whole pot. I have a few to feed. I'll need a dozen bowls and spoons as well."

Billie disappeared. Calder glanced at the four in the corner, leaned over and whispered, "Four men sitting across the room. Not from around here."

"I saw them. One doing most of the talking has white hair under his hat. Did you notice?"

"I saw."

Billie returned with Maude.

"You feeding an army, Calder?" Maude asked.

"No. My crew has some prisoners over at Wesley's. Haven't eaten since early. I'll bring your empty pot back, Maude."

Houghton noted the four across the way momentarily stopped their conversation and looked up at the name *Calder.* Their discussion continued, he thought, with more animation. He was struck by the furtive, yet obvious glances and the occasional guffaw.

"Well, let's see," Maude was saying, "pot's almost full. I figure thirty bowls left. Should be somewhere around four dollars worth."

"That's fair enough. I'll bring all your dishes back in an hour or so and your money in the morning."

"Just a reminder, Buzz, you know I close up at 8 p.m."

"Oh, I'll be here, Maude," Buzz raised his voice just enough to make sure the four heard him. "Wesley's barn isn't that far."

"I'll put the bowls and spoons in a gunny sack. You'll have to carry the pot by the handles."

"Ha!" Calder laughed. "What you're saying is 'don't trip over anything on the way to the barn'."

The two men stood at the counter as Billie put bowls and spoons in the sack. Maude brought the pot from the kitchen and opened the door. Houghton turned to say goodnight to Billie, making sure he scanned the entire room.

"They'll be coming out in a few minutes, Calder. We'd have to run to beat them to Wesley's. Best bet is to cut through the alley and double back behind them. Problem is, I left my rifle in the barn."

"Yeah, mine, too," Calder admitted. He thought for a moment. "I have an idea. Give me the bag. You take the pot and hightail it to the barn. I'll delay those boys long enough for us to bring Chuck and the others running."

"You sure?"

"Bernard Medders and his wife are dining in there right now. He owes me a favor. Now go!"

Calder turned and poked his head in the door. Looking around he spotted the Medders and walked directly toward their table.

"Hey, Bernie! It is you!" Buzz kept his voice low, but just enough to make the four curious strangers aware. "I thought I saw you."

He let out a wheeze and continued, "Sorry, I've been so far behind I think I can see my butt up there ahead of me. I'll be working on your project next."

"Hi, Buzz. What's up? Haven't seen you in a while. What project is that?"

"You know." He turned to Mrs. Medders, "Hi, Ma'am, may I borrow Bernie for a minute. I need him to refresh my memory on that, uh, on a project I'm doing for him. I won't keep him long . . . promise."

"Sure, I suppose," she said, frowning. Bernie shrugged his shoulders, stood, and followed Buzz out the door.

"Keep your voice down, Bernie," Buzz whispered. "Two things I need: your gun, and to know your wife's birthday."

"What on earth are you talking about, Calder?" he screwed his face into a question mark as he whispered back.

"Your wife's birthday, Bernie. When is it? I need to create a believable story when you go back inside. When June asks you, tell her I'm making something for her as a surprise, and I needed final dimensions."

"December 4 . . . but why the gun?"

"Don't you even breathe a word to June about the gun."

"It's them four fellas, ain't it? They look mighty hard, Buzz. Not from around here for sure."

"I have five of their men in the Wesley barn, but like a damn fool, I left my rifle in the barn as well. Didn't figure on running into trouble just now."

"Okay, Calder, but ain't no bullets in it."

"What?" Buzz exploded. "No bullets? Shit -- never mind. Give it to me anyway!"

Buzz slipped the gun into his belt. "When you go back inside, have a smile on your face. June's going to ask, but just let her know it's a birthday surprise. Don't go staring at those four fellows."

The blacksmith turned and trotted in the direction of the Wesley barn, cursing Bernie Medders under his breath.

"I don't think they're coming, Buzz." Houghton was sitting on the back of an old hay wagon, finishing his second helping of Maude's stew.

The blacksmith strapped on his big handgun. "I think you're right," he agreed. He checked his watch and scanned the street for any movement. "It's been fifteen minutes; wonder what brings them to Warm Springs?"

Brody, one of the young men, chimed in, "Maybe they're waiting for the cover of darkness -- as my mother used to say -- to do their evil deed."

"Damn!" Buzz almost shouted. "Of course! Margaret's place! "

Houghton was quick to agree. "I'm not much of a gunslinger. Leave one of the fellows with me to watch over these prisoners; take the others and get moving."

"I'll stay," Chuck volunteered, "my arm is feelin' a mite wore out from bein' shot. Ain't as tough as I thought."

"Fine. You two ready to ride?"

"Yessir, Mr. Calder," Brody and Petch affirmed. The three men cinched down their saddles and rode out of the old barn, headed for Margaret's.

Houghton gathered the pot, bowls and spoons. "I'll take these and that gun back to Maude's, Chuck."

"You going to be okay?" the young man asked.

"Oh, sure. Be right back."

Chapter 58

Calder and his two companions trotted up Margaret's drive. Strange! There were no hoof prints showing on her snow-covered drive. Petch tossed all the reins over the hitching post rail while the others rapped on the side entry.

Molly answered. "Hi, Uncle Buzz, fellas, come in. Shut the door. It's cold out there."

"We won't stay, Molly; we were afraid those trying to kill you and Margaret were on their way here for another try."

"We're safe so far. What made you think they might be heading here tonight?"

"We think we saw your white-haired killer at Maude's tonight, having supper with three other ruffians. We didn't recognize any of them, but your description of that fellow fits, right down to the scar on his cheek."

"He's in town?!" Molly's face grew suddenly stormy. She ran to get her coat and gloves.

"Margaret!" she shouted. "Margaret!" she ran into the bedroom, handed Margaret a loaded shotgun and announced, "Uncle Buzz is here. I need to run to Warm Springs. I'll be back as soon as I finish some long overdue business." She grabbed her rifle.

"What are you talking about, Molly? Come back here! Buzz! Are you here? Please come in here!

Now, what is all this?" Margaret demanded.

"Good evening, Ma'am. I have a few fellows with me trying to chase down some killers. We thought they were headed this way, but it seems they are still in Warm Springs. We're on our way back, Molly is determined to accompany us. That's it in a nutshell."

"No, it's not!" Molly said defiantly. "One of those killers is the white-headed gang leader that killed my whole family seven years ago. I even the score tonight!"

"Oh, Molly! You can't go up against a killer like him and his gang!"

"I am! I will! Believe me, Margaret! I've been waiting for the day, and this is it! You can't stop me, and neither can you, Uncle Buzz!

If you want to stay away, fine, but I'll gun him down the second I see him. I've promised Mom and Dad, and I won't let them down!" She flew out the door and went to saddle her horse.

"Margaret," Buzz placed his hand on her shoulder, "I know your relationship to Molly. I'll try to watch over her," he said, shaking his head.

"Thank you, Buzz. Strong-minded girl, that one."

"I can leave one of my young men here to be with you if you'd feel safer, Margaret."

"No. I'll be fine. You'd best run along if you're going to catch that young lady."

The three men and young lady reached Warm Springs just in time to join Maude as she locked up.

"No, Mr. Calder, I don't know where those four mean-looking fellas went when they left here." Maude chuckled. "My, they were mean-looking, weren't they? But their money was as good as the next guy . . . ha! actually better. You haven't paid me yet."

"I told you I'd" . . .

"Buzz! Just kidding! I know you'll pay me tomorrow. Those four fellows were still here when the judge brought my pot and bowls back. They left shortly after."

"You notice if Medders got his gun back?"

"He didn't. I have it under my counter inside. Do you want it? It's not loaded."

"I know," Calder shook his head. "Bernie gave me an unloaded gun to defend myself! I don't know why a fella would walk around with an empty gun on his hip. But then . . . I did it myself, didn't I?" Buzz shook his head at the thought. They all bid Maude a good night and walked their horses to the Wesley Barn.

"Coming in!" Buzz announced when they reached the entrance to the barn.

<><><>

"Come ahead!" Houghton responded. "Didn't you meet up with them?" the judge asked.

"No. They've disappeared. Maude says they left shortly after you." Calder turned to the young men. "You may as well head home, fellas. It's been a long day. Be back by 7 a.m. tomorrow if you want to join the group headed for the *Snake Eyes*."

The three agreed; they stood to leave when a bundle of flaming straw burst through the sliding doorway, casting shadows and illuminating the first twenty feet inside the barn, ending harmlessly on the dirt floor.

Gunfire erupted from outside; more bundles of burning straw came flying inside. Brody dove for cover just inside the barn wall out of sight, Calder did the same on the opposite side of the door.

"Hey, Blacksmith!" came a raspy voice. "We waited for you to git back, Blacksmith!" the screeching from outside continued. "Wouldn't be a party without you! I don't like leavin' a job half done!"

More gunfire came through the open door. Most of those inside scurried to the rear of the darkened barn for something to offer cover. There was very little. Buzz pulled the big pistol from it's holster and waited for a target. *C'mon, show yourself!* he thought. He worried the shooting from outside could wound -- or worse -- the five prisoners as well as his crew or the judge.

"And that little girl that came in there with you, Blacksmith," the voice went on, "she's the daughter of those sheepherders, ain't she? A bonus fer sure. After we do you, we'll be ridin' out to the old lady's place and take care of her as well. It's gonna be a great night."

Another volley of shots brought a yelp of pain from inside. Houghton called out, "Who's hurt?" just as a cry of triumph from outside: "I got one!" could be heard.

"They shot me -- Reginold Montgomery. Hit me in my belly. I'm hurting real bad."

"Whitey! Is that you?" Abbot yelled at the shooters outside. "Boss, you jus' shot Reggie! You can't jus' shoot in here like that. They's Moe, me, an' the others, an' our horses!"

"You shouldn'ta got caught, Abbot!" came the reply as two more slugs came flying inside.

"Untie me," Abbot whispered at those around him, "filthy swine! They'll pick us off sure as shit! You need my gun. I'm a better shot than most. Untie me! Give me a gun!"

Houghton looked to Calder, faintly visible -- leaning against the door. Calder nodded his head.

"Against my better judgment," the judge said, "but we are in a desperate situation." Houghton untied Abbot and handed him a rifle.

Bullets kept slamming into the back walls or zinging off pieces of rusting equipment; a horse was shot and was thrashing on the dirt floor.

Another large, fiery bundle of straw approached the entry, ready to be thrown inside. Abbot caught a glimpse of the torch lighter and fired. A look of surprise flooded over the man's face as he fell.

A fellow gunman tried to pick up the torch to throw it inside. Calder took the opportunity. The big .50 calibre gun roared. Their opponents were down to two. The blacksmith rubbed his sore arm where the recoil tried to tear his shoulder from its socket.

As the man was screaming, the other two outside were trying to determine their next move.

Abbot chose the moment. He ran outside, looking for Whitey. Instead, he found the other killer. "You tried to kill me and Moe, Flint." Flint was trying to process what Abbot said as Abbot pulled the trigger. Then, with Flint's rifle he aimed and fired at a fleeing Whitey.

He walked back inside; handed Calder both weapons.

"Think I winged him, Mr. Calder, but I'm not sure."

Brody looked outside. "I guess that's all of them. You think Whitey will head to Margaret's place? I'm ready to ride there right now. Let's finish it tonight!"

"I won't be going anywhere," Chuck said. "They shot my horse."

"I'm going!" Molly was adamant.

"I think we should, just to be on the safe side," Buzz agreed. " Molly, I'll take you and Brody. That's all we need fellas. The rest of you get some sleep. With luck we're going to end this thing tomorrow at the *Snake Eyes.*"

"Is that you, Molly?" Margaret asked, clutching her double-barreled shotgun. "Is Buzz with you?"

"Nobody's here, Maggie." The raspy voice came from the kitchen. "Just you an' me. I'm takin' you back to Brendan tonight. I can make it easy for you. I can also cut your liver out and haul you to the ranch over a saddle. Your choice, Maggie."

"Oh! It's you, Whitey!" Margaret stiffened at the voice.

"I'd recognize that raspy screech anywhere! How long has it been, Whitey? Twenty-two, twenty-three years? Still Brendan's same little, chicken-shit puppy dog, huh?"

"Hey, Maggie! I understand you don't get outta bed very much these days," he laughed, wincing at her insults as he came down the hallway toward the bedroom. "Shame you're in such pain. Brendan hoped you'da died in that fire an' be done with it, but" . . .

A hand showed itself on the door jamb. Margaret pulled one trigger. Blood spattered against the door.

"You bitch! You shot me! Now I ain't givin' you no courtesies."

Whitey rounded the corner, thinking Margaret's shotgun was a single-barrel. He saw the second barrel just before the twelve gauge almost took his head off.

Calder and his companions were just fifty feet from the house when they heard both reports of the gun.

<><><>

Calder walked into the bedroom. "Are you alright, Margaret?"

"I think that gun ripped out all the stitches the doc put in my back, Buzz." She sighed a long sigh and began to cry. Once she started she couldn't control the sobbing. Buzz sat on the side of the bed and held her hand. "I'm so sorry you're in such pain, Margaret."

"Oh, Buzz, it's nothing to do with the back. Just years and years of anguish. It's still not over, is it?"

"Not yet, Margaret, but soon."

He turned to Molly. "She could probably use some of that pain killer, Molly. Sorry for leaving you to clean up the hallway."

Calder dragged the lifeless body to his horse, roped it over the saddle, and bid both women good night.

Chapter 59

It was 5 a.m. In the Wesley house. Annie first lit a candle from a red-hot ember still glowing in the potbelly kitchen stove. With the candle she lit the kerosene lantern and the various candles throughout the house. Back in the kitchen she stoked the embers into flame and added two more chunks of split firewood. Her day had begun.

Annie checked on Wally, tucking the quilt around his frail body. He looked the ghost of his old self, but he was still breathing. She shook her head; *it wouldn't be long, now, poor old bugger.* Wally wouldn't last more than a week, she as sure of it. In his prime, Wally was a stalwart; time and trial had taken his strength and his will.

She had heard gunfire in or near the barn the previous evening. She considered investigating as she trudged through the snow to the outhouse shortly after midnight, but decided morning would be soon enough; no sense in sticking her nose into other folks' concerns. As she carried her lantern to the outhouse she noted with satisfaction that the barn was still standing. Back outside, she began to pick her way the short distance toward the barn. *Now I'll snoop*, she thought.

Several riders were approaching -- one was Calder. "Mrs. Wesley! Are you alright?" He pulled the roan to a stop and dismounted. "Lady, what are you doing out here this time of morning? It's only a few minutes after 6. You'll catch your death a'cold!"

"Mr. Calder, what's going on in our barn? Gunfire last night, and now looks like you're getting ready for a meeting. Did you find out who killed those teamsters? Did you find the wagons?"

"We're getting closer, Annie. We're putting a group together this morning to follow up on a hunch. How's Wally?"

"Wally's fine for a dying man. A light wind will blow him into heaven. What was the shooting last night?"

"Might as well come on in, Annie." He set her on the horse and walked her into the barn. Leaning against the open door were four corpses. One was unrecognizeable, except for white hair. Calder jerked a thumb in their direction. "Part of the crew responsible for Margaret's fire."

Annie was shocked to see inside the barn about a dozen riders sitting astride their mounts. Most of them she knew. Next, her eyes focused on the four sitting in a circle roped together with guns trained on them. "And these?"

"The rest of the crew."

"Oh! The lucky ones, eh?"

"Except for him, Ma'am," Moe said, pointing at the young fellow lying in the dirt toward the front west wall.

"Boy's not dead," Calder told her. "We sent Chuck for Doc Ford. Should be here any time now."

"Boy looks bad," Annie said. "Perhaps Doc can look at Wally while he's here. Just a visit, mind. Not much he can do."

The troupe of twelve, with Calder at the front prepared to head for the *Snake Eyes Ranch*. They left Chuck behind to guard the prisoners. Houghton had retired to the hotel the night before, and today he had some business to

The BLACKSMITH   and   *The Sheepherder's Daughter*
attend with Royston.

Doc Ford and Annie Wesley stood with Chuck and bid the riders goodbye.

"Chuck, I'll escort Annie up to the house to have a visit with Wally, then I'll be back to look at your arm."

Pointing at the young outlaw on the floor, Annie, protested, "You take care of this youngster, Daniel. I'll make my way up to the house. Come see me after. Wally isn't going anywhere."

"I'll walk you up there, Ma'am," Chuck volunteered.

"Young man," Annie argued, "I've been in blizzards and floods more times than I can count. I don't need your assistance getting to my own house with 5 inches of snow on the ground; thank you just the same."

Chuck smiled, "Take my arm, Mrs. Wesley. I could use a hot cuppa coffee." She took his arm and squeezed it.

"You know how to make coffee don't you, Sonny? Bag of coffee is on the counter beside the pail of water. Ladle is in the pail. Make enough for me. Put the kettle on the stove; I'll check on Wally and be back in a minute."

She was back in less than five minutes. "I'll finish up here, my young friend." She poured the steaming coffee through a sieve into two mugs and handed one to Chuck. "My! You make strong coffee! Wally used to make the strongest coffee I've ever tasted. Yours would give him a run for his money! I have some cookies. Would you like one?"

"Yes, please! Ma'am. How's Wally doin' this mornin'?"

Annie brought a ceramic cookie jar to the table, took one for herself and pushed the jar toward Chuck.

"Wally loved my butter cookies. When we were courting he rode seven miles; told Ma he only came for my butter cookies. Have another, Son. Wally won't mind."

The smile disappeared from Chuck's face. The cookie he was dunking disappeared to the bottom of his mug as he stared at Annie. She sat in pensive resolve, both hands wrapped around her mug.

"You mean" . . .

Annie only took a sip of coffee and nodded.

"What will you do, Annie?" Chuck asked.

"What every other widow does, Son. Get by. I've gone to see Royston; he tells me there are a couple of people interested in buying the farm. I don't owe anyone anything -- not a nickel -- and God is good. He's taken care of Wally and me over the years. He's not about to discard an old widow woman at this point in her life." She took another sip from her mug.

"Go tell Doc Ford there's no sense in coming up here, just take care of that young man that was belly-shot. I have a few things to do for Wally before I put him in the ground." She drained her coffee and stood.

Chuck knew his visit was over. He stood, picked his hat off the table and gave her a nod. "I'll let Doc know. And, Ma'am, I'm sure sorry." He walked back to the barn and informed Doc Ford.

"Couldn't save the boy, either," Doc Ford shook his head -- "lost too much blood. Help me drag him over with the others, Chuck, then I'm heading home.

I have another would-be killer there. His name's Buster. Been keeping him alive; should be well enough to sit a horse by now. I'll stop by Maude's to see if I can find someone to escort him over here." He stopped long enough to shake his head at the five deceased men leaning against the door. "Too much killing, Chuck."

Chapter 60

One of the servers from Maude's was on her way to work; Chuck flagged her down.

"Miss Alice!"

"Hi, Chuck! Whatcha doin' in the Wesley barn?"

"Guarding prisoners."

"Guarding prisoners? What prisoners?" she took a few steps, laughing, then stopped short upon seeing the five lifeless chaps against the door. "Chuck!" she screamed, "they're dead!"

"Not those, Alice. These fellas," he said, pointing to the four in the circle. "And that's why I called out to you . . . would you ask Maude to whip up enough scrambled eggs, bacon and coffee for five starving men." Chuck turned to the bound men, "Scrambled eggs, fellas?"

"Bread and butter, too?" one of them asked.

Alice took one last look at those lined up along the door and nodded her head.

"Oh, Alice, please have a fellow deliver the food. I need to be relieved for a half hour to go to Doc Ford's place."

"I'll see who I can rustle up." She walked a few steps, turned back, "Scrambled eggs and bacon coming up."

Half an hour later Chuck saw two figures coming from the direction of Maude's carrying some platters and a big pot of coffee. As they approached he recognized the young kid, Elmer, but the other one evaded his memory until the fellow spoke -- Orren Juneau, the mail wagon driver.

"Orren! When did you hit town? I didn't recognize you at first. Hi, Elmer!"

"Grossinger, right?" Orren greeted him.

"Good memory! Just Chuck will do. Didn't mean to rope you into bringin' the grub over."

"Ha! Just got in long enough to have one bite of steak, then some gal came in looking for a rough, tough jailer-type to watch over five dead guys for a half hour," Orren laughed. "I knew I was the guy that could handle the job."

"Sorry. Didn't mean to take you away from your steak."

"Brought it with me; now where are these *mal muchachos?*"

"I brung the coffee an' mugs," Elmer interjected. "Mugs, plates an' stuff is in the bag."

"I need to go have a pee first," Moe said. They all voiced their needs after sitting for so long. "We ain't gonna try to run off, Mister."

Chuck allowed them, one at a time, to use the outhouse. He sent Elmer to stand guard twenty feet from the facility, with strict instructions to yell if a fellow tried to run.

"When you come back, wash up at the horse trough outside, wipe your hands on some straw, and come in for breakfast."

Everything went smoothly. As the prisoners were eating, Chuck picked out a horse -- a big black, still saddled, with sheath but no rifle.

"Who's horse is this?" Chuck inquired. No one knew. "Mine now." He pushed his rifle into the sheath and left Orren and Elmer to guard the others while he rode to the Ford's to pick up Buster. The horse sported a *Snake Eyes* brand on its rump.

An hour later, while taking the dishes back, Elmer stopped and watched as Doc Ford returned to the Wesley barn with a companion in his buggy. Trailing behind was Chuck on his black mare.

Fifteen minutes later two more visitors joined the group -- banker Royston and Judge Houghton.

"Orren!" Judge Houghton smiled and shook the mail carrier's hand. "Saw your wagon in front of Maude's. Have any mail for me?"

"I think so. I haven't opened my bag yet, but I think I saw your name on two or three packages."

"Don't leave town. I hope to add more to the bag."

"I'm heading for Tucson. Why don't I catch you on my way back north?"

"Okay," the judge agreed. "While you're grabbing my mail, Royston and I will go up to see Wally."

"You haven't heard?" Orren asked. "Wally's dead."

"Died this morning about 8 a.m." Chuck added. "I was with Annie at the time."

"How's Annie taking it?"

"Expected it at any time. Told me without shedding a tear."

"Damn shame," Houghton said looking at Royston. "Really doesn't change anything I suppose. You ready?"

"Sure," the banker replied.

The two men walked to the Wesley home. Annie invited them in. Over a cup of coffee, they signed a purchase agreement for the Wesley farm to be used as a New Mexico Territorial facility -- housing government offices, sheriff's office, jail, and more -- operated and managed by Warm Springs personnel yet to be determined.

The sale included certain rights for either or both of the Wesleys to maintain their homestead to their last days. The barn would be converted or rebuilt as soon as possible to house the physical Territorial space as deemed necessary.

Annie signed the papers willingly and sighed. "I wondered how I would be able to carry on," she said. "I have no one else in the family to inherit our farm. I'm happy this place will be used for the good of the town."

"I'll send someone by here every day, Annie. Anything you need you just tell him. He'll make sure you get it."

She laughed. "I'm not a cripple, Mr. Royston. Maybe once a week for now. That would be fine, I suppose.

Since you fellows are here, would you help me bring Wally out to the living room? I've already put some blankets on the divan, but I can't move him by myself."

The two men accompanied Annie into the bedroom. Wally was laid out in bed dressed in his Sunday best -- a dark gray suit, black tie, and polished shoes. The banker looked at Judge Houghton, shrugged his shoulders, and smiled at Annie.

"We'll be happy to, Ma'am."

They each took an end of the lifeless body and carried Wally to the divan.

"You have a wake service in mind, Mrs. Wesley?" the judge asked.

"I think so. Can you let Pastor Marshall know?"

"Of course," the banker assured her. "Doc Ford is still at the barn. We'll let him know."

Houghton picked up all the signed documents; the two men said their goodbyes. Turning to Royston, Houghton said, "Maybe Ford can stop by and see the undertaker as well; should make him happy to know he's being paid out of the territory coffers. A guaranteed $12.00 each."

"He' going to receive $12.00 for each of those criminals?"

"Yes, but he's responsible for building the boxes, digging the graves, burying each fellow, and supplying markers. How have you handled it before?"

"I've never asked, but the bad ones were probably dumped over a cliff for the coyotes. With someone like Wally, the cabinet maker will build a fancy coffin, some of the boys will dig the grave, and a collection will be taken up for all the work done."

"I like the community effort for residents, but $12.00 sounds more refined than coyote chow for a city, don't you think?" They both laughed and agreed it was.

Royston had a word in private with Doc Ford who nodded his head then climbed into his buggy and headed his horses toward the cabinet maker's shop.

Orren handed Houghton two packages, one thicker than the other. The mail carrier then bid the group a goodbye and walked away, Elmer at his side.

Houghton ripped the thin one open and smiled broadly. "Title deed came through for the young lady, Royston."

It was the deed to the six hundred-forty acre parcel -- now with Molly Broderick's name on the title.

"Well, don't that beat all," Moe had been listening to the conversation. He turned to Abbot and the others. "King don't even own that land! Sounds like he's been buildin' that bunkhouse fer somebody else."

"I'll bet it's that girl," said a pale Buster, who had joined the other culprits after having crawled down from Ford's buggy. "The girl that shot me out at that woman's place."

"Open up that other package, Judge," the banker said, smiling, "did the bank get the money?"

Houghton opened the bulky package. It indeed contained a Treasury note in the amount of $35,000.00 made out to The Territory of New Mexico-Southwestern Office-Warm Springs.

"Perfect!" Royston exclaimed. "I'll set up the draws for the widow and the building fund this morning."

Other papers were in the package as well -- directives, territorial procedures and regulations, selection of officials, chains of authority, and on and on...

'Take these as well, Abel. Put them in the bank's vault for safe-keeping. I expect to come down for the dedication of the building, but plans change . . . I can only hope so at this point. For now, let's get the building started. Oh! Before I forget, I'm heading out to see Margaret and Miss Broderick after lunch; do you want to ride out with me?"

"No, but you might tell them we need to open the general store soon. It seems like a year since the folks have been able to buy the goods they need. Maybe Molly can run half-days or some such arrangement for a few weeks. People are hurting for day to day necessities."

"I can certainly agree, Abel. I'll ask."

Elmer came running toward the barn from the center of town. "Floyd's back!" he shouted, "Jake's back, an' that young fella came back with him. He says he had a safe trip back and forth. He really likes Albuquerque. He's says he an' the kid are goin' to Jake's to worsh the dust outta their throats."

"I think I'll join them," the judge said. "I need to head back to Albuquerque in the next day or two myself; perhaps Floyd will ride shotgun for me. He likes Albuquerque."

Chapter 61

The band of riders neared the residence of the *Snake Eyes* spread. They had increased to sixteen men as Ted Willitson and three others from the *Eagle Spread* joined them above the fork which split off to the old *Dammer Homestead* -- now of course, Molly's 640 acre ranch.

The *Snake Eyes* ranch house sat atop a rock-faced knoll overlooking an open meadow that sloped upward to the base of the Black Mountain range to the north. Today it was dusted with the first snow of winter, but in the spring it would be transformed into a yellow and purple carpet of Mexican Poppies and Lupines as far as the eye could see.

As they approached, Buzz recalled happier times, sitting on the veranda enjoying a tea or something stronger with Ida Ingraham, looking out over God's tapestry.

Ida had always been a bit quirky. She had told him once that she had designed the meadow, right down to the color combination. She had walked out on the veranda, told the Creator exactly how she wanted it, He took notes, and the next spring her meadow popped up to perfection. Calder smiled. *Dear, sweet Ida -- she must be 80 by now -- if she's still alive.* He prayed so.

He was jolted from his idle musings when someone fired three rifle shots in the air. Calder held his arm up to halt the riders. "Looks like we won't have the warm welcome we were hoping for. They may have sentries posted all around this place. Spread out; find this sentry and disable him. Then let's regroup and decide how to proceed."

Brody whispered to Petch, pointing to a boulder above, "Puffs of white smoke. Gotta be the spot where those three shots came from."

"You behind the rock!" Petch yelled out. "Toss your rifle and come down here! We've killed four fellas in town, including Whitey!"

"Whitey's dead?" the man shouted, obviously in shock. "Cain't be!"

Calder moved up a ravine about fifty feet from the shooter, until he was almost parallel with the man. From this vantage point he could see movement from behind the boulder.

"Last evening, about 8 p.m. Mister," Buzz called out. "All four of them, and yes, Whitey was blown to kingdom come by a 12 gauge scattergun. Now, I can see you. I don't relish the idea of any more killing. Toss your rifle over the side of that rock and come down, please, or I'll be forced to put a bullet in your head!"

There was a brief hesitation, then, "Don't shoot!" The rifle clattered down the boulder's face. A youngster of no more than sixteen skidded and slid down the shale, landing on his rear no more than four feet from Brody. Brody tied his hands as the others gathered around.

"What's your name, Son?" Calder asked

"Fred Norton -- or Freddie."

"How many are up there, Freddie?"

"I think ten including me, but Shorty went to get the other six fellas over at the new bunkhouse, so we'll have fifteen or sixteen up there soon."

Willitson broke in, "Freddie, you ain't up there no more, an' those six ain't comin'. I suspect Shorty will keep ridin' once he sees the tracks of our horses in the snow. That leaves eight or nine at best. Now if you want to go back up and defend the place" . . .

"That won't happen!" Buzz cut in. He looked at the lad, "Son, who do you belong to? I expect you have kin up there."

"No family a'tall -- been driftin' on my own. Joined up with Flint, a fella who was workin' a sawmill on the *Little Black*, an' been sawin' with him ever since -- 'bout four months."

"You say Flint?" Petch asked.

"Yeah. Flint, Shorty, and Carlos. Whitey comes along ever so often and works half a day with us -- hard worker for an older fella -- you sure Whitey's dead?"

"Sure is, Freddie, an' so is Flint. Probably Carlos, too, but we didn't hear any other names," Petch said, soberly. "You can tell us when you get into town."

Calder had more questions. "Are Mr. King and Ida Ingraham up there this morning?"

"I don't know about no Ida Ingraham, but I'm sure Mr. King is there. I saw him earlier."

"Last question, Freddie. What do you know about four wagons full of merchandise?"

"We have an awful lot of stuff -- all sorts of things in our new storage barn. I don't know when it came in or how. I was out at the sawmill until two days ago."

Buzz turned Freddie over to an older gent in their group.

"Okay, fellas, Freddie, here, fired a warning to those at the ranch . . . they know we're here. From what the kid says we outnumber them about two to one. One or two of us should go down the trail toward the bunkhouse and cut off that Shorty fellow. Any volunteers?"

Two riders agreed and disappeared down the trail.

"We leave horses down here and work our way up slow and easy. Subdue these bastards without gunfire if at all possible, but defend yourself as you see fit. From what we've seen, almost all of King's people are hired killers. They won't give you any courtesies."

Buzz started up the craggy incline. Progress was slower than he would have liked in the ravine he chose -- snow had drifted into the low spots, in some places as much as a foot.

As he gripped his rifle he wondered if perhaps his posse of more than a dozen would have been smarter riding straight in from the east on the open trail. *These gloved hands don't add much comfort,* he thought. *It's damn cold!*

Shots rang out somewhere to Calder's left. He heard a cry of pain and more rifle fire. He decided to move up at a faster pace.

He heard voices above him -- at least two men in a heated conversation as they neared. He couldn't make out everything that was said, but by the tone and cursing, Buzz was certain the expletives were not directed at his outfit. In fact, he thought he heard them speak of mounting up and heading for California -- a thing he would applaud.

Being a fair poker player, Calder called out, "You, up there! Toss your guns down here, both of you! Then follow them down! Do it! Nice and easy! No one'll get hurt!"

The conversation above stopped. Calder waited a few seconds, then he shouted, "Hey, Tim! Looks like they'd rather die! They're coming straight at you!"

To his surprise a voice answered, "We're ready for them, Mr. Calder."

One of the two above shouted, "Hey! Wait a minute! You, down below! You the Warm Springs blacksmith?"

"I am! You coming down here so we don't have to hurt you?"

"Yeah, I think so. Me'n Sully, we didn't do nothin' bad, but Mr. King will say we did just to lay the blame on us. He's a murdering son of a bitch, that one. We gonna be okay, we come down?'"

"You're going to be just fine, unless we find out anything different."

"What do you mean , Mr. Calder?"

"Once we round up the entire crew, we'll ask questions about you and the others, but I think we've killed the worst of King's lot except the man, himself."

"Did you kill Whitey?"

"Lined up with four others against a barn door, all dead."

"Did you hear that, Sully?" the fellow said to his partner, "they killed Whitey."

Two rifles slid down the slope and buried themselves in the snow. The two men followed. Buzz roped their hands behind their backs and led them further down the hill to the fellow guarding Freddie.

"How many more up there?" Calder asked. "Freddie, here, figures nine were up there to begin with. Shorty went to bring Moe and his boys back from the new bunk, but we've already rounded them up and taken them to Warm Springs. So who's left?"

"Not sure now," one of them answered, "King an' Rodriguez for shore, Chico, Eddie, Porter, maybe Calhoun -- but there was a lot'o shootin' a few minutes ago, an' I think I saw Calhoun drop his rifle. I think he got hisself shot. Don't know who else."

"I'll be back," Buzz said. "Just make yourselves comfortable here with Vern."

He started to walk away when they all heard horses whinny. It was the *Eagle Ranch* riders that had gone to intercept Shorty. Ramos was leading a sorrel mare with a body tied over her saddle. Shorty.

"You boys should be happy you followed Mr. Calder's advice," Gerardo, the other rider, sighed. "We would have been forced to shoot you both. We heard you comin', an' had rifles pointing straight at you when he called out."

"You fellas ready to go up with me and finish the job?" Calder asked the newcomers. They nodded their heads, dropped the sorrel's reins, dismounted and followed the blacksmith up the hill.

Chapter 62

Molly was in the parlor, reading, when the judge rode up. There was no security in the barn. Houghton frowned. He walked his horse to the back porch, tied her off and knocked, his satchel in hand. Molly picked up her rifle and went to the kitchen window and saw Houghton at the outside door.

"Coming!" she sang out. "It's Judge Houghton, Margaret!" She opened the door to receive Houghton into the kitchen.

"You're here to see Margaret? I know she's awake. We were just talking."

"Good afternoon, Molly. Actually, I'd like to speak with both of you. Let's join Margaret in the bedroom."

"Margaret," Molly said, "are you decent? We're coming in."

"Sure . . . come in."

After greeting Margaret, the judge told them the latest news in town -- Wally Wesley had died at 8 a.m.; Santa Fe had approved funding for government offices in Warm Springs; the Wesley property had been purchased for construction of those offices. He went into the details of the purchase and the outline for the property's use.

The last piece of news was the *Dammer Homestead*. Houghton pulled the title deed from his satchel.

"Here you are, Miss Broderick. Signed, witnessed, and stamped with the seal of New Mexico in Santa Fe. You are officially the undisputed owner of that quarter-section. I don't know what your plans are for the property, but it has a brand new bunkhouse and corral."

Molly read and re-read the two-page document, almost in disbelief. She looked up at Houghton, "I don't know how to thank you and Uncle Buzz," she cried. "So I could sell it tomorrow if I want to, or put a herd of cattle or sheep on it?"

"You may do whatever, Molly, it's yours."

"Any ideas for the land, Molly?" Margaret asked.

"I'm going to think about it for a long time before I decide," Molly assured her.

"Now," the judge continued, "there's one more thing we need to discuss, and that's your general store. It needs to be up and running soon, ladies. A town will die without commerce, and" . . .

Margaret and Molly looked at each other and laughed.

"We were discussing that a half hour before you rode up," Margaret chuckled. "Molly will be in town tomorrow morning by 9 a.m. directly after she does a few chores around here."

"Right!" Molly chimed in. "I'll make known in town we are open for business. I was hoping Antonio would be back from his trip to *del Cobre* so we could start on the new building, but we'll be fine in Uncle Buzz's barn."

"Good! Good! Okay, ladies I'll be off. Incidentally, I'll be leaving for Albuquerque when the teams return to town. I do believe King will no longer be a problem, Margaret. I'll try to make another visit before I leave."

"Can you stay for a cup of tea, Judge?" Margaret asked.

"Afraid not. I have a few more things to do before day's end."

"Wait up!" Molly cried. She turned to Margaret. "I'm going to ride into town with the judge. Will you be okay? I'll be back before supper."

"Of course, Dear," Margaret laughed, patting her shotgun.

Molly raced into the parlor for the pricing sheets and inventory list, then scurried out the door.

Chapter 63

Calder and his two companions chose the same route up the slope that the horses had used coming down, and found the going quite negotiable. The house was now just a hundred yards to their left and perhaps thirty feet above them.

The rocks were straight up at this point; they looked for a spot to ascend. "We should go up next time we see a ravine," Ramos suggested. They all agreed. They took a few more steps, walking abreast; a rifle cracked from somewhere above, sending Ramos to his knees.

"My laig! My laig got hit, bad!"

"Did you see where the shot came from, Gerardo?" Buzz whispered.

"Just above! A red shirt in the trees!"

"Help me drag Ramos off the trail, behind that tree; you stay with him, I'm going up there."

Buzz got a foothold on a rock and pushed himself partway up; he looked for another rock to grip, either his feet or his hands. He reached for a jagged rock two feet above his head; a rifle report sounded. Instantly its projectile struck the snow just inches above his head, making an ominous *thunk* as the shell buried itself in the white powder. Calder said a silent prayer of thanks.

He scanned the trees above him, searching for the red

shirt. Not spotting it, he started a second attempt at the jagged rock, then stopped. He saw a glint in the trees above. He eased himself back down to the trail, crouched and snaked forward about fifteen feet along the four foot rock face.

Hugging the rock wall, he peered back to where he had seen the sun gleaming off the barrel of a rifle. He couldn't see all of the shooter, but he saw enough of the red shirt to take a shot. He pulled the trigger.

Calder didn't wait to watch the sniper in the red shirt tumble down from his perch; instead he crouched and ran forward to a ravine created by a wash between the rocks that led up to the level of the ranchhouse. Seeing no one, he relaxed for a moment to reload his rifle and determine his next move. He proceeded up the hill using the trees and boulders along the ravine to provide cover.

Gunfire erupted. Calder flattened himself against a rock then proceeded cautiously -- no lead was heading toward him. He reached the top of the ravine and poked his head up. Willitson and Petch were in a gun battle with three of King's men. All three were in plain view to Calder while crouching behind boulders. None of the three saw the blacksmith as he crept behind them.

He settled himself behind a tree, only 25 feet behind them, aimed his powerful handgun at the burly one on the end, and shouted "Drop your guns!"

All three started to turn around. "Do not turn around!" he warned. "Now drop your weapons!"

The big man in front of him whirled, rifle in hand . . . Calder's gun boomed before the rifle could even come to the man's shoulder, blowing him backward dand smashing against the rock he had been crouching behind. The other two immediately dropped their rifles and raised their hands in the air.

Petch stood and walked forward. "Shoot'em or shackle'em, Boss?" he asked.

"You have rope, Petch?"

"Enough'ta hang'em both."

"No hanging today, Petch. We'll hog-tie them, hands behind their backs, and tie them to two separate trees. Ted, come on down here and give us a hand."

While they were binding the two to the trees they heard distant gunfire -- several rifle reports and a handgun.

Task done, Buzz questioned the two. "Your names?"

"I'm Porter, an' he's Chico; an' you jus' shot our frien' Arturo with thet big cannon a'yourn."

"Where would that shooting be coming from, Porter?"

"Sounds like the barn or the warehouse; whaddya think, Chico?"

"Barn, I bet," Chico said, nodding his head. "Good places to hide . . . and shoot."

"Who else is with King besides Rodriguez?"

"Since Whitey's not here, just Rodriguez. Then two-three others up there in the barn." Chico scratched his head. "Wonder why Whitey didn't show up yet," he mused aloud.

"Because he's dead!" Porter blurted out. "These fellas shot'im. Ain't that right, Mister?"

"No," Buzz answered nonchalantly. "Oh, he's dead, all right. Happened just last night. A woman shoved a scatter gun in his face and pulled the trigger." Calder casually reloaded his .50 calibre pistol. "So, like I said fellas, I didn't do it, but he is quite dead."

Porter looked with amazement at the size of the cartridge. "Holy cow! Look at the size of them bullets fer that cannon, Chico! No wonder Arturo was tossed back, ass over teakettle!"

"Shall we head to the barn, Boss?" Petch asked.

Buzz thought a moment. "Ramos was leg-shot back a little way on the trail. I left Gerardo with him and came on ahead. I need one of you to go back and help Gerardo carry Ramos down where a few others are being held. Vern's watching over them."

"I'll go," Petch said.

He started to trot down the trail when Calder sang out, "Hey Petch! Just above the spot where the group is gathered there's a red-shirted body; drag that ol' boy down and stack him up with the rest of them down there. Rascal nearly got me! You can keep his rifle!"

"We'll find him!"

Calder and Willitson checked their prisoners one last time, then began to pick their way toward the barn and the newly-constructed storage shed.

"I have the feeling King and Rodriguez are holed up in the ranch-house," Calder said, "but let's set our sights on the hired help first. Petch and Gerardo should be joining us in ten or fifteen minutes, and we should be joining up with the main party of our men from Warm Springs."

"What baffles me, Calder, is how King can attract so many riders, willing to defend his violent behavior. Just who does he think he is?"

"I suspect he's made promises that he doesn't intend to honor. A couple of the boys we rounded up at the new bunkhouse were promised a *huge bonus once the job was done,* as one of them said."

"Yeah," Willitson shook his head, "but we're talking twenty, maybe thirty men! How in hell is that possible?"

"I suspect, though I'm not a hundred percent sure, King has a deep-seated jealousy and hatred for the folks of Warm Springs. He had Whitey and some other of his goons going to Mozura and different places to recruit all the lowlifes and layabouts they could find with promises of great rewards for joining his ring of killers. We have one in Warm Springs right now by the name of Buster who" . . .

A bullet whizzed so close to Calder's head he began to

perspire as he flattened himself on the snow. The bullet made an ominous *thud* as it slammed into an aspen tree just behind his left shoulder.

"You were saying?" Ted asked, smiling at the blacksmith. The *Eagle* drover was crouched behind a boulder, rifle at the ready. "Sorry Boss," he continued, soberly, "we weren't paying attention."

"I am now!" Calder said as he rolled behind the boulder next to Willitson. "Don't think I've ever had a scare like that before," he said, brushing the snow from his beard and clothes. "My fault, Ted. I'm the one who's sorry!" *That's the second time today I've had a close call with a bullet!* he thought. *Be more careful, old man!*

"Hey! You up there!" Buzz yelled. "What's your name?"

"Who wants to know?" came an answering voice.

"Buzz Calder from Warm Springs! You just shot an aspen tree -- it's not hurt bad, but it may require some attention. So, what's your name?"

"What the hell's the matter with you, mister? Why'd ya' wanna know my name, fer?"

"So I can mark it on your tombstone!"

"Yer a funny son-of-a-bitch, ain'cha? Poke yer head up'n I'll tell ya my name."

"Poke your head up, toss your rifle, and I'll save your life, Son."

"Just keep flappin' yore lips, Mister. I'll boot yore sorry ass over a cliff into the river. You an' yore friend! . . . Hey! an' don't call me son!"

"Okay, I'll just write, 'Here lies a gunfighter -- at least a would-be gunfighter -- no aim, no name, a shame -- now just dead'. How's that sound, Sonny?"

"Asshole!" came the reply. Another rifle report. Snow flew off the rock above Calder's head. Willitson rolled to his left to see where the shot came from -- Calder to the right. Ted aimed and fired near the puff of smoke, Calder waited.

They heard laughter as the culprit shifted to again raise his rifle. Calder saw an arm and pulled the trigger. A cry of pain was followed by a figure staggering from behind the rocks.

"Aghh! You bastard! You just shot my wrist half off!" he screamed.

"Can you still shoot, Son?" Calder asked him.

"The man lurched forward, dropping the weapon as he plowed toward them, leaving a trail of scarlet in his wake. He mouthed something, then fell headlong into the white stuff, not thirty feet from them.

Ted was astounded. "Is he dead, Calder?"

"I don't think so, Ted. Fainted I expect; a lot of blood in the snow. I'm going to go get him and drag him back. Cover me in case he has a partner."

Buzz scrambled to the fallen outlaw; there were no others in the vicinity. He flipped the culprit on his back and took a look at his whiskered face. Mid-twenties, he surmised. The eyelids were fluttering. "In shock are we?" he asked the young, would-be killer. There was no response. His wrist definitely needed medical attention.

Buzz grabbed one of the fellow's boots and dragged him behind a boulder. Ted joined them. "Look at the way that bullet hit him, Calder. Freaky shot for sure. Looks like your bullet hit him between his fingers, busted up most of the bones in his hand and came out at his wrist! An' he's bleedin' like a stuck pig. I think he's gonna be dead inside an hour."

"Damn shame," Buzz said, shaking his head. He took his long coat off and ripped a sleeve from his shirt. He tossed the sleeve to Ted. "Wrap this around his arm just below the elbow and tie it off, tight!" He put his coat back on.

"We get to a stove soon enough we can save him, but that hand is gonna have to come off."

"Why you doin' this, Calder? That feller woulda killed

you if he had the chance!"

Before he could answer, Petch and Gerardo caught up with them.

"Who's your friend?" Petch asked.

"Never got his name. Need to take his hand off and cauterize the wound. He's in shock right now, but his hand will never be right again -- you can see how mangled it is."

"This coterizen' thing -- it's put in fire, yes?"

"Yes, Gerardo, fire. *Fuego,*"

"We have fire, Señor Calder," he declared.

"Yes, we do," Petch joined in. "The boys have a little campfire going -- to keep the chill off. I guess I can take him back and do the deed, I have a hatchet in my saddle pack. I can take care of his arm and cauterize it. Then I guess just wrap it in a cloth, right? I've seen fellas with stumps before. I can do it."

"Good. I doubt he'll wake up."

"Just one question, Calder," Petch shook his head, "why are you so interested in saving the kid? He'd a killed you and every one of us, given the chance."

"Conscience, I guess. I was taunting him just a bit ago, now it's not so funny. Hell, look at him. He's just a kid; barely old enough to grow whiskers. I figure he was talked into being a shooter by King or Whitey and got sucked into the thrill of it."

"Gerardo, c'mon, I need your help again," Petch said to the big Mexican drover from the *Eagle Ranch.* "By the way, we found your 'red shirt', Calder. Nobody recognized him. Just another drifter I expect."

The barn loomed in front of Calder and Willitson as they continued up the hill. They turned to see Petch and Gerardo dragging the young fellow over the side of a hill and disappear.

"You're late, Ted!" Wilbur, one of the *Eagle* hands cried out. "They're all rounded up, nice and tidy-like."

"Any of 'em still breathin'?" Ted asked.

"I don't know fer sure but I don't think so. Why'd ya ask?"

"Calder, here, has a soft spot fer killers; thinks a kind word will turn 'em. All we need to do is bust 'em up some first, then he takes over, asks the doc down in Warm Springs to fix 'em up, so's he can turn 'em into deacons at the church."

"Alright, fellas, you've had your fun. How many, Wilbur?"

"Five of 'em, Mr. Calder. Never seen any of 'em before. Strange, cuz you'd think we'd run into 'em on the trail or sum'thin'."

Buzz nodded in agreement. "And our boys?"

"Cezar got hit bad. Couple of fellas took him down to the horses. They took him back to the ranch. Sarah will take good care of him. She's 'most as good as a doc. Smitty went with 'em. Broke his damn laig, climbing over some boulders and slipped on the ice. Might be just a sprain, but we sent him on home anyway. We had enough guns."

"Hey fellas!" Maxie yelled, waving at them, "come take a look at the goods they got in this lean-to they built. Must be the stuff them four teamsters was killed over."

"I'm sure it is," Calder agreed. "Anybody know where the wagons and horses are?"

"Wagons are at a line shack we spotted on the way over here," Ted answered. "Figured as much; just didn't say anything until we knew for sure. Horses are probably right here in the barn."

"So, how many are here?" Buzz asked. Looking around he counted, including himself, seven men. "Now inside the ranchhouse are at least two serving ladies and Ida Ingraham; we need to be very careful -- make sure of your target before you pull a trigger. Take a good look at everyone in this circle, fellas, so you know who's with you."

Ted piped up, "We think King and Rodriguez are in the main house. We hope there's no one else to worry about."

"Anyone else have something to say?" Buzz asked.

"Do we shoot to kill or take them as prisoners?" Wilbur asked.

"King is a monster. Do as the circumstances present themselves, but if he ends up dying today, it won't be a loss to mankind."

"Explain what you just said, Boss," Maxie said, shaking his head, laughing.

Wilbur poked Maxie in the rib, "He said if you see him, shoot him like a rattler."

"Let's go up and end this, fellas," Ted said.

Chapter 64

Molly kissed Margaret on the cheek and walked out the door with Houghton. She saddled her pinto; they headed for Warm Springs, he to the bank, she to Buzz Calder's barn to reopen the general store in it's temporary location.

"I'm going to stop at the Iversons, Judge. Go on ahead. If Jimmy's home I'll have him announce to the town that we're opening this afternoon until 6 p.m. and tomorrow starting at 8 a.m."

Houghton tipped his hat. "Good plan young lady. I'll have a notice put on the wall inside the bank as well."

Mrs. Iverson didn't know where Jimmy was. "He stopped goin' to school reg'lar -- only goes on occasion. He might be fishin' the *Little Black*, might be shootin' varmints with his sling shot; Lord knows where that boy is these days, but he will surely show up fer supper."

"When you see him would you tell him to see me at Buzz Calder's place, please? I may have a job for him."

"When you gonna be open?"

"This afternoon, Ma'am."

"Thank the Good Lord!"

Molly said goodbye and continued toward the blacksmith's barn. She opened it up and began walking through the rows and aisles to re-acquaint herself with the stock on hand. She had been there only ten minutes before residents began coming through the door.

"Can you give me about ten more minutes? Then I'll open up. I'll be here until 6 p.m. and tomorrow at 8 a.m. I promise!" she laughed as she shooed the eight or nine folks out the door. No one was upset; all were excited that the general store was finally coming back. She turned to set up a counter when the door reopened

"Give me another few minutes!" She laughed, then turned to see an unexpected pair of fellows standing there.

"You need some help settin' up, Missy?" Floyd Banner smiled at her. Standing at his side was that young fellow Uncle Buzz had brought back from Albuquerque, Ben Draper. She felt her face begin to flush red. She turned quickly to fumble with a whisk broom.

She cleared her throat, "Oh, Floyd! Yes, please!" And without raising her eyes to meet Ben's, she apologized. "I've forgotten your friend's name, I'm afraid," she lied. She remembered very well his name. She had doodled it dozens of times while sitting in Margaret's parlor. She had thought many times of young Ben working with her at the general store.

"Ben, here, tells me he needs a job real bad."

"I didn't say that, Floyd! I simply said" . . .

"Mind yur elders, Sonny! I'm talking right now. Like I said, Missy, he wonders if you might have an opening when you git yurself set up. Damn near wore my ear off bout it, comin' back from Albakerk."

Now she was really embarrassed. "I haven't even opened up yet, Ben," she managed to look at him directly, "but help me this afternoon; let me think about it tonight.

Come by tomorrow morning, I'll see if I can use you for a while. I'll be here early -- say, 7 a.m."

"I'll do my best. I hope you'll see good results, Ma'am."

"Call me Molly."

The afternoon went fairly smoothly. Several folks tried to meander up and down aisles as the custom was in Margaret's general store; Ben had quite a job keeping them in the front of the barn. "This is a temporary situation," he explained, "until we rebuild at the old site."

Molly counted twenty-six sales receipts and three orders to be delivered the next day. She would have completed another four orders, but neither she nor Ben could find the items, even though the bill of lading showed the items were checked off . . . should be here.

"I'm coming in early tomorrow. I'll find your items," Molly promised, "and have your order ready at the counter for you, let's say by ten a.m."

There were a half dozen folks still hoping to purchase merchandise, but even with lanterns it had become too dark for Ben to see the stock. It was a few minutes before 6 p.m.

"Sorry! You'll have to wait until tomorrow, folks," Ben said. He ushered folks out and locked the big doors. Molly gathered their lanterns, set them on the counter.

"We did well today, Ben," she said. "I appreciate your help. If you show up tomorrow, you're hired."

"I'll be here," he beamed as he walked out the side door. "Good night."

Molly sat for a few minutes in the quiet semi-darkness analyzing the general store's first day back. "Margaret is going to be so pleased."

A horse's whinny interrupted the calm, and for the first time, Molly began to notice and exaggerate the various creaking and rustlings within. A shiver ran down her spine. In the dark, even Uncle Buzz's barn was frightening. Lantern light sent grotesque, long-eared figures playing across the barn ceiling and walls.

"I must find Elmer for tomorrow's deliveries," she said to Spirit as she saddled him. She cinched down the pinto's belly strap.

"I think my winter hours will be changing," she told the pinto with conviction.

Mrs. Grumps suddenly joined Calder's draft horses, making a fuss in the rear of the barn; the animals were anxiously snorting, kicking at the stall rails and pawing, obviously annoyed at some major disturbance.

Huh, Molly thought, *wonder what their problem is now? Ben took them to the corral earlier in the day to exercise and play in the snow for an hour or more . . . Plus, they had plenty of oats and hay . . .*

Molly picked a lantern off the counter and frantically searched for a defensive weapon from among Calder's tools. No hammer, but she found a pair of long-handled tongs. Thus armed, she began to make her way toward the nether region along one of the corridors the teamsters had laid out.

She made soothing sounds as she inched her way, swinging her lantern, through the cavernous recesses of the barn to calm the panicky horse-flesh. "Whoa Boys. Everything's okay. What's the matter, Girls? What's the problem back here, huh?"

From the corner of her eye Molly thought she detected movement. She wheeled! In the eerie shadows she could see almost nothing! A rustling, scraping sound from the catwalks above added to the distress of the animals.

"Who's up there?"

"Yeah! Who's up there?" A raspy, mocking voice! Very near! Molly dropped the tongs and ran with the lantern as fast as she could toward her pony.

Chapter 65

"They're not here, Mr. Calder! Ain't no menfolk here a'tall," Maxie announced. "Me and Wilbur been all through the house; only ones here are a couple of young Mexican women and one old, sick lady. Must be your friend, Mrs. Ingraham. We think she's gone a bit cuckoo."

Buzz had come to the same conclusion. King and Rodriguez must have taken to their horses when that youngster, Freddie, sounded the alarm shots early on. *Cowardly chicken shits!*

As he and Ted went from room to room they saw Gerardo speaking to the two younger women in their native tongue; Buzz considered stopping to listen in on their conversation, then decided he'd ask them later.

They found Ida singing *Oh! Susanna* while staring out the parlor window. She looked up but kept singing. When Willitson and Calder stood watching her, she motioned for them to join her. They declined. She stopped abruptly.

"Michael! You and . . . let me get a closer look at . . . Arnie!" she shrieked. "Arnie, you've come home! Oh, Arnie, you've come home! My little boy has come home, Michael ... now both my boys are home!"

Ida returned to her place in front of the window, turned, and immediately demanded, "Who are you? Get out of my home, this instant!"

Calder walked into the parlor. He draped his arm around Ida's shoulder. "You'll need your heavy coat, Miss Ingraham; it's mighty cold out there."

"Are we going to Santa Fe again? I went there once, you know. I must get my hand bag. Brendan will be so angry with me if I forget my handbag."

"Who is Brendan, Miss Ida?" Buzz asked.

"Silly man!" Ida cooed. "Don't tease me, Brendan. Mrs. Ida King! Oh, I've longed for my own ranch, and you've given it all to me."

"Bring your handbag," Ted instructed, staring at Buzz.

Ten minutes later Ida Ingraham, ten friendlies, seven prisoners, and six dead headed for Warm Springs. It was 5:20 p.m. when they stopped in front of the Wesley barn. Aside from Ida's ramblings, the trip was without incident.

Inside, along with two fellows guarding the prisoners, Jimmy Iverson was sitting cross-legged across from Floyd Banner, listening to tall tales as only Floyd could rattle off. They all looked up when the troupe of riders arrived.

They had a bonfire warming the front area, probably five feet inside the door, dangerously close to one of the barn's upright poles. A stack of wood could be seen beside it. The four prisoners seemed content to be tied in a semi-circle around the fire. The two armed guards looked half asleep opposite them. *Cozy picture*, Calder thought.

He noted the five dead had been removed. *Good*, he thought, *there wouldn't have been enough room for the new arrivals*.

"Jimmy!" Calder sang out, "go get Doc Ford please. Hurry up now! We have two, three in tough shape."

"Yes, Sir!" Jimmy scrambled to his feet and bolted down the road. Floyd sat polishing his shotgun.

Those already inside, both the guards and the guarded, expressed disappointment. Buzz looked around at their faces. "What?"

"Damn, Calder, you spoiled a good story! Hey Floyd, what happened to that fellow in the cabin? Did the bear tear through his roof?"

"Oh!" Buzz apologized, "I didn't think any of you were awake. The mama bear story. Sorry, fellas, but I need Floyd for a few minutes. Floyd, would you take Ida across to Maude's, get her taken care of . . . get some soup in her so she doesn't freeze to death. Ask Maude to keep her for a day or so until we figure out what to do with her.

You fellas," he motioned to the prisoners, "down off your horses. Drag these six down off theirs and lean'em up against that wall over there," he pointed. "That one there still alive?"

"Yeah. Bloody stump, though," one of them said.

"Bring him over by the fire, then the rest of you crowd in around your four buddies. You probably know them all. Ramos, can you walk? somebody give him a hand, over there by Maxie."

Floyd stood watching. "General store opened up this afternoon, Calder," Floyd smiled as he put his arm around Ida and lifted her into his arms. "Molly an' that new fella, Draper's doin' a good job. Still got a line of folks tryin' to get in. Spozed to quit at 6 p.m., but I don't see how. Too damn dark. Dark a'ready," he laughed.

"I'll have to go take a peek in a few minutes," Buzz laughed, "now hustle Ida over to Maude's, please."

"Riders comin' into town from the east," Willitson sang out. "Five of 'em. Too dark ta make'em out."

Chuck walked to the barn entrance. "Maybe Antonio and his boys or Lamar's group," he announced. "Jake wouldn't be back from Mozura yet."

It was, indeed, Antonio and his four man crew. They stopped long enough to learn the news -- the wagons and merchandise had been found, most of the bad guys had been rounded up, only King and Rodriguez had dodged capture.

"Guess we're the first ones back, side's you," Antonio observed. "Goin' over to Jake's. Bring you back a bottle?"

"No thanks," Buzz responded, "couple of us might see you over there in a bit."

Doc Ford's buggy could be seen coming down the road. *Good man,* thought Buzz. *Doc could have said, Piss on it! But he felt the responsibility laid on him by being the only doctor in the area. Wait until I throw Ida Ingraham at him!* Calder chuckled to himself.

Doc jumped down, Jimmy at his side. "Understand you have need of my services."

Ben Draper came riding in from the east end of town about the same time. "Mr. Calder! I've been working with Molly at your barn! She opened the general store today!"

"I heard, Ben. Busy?"

"Oh, yes! Shouda seen it! We worked until it was too dark to work any more," he said excitedly. "Molly should be along any minute. She said I have a job with her, so starting tomorrow I'll be working!"

"Hang in here a moment, Ben. Doc may need some bandages or medicines from my barn. I remember seeing some the other day when I walked through the place."

Calder turned to Doc Ford. "Anything you could use right now, Doc?"

"Yes, as a matter of fact," . . . Ford gave Ben a short list of items; the lad headed back to Calder's barn. The doc turned to Buzz, "That boy's arm is bad, but there's enough skin to wrap it. You did a good job."

"I mangled it, Doc. Petch, over there, he performed the hatchet surgery."

Two riders came from the direction of Buzz' barn, horses at a leisurely pace.

"Boy's back a'ready?" Maxie commented with a question in his voice. "Cain't be. Too damn fast."

The riders tipped their hats and kept riding. In the

dark Buzz couldn't make out who they were as they passed. "So many newcomers in town these days, Doc. Town's growing, like Houghton said."

Doc was bent over Ramos' leg wound, and only nodded, with an, "Um-hmm. Bullet needs to come out, Calder; I could use better light." Doc reached for his bag.

Calder took a branch from the fire to use as a torch when he noticed some of the prisoners were jabbing each other and whispering among themselves. "You fellas, don't even think about making a move. You wouldn't even make it out of the barn."

"We wasn't even thinkin' 'bout makin' a break, Mr. Calder," Moe almost whispered. "We was jus' thinkin' them two riders jus' rode by sure looked like King and Rodriguez."

Buzz bolted upright, jerked his head toward the road. Riders had disappeared. "What?" he bellowed in disbelief, turning back to the prisoners. "Are you sure?"

Now everyone was wide awake, looking at Calder.

"Sure looked like 'em, Blacksmith," Chico piped up, "the way they set their horses. Course, in the dark, can't say for sure."

"The light!" Ford yelled. "Hold the light still!"

"Chuck, come over here, please, and hold this torch for the Doc!

Who's ready to ride?" Calder thundered. "That was King and his buddy that just passed us. Even waved at us, the wily bastards! I want five riders with me; let's go get that murdering pair of A-holes!"

Calder had just thrown a leg over his roan in pursuit of King when a lone rider shouted his name. He turned back in the saddle.

"Mr. Calder!" Draper shouted as he raced up the road. "Mr.Calder! It's Molly! She's hurt real bad! Come quick!"

"Shit! Shit! Shit!" Calder roared. "You boys go on

ahead! Find those piles of crap and finish them for good, I'll catch up if I can!" He spurred the roan toward his barn, Ben Draper at his heels.

Door was still open as Buzz dismounted. He raced inside to find Molly shriveled against the counter. Her pinto stood close by, a long-handled pitchfork had been driven into its saddle. The pitchfork still dangled from the pony's side -- one prong stuck up near the pommel.

"She was under the horse when I got here, Mr. Calder. I was afraid she'd get trampled, so leaned her up against the counter and came a'runnin'."

A quick analysis told Calder the tough saddle leather had saved the girl's life -- two tines of the long pitchfork had punched into Molly -- one in the side of her gut, one in her left thigh. The straw floor was covered in blood. She hadn't quite got away.

"We'll take her back to the Wesley barn, Son. Back on your horse." Buzz lifted the unconscious Molly into Draper's arms. "Carry her steady now, and we'll walk the horses back, easy-like."

Buzz took the reins to Ben's horse and led the way. Ben kept looking down at the young lady cradled in his arms. Almost at the Wesley barn her eyes fluttered open; a smile, "Oh, Ben, I" . . . a painful gasp. She fainted again. Ben cradled her closer. *Please, God, help her get better.*

Chapter 66

Morning came, bright, cloudless, and bitterly cold. a.m. Thursday, October 2nd, 1851.

Antonio had a crew laying out the new general store. Three wagon-loads of timbers were already stacked neatly in the center of what would become the structural mainstays of the premises.

The cabinet maker came by, having heard there was more need for his services. He had brought a hay wagon to collect the six corpses -- four of whom would even have names on tombstones, the other two were simply faces in King's assemblage of ruffians.

Molly and the amputee had been transferred to Doc Ford's surgery the evening before -- to his own equipment, his own medications. Much warmer, too.

Ben Draper was at Calder's barn, searching through the inventory for the misplaced merchandise from the day before. Calder had given him one of the pocket watches he had bought from the widow Marcussen in Albuquerque. Ben kept looking at it, wondering how he would handle a day manning the store he knew almost nothing about. To make matters worse, Calder had disappeared!

Elmer walked into the Calder barn. "Mr. Calder says you got work for me," he said as he dropped hay into the mangers and filled the oat bags for Mrs. Grumps and the horses.

"Yes, Elmer. Deliveries. I'm not open yet," Ben said, looking at his watch, "go ahead with your chores. Oh, Elmer" . . .

"Yeah?"

"Where did Mr. Calder go? I saw him this morning with Doc Ford's buggy. He passed the Wesley barn before first light."

"Goin' to see Molly and that kid he shot," he said. "Back by 9 a.m. he said."

Buzz passed by Doc Ford's place without stopping; he pulled into Margaret's drive, waved to Lamar Jefferson who had stopped there the night before, just in case the criminals would stop there, and continued to the house. He stepped in.

"Hello the house!"

"Buzz? Is that you?"

"Good morning, Margaret!" he continued. "Rise and shine!"

"You stay in the kitchen, Buzz! Make a pot of coffee! I'll tell you when you can come in here!"

"Time you come out here, Margaret! When you're up and decent, you come out here for your mug of coffee!"

"Is that a challenge, Buzz Calder?"

"Probably!"

Calder made coffee, found a full cookie jar and waited.

"Do you realize this is the first time I have walked into my own kitchen in weeks?"

"Sit down, Margaret." He handed her a steaming mug of coffee. "Have a cookie. We need to talk."

"Molly's hurt? How?"

"Your husband, Margaret. Came into town yesterday while we were cleaning out his nest of vermin. I expect he and Rodriguez ran as soon as we started up the hill to their rat hole at Ida's place."

"Ida's place?"

"Yes. Anyway, they came to town, probably thinking you or Molly, or both, were somewhere in town, and heard the new general store was open. Hid out. Tried to kill her with a pitch fork. Only thing saved her, I figure, was maybe the pommel of her pony's saddle as she tried to ride out."

"Why are you here, Buzz?"

"Take you to town, Margaret, to run the general store. That young Ben Draper is there, but he can't run it. You've done enough resting. Time you get back to work."

"Is Molly okay?"

"We'll stop and see on our way. She's at Doc's. Buggy's waiting."

"Can you go get my coat and handbag, please?"

"No, I'm going to have another mug of coffee. You'll have to go get them yourself."

Margaret laughed. "You can be a real son-of-a-bitch at times, Buzz Calder!"

"Hurry up! I promised I'd be back by 9 a.m."

<><><>

Margaret leaned over the sleeping Molly, her hand on the feverish forehead. "My sweet baby. He had to drag you into our personal battle, didn't he?" Turning to Doc Ford, "She going to be alright, Doc?"

"No reason to think otherwise, Margaret, unless the pitchfork pushed something into her. It went into her leg to the bone and, I figure -- probably two, two and a half inches into her tummy. Missed everything vital. I gave her a sedative just before you came, so she'll be out for a couple of hours.

Now, your boy," Ford said to Calder as the blacksmith sat listening to the exchange between the doc and Margaret, "he's in my examining room. He fought, screamed and struggled all through the night with the pain and the idea of having no hand. I finally gave him chloroform this morning at 4 a.m. so the Missus and I could get some sleep. I think he'll be coming around soon. Go check. You know where."

Buzz opened the door, walked to the table and peered down at the young man. Doc had taken the fellow's boots off and tied his legs and arms to the underside. He walked back out.

"He's still fast asleep. Got smelling salts around here somewhere?"

"Yup. Six drawer cabinet, second drawer on right, toward the back on right side. Green cap as I recall; can't miss it. Better take some ether as well in case he wakes up." He handed a corked bottle to Calder.

As it turned out, Calder didn't need the jar of salts -- the lad was coming around . . . and in pain. Calder stood over him.

"Who are you? You chicken shit! You tied me up! You . . . oh, Damn! That hurts! My hand hurts! Doc! Make it stop!"

Calder took the cork off the ether and put it under the lad's nose. He watched as the eyes rolled back a bit, then pulled the bottle away and re-corked it.

"I remember when that asshole shot my hand, but I don't remember anything else, Doc. Where am I, and how did I get here?"

"First off, Son, you are in the doctor's office in Warm Springs. Six of your buddies are dead, seven are in custody -- you being one of the seven. Your hand was shattered and you would be dead had emergency surgery not been performed immediately."

Fear crept across his face, "What kind of surgery, Doc?"

"You were in shock. Blood was spurting from your

wrist like a son-of-a-bitch. We dragged you down the hill, took a hatchet and cut your hand off and cauterized it. Then wrapped it and brought you here."

The fog was lifting, his memory of having his hand badly injured was returning, though he fought with that realization. "My hand? Oh, shit! No! Not my hand, Doc!" Despite his attempt at stoicism, tears welled up; he began to bawl.

"Now, son, Doc's taking good care of you, and so long as you don't get an infection, you're going to be just fine -- live a long, productive life."

"You ain't the doc?" he blubbered. "Then, who the hell are you, mister?"

"Buzz Calder, the asshole that shot you." Buzz left him to moan over his lost limb, and returned to the others.

"Ice! Of course!" Doc exploded. "Why didn't I think of ice!" Turning to Calder, Ford said, "Margaret just reminded me that a good pain reducer for burns and swelling is an ice pack, Buzz. I have a rain barrel out back. Would you be so kind as to fetch me the slab of ice that's sitting on top?" Calder stepped out and returned a few minutes later with a 20" round slab of ice, almost 4" thick. "Ha!" Ford laughed. "Need it broken up into smaller pieces."

"Got any sacks, Doc?"

"Ask the Missus."

Ten minutes later Buzz came into the kitchen with bulging cloth bags of chipped ice.

"We'll be off, Doc," he said, steadying Margaret to her feet. "Bring the buggy back this afternoon, talk more then."

"My new store!" Margaret and Buzz were stopped in front of the general store construction site. She gripped Calder's arm. "Oh, thank you, Lord! thank you, Warm Springs!"

The buggy drove slowly by the Wesley barn. Margaret studied the faces of the shackled prisoners for a moment as they passed.

"So this is where Warm Springs is going to become more than just a township," Margaret said exuberantly. "We knew it would happen. Not just a flash in the pan any more, Buzz. We have a good mix of industry, and with a Territory Seat or whatever they call it, we'll be considered a city before long.

The judge says we'll be needing a judge here soon. I can think of no more qualified person than you, Buzz Calder, to be the territorial judge of this southwest sector of New Mexico."

"Stop the nonsense, Margaret! I'm very happy to be the Warm Springs blacksmith. I left my law books as a young man, and I'm not the least bit keen on the idea of looking at another one."

"I guess you're right. Easier to just hang those 10-12 fellas back there without a trial. They're all guilty, even that one the doc has in his surgery. Hang'em and be done with it without any remorse."

Margaret broke off any further conversation. Calder started to offer a rebuttal but she only said, "This buggy is beginning to kill my back, can you push that nag a bit faster, Buzz?" She had said what she wanted -- planted a seed. One way or the other, Buzz Calder wouldn't let the town grow into a city without him.

Margaret was grateful when the buggy pulled inside the temporary general store. It was 8:35. Already the place was jammed with customers. When they saw Margaret, there were cheers and cries of joy. Calder stepped down, walked around and assisted Margaret to the wooden floor.

Ben Draper stood watching, not knowing what to do.

"Don't just stand there, Son. Get her a soft chair to sit on. The one on my veranda will be perfect."

<><><>

Calder looked around his shop. He hadn't used his tools in months, hadn't fired up the forge, picked up hammer or tongs. Time he went back to work.

He loaded coal into his furnace and used hot coals from his home fireplace to ignite it. Once the coals took, he used his bellows to bring the coals to a hot fire. He sighed. He felt like a blacksmith once again. He grabbed a hammer.

Margaret's strength began to wane around the noon hour; Maude brought over some of her famous stew which was accepted gratefully and disappeared swiftly, but by 2 p.m., despite fighting against it, her strength was noticeably at the end.

"I'm sorry, but I need to go home, Ben," she informed him. "I'm all tuckered out."

Ben had been filling orders steadily, everything from kitchen utensils, pots and pans to rain barrels, from guns and rifles to bags of bullets, from soaps to medicines, from seed potatoes to chicken feed, several bolts of fabric, patterns, yarn, needles, barrels of whiskey and rum, salt, sugar, spices, pickling jars, paraffin wax, buggy whips and much more. Elmer had made five deliveries thus far, with probably more to come before the day was out.

"Certainly, Miss Margaret. I'll run, get Mr. Calder." Turning to the folks waiting to order, Ben held up his hands, "Give me a few minutes, folks. Miss Margaret is worn out. I'll be back in a few minutes."

"Mr. Calder, come quick," Ben said when he found Buzz standing over a barrel of water. "Margaret wants to go home. She's done."

"Tell her I'll be there in a few minutes!" the blacksmith answered, holding a red hot piece of metal in his long-handled tongs. "Just about to quench this ax head."

He looked out at the skies in the north and shook his head.

<><><>

Doc Ford insisted that Margaret spend the night in town. Arrangements were made with Annie Wesley. The old widow brightened, delighted to have Margaret stay with her. Annie and Wally were among the first settlers to set down roots in Warm Springs. They had bought just about the same time Margaret had made her purchase.

Annie made a pot of tea, invited Buzz to join them but he smiled and declined.

"Thanks, but no. I had a look around my shop earlier today, ladies. I'm so far behind" . . . both ladies chimed in, "You think you can see your butt just up ahead." They all laughed. Buzz excused himself and returned to his shop.

The two ladies settled in the parlor and began to chit-chat. The many memories they shared in their twenty-five or more years in the valley.

Ben finished the day alone. The waiting crowds that had flocked yesterday afternoon and this morning had finally thinned to an almost *pre-fire* general store day, and by 3:30 they had thinned out to only a dribble.

He walked outside to see if anyone was coming; the street was empty except for five riders coming from the west. Ben couldn't remember names but recognized the faces of a few. He waved, then went back inside.

While waiting for customers, Ben counted the day's receipts -- sixty seven! Margaret had run him ragged. Elmer was equally busy. At present he was out on his sixth delivery. The young storekeeper was ecstatic.

He put together his tally sheet and the money pouch for the bank. Looking at his handiwork, Ben smiled, so grateful to Mrs. Marcussen and Mr. Calder for his education.

He sat back and stared around the blacksmith's barn. His eyes spotted the saddle with the two punctures, and his thoughts immediately turned to Molly, thinking of finding her under her pony, cradling her in his arms the night before, praying she would be okay. *The pinto is fine*, he thought, *Molly surely is, too.*

A female voice brought him back to the present.

"You're that kid from Albuquerque, aren't you?" Without waiting for a reply, "We need salt and sugar. Can you get them over today, please?" It was Maude's waitress, Billie. She was bundled in a heavy parka and a woolen cap pulled down over her ears.

"I'll make sure of it," he smiled as he wrote it down. She smiled back and was gone. He blinked and followed her outside, but she was already galloping back to the cafe. He yelled after her, "I'm not a kid!" *Hell*, Ben thought, staring at the horse and rider, *she's barely older than me.*

He walked back inside, pulled fifty pound bags -- one of salt, one sugar from the storage shelves and set them beside the counter. He changed his sales figures, added the items to the accounts receivables column and reduced the bags of sugar and salt by one each on the inventory sheet. He felt quite pleased with himself. "Kid!" he muttered.

After waiting another ten minutes he walked around the barn and headed for the blacksmith shop. "I'm waiting for Elmer," he explained to Calder. "He's out on his last delivery. Then I'm headed for the bank with the receipts, then to Jake's. You about finished up here? Join me?"

"Maybe I'll meet you there. I need to see the fellows at Wesleys. We may need to shift the guards around so they can get some rest. Also need to check on Ida. She seems to have gone a bit batty. I'll probably drop by Maude's to get her assessment. Have you seen Jake or any of the fellows we sent after King?"

"Nope -- I saw that group that went toward Tucson, Mr. Calder. You know, that Lamar fella and his boys. You say you're headed for Maude's?"

"I think so, why?"

"If your pony can handle another hundred pounds can you take a couple of bags over there? Billie ordered, then she rushed off without them."

"Sure thing. I'll go there first. I'll be happier when our fellas get back, especially Jake's bunch. Look at the cloud above those mountains, Son! Storm's coming our way. Looks bad!"

It was almost 4 p.m. Calder rode to Maude's, carrying two bags in through the kitchen door. Maude, herself, was washing dishes, Ida was at her side, drying and stacking them in a cabinet.

Maude smiled, "Thank you, Buzz. We would have been out of sugar in a week and salt not far behind. Tell Margaret I'll put in a regular order in a few days, but this will give me peace of mind for right now."

"Sweetheart!" Ida cried out. She set a plate on the counter and ran to Calder, throwing her arms around him. "I knew you'd come!" Turning to Maude, she said, "I just knew he'd come, Mother."

"Been saying that kind of nonsense all day, Buzz. I had to bring her in here and put her to work -- keep her out of trouble. Claims she's Mrs. King . . . claims she has proof. And by the way, Buzz, you're the third Mr. King so far."

"Interesting," Calder said, peering at Maude over Ida's hair as the *Snake Eyes* owner held him close. He reached down and took Ida's shoulders pushing her out in front of him.

"Ida, can you prove to me that you're Mrs. King?"

"I could, but somebody stole my purse. I've looked everywhere."

Maude laughed. "So that's what you've been doing!" She turned to Buzz, "She gave it to me for safekeeping. I'll get it."

She was back in just a few minutes, but in that short time Ida's mind cleared. She and Calder spoke of happy times of years gone by. Buzz was a friend, no longer her husband.

When Ida spotted the purse her face lit up. "Where did you find this? I'll show you that I'm Mrs. King, Buzz." She took the purse and dumped it out on a counter. Several legal-looking papers spilled out. "Here," she said proudly. "Look through those, I'll look through these."

She handed Buzz a half dozen papers, two stamped with the seal of New Mexico territory. Buzz recognized them immediately; he whistled and looked up at Maude, shaking his head. "I think I have all the papers you're looking for, Ida, and it seems you weren't fibbing."

"I told you, Buzz! Let me see!" she leaned over the blacksmith. "Read it to me. I don't read so good," she smiled at Maude. "See? I knew I was in Santa Fe!" She clapped her hands gleefully as Calder read that on August 11th, she and King were duly married in Santa Fe. The following day they had gone to the Territory offices for a title change on the *Snake Eyes* spread from Ida Ingraham, sole owner, to Mr. and Mrs. Brendan and Ida King, husband and wife.

"I have some here, too," she said gleefully, handing Calder the papers she had taken from the purse. It was concerned with banking. Buzz looked through the papers and determined it was a form to change Ida's account to include Brendan.

"Did you and Brendan go to see Mr. Royston?"

"Not yet. I'm waiting for him to come home. Then we're going to the bank together to see Abel. Brendan wants to buy me a new Sunday outfit for my birthday."

"Don't lose those papers, Ida. You might want Maude, here, to put them somewhere for safekeeping."

"That's a good idea. Maude, would you?"

"I'm heading for the Wesley barn," Buzz announced. "If you see the judge send him over, please. Otherwise, I'll catch him up at the hotel. Oh, almost forgot! Send Billie over for our supper orders."

"I'll just send a few fellas over with enough of my stew to feed an army," she laughed. "Shall we say fifteen bowls and spoons -- will that be enough?"

"Perfect."

<><><>

Large flakes of snow were beginning to fall as Buzz stepped outside Maude's kitchen door. He looked at the sky and swore as he grabbed his roan's reins. "Where are our boys, huh?" he asked her as he walked her across the road and south a hundred yards to the Wesley barn.

"We'll take over from here, Ted," Calder told the *Eagle* boys. "We just may be snowed in by morning from the look of the sky. You three should probably be on your way. Run on over to Maude's for supper first -- put it on my tab."

He then looked at the ten prisoners tethered together. "You fellas should be warm enough in here. There's lots of dry hay. We'll pull some more down so you can make up more comfortable beds."

"We gotta stay in here ferever, Mr. Calder?" asked the young fellow who had fired that first warning shot at the *Snake Eyes* yesterday.

"Where would you like to go, Son?" Calder asked, something approaching a smile on his face.

Before Freddie could answer, "Oklahoma!" came from one of the other prisoners. Others chimed in with various answers, ending in a barn-full of guffaws and chuckles, all coming from those tied together around one of the uprights supporting the mezzanine. Even Calder joined in.

"Better'n swingin' in the wind, Freddie!" Moe sang out. The barn became suddenly silent.

Chapter 67

The boys from the *Eagle Ranch* bid them goodbye and left for home. Ten minutes later Petch and Brody rode up the road.

"Hey, Mr. Calder! We heard you might need a hand with these fellers. We'll spell you for a few hours. Rules are still the same, right? They move, we shoot?" Brody said, brushing the snow off his hat and shoulders, smiling around at the ten sitting in the hay.

"Thanks, fellas," Buzz said as he saddled his big mare. "Glad to see you back. I take it you boys had no luck finding King and Rodriguez."

"Naw, tracks jus' got mixed up with all the others, an' after a day lookin' we jus' gave'er up. Storm's comin' anyway, an' we figgered we'd go lookin' fer'em after."

"So you're all back, then?"

"Yup. All six of us."

"You seen anything of Jake and his boys?"

"Nuthin', Sir."

"Supper's coming in a few minutes if you're hungry," Buzz told them. "Thanks again."

Calder caught up with Judge Houghton at the hotel. The judge waved a welcoming arm at him, followed by a tall whiskey.

"So, what brings you by, Buzz? I was about to head over to Jake's for a steak dinner. Care to join me?"

"I might, but before you head off for Albuquerque we need to do some paperwork to protect Ida Ingraham. She's gone a bit wacky, I'm afraid, and she went and married King, and put him on title to her ranch."

"We can't do anything about that, Calder. She has the right to marry him and do with her ranch whatever she wills to do."

"Just sit with her for a half hour, I think you'll change your mind."

"Okay, let's go take a look at the marriage papers if there are any. Your pastor Marshall must have kept a copy."

"Not that easy," Calder said, sipping his whiskey, "Marshall had nothing to do with it. King took her all the way to Santa Fe. Put it in the territorial records so there'd be no argument."

"Sneaky bastard. Must have been the same time he put down the deposit and bid on Molly's place. How old did you say she is?"

"Late seventies, maybe even eighty by now."

Houghton almost choked on his whiskey. Instead he coughed, and cleared his throat. "He dragged her all the way to Santa Fe and back at her age? So where is your lady now?"

"Over at Maude's, scrubbing dishes," Buzz laughed.

"Let's go have a talk with her. Damn! I had planned on heading home tomorrow."

As the two men stepped out into street, an east wind was swirling small flakes of snow sideways. Houghton grabbed his hat and pulled it down over his ears. "Looks like a bad one coming. There goes my plan to head out tomorrow. Are all the boys back?"

"All except Jake and those with him from Mozura," Buzz answered. "And I don't think a bad one's coming,

Cedric, I think it's already here," he said, pulling his collar up to shield against the biting wind. "Hope our boys are hunkered down somewhere safe."

"It's too early in the season, Buzz. We don't get the serious storms until January or February. Should die down, soon, don't you think?"

"Not unheard of. I remember mid-October, 1839, Cedric. Snowed four days straight. Folks couldn't even open up doors or windows, snow was so high. Roofs caved in, livestock froze in the field -- even chickens and hogs. Froze toes, fingers, and noses within minutes. Lost five folks right here in Warm Springs. As I remember, it hardly touched your area . . . just the Black Mountains and the area down here along the *Gila*."

"A real freak of a storm," Houghton agreed.

<><><>

"Sweetheart! I knew you'd be back!" Ida cried as Calder and Houghton stepped through Maude's kitchen door. "I'm so tired, Honey, can we go home now?"

Houghton pursed his lips and raised an eyebrow toward Calder when she reached, not for Calder, but for him. Calder only shrugged.

"Let's talk about home, Ida. Where is home?" he asked her, holding her arms at a distance.

"I don't remember. You bought it for me, Benjamin."

"Benjamin?" Calder whispered to Maude. Who's Benjamin?"

"I don't know. Perhaps Ida's dead husband? Margaret would know."

Houghton was satisfied. "Let me see the paperwork, Buzz. I can annul both transactions for cause, and once home, I'll dispatch new paperwork to Santa Fe."

"She wants to go home, Cecil. Why don't I take her to Annie's? The three ladies can visit, Annie has room, and it would give Maude a break."

"Let's both take her over there. Bring her purse and all

her papers. I'll write everything up and the ladies can witness. I'm going to have quite a bundle to dispatch to Santa Fe."

"You may be spending the winter here in Warm Springs if this storm turns into a full-fledged blizzard."

The snow was above their boots as they stepped out of Maude's. Buzz set Ida on his roan and the two men walked the short distance to the Wesley farmhouse. Annie invited them into the parlor where it was warm and cozy. Houghton set to work at the kitchen table.

Chapter 68

"I feel fine, Doc, I'm ready to go home," Molly insisted as Doc Ford came in from a call, puffing as he entered a side door. He brushed snow off his coat and hat, peeled the scarf from around his neck, and added all three items to the hooks on a beautifully carved walnut hall tree.

Molly had been sitting at his desk in the study, thumbing through a dog-eared medical journal. "I can walk just fine, see?" She stood and walked the room and back.

"I'm not going to hold you here, young lady," Ford answered, sitting on the hall tree bench, removing his boots. He had been out on a call. "I'm satisfied there is no infection in those wounds. But before you leave, would you ask the missus if she'll bring me a cup of tea?"

"I'll make it and bring it in." She turned to go, then heard, "I'll take one, too!"

"You're awake!" Molly chirped. She ran to the young amputee and held out her hand. "Hello there! I'm Molly."

The young ruffian looked at her, obviously perplexed. "Mo . . . Molly?"

"That's me!" She smiled broadly. "Be right back." She departed for the kitchen.

"That's Molly? The one, runs the general store in Warm Springs?" the young man asked Doc Ford.

"Yes, that's her. How do you know about that?"

The outlaw didn't answer, simply shook his head. Then, "She's got bandages on her leg. What happened to her?"

"Your boss tried to stab her with a pitchfork. Luckily she escaped serious injury."

Molly returned with a tray -- complete with tea pot, two cups with filled infusers, sugar, and milk. She curtsied.

"How do you take your tea, m'lord?" she asked the doc. He laughed at her antics.

He stood from his seat on the hall tree, bowed, and answered in kind, "Just a little milk, m'lady." Then he took the saucer and sat at his desk, stirring the infuser through the boiling water. Molly added the milk, then turned, "And you, kind sir?"

"I'm not a *kind sir!*" he almost shouted at her. "Forget the tea as well!"

"I'm sorry. I was only trying to keep a friendly tone. I didn't mean to offend. Did I do something wrong?"

"No. Just go away," he said.

"Not until you tell me why, all the sudden, I'm the enemy!"

"You ain't," he almost whispered, shaking his head. "I'm awful sorry about your pa, Miss Molly."

Undeterred and more adamant, Molly walked to his bedside and handed him the tea. "My pa's fine. Leg wound healed up real good. Now, take this!" she ordered. He obeyed, balanced it in his lap, and stirred it with the infuser.

"Milk? Sugar?" she looked at him with slits for eyes.

"Both, please."

"So, tell me," she said as she poured a splash of milk into his cup and a spoon of sugar, "what's your name, and where you from? And how'd you know about my pa?" He continued to stir his tea.

He took a sip. "Sonofabitch! . . . Molly! You're Molly! . . Huh!" He shook his head, almost sobbing. "My name's King!" he blurted. "Brendan King, Junior!"

Doc Ford and Molly suddenly realized what he had said. Molly frowned and backed away. "You weren't talking about my adopted pa! You're talking about my real pa! You're talking about my whole family!"

"Yes!" he exploded. "The sheepherders!"

"You involved, Junior?" Ford demanded.

"Hell no! I was a kid living in Tucson with my ma. She left him when I was just a baby. Anyway, she got sick; she asked that mail wagon driver, Orren, to pass the word along, hoping someone could find her sister -- my aunt Louisa. She thought Auntie was in Santa Fe. I don't know how, but Pa found out and sent Whitey down there to find us. Ma was already dead by the time he got there."

"How did she die, Son?"

"I'm not sure. Doc in Tucson said Melancholia."

"Was she sickly?"

"Long as I can remember. Couldn't get around too well the last few years. Useless arm, too."

Molly, listening to the back and forth exchange, decided to join in. "How'd you know about my pa?"

"Different stories come up at the ranch; that was one. But it wasn't until just recent I heard the family got killed. I was led to believe the guys shot up the sheep and sent the sheepherders packing back to Utah." The young man looked at Molly through teary eyes, "Miss Molly I swear I didn't know! I just didn't know."

"Your dad sure did! He's a cruel, wicked man!" Molly almost screamed at the young Brendan. "You said your mother was crippled? How did that happen? And why did they split up? He probably beat her! I'll bet he broke bones -- destroyed her spirit until she had to leave the bastard, packed up her baby, and disappeared."

Molly wasn't yet finished. "It wouldn't surprise me if it was he that murdered her and grabbed you up as one more vassal to do his bidding . . . ha! I just thought of this, I'll bet he demanded that you go out and fight while he slinks off like the coward he is! He is *The King* after all. He cares about no one or nothing but himself!

I'm leaving, Doc. Good night." She turned to the young man, "Enjoy your tea, Mr. King!" she spat. "I put no poison in it!"

Chapter 69

Snow continued through the night and threatened to continue with no let-up Friday morning. It had already reached as high as horses' bellies, drifting even higher in places.

Buzz Calder made his way to the Wesley barn early, the big roan labored, but pulled a sled loaded with snow shovels and warm clothing from the general store.

After conversing with Antonio and Chuck, the two now on guard, Buzz turned to the prisoners.

"Fellas," he told them, "listen up! Here's what we're going to do. We're going shoveling snow."

"You turning us loose?" Moe asked.

"With certain rules," smiled Buzz. "You'll be in teams of two, each with one guard. You'll shovel from houses' front steps to all the outbuildings of the residents. The only building you will enter is the outhouse, and then only with your guard's knowledge.

Anyone of you that tries to escape, overpower a guard, or enter any building without your guard's permission will be shot, and that will be the end of it! Understood? So how many of you are willing?"

They all agreed to the task. "Good!" Buzz said. "I'll be back in a while with a few more fellas."

Knocking on doors produced six men, willing to

watch over the men with the shovels, and two or three more who volunteered to wield shovels themselves. By this time many of the folks able to exit their doors were out clearing their own trails as well.

Buzz fashioned a wide V-plow from boards Antonio had sawn for the new general store, then hitched it behind his team of buckskin draft horses and set Elmer and Jimmy to work clearing the main roads.

Convict crews set, they worked until noon, stopped for lunch at Jake's -- sitting at three tables and surrounded by their guards -- then continued until just before dark, exhausted but jubilant with their success. Almost every property had trails to the important out-buildings and woodpiles.

As they returned to the Wesley barn and their shackles, snow flurries had increased, along with a fierce, prevailing north wind. Buzz, along with old man Banner and young Chuck stayed behind to keep night watch.

"Another night of snow means another day of shoveling. Same rules. Anybody opt out?" Buzz asked.

"No, sir," Porter replied, "most honest work any of us guys has did in weeks."

"You probably should hang your wet clothes next to the fire. Anybody need thermals?"

"What's thermals?" Porter asked.

"Drawers under your reg'lar pants to keep you warmer in weather," Banner laughed. "Goes from yore neck to yore feet. Got buttons in front an' buttons with a flap in th' backside to take care'uh necessaries."

"I'd like some'a them thermals," Eddie said. It was cold out there today."

"Me, too!" someone else said, echoed by several others.

"I'll be back in fifteen minutes with a pair for everyone," Calder laughed. "Take off what you have on and change. I'll take your old clothes to be washed. Don't worry, I'll bring them all back by tomorrow morning."

"We gonna be nekkid when that girl comes with our supper?" Freddie asked, snickering.

"Nope!" Calder shook his head . . . "sorry."

"Shucks!" someone moaned.

<><><>

The blizzard of October, 1851 lasted three full days -- probably not as severe as the one Calder remembered from 1839 -- but this time the town was much better prepared; old-timers had come to realize that New Mexico's early mountainous storms could last more than an afternoon. Margaret had equipped the store with snowshoes and toboggans as well as severe weather clothing.

Buzz sent Elmer and Jimmy out to clear the road southwest as far as Margaret's drive and then all the way to the rear entry of her house.

Lamar Jefferson walked outside to greet them. "Hey fellas, much obliged! You saved me at least two hours with that contraption. Sure beats a shovel. You gonna plow further southwest -- down toward Tucson?"

"Nope!" Jimmy piped up, "Uncle Buzz said to go as far as Margaret's. Then we gotta go back through town and go as far as Floyd Banner's place, east end of town. Spozed to do it twice today."

Lamar had shoveled a path from barn to house on the first day of the blizzard to care for Margaret's livestock, and now he spent most of his time hunkered down before the fireplace in the parlor, enjoying Margaret's books.

"Hard work, eh, fellas?"

"Only fer the horses, Sir," Elmer supplied, "me'n Jimmy's jus' havin' fun."

"Did the boys catch up with King and that Rodriguez fella?"

"No, Sir. Looks like they's plum disappeared."

"Hmmm," Lamar replied. "I was sorta hopin' they'd show up here. How about the fellas the judge sent out to find them . . . they all back?"

"All except Jake and his crew that went up to that ghost town -- Mazurry."

"Mozura," Lamar corrected. "Tough town, tough area," Lamar said, almost to himself. "Okay fellas. Tell Calder I'm doin' fine here."

"Oh," Elmer said, "Almost forgot. Pastor Marshall said to tell everyone we're gonna have a Sunday afternoon service and potluck tomorrow at 2 p.m. Bring a dish."

Lamar smiled as he waved them goodbye, then shook his head. *Bring a dish?*

Chapter 70

Before 9 a.m. Sunday morning three things happened: the winds abated, the snowfall ended and the sun peeped out from behind the highest ridge of the Black Mountains to the northeast of Warm Springs. Residents emerged from their homes with smiles and cheery greetings to one another.

A few were atop their homes, barns and chicken coops shoveling off the white stuff -- a few had roof repair to attend, but all agreed they had avoided catastrophe through preparedness. No fatalities and only a handful of injuries needing Doc Ford.

Houghton sat with Floyd Banner at a table in Jake's, discussing the judge's return to Albuquerque. Jake's was a great meeting place, always open on Sundays for meals, but never for drinking.

Floyd motioned for Petch and Chuck to join them. They dragged their chairs over. The four shook hands, agreeing to start out Tuesday morning as a protective detail for the judge. The judge was anxious to begin the trip.

"I'll put you up at a bed and breakfast for a few days while I put together a dispatchment of building engineers you'll escort back."

"Yore gonna pay us fer doin' nuthin'?" Floyd's brow furrowed.

Houghton nodded. "I'll have more to say this afternoon at the church." He stood, smiled, and waved a welcoming arm to Margaret who had just come in.

Margaret was walking quite well with aid of a staff Jimmy had fashioned from a hickory limb.

"Good morning boys," she smiled, "great to be alive!"

All four men stood, removed their hats and almost in unison asked how she was mending.

"I'm so grateful to be walking. I almost gave up but for the good people of this town."

"Good lookin' pole you got there, Margaret," Floyd commented. "Looks a bit like that feller, Moses, in the bible . . . 'ceptin' fer the skirt," he added, smiling.

She stared at him in mock anger, narrowing her eyes to slits. "This happens to be a staff, used by many country folks as their legs begin to give them trouble. You ought to consider one, Floyd. Better than a cane." She sat in the chair offered, and let out a tired sigh. "Jimmy Iverson made this one for me. Hickory. In fact, Floyd, I'll sell you one for a dollar. I'm having Jimmy make me six more."

Floyd made a face and stuck his tongue out at her.

<><><>

The sun was warm -- the two o'clock meeting came together as scheduled -- almost 300 folks showed up. The service was minimal. The sanctuary could hold fewer than 100; Pastor Marshall stood on the church steps to send up a brief prayer to The Almighty:

'Thank You, Father for Your safety during the storm; for sustaining us, and protecting us; and thank You for the pot luck we're about to enjoy."

Then he led the congregation in a hymn.

"Now I'm going to have Judge Houghton say a few words about plans for our town. Then we'll eat!" Pastor Marshall said.

Houghton greeted everyone. He spoke about procuring the Wesley property for official New Mexico purposes, that a construction team would be coming, that locals could apply for paying jobs, jobs would be posted when the team arrived.

"We need a General Store here in Warm Springs -- it was lost through no fault of Margaret Chisholm. We intend that it be replaced as soon as possible. That means, Antonio," he pointed to the builder, "to meet your payroll, lumber or other supplies, you go to Abel Royston for a draw. Whatever is left over will be transferred to the Warm Springs general fund. Now, does that make sense to everyone?"

Those in attendance, as one, voiced their approval.

"One last order of business needs to be aired," Houghton said. "In the spring, Territory buildings will be ready to be occupied. Voting will take place for city managers, sheriff, and mayor. I'll be here to oversee the swearing-in of the winners.

There are two posts that are Federally appointed: a Federal Judge presiding in southwest New Mexico, and as well, a Federal Marshal. Now, I intend to make those appointments when I come. Let's set voting to be on the first Tuesday in June of 1852. That gives you men over half a year to decide. I want you to think about all of this. New Mexico is nearing statehood. It's inevitable, folks. Now here's your pastor."

"Lot's to think about, folks," Marshall said. "Okay, time to eat. Please form a line at the left door. Once inside help yourselves -- food's on the tables -- then come out the right door and find a spot outside. Plenty of food, just remember to leave some for the person behi" . . .

"Riders comin'!" Petch yelled, "looks like eight or nine horses, only four riders!"

Chapter 71

"Bring them through here fellas," Doc Ford instructed as Mrs. Ford hurried to push open the door into the doctor's home surgery. "Brendan, you're goin' to have to make some room for . . . Brendan?" . . . Doc turned. "Brendan, where are you? Damn! The kid's missing, Petch!"

As Ford motioned for the men carrying the female to lay her on the bed, and the older man on the goose down pallet, he continued, "I shouldn't have left him. I thought I could trust him."

"You mean the kid I did the hatchet job on?" Petch turned from the unconscious woman to Ford, "he didn't run out on you, Doc. I saw Mr. Calder and Floyd Banner taking all the Wesley barn prisoners through the church door to get food, an' he was amongst'em."

"That's good. Now where's the missus?"

"Right here, dear. Molly and I were getting blankets."

"Good! Bring them through. Jake and his team -- are they okay?"

"They look plumb tuckered out and cold, Doc, but I don't think they got themselves froze at all," added Willie, who had helped Petch bring in the unconscious old woman. "Not like these two anyways. Jake's taking them to his place to dry out. Chuck's on his way to get'em dry clothes."

"All of you, get over to Jake's place," Molly told the men. "Best to simply get out of wet clothes and wrap up in blankets, warm but not too hot."

Petch looked at Doc Ford questioning Molly's directive. The doc simply nodded and began cutting the frozen leggings from the old Indian.

"Thanks, fellas," Ford said. "We'll take it from here. Head on back for some pot luck lunch."

Eversole, another of the four who did the transporting, turned and gave Ford a strange look, "Why'd they bring'em back, Doc, an' why'd we bring'em here? Hell, theys jus' injuns?"

"How long have you been in Warm Springs, Son?"

"Six months, why?"

"I don't like you, but if you're hurt, I'll drag you in here and heal you the best I know how -- you understand? Now, these two Indians, well, they're friends of mine. I'll drag them in here and heal them the best I know how, then I'll cook them a meal and sit and eat with them."

"Why don't you like me?"

"No reason at all." Ford looked him in the eye, "but do you see what I mean, Son? Now, go grab yourself some grub."

<><><>

Calder stomped the snow off his boots and followed Jake and the others inside the house. "Just go take your clothes off fellas. Where's your blankets, Jake? I'll get a fire going for you, then I'll rustle up some coffee."

"Stop right there!" Jake protested, "you just get a fire goin', that'll be fine."

"Okay, okay," Buzz smiled, "then you'll have to tell me how you happened upon Red Hawk and his woman and brought them here."

"Snow was so heavy up in the high country, Buzz," Jake said, grabbing a bottle of whiskey from the cabinet.

"Must'a been twelve-fifteen foot deep in some places. You could hardly see your hand in front of your face. Came upon three Indian ponies 'bout hundred foot or so off the deer trail we was coming down, checked the area, our horses almost stepped on their wickiup but shied away, so we knew there was something under. Top of their little hut was -- what, Foss, four feet under?"

The bar owner took a swig and passed the bottle to Calder.

"Yeah," the other man nodded, "woulda been nice'n cozy inside, but snow caved it in on'em, we had to dig'em out; good thing snow had stopped by then."

"That was early this morning on our way back," Jake continued, "couldn't'a been more'n fifteen, eighteen miles from here, but rugged terrain along the *Little Black*. They're in pretty tough shape, but still breathin'."

By this time the men had shed their wet garments and were wrapped in warm blankets, sitting with Buzz around the fireplace. The bottle had gone around the semi-circle twice as they shared their stories: the weary travelers of their trip, Buzz of the gunfight, of finding the wagons and merchandise, of Ida, and finally of the escape of King.

Buzz stood. "You had quite the adventure, fellas. Glad you're home safely, and with Red Hawk, to boot! I'll be off now." He bent to pick up the stack of dirty clothes.

"You leave those dirty clothes right there, Calder! The widow Iverson always does my wash; I always split her firewood . . . we have this agreement, ya see?" he winked at Buzz.

"Ah, I see." Calder smiled. He stepped outside, leaving the four men sitting, wrapped in blankets, staring into the cheery flames, and at times glancing at Jake.

Floyd Banner walked alongside the eleven manacled miscreants, escorting them back to the Wesley barn after the potluck. Antonio Muñez took up the rear position in case they decided to overpower the crippled old-timer and make a run for it.

"How'd you lose your hand, kid?" one of the others asked young Brendan.

"That Mr. Calder gave me a choice -- my hand or my life."

"That son-of-a-bitch! He did that to you?"

"Hey!" Brendan retorted, "I can live with it!" He laughed at his own statement. "I'm not happy, you understand, but I've had time to think about it. I've only got myself to blame."

They filed into the barn, laughing and fully sated, lying back on the straw around the post. Antonio looked at them with a curious grin.

"Yeah?" Porter grunted, "Whadda you lookin' at, Friend?"

"Uh, nuthin. Jus' wun'drin' if any'a you fellers would help me out. I know you kin shovel snow; my project is covered in the stuff; mebbe you could help me out tomorrow."

"Depends on that Calder fella."

"Why jus' tomorrow?" Freddie asked. "We can help you build the whole building."

"Again, fellas, that would depend upon Mr. Calder . . . along with Judge Houghton," Antonio said.

<><><>

While Doc Ford cut away Red Hawk's frozen clothing, Molly followed suit, using the hunting knife Calder had made and given her, cutting the leggings and tunic away from the wife's small frame.

Warm, dry blankets came next, then Molly began to gently massage the woman's feet which had turned almost blue with the cold and lack of blood circulation.

"Bring my medical book over, Molly," Doc instructed. "There's something in there about frostbite and extreme cold. Can't remember exactly, but something sticks in my craw. I don't see anything black, so nothing's frozen and ready to fall off."

"Oh! I remember reading something in Margaret's medical book about treating someone exposed to extreme cold," Molly exclaimed, handing Ford his medical book. "As I remember, the advice was, 'No aggressive rubbing or massage; severe cold causes heart to become faint and slow; blood circulation almost stops. Bringing it back too quickly could damage the heart'. I think we're doing everything right, Doc."

"So do I, Lass," Doc smiled triumphantly, "Look!" He pointed to Red Hawk.

Molly watched as the old Indian's eyes twitched. She ran to him and hugged his shoulders.

The old Mescalero native's eyes continued to flutter, then opened and stayed open. He looked up to a smiling Molly. "Spirit Woman . . . you come."

"No, Red Hawk. You are in Warm Springs. A group of our men found you and your wife buried in the snow."

"Woman!" Red Hawk grew anxious. He started to rise from the pallet.

"She's sleeping," Molly assured him, "but she'll awaken like you just did; her vital signs are good. Now you rest for a while, your insides need to warm up slowly, so I'm going to bring you something warm to drink. You might not like it very much, but it will be good for you."

Red Hawk simply nodded his head, and started to rise. "Best not try to get up yet," Molly advised him, "you can do damage to your insides; at least lie still until I bring you back that drink."

"Umm,"the Mescalero said. "Woman not awake yet?"

"Not yet, but soon, Red Hawk. I'll be right back. Maybe your wife will be awake by then."

Molly joined Mrs. Ford in the kitchen. "Do you have anything savory, like a beef broth, Ma'am?" she asked.

"I sure do, Molly. I canned venison earlier this year. It's cold -- in fact, probably frozen, but I can heat it up and come up with a nice, savory broth."

"Enough for two cups?"

"Even more," the doctor's wife assured her.

Minutes later two mugs of broth were set on a small table in front of Molly. She handed one to Red Hawk. He leaned on an elbow as he lay on the pallet and sipped.

"Good venison. Need only one thing," he smiled, "more."

"Okay, but just a little. You had a very bad experience and you must recover slowly."

"Umm. Mescalero brave well quick," Red Hawk started to get to his feet just as Doc Ford directed their attention to the woman, who was just stirring.

"Let her waken and regain her senses slowly," Ford encouraged Red Hawk, "then let her sip some of that venison broth, but slowly."

"Umm."

<><><>

Sunday, October 5th, 1851 ended. The Almighty did indeed watch over the little town of Warm Springs, answering the pastor's prayerful requests:

Thank You, Father for Your safety during the storm; for sustaining us and protecting us'.

Chapter 72

As Calder exited his house Monday morning he was met by Elmer.

"Hi, Mr. Calder," the lad said. "Antonio is lookin' fer ya. Sez he wants all them bad fellers to shovel all the snow at Margaret's."

Buzz okayed Antonio's request; the prisoners donned their warm outer clothing and went to shovel the snow at the general store building site. Two guards watched as they began. The blacksmith then joined Houghton for a steak and egg breakfast. Jake turned the kitchen chores over to an employee and joined them. They noticed others of the town's stalwarts: Doc Ford with his wife, and the banker, Abel Royston. Houghton waved them over as well. They pulled up another table and chairs.

"I'll be leaving tomorrow morning, fellas, ma'am," Houghton told them. "Not sure how soon I can round up some army engineers, but you can expect them probably within two weeks or so.

Now, I've been thinking about those boys you have in custody, Buzz -- you know, those Texas cowpunchers -- Moe, Abbot and the bunch that ended up doing King's bidding."

"Yeah?"

"What are your plans for them? Remember they

killed old man Tyler and his men."

"You asking out of curiosity or as a litigator, Cedric? . . . because, as you know," Buzz laughed, holding up his fork, "you're asking simple shop-keepers a question that should be asked of an attorney or judge."

"Let's say all of you, Mr. Blacksmith," Houghton smiled back.

"Okay," Buzz thought for a moment, "I'd give them a choice."

"Hang 'em," Jake broke in, "no choices! Hang 'em all. Eye fer an eye the Good Book sez."

Buzz looked sideways at Jake, squinting at his friend.

"That's pretty damn final, Jake."

"Damn right!" the bar owner said. "They killed the Tylers, tried to kill you, Buzz, probably had a hand in killing those teamsters . . . They're a no-good bunch! Get rid of 'em."

"Or?" Houghton asked, frowning, "Is there no other way?"

"Sure," Buzz looked around the table, "make them return or replace that 400 head of cattle to the Tyler spread and then all of them work for the Widow Tyler for two years with only grub and bunk for wages, after which they head back to Texas with the stipulation they never return to New Mexico.

We could also consider using their manpower in building the general store and the federal buildings that are slated to be built here soon - make it indentured service until the Tyler's debt is satisfied, as determined by a fair-minded jury."

Just then Molly came through the door looking for Doc Ford. She spotted them and walked in their direction in time to hear Jake's loud rejection of Calder's suggestions.

"Oh, right!" bellowed Jake, "and who's gonna pick up their bunk and grub tab while they're a'workin'? Jus' hang 'em, I say, an' be done with it!"

The banker, to this point, had said nothing. He now spoke up. "I'd have sided with Jake five years ago," he said, "but times are changing, and we should look at things through a different lens.

Now, I have no problem hanging King. He's the lying no-good that has caused all the recent bloodshed. But the others -- well, I've talked to a few of them, and I see young men who, for adventure and a big payday, thought they'd have a bit of fun -- playing with dynamite, shooting up a homestead, defending against a lawless bunch -- not realizing they, themselves, were the lawless ones.

Eye for an eye was the rule of law, yes, but Jesus came along and said, *'Justice tempered with mercy'*. As a fledgling city within federal jurisdiction we need to be careful, fair, and within the law."

"Let me just add," Doc Ford piped up, smiling at Molly, "I treated three of those fellows. They all expressed remorse, none of them tried to overpower me or escape. I think it's workable."

"What's the big decision you're making?" Molly asked, dragging up a chair and sitting next to the doc's wife.

"Hanging the outlaws or putting them to work -- unpaid of course," the doc said. "Problem is, they can't stay in the Wesley barn, so where could we bed them down?"

"Well, if I may, don't I have a bunkhouse that'll house twelve or fifteen?" Molly exclaimed. Why not hire a guard to take'em out there at night, lock'em in, then bring'em back in the mornings? At most it's an hour each way, and it would be only temporary. If in a jail they would still need to be guarded and fed, right?

Anyway, I came to tell you, Doc, that Red Hawk and his wife left. I gave them blankets and enough provisions for two days; they wouldn't accept anything more."

Doc Ford shrugged, "Tough old bastard. Wife, too."

The others at the table nodded their heads or mumbled in agreement.

"Gentlemen," Houghton said, getting back to the topic, "there you have some options. I appreciate the input from all of you. Let me just say, hanging would not be allowed now, not without a trial. Abel is correct. You are no longer an isolated little burg in the wilderness making up your own rules vigilante style."

Jake reluctantly acquiesced. After a half hour they shook hands on a plan with the following determinations:

1. Once Houghton reached Albuquerque, he would send out the request for a construction outfit, then he and his associates would head over to the Old Horse Springs area to present the option as Buzz had offered to the widow Tyler. In the event she wanted the cattle back and those miscreants to be under her thumb, they would send them. Otherwise, they would proceed with option 2.

2. A generous price for the 400 head of cows was $2,600, or $6.50 per head -- sum to be paid immediately to the widow Tyler from funds fronted by Calder in lieu of the physical cows -- (cows were selling for $4.00 per head in Oklahoma making $6.50 a premium price) Jake assured those around the table that many of the locals would take a few cows to repay Calder.

> **A. Molly's property would be used to house the prisoners until a jail could be built. She would be paid $10.00 per month for the use of the bunk house on her property.**

> **B. The prisoners would work at hard labor at the rate of $2.00 per month per man at whatever task the town leaders determined would satisfy the community obligation and assist in repaying Calder.**

Breakfast over, Buzz went to see the three ladies at the Wesley homestead. Margaret wanted to go home this morning. He agreed to escort her.

"Ida will never be able to run her ranch anymore, Buzz," Margaret shook her head. "Her mind is going."

"Yes, I know," he agreed. "Do we have any idea how many cows she has up there, besides the 400 head Moe and his bunch brought down?"

"I certainly don't, but ten years ago she bragged about more than 3,000 head. I know that over the years she sold some to settlers passing through who lost cows on the trail."

"Yeah," Buzz agreed, "I remember. I wonder if she has any of her own cowhands still anywhere on that ranch, or if they were all replac"Time I made a visit ed by King's own bunch," Calder mused. up there. Maybe Molly would like to go along, see her own little acreage as well."

Tuesday morning at sunup saw the judge and a four-man escort leave for Albuquerque. Floyd Banner, Lamar Jefferson, Chuck Grossinger, and Petch rounded out the escort crew. It was a wondrously beautiful morning -- crisp, but promising a day full of sun.

They chose the regular trail which was safer than the higher, more treacherous *Gila Cutoff*. Their route added at least a day, but they were in no desperate hurry.

The judge carried with him Molly's title deed, signed and witnessed nullifications of Ida's marriage and joint ownership of her land, papers for her reinstatement as sole owner, as well as the written offer and cash to the widow Tyler for her loss, should that be her choice.

Daylight also saw Ben Draper arrive to open the general store -- the first time after the storm. Calder was enjoying a second mug of coffee as the young man rode into the driveway.

"You're early, aren't you?"

"I need to check inventory. Do you have a list of the stuff you took? You know, the meds and blankets and such?"

"Should be on the desk; I think I included everything."

"Is Molly coming in today?"

"No," Calder said, "Molly and I are taking a trip. Elmer will be in shortly to get the delivery wagon. He'll go out to pick up Margaret. You'll be working with her today."

"Where are you taking Molly?"

"Up-country . . . we're going to a few places. Ida's place for one to see how her two Mexican-Indian housekeepers are doing . . . Then we'll head to the *Eagle* spread and perhaps a few other places."

"You're going to look for King aren't you?"

"I didn't say that, and no, Son, I'm not. I'm actually on my way to see Willitson and the old man that runs the *Eagle*. Ahh, here's Elmer now. Bring a couple of pillows around, Ben. Margaret's back is still hurting her. Can't say the wagon will be easy on her."

"You want me to do the chores before I go, Mr. Calder?"

"Not this morning, Elmer. I'll take care of the animals. Just hitch up the team and get started. Margaret's waiting for you, Son."

<><><>

"I'm ready, Uncle Buzz!" Molly said excitedly. "Will we be able to get through to my acreage?"

"According to Jake, we should have no problems. He said Warm Springs snow levels were much deeper than where we're headed. We'll take the right fork where the *Little Black* cuts west."

"So, we'll visit the *Eagle Ranch* first, then?" Molly settled on her pony and urged it alongside Calder's big roan.

"Yes, we'll start there."

Chapter 73

"Hey, Calder! What brings you two out here? You lost?"

Ted was at the head of a chorus of cowpunchers spilling out of the bunkhouse. They greeted Buzz and Molly as they pulled up to a hitching post at the *Eagle Ranch*.

Buzz stepped down from his roan just as Jaime Gallegos, using two sticks, hobbled around the veranda of his home.

"Buzz Calder! Welcome! How's my metal-bending friend?"

"Doin' just fine, Jaime, just fine. Like to introduce you to your neighbor."

"Ahh!" Gallegos nodded his head with a broad, open smile. "Heard good things about you. Heard horrible things about your family. Welcome to the *Eagle*," he said, waving his arm out in a friendly gesture. "What's left of it," he added with a grin, looking into her eyes.

"Sorry, Sir, I don't follow you."

"Both the *Snake Eyes* and the *Eagle Spread*, and the town of Warm Springs for that matter, were originally part of a Spanish land grant in the early 1700's. When Mexico gained its independence from Spain, old land grants were split up into smaller sections, but the idea was the same -- they were usually awarded for military service resulting in duplicate and overlapping claims.

When Mexico signed a treaty ceding most of the southwest above the Rio Grande to the U.S., stipulations were in place guaranteeing the land grants were to remain," Gallegos smiled and shook his head; "however, my family's grant of 70,000 acres originating in the 1720's has been split and re-split many times over.

I ended up with a fractional 12,500 acres, Ida's family was granted 8,800 acres, cut out of mine, by the way -- and then Dammer comes along and picks up a section that was left over between our two ranches. Still don't know how the surveyors up in Santa Fe figure these things but seems they're the experts. Both Ida and I went up to Santa Fe to argue back in '43, but didn't do us any good."

"This was originally a 70,000 acre family grant?" Molly asked.

"That's right, neighbor.

Buzz cut in. "How many head you runnin', Jaime?"

"Cows? 'bout 6,000 head, I guess. Thinking about bringing in sheep, goats, setting up a butchering operation, sell to all those passing through. Why?"

"See any cows with two brands? *Snake Eyes* and one other?"

"You mean that King bunch, brought in those 3-400 head from up-country?"

"Yeah, Jaime, that bunch."

"Ted and some of our boys cut'em out and penned them off. Ida has nothing to worry about. No one's blaming her for rustling them cows.

Have you caught that murdering son-of-a-bitch King, yet?"

"Not yet. We chased him, but he and his buddy Rodriguez got away.

Came here for another reason as well. As you know Warm Springs is growing -- it's going to be the county seat here in the territory very soon, Jaime. Crew's coming in from Albuquerque to start building -- Federal office Complex: courthouse, jail, the whole shebang.

Oh! before I forget, how's your fella got shot up there at Ida's? What's his name? Cezar, was it?"

"Yeah, Cezar. He didn't make it, Buzz. Good man. He was dead before the boys got him home. Buried him at his favorite fishing spot up along the lake.

So you're bringing law and order to Warm Springs. How can I help?"

"Be there when we need you, Jaime. Looks like Ida's whole crew has been killed off, replaced by ruffians and scoundrels to do King's bidding," . . .

Gallegos' mouth dropped! "What?" he almost shouted in disbelief. "She had fifteen permanent riders over there, Buzz. I should have paid more attention to what was going on. I recall some of my boys said they had met some *Snake Eyes* fellas, came back and said they didn't recognize a one of them." He shook his head, "Should have paid more attention."

"I have eleven culprits in a barn in town; I'm bringing them out to Molly's new bunkhouse, under guard, of course. They're the last of the bunch. Would you believe, Jaime, we've buried close to fifteen of those bastards?"

"Heard about that bunkhouse. Haven't seen it."

"Ride with us, Mr. Gallegos. We're going there today, aren't we, Uncle Buzz?"

"Yes. *Snake Eyes* first, then your place."

"Sounds like fun," Gallegos smiled. "Hey, Maxie!" he shouted, "saddle my horse!

<> <> <>

hey traveled the distance to Ida's ranch along a tree-line, skirting the open country where snow depths continued to increase the further west they rode. Molly noticed her Indian pony was finding the way increasingly difficult.

"Glad we chose this route, rather than that *Little Black* trail where they tried to dynamite you, Uncle Buzz; Spirit's beginning to struggle a bit."

"Step in behind us, Molly. Let my roan plow the trail for you and your pony."

"So," Jaime continued a previous conversation, "you're saying Ida has gone loco, Buzz? Haven't seen her in two or three years. So sorry. Wonder what's going to happen to her spread, cows and all."

"Way too early. She doesn't even know, Jaime. She slips in and out. Sometimes she's right-minded, next minute gone."

"Who's up there now?"

"Not sure. Last we knew, only two young Mexican ladies -- cooks or housekeepers. Who knows, may even run into King hiding out there with Rodriguez."

"You boys must have been hit with quite a dump in Warm Springs, Calder. Snow here is two feet higher than at the ranch."

"How much further, Mr. Gallegos?" Molly asked.

"Bout a mile, more or less. As I remember, there's a big, open space along the ridge and then a stand of white birch. Ida's barn is almost directly below those trees."

"Yeah, that sounds about right. It's a coupla hundred yards above and to the right of the ranch house. Just above the barn is where Cezar was hit, and just below is where I shot the King kid."

"You shot King's son?"

"Yeah. Just a stupid kid thought he was protecting his old man's rightful business endeavors."

"He dead?" Jaime asked

"Nope, took his arm off."

"Where's he now?"

"Waiting in a barn in Warm Springs with ten others."

Chapter 74

It was Thursday evening, October 9th. Mrs. Marcussen was delighted to have four new tenants in her bed and breakfast -- a week, paid in full by Judge Houghton.

"Any of you fellas interested in buying my business -- lock, stock and barrel?"

"You thinking about selling, Ma'am?" Chuck asked.

"Had it up for sale for months," she said, pouring a second round of brandy to the four men. "Ever since your blacksmith came through here on his way to Kansas. Fact is, I almost asked him if I could ride along with him."

"You did what?" Floyd looked up, almost choking on a mouthful of brandy, a shocked look on his face.

"Oh, just for the adventure of it. Life is pretty dull around here. I'm still young. Maybe California would suit me."

"Maybe so, Ma'am," Lamar Jefferson threw her a quizzical look, "but I think Warm Springs would suit you perfectly."

Her cheeks reddened, but Lily Marcussen said nothing.

<><><>

The following morning they rode to Widow Tyler's small ranch near the area called Old Horse Springs. The lady welcomed Judge Houghton and the others into her home. She gathered her two young sons and three daughters to her side as Houghton presented her with the choices the Warm Springs folks had offered.

"Me'n my last young'uns only have a half section -- 320 acres," she said. "Boys, girls, what do you think? I ain't even gonna consider havin' them murderers work fer me -- so, you think we should get them cows back, or do you want the $2,500.00 an' we go out and buy new cows?"

The eldest son, a slight lad of fourteen looked around, then spoke up, "We'd be better off with the money, Ma. Ain't none of us ready to herd 3-400 cows. Need money to build a chicken coop and buy chicken feed. Maybe buy a milk cow or two an' a couple head fer butcherin'. Maybe a plow an' other farmin' equipment."

All the children looked at their mother in agreement with their brother -- the money changed hands and the widow signed a release on any further demands -- witnessed by all concerned. When it was all said and done, she sat and cried. Then she dried her eyes and pulled her children to her.

"We can make it now children, we can make it."

After a few minutes Houghton stood. "We've done what we were sent to do, Ma'am. We'll be on our way."

As they mounted to return to Albuquerque, Floyd tried to hide his moist eyes, "That was a good thing what we just done, fellers. Makes me proud." Everyone nodded or grunted their agreement.

From Tyler's, Houghton went directly to the Albuquerque Army Corps of Engineers to assemble a building crew to design and build the Warm Springs complex. Chuck and the others decided to look around the city before heading back to the bed and breakfast.

"Another run to Santa Fe, Sir?" the young man's eyes twinkled when he came in.

"Yes. I need this packet in the hands of Norm Calhoun, attorney at Government House, as soon as possible, please, and this packet," Houghton said, handing the federal deputy marshal a second packet, "goes to my brother's office. Oh, by the way, I heard about that dark-haired beauty you've been seeing on your trips up there. That's okay, so long as you take care of business first," the judge winked.

"Right away, Sir."

Houghton leaned back in his chair and sighed. It had been quite a day, and it still wasn't finished. Was the territory really ready for a southwestern seat with yet more opinions in the federal mix? His brother, Joel was skeptical, but finally acceded to Cedric's future-looking thoughts. After all, statehood was rapidly approaching.

He sat for another moment, then sighed and called his assistant once more, "So, Ferdig, I've been gone half a month or more, what have I missed?"

The assistant brought a ledger with three pages full of cases. "Shall I begin scheduling for Monday, Sir?"

The judge flipped through pages and sighed, "No, no. Not yet. I'm going to take a week. Let's set the first case for Monday the 20th."

He leaned back in his stuffed leather chair, put his feet up on his desk and closed his eyes -- *so the widow Marcussen wants to sell her bed and breakfast*, he mused. The judge let his mind drift with thoughts of making the widow an offer . . . *I think I'll talk it over with Robin tonight* . . . then he fell asleep.

<> <> <>

Three wagons, two filled with tools and supplies, one with the personal effects of the widow, a construction crew of nine, the four man Warm Springs escort team and the widow Marcussen started home on Thursday, October 16th. Snow was beginning to fall.

Chapter 75

"Ranch is just below," Gallegos pointed. "There's the barn with that new lean-to storage shed Ted described to me. That's where all the goods are, huh?"

"Yeah," Calder replied as he plowed his way down the sharp decline, snow almost to the big roan's chest plate. Jaime took his horse down next, the way being somewhat cleared by the roan. His black mare stumbled, caught herself and cautiously continued down the slope.

Then Molly encouraged her pinto down the cleared path. The surefooted pony managed easily, and the three riders found themselves adjacent to the barn.

"Aren't we going to look in the barn, Uncle Buzz?"

"House first, Molly. We're going to check on the two young ladies, perhaps they'll go home with us."

They proceeded to the house. Molly dismounted and knocked, the two men pulled their weapons just in case. It seemed like an eternity before the door opened.

"Si?" a dark-skinned lady asked.

Gallegos took over. In the course of their conversation the other lady joined them. They were a mother-daughter pair according to Jaime. They had seen no one since the gunfight, in fact, King and Rodriquez had disappeared when the first gunshot sounded.

"Ask them if they wish to leave the ranch and come to

Warm Springs."

"Already did. They said, no, they were waiting for Ida to return."

"Did you tell them she would never return?" Molly asked him.

"Not yet. I was getting to that," Jaime grinned, "but I will now. How do I tell them she's gone . . . uh. . ."

"A bit crazy?"

"Yes."

Gallegos turned back to the two women and gave them the bad news. They looked at each other and erupted with stories of their own, confirming Ida's recent confused state. Five minutes of conversation with Jaime showed the relief on the two ladies' faces. They changed their minds. They were ready to leave within a quarter hour.

In the meantime, Buzz and his two companions visited the storage lean-to, then the barn. They saddled horses for the two Spanish ladies, dropped hay for the six other stalled horses and broke the ice off the horse trough for those they left behind. They would send a few riders back at a future date to pick up all the animals for housing in Warm Springs.

<><><>

The last leg of their journey was Molly's acreage. Buzz looked at his watch -- it was 1:44 p.m. The two Spanish ladies prepared a fine meal at the ranch house before they started. Then, warmed by the meal, they mounted up.

"Perhaps we should forget going to Molly's today," Buzz suggested. "The snow here is very deep, the trail is treacherous, and increasingly more-so just below Molly's bunkhouse."

"We'll be alright, Uncle Buzz," Molly protested. "I'm sure we will. I say we go on."

"Let's see what the others say."

<><><>

The big roan picked her way carefully as they dropped down on the trail along the *Little Black*. Within the hour Gallegos found himself shaking his head and cursing under his breath for siding with Molly. *How much deeper could these snow drifts get*, he wondered. The horses were struggling as it was.

"Careful and quiet now everyone," Buzz cautioned to those behind him. "No loud noises. We're getting close to the short trail up to Molly's."

"You think King might be there, Uncle Buzz?" Molly whispered.

"Not sure what to think just yet. Be prepared for anything. Ahhh, here we are," he said and started up between two boulders.

Gallegos smiled, "This is a trail, Amigo?"

"Yes, I remember these boulders and that old Bristlecone Pine from that day we were dynamited," Buzz said, pointing to a gnarled, dwarf outcropping of bark and leathery limbs thirty feet above them.

"That old boy is 2-300 years old," Jaime whistled. "I'd remember that as a landmark, too, I suppose. Bristlecone Pine, eh? Only one I've seen in these parts."

"2-300 years? That would be a sapling!" Calder smiled. "Try 2-3000 years, Jaime." Molly's mouth dropped as Buzz continued, "They're usually higher up!"

Molly was dumbfounded. "You mean that tree may have been growing there when Jesus walked on the earth?"

"Absolutely. That's what some of the scientists say."

They came out on a knoll. In summer it would provide a spectacular viewpoint; however, now with the exception of the occasional tree or rock face, it was solid white. The *Little Black* could be seen as a frozen ribbon far below.

"See that stand of birch trees?" Calder pointed, "the bunkhouse and corral are just beyond."

"*Compadres*," Jaime pointed, "look! They're here."

They could now see smoke coming from a tin stove pipe above the roof. Jaime pulled his rifle from its scabbard, the others did the same. They continued cautiously.

A horse in the corral whinnied; one of Ida's maid's horses returned the greeting -- followed by another. Calder urged the roan forward through the deep snow.

They were still plowing through the snow when they glimpsed the two fugitives heading down the eastern decline to the trail below, heading toward the area where the cliff had been dynamited.

The blacksmith's roan had finally plowed to the stand of birch trees overlooking a section of the trail below. The two fleeing riders slowed and looked back; their eyes met. Calder raised his rifle, but one of the two below was quicker to pull the trigger.

The bullet missed it's mark, thudding into a birch tree about two feet to the left of Calder -- close enough to raise the hair on the back of the blacksmith's neck; but the resulting percussion resounded throughout the gorge.

Snow began moving downhill immediately. It picked up speed and roared down the mountainside dislodging everything in it's path.

Buzz and the others sat on their mounts and could only watch in awe and horror as the two below -- both horses and riders -- disappeared into oblivion.

For a full two minutes the entire mountain seemed to move downward, and the five watching seemed not to breathe. Finally, the movement stopped, the white dust-like cloud settled all the way to the canyon floor. The five could only look at each other, wide-eyed.

Gallegos finally found his voice. "Can't go back that way, amigos," he said dryly, and turned his black mare away from the ridge edge, pointing her toward the bunkhouse; the others followed.

They spent the next hour in the bunkhouse, warming themselves before the pot-bellied stove, discussing the cataclysmic avalanche, the demise of King and the obliteration of the trail.

Molly walked the bunk from one end to the other. "It's well-built, but we can't use it now, can we? For a jail, I mean. That trail won't be usable until next summer the way it looks."

"Too far around," Buzz agreed

"Speaking of which," Jaime added, "we should be heading back."

Chapter 76

The construction wagons arrived from Albuquerque mid-morning, Tuesday, October 21st. Their first order of business was a hot meal at Jake's. Lily Marcussen was among the men.

At the time, Margaret and Molly were tending the general store, Calder was busy in his shop, unaware of the newcomers until Jimmy came running.

"Uncle Buzz! Uncle Buzz! The wagons are here with Floyd an' them. An' there's a woman with'em, too."

"There's a woman?"

"Yessir!" Jimmy confirmed. Then he was off to report to those at the general store.

A woman? Buzz mused. Who could that be? The widow Tyler? He set his hammer down and took his apron off. *This I gotta see,* he told himself.

Calder walked over to the general store, "Either of you want to join me for lunch at Jake's?"

"Go ahead, Margaret. I'm fine here," Molly said.

<> <> <>

Buzz assisted Margaret through the door into Jake's place. He guided her to where the large group had pushed tables together and were enjoying steaks. Jake saw them, stood and welcomed them. "Pull up another table, Buzz. Steaks are on me; drinks are on you."

As he was seating Margaret, Buzz felt someone at his elbow. He had recognized her when he first walked in, but he needed to focus on making sure Margaret was comfortable. He took a deep breath. Now he was ready.

He turned. "Lily! What a surprise!" he sang out. He reached out to give her a quick squeeze, but that didn't satisfy -- she closed in on him with a bear hug and a kiss on the cheek.

"Mr. Blacksmith! Here you are! Jake's been telling us of all your exploits."

Calder then turned to Jake. He raised an eyebrow and glared. Jake simply shrugged.

The sergeant in charge of the construction team, sensing an awkward moment, scooted his chair back. "Fellas, time to look at our jobsite. I understand it's housing some prisoners at the moment. . . so, first order of business will be to tear the barn down and set up a large tent at the same time."

"I'll show you," Floyd stood. "It's a ways down the street. Good seein' you walkin' so good, Margaret." He tipped his hat and led the building crew out of Jake's.

Margaret stood as well. "Thanks for breakfast, Jake. I'll be heading back to the store, now." She turned and gave Lily Marcussen a hug, "Lily, welcome to Warm Springs. I'm sure you'll fit right in here.

And by the way," she pulled Lily close so the next few words were for the newcomer's ears only, "no one's nose will be twisted out of joint if you have any designs on Calder. That old man could use someone in his life."

<><><>

"So, Lily," the banker asked with incredulity, "you sold your little traveler's inn to Cedric?"

"Surprised me, too," Lily told her friend. "Cedric and Robin just walked in the other day, walked through the place, looked over my books, took me for a quick lunch at the Pigeon Hole and made an offer. Sounded fair -- I didn't even counter. So, here I am, Abel.

Set me up with an account. I'll be living hand to mouth for a few weeks until something opens up for me. I can see why you and Beryl moved down here. I can only imagine what spring will be like."

"You just got here, Lily. Take a few days or weeks to look the town over. There are a few opportunities I can think of here for you to consider. The *Clarion Call*, that's the newspaper, may have a job opening soon. Old Howard Lange has been talking about retiring. Says his eyes are failing him; Mrs. Brighton at the school is another -- getting on in years.

And, of course, the new Federal offices will require staffing. In the meantime, Lily, may I show you our little town? My carriage is just outside."

"I would be delighted, Mr. Royston," she replied, taking his arm.

"I'll be out for a couple of hours!" Royston yelled to his staff.

<><><>

"Molly is delightful . . . and bright!" Lily commented to Calder as the two sat on his veranda sipping a hearty port. "A real bundle of energy, that one. And her calling you Uncle Buzz . . . so sweet."

"Sweet? humph!" Buzz cocked his head, wrinkled a brow, and chuckled at her description. "Okay, *sweet*. I'm sweet! I'm Uncle Buzz to half the kids in Warm Springs.

But you're right about her. She is an important part of our community. A local rancher, Jaime Gallegos, is considering starting up a commercial meat processing business -- butchering, making pemmican and smoking. He has a big smoke-house at his ranch. We recently sampled some of his beef. Really good. Molly discussed with him the idea of running sheep on her property --

which is close to his ranch -- and selling the critters to Jaime. He doesn't want to mix sheep and cows together on his ranch.

Far-fetched idea, but damned if it might not just work. Spanish used to run sheep in New Mexico 200 years ago -- so, why not? She even figures she has the guy to herd them. Older kid named Elmer."

"My goodness! Talk about industry!" Lily was amazed.

"Now, Lily, I'd love to have you stay here, but you can't. I've made arrangements for you to stay at Annie Wesley's place. She has the farm house behind the construction site where the Army Corps is working."

"Did you see what they've already done, Buzz? Surveyor stakes up all over the place."

"I did," Calder acknowledged. "And, I'm especially happy with the general store. Antonio's crew is moving right along."

"Yes! I saw Ben with a wagon load of sawn lumber. I waved at him . . . don't know if he recognized me."

"Antonio's keeping him pretty busy. They have four pit saws set up in a stand of Ponderosa Pines just out of town. Right now they're staying ahead of the carpenters, but not sure how long that will last. I'll just be happy when I can use my barn again."

The last rays of the sun were disappearing. It turned suddenly cold. Buzz refilled their glasses and put a shawl over Lily's shoulders. "Such a nice surprise, Lily; I'm happy you're here! " he said taking her hand in his.

"I'm so glad, Uncle Buzz," she laughed as she squeezed his fingers . . . "and I'm very happy I made the move."

They stood and walked to Calder's wagon, hand in hand. He assisted her up to the wooden seat, then walked around and hopped aboard. He pulled her to him. They shared a long, drawn out kiss -- then he urged the team forward.

The
End

Epilogue

Maggie was running late. She dropped her three children off, kissed her mother on the cheek, hopped up to her buggy seat and urged her big bay toward the general store.

Molly handed the two seven year old twins their tools: to young Evelyn the gallon scoop of egg mash to feed the chickens, to Benjamin the empty eight quart pail to the pump house for water. But as she turned to young five year old Carlton, the lad was already halfway out the back door, wire egg basket in hand.

"I know, I know . . . get all the eggs," he yelled as he raced outside.

"And don't you break a one of them! Walk slowly and carefully when you return!"

"Yes, Ma'am!" he shouted over his shoulder. She could only follow him with her eyes, shaking her head, grinning broadly.

She finished making breakfast for her "ranch hands", then watched as they returned, one by one. The scoop was hung on a nail, pail of water was left on the porch floor, and finally the egg-man came, beaming, and with both hands, he held up the basket of eggs; Molly took it from him with a curtsy and a "thank you, kind Sir."

Before the three filed in, they washed their hands in the enameled wash basin on the porch and wiped their shoes on the ribbed wooden steps just as they had been instructed.

"Gramma, are you going to read us some more of your story?" Melissa chirped as the three children sat at the kitchen table.

"We gotta say our prayers first!" Carlton piped up -- "And *then* we can eat! And, boy, am I hungry!"

"And *then* we do the dishes," Benjamin reminded the others.

Carlton covered his eyes and forehead with his little palm, "Oh, boy! We'll never get to the story!"
Molly laughed and tussled the boy's sandy hair. "Yes, we will. I promise. And this afternoon I have a surprise for you. Now, whose turn to say grace?"

<><><>

"Who remembers where we left off yesterday?" Molly asked her audience of three bright-eyed youngsters.

All three raised their hands excitedly with, "Me! I know!" as they snuggled around her. Melissa was quite verbose:

"The widow, Mrs. Marcusson came to town. She was in love with Uncle Buzz, and they were kissing. Then" . . .

"Then he took her home, cuz he was tired of kissing her!" Benjamin cut in.

"Yeah! Oohh, yuk!" Carlton agreed, with a screwed up look of disgust.

Molly hugged them, chuckling at their antics, and continued reading her memoirs -- omitting some more difficult to understand memories -- adding a few memories not included in print.

"Snow finally melted in the valley, and when spring came things became normal once again. The new general store was built just the way we wanted, and business was good.

The federal buildings were built, including a U.S. Marshal's office and courthouse, a sheriff's office with a jail, a fire station, and offices filled with records and clerks. Your grandpa's office is there."

"I forgot what Grandpa does, Gramma. Tell us again, please," Melissa begged.

"Yeah," Carlton echoed. "We forgot!"

"He's the district attorney for this whole part of New Mexico. He had to go to Santa Fe last week, remember? He picked up the train at Socorro and went up to meet the Governor. I think the Governor is going to make him Judge Benjamin Draper. We haven't had a judge here since Uncle Buzz died.

Anyway, back to the story. Since all the buildings were finished, Uncle Buzz got his barn back."

Ben Jr. raised his hand. "Yes?" Molly asked.

"Did those bad men have to go to jail when the jail was built, or did they stay in that lady's barn?"

Molly smiled. "That lady's barn was torn down to make room for all the federal buildings. And yes, those men spent nights in jail, but they helped with the building during the days. Turns out, they were real hard workers."

Carlton raised his hand, but asked his question immediately. "Even the man who got his arm chopped off?"

"Yes! Even him. But we're getting ahead of the story."

"Don't ask so many questions!" Melissa scolded her brothers, "Gramma will come to that part. Go on, Gramma."

"Well, children, a lot of things happened that spring: Buzz married Widow Marcussen. She became the school teacher, taking over for Mrs. Brighton who retired -- she even made house calls to folks whose kids weren't coming to school and encouraged them to send their kids to school -- even Jimmy Iverson went on a regular basis."

"Jimmy is the boy who saved that Indian woman from the cougar isn't he, Gramma?" Melissa asked.

"With a fishing pole!" Benjamin added.

"Yes, he is."

"How come you get to ask so many questions, Melissa?" Carlton asked, with a sour expression.

"Where does Jimmy live now?" Ben Jr. asked, ignoring the others.

Molly laughed and set her writing aside, deciding to tell her story as opposed to reading it. "I'll get to that in a bit, but speaking of those Mescalero Indians -- my friend, Red Hawk and his wife came to town one more time. It was early that spring.

He brought Margaret and me two saddles and some guns that he said he found on the banks of the *Little Black* -- said they were just laying there in the snow. Of course, we knew he had really found them with the bodies of the two bad men: Mr. King and Mr. Rodriguez."

"Oh! Because of the avalanche!" Ben exclaimed.

"Were the horses okay?" Melissa asked, with a worried look on her face.

Molly shook her head, gravely. "I'm afraid not, Honey. I think the snow was too deep." The older woman bit her lip as memories came flooding in. "That was the last time we saw my Indian friends."

"Did Red Hawk die, Gramma?" Melissa asked.

"Yes. You see, everyone is supposed to live a long life, learn to work hard, be kind and care about everyone else -- then, when the time comes, God says, *'okay, you're tired; It's time to rest'*. Just like Grannie Margaret, Uncle Buzz, and others -- and, yes, Red Hawk . . ."

"What about those other guys: Chuck, Petch and Elmer, Gramma? They died in the war," Benjamin frowned.

"That war was the worst thing that's ever happened to our country. They never should have joined up, but they did what they thought was right, I suppose. We tried to talk them out of it, your Ma, Uncle Ben, Uncle Buzz, your Grandpa and me.

Union troops came through Warm Springs and said Rebels were trying to take over New Mexico and destroy everything and everybody that disagreed with them.

The leader of the troops signed quite a few from town, Elmer and the others among them; went to a place called Glorietta Pass, up near Santa Fe. Rebels were pushed back, but a lot of Union troops died, including my friends."

Enough of this, Molly thought. *I need to get back on a positive vein . . . stop thinking about that dreadful war.*

"Now I've gone way ahead of myself, children. That war was in 1861, but let's go back where we were in our story, back to early 1852."

Carlton waved his hand in the air; Melissa grabbed it and pulled it down. He jerked away and raised it again.

"Yes, Carlton?"

"How old were you when you and grandpa were married?"

"I was just 19, your grandpa was 20, almost 21. Our wedding day was on my birthday -- July 10th, 1854. Anything else before we continue? Actually, maybe we should stop for now."

"No, Gramma! we won't interrupt anymore!" Melissa frowned at Carlton, "will we?"

"Sorry!" the youngest of the three said apologetically.

"Okay, then," Molly said, "I'll finish. We're still in 1852."

Judge Houghton came as he promised he would, and the elections were held in June. The people voted, and Judge Houghton appointed Uncle Buzz as first judge of the Tucson district, Floyd Banner was voted in as sheriff, and Abel Royston, our banker, became our first mayor.

Uncle Buzz appointed Ted Willitson, one of the ranch hands out at the *Eagle Ranch*, the first Federal marshal in the Tucson district. Ted is still alive. He married Billie, a waitress at Maude's. They had five kids and there must be fifteen grand kids. You'll meet some of them when school starts this fall.

Let's see, what else," Molly thought a moment . . . "oh, yes. . . about a year later, three outlaws rode into town and tried to rob the bank. One of them shot and killed old Floyd Banner, our sheriff.

Now, remember the prisoners who worked during the day and spent their nights in jail?" The children nodded their heads.

"Well, they happened to be working near the bank; they heard the shooting and ran to see what was going on. They saw the outlaws, ran after and tackled them. Then they took them to the jail and locked those three 'would-be' robbers up.

As a consequence, the town leaders voted in one of the heroes, Garfield Abbot, as sheriff and two others were made deputies that very day! One of those fellas was the man whose hand was chopped off!"

"Wow!" Carlton exclaimed. "He was a hero!"

"Yes, actually, they were all heros that day. Uncle Buzz commuted their sentences -- which means he forgave them from working off any more jail time. Some of them left town, some others stayed in Warm Springs.

You also asked about Jimmy. He bought the *Snake Eyes Ranch* from Ida's estate in 1859, then my little sheep ranch in 1866. He's still out there, running it with his sons.

Once in a while he comes to town, sits on the veranda at the blacksmith's, chatting with folks that come by, or just watching your Uncle Ben at work."

"When did Uncle Ben take over for Uncle Buzz, Gramma?" Melissa wanted to know.

"Well, let's see . . . this is 1899. As I remember, it was on his 21st birthday which was 1877. Grandpa wanted him to be a lawyer like him, but it seems my son -- your uncle

Ben -- loves working with his hands, so Uncle Buzz said he'd teach him the basics of the trade. They worked together until Uncle Buzz retired in 1888."

"Wow! Uncle Buzz was a blacksmith and a judge!" Ben was impressed.

"Yes, he said one job was work, one was fun. He was a very bright man, with several recorded patents."

There came a knock at the front door. "That's our surprise! Put your coats on, children. Benjamin, open the door, please."

Two men stood on the front porch with fishing poles, a picnic basket, and cans of worms.

"Gramma! It's Uncle Ben and some fellow with him!" he yelled.

"Kids! this is my friend, Jimmy Iverson!" Molly beamed.

"Did you really poke that ol' cougar with the fishin' pole?" Benjamin asked.

"I sure did! You must be Ben." He stuck his hand out. "That ol' cat was no match for me!" He tussled Ben's hair, then turned to Molly.

"Molly! Kids! Fish are bitin' real good on the *Little Black* up by the beaver dam! Don't just stand there," Jimmy Iverson grinned, "let's git goin!"

Molly stood on her tip toes and gave her friend a bear hug and a kiss on the cheek. "Kids! You heard Jimmy! I can't think of anything better! Grab your poles! Let's all go fish the *Little Black*!"

About the author

Myron Ferdig lives in southern California with his wife, Darlene, and two rescue dogs, Thatcher and Shylow. When he isn't writing he might be found playing guitar and singing.

"My love for books began early on in life. Education in primary years was in two-room rural Michigan and Minnesota schoolhouses -- grades one-three in one room, four-six in the other.

Books were precious commodities, purchased by parents, and traded in at year's end for the next year's subjects -- and the fewer doodles inside or out, the more the "trade-in" value. I wrote in my books almost never.

I read almost everything I could lay my hands on, from Men of Iron to Bambi; from Bomba the Jungle Boy on Jaguar Island to

A Tree Grows in Brooklyn and *The Foundling*; I could check out twelve books at a time from town libraries, and almost always had my card 'maxed-out.'

My first book -- other than short stories, poems, and songs, of which there were many -- was the 300+ page *A Lad from Sardinia,* which I self-published at the age of 73 in 2015."

The Blacksmith and the Sheepherder's Daughter is his 8th book.

It's a story of good versus evil, but so much more.

In this fictional account he brings a strong Christian or moral ethic into view; he makes the characters come alive, to be believable -- showing the struggles and hardships they face, making and adapting to change In the 1850s fictional frontier town of Warm Springs, New Mexico.

Myron hopes his creation will have an appeal to all age groups   and worthy of shelf space in your library.